PRAISE FOR

PRIEST OF BONES

"A charismatic and very moreish book v
Priest of Bones is a story of organized cri
sounds grim and dark . . . and it is . . . b
humanitarian for a ruthless crime lord.
very fun to read."

—Mark Lawrence, author of *Red Sister*

"McLean's writing is punchy and fast-paced. . . . Anyone itching to read a high-stakes story should pick up this delightful combination of medieval fantasy and crime drama."

—*Publishers Weekly*

"A pitch-perfect blend of fantasy and organized-crime sagas like Puzo's *The Godfather* or Pileggi's *Wiseguy*, this novel . . . is very, very hard to put down. Piety is a captivating narrator, coarse and abrasive but also smart and intuitive, and the author has built a world that's a mixture of the familiar and the wildly different. . . . Expect word-of-mouth support from fantasy fans to turn this one into a genre hit."

—*Booklist*

"*Priest of Bones* is a fresh and compelling take on grimdark fantasy and has done something I haven't before seen in the genre. Mashing together soldiers, gangsters, magic, and war into a heady mix that is a hulking big brother to *The Lies of Locke Lamora*, this is the first in an unmissable series."

—Anna Stephens, author of *Godblind*

"*Priest of Bones* is sure to be among the favorite reads for grimdark fantasy fans this year. . . . If there's one thing that puts *Priest of Bones* above your everyday, run-of-the-mill fantasy novel, it's the narrative voice of Tomas Piety. . . . Told by Piety in a charmingly low-key voice. . . . It's intimate, subtle, and flows like a lazy river. The prose is rhythmic and captivating."

—*Grimdark Magazine*

"Swiftly plotted and presented in a smooth first-person narrative, this novel will appeal to those who like their fantasy light on magic and heavy on violence and intrigue."

—*Library Journal*

"[McLean's] got a keen eye for flawed characters and moral quandaries that gives this story depth and emotion to go with the swagger, swearing, and gore. . . . The action is gripping and well-handled, the characters are vivid, and there's obviously a lot more story to tell." —*SciFiNow*

"What I originally thought was going to be a grimdark battle royal became in reality a multi-textured, mystery-infused, character-driven novel that shows you the best and worst that human nature can exhibit under extreme duress. . . . *Priest of Bones* defies classification in that it is a phenomenal story with sensational characters and should be read by everyone who enjoys bloody great books." —Out of This World SFF Reviews

"An enjoyable read for lovers of small-scale fantasy, with a diverse cast of crooks. *Priest of Bones* can be effectively summarized as 'gangsters in fantasyville.' . . . McLean manages to combine two of my most liked elements in fantasy—a quick-moving plot and characters with realistic relationships."
—Ed McDonald, author of *Blackwing*

"*Priest of Bones* is a fast-paced fantasy filled with magic and combat, but with the intrigue and strategy of a crime thriller. McLean writes soldiers and their experience of returning from war like someone who has been there. There is excellent character development throughout; I'd follow the Piety brothers through any story." —Michael Mammay, author of *Planetside*

"Managing to be exciting, narratively taut, and a commentary on the terrible things war and violence do to people is no mean feat, but Peter McLean manages it with *Priest of Bones*. I wish I had written this."
—RJ Barker, author of *Blood of Assassins*

"Absolutely sensational. . . . The prose is smooth and easy to follow, and that combined with a flowing story, an even pace, and a rising tempo results in one of those books that you could easily read in one go. All in all, *Priest of Bones* is low fantasy at its finest, and I wouldn't hesitate to call it the Fantasy Debut of the Year." —BookNest.eu

"*Priest of Bones* is built on the voice of Tomas Piety, and from the very get-go you know the kind of man he is. . . . If violence and planning, honor among thieves and treachery among lawmen, blood and profanity and spies and explosions are your thing, *Priest of Bones* is the book for you. Get it. Read it. Wait impatiently for the sequel." —J. C. Nelson, author of *The Reburialists*

"The literary version of an action/mobster flick. . . . Very fast, very readable, and it stuck to its plot like concrete shoes. If you're looking for an accessible, darkish fantasy, particularly if you're not a die-hard fantasy fan, this would be a great place to start. . . . I can safely say that this will be the book dark fantasy and grimdark fans will be raving about at the end of this year. . . . *Priest of Bones* will be one of the finest grimdark books of the year. . . . [McLean] has presented a brilliant debut grimdark outing that is fascinating, gripping, and has everything that I look for in a crime-focused novel."

—Fantasy Book Review

"Peter McLean's rendering of battle fatigue as well as the traumas of physical and emotional abuse fosters an emotional investment for readers that elevates this title above other 'run and gun' adventures. . . . With its charismatic merging of backstreet magic, gangland conflict, and political power struggles in a city teetering on the edge of destruction, *Priest of Bones* launches a breathtaking opening salvo in the War for the Rose Throne series."

—*BookPage*

Ace Books by Peter McLean

PRIEST OF BONES
PRIEST OF LIES

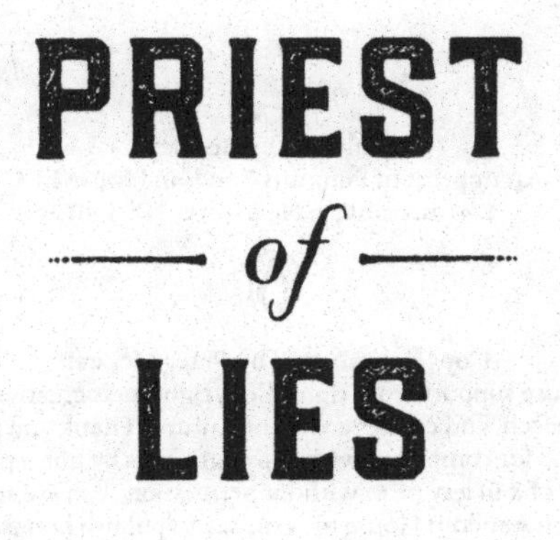

PETER McLEAN

ACE
NEW YORK

ACE
Published by Berkley
An imprint of Penguin Random House LLC
1745 Broadway, New York, NY 10019

Library of Congress Cataloging-in-Publication Data

Names: McLean, Peter, 1972– author.
Title: Priest of lies / Peter McLean.
Description: First edition. | New York: Ace, 2019.
Identifiers: LCCN 2018045399 | ISBN 9780451490230 (paperback) |
ISBN 9780451490247 (ebook)
Subjects: | GSAFD: Fantasy fiction.
Classification: LCC PR6113.C543 P77 2019 | DDC 823/.92—dc23
LC record available at https://lccn.loc.gov/2018045399

First Edition: July 2019

Printed in the United States of America

Cover design by Katie Anderson
Cover art: image of house by Neil Holden / Arcangel Images;
dagger image by n_defender / Shutterstock Images
Book design by Tiffany Estreicher
Map by Cortney Skinner

For Diane,
forever.

Nearly all men can stand adversity,
but if you want to test a man's character, give him power.

—Attributed to Abraham Lincoln

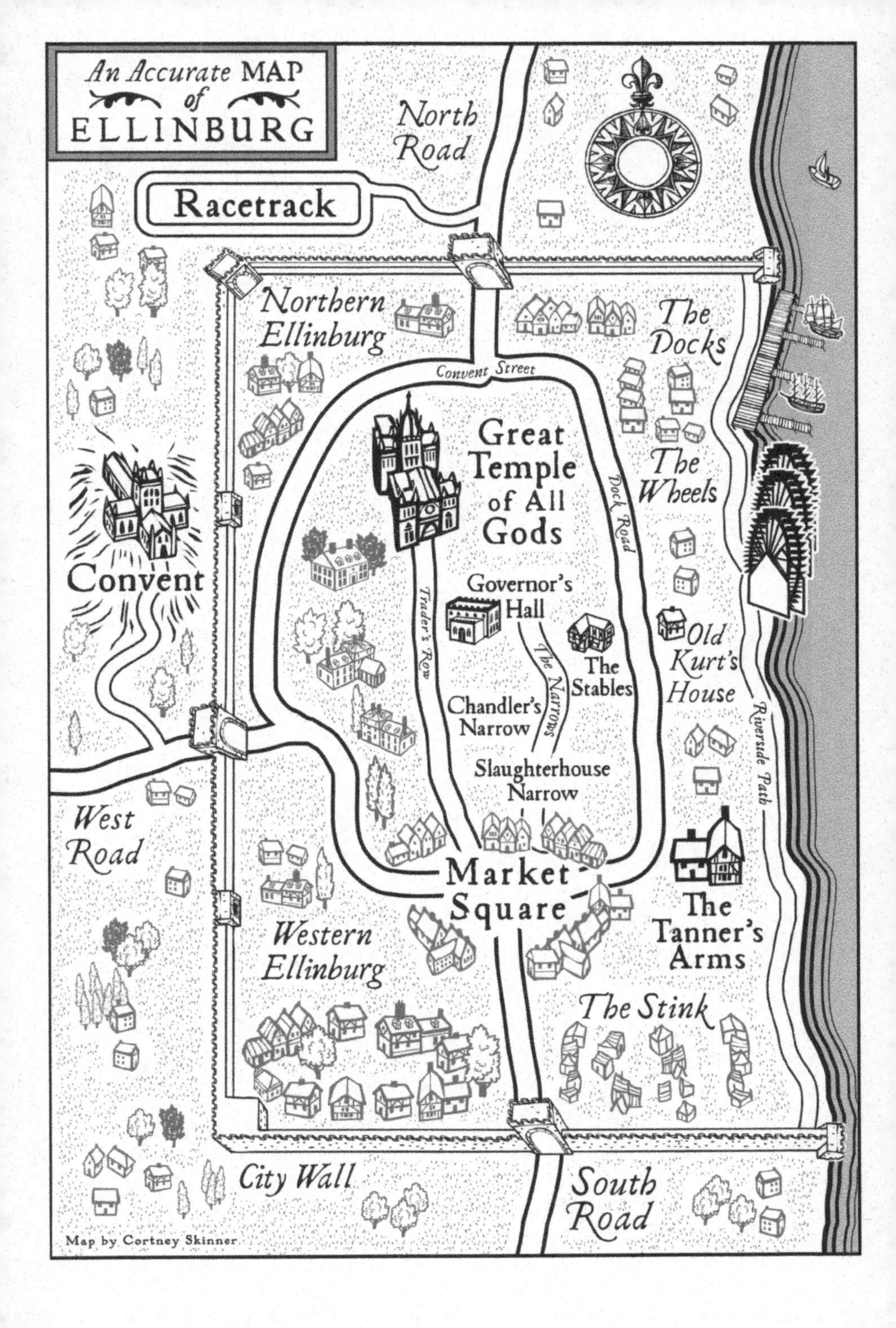
An Accurate MAP of ELLINBURG
North Road
Racetrack
Northern Ellinburg
The Docks
Convent Street
Great Temple of All Gods
Dock Road
The Wheels
Convent
Governor's Hall
Trader's Row
Old Kurt's House
The Narrows
The Stables
Chandler's Narrow
Riverside Path
Slaughterhouse Narrow
West Road
Market Square
The Tanner's Arms
Western Ellinburg
The Stink
City Wall
South Road
Map by Cortney Skinner

DRAMATIS PERSONAE

The Piety Family

TOMAS PIETY: Head of the Pious Men, a businessman and former army priest. Your narrator.

AILSA PIETY: His wife, and a Queen's Man.

JOCHAN PIETY: His younger brother, a very disturbed man.

ENAID PIETY: Their loving aunt, grand matriarch of the Pious Men.

The Pious Men

BLOODY ANNE: Tomas's second in the Pious Men and his most loyal friend. Bloody Anne had lived through a lifetime's worth of horror before she ever went to war.

BILLY THE BOY: A lad of some fourteen years, strong in the cunning and touched by Our Lady. Tomas and Ailsa's adopted nephew.

FAT LUKA: Head of propaganda, master of listeners.

SIR ELAND: A false knight but a loyal follower.

BRAK: Lover to Aunt Enaid, despite being a third her age.

SIMPLE SAM: Tomas's self-appointed bodyguard. A slow lad but a faithful one.

BLACK BILLY: Black Billy was proud of his arms, and rightly so. Good with his fists, too.

STEFAN: A soldier. There was little more to be said about Stefan.

BORYS: A thoughtful, older man who said little. He could move quiet when he wanted to, for a big man.

WILL THE WENCHER: Will runs the bawdy house on Chandler's Narrow.

HARI: Tavernkeeper of the Tanner's Arms.

MIKA: A useful lad who could think for himself.

CUTTER: A professional murderer with a mysterious past. When even sappers fear a man, that man is to be feared indeed.

DESH: An Alarian lad from Hull Patcher's Row. As far back as he could remember, he always wanted to be a Pious Man.

Various other ruffians and hired men whose names are not recorded here.

NOTABLE PEOPLE IN ELLINBURG

GOVERNOR HAUER: The city governor of Ellinburg. A frugal man, or so he let it be thought. Overly fond of wine.

CAPTAIN ROGAN: Captain of the City Guard. A hard man and a ruthless bully, but he was greedy and he had his vices.

ROSIE: Boss of the Chandler's Narrow girls and an agent of the Queen's Men. Bloody Anne's woman.

OLD KURT: People called Old Kurt a cunning man, and that had two meanings.

FLORENCE COOPER: A former soldier, and the boss of the Flower Girls.

EMIL: A veteran, and a hired man.

MATTHIAS WOLF: A cunning man.

MINA: A young woman with the cunning.

HANNE: An undercook.

COOKPOT: A groom.

SALO: A steward.

JON LAN BARKOV: A wealthy man and a patron of the arts.

KLAUS VHENT: A man also known as Bloodhands.

NOTABLE PEOPLE IN DANNSBURG

MR. GRACHYEV: A gangster.

IAGIN: His second. A very well-connected man.

LEONOV: An underboss.

DIETER VOGEL: The Lord Chief Judiciar. Among other things.

MR. AND MRS. SHAPOOR: Ailsa's parents.

THE PRINCESS CROWN ROYAL: A little girl of eleven years. The heir to the throne.

LORD LAN YETROV: A man overly fond of bear baiting, and worse things.

LADY LAN YETROV: His wife, who married above herself for money.

LORD LAN ANDRONIKOV: A man who did not fight in the war.

LADY LAN ANDRONIKOV: His wife. Very fond of the poppy, it is sad to say.

MAJOR BAKRYLOV: A veteran and a war hero, from a certain point of view.

LADY REITER: A courtesan.

ABSOLOM GREUV: A magician.

MR. FISCHER: A tutor.

PART ONE

ONE

Five hundred corpses.

That had been my wedding gift from Ailsa and the Queen's Men. From this woman I called my wife. Five hundred or more burned and blackened corpses had been pulled out of the smoking rubble of the Wheels after we bombed it into Hell, that Godsday afternoon.

I still hadn't forgiven her for that.

I hadn't forgiven myself.

That was six months past now, and Ellinburg was in the grip of a summer heat. The river stank even worse than usual, but still the people of Dock Road came out to watch us pass. We were on horseback, Jochan and Bloody Anne and Fat Luka and me, and everyone had come out onto the streets to see us. We were the Pious Men, and in Ellinburg we were received like princes.

Six months ago the Wheels had been a wasteland of devastation. On my wedding day Ailsa's company of army sappers had all but destroyed the district with enough blasting powder to start a war. Or perhaps, as I hoped, to prevent one.

The butcher's bill had been horrific, and to my mind that bill was laid squarely at Ailsa's door.

If we cannot stop this infiltration, there will be another war and we will lose. *There will be another Abingon, right here in our own country.*

Ailsa had told me that, and she had swayed me to her cause and to the service of the Queen's Men with those words. With those words, and with threats. It was that or hang, I knew that, but when I thought of how the streets had looked the day after our wedding I couldn't help but feel that Ailsa had brought Abingon to the Wheels herself, in the service of the crown.

My wife had done that, this murderous stranger I was forced to share a house with. To share a *life* with, whether I liked it or not. It was that or hang, and that was no choice at all. That was what the Queen's Men could do.

I had vowed then to rebuild, and I had done that.

Dock Road ran through the heart of the Wheels, and a year ago it would have been unthinkable for me to be there. The Wheels belonged to the Gutcutters, everyone knew that, but on my wedding day all that had changed. The Wheels was mine now, and the docks too. All of eastern Ellinburg belonged to the Pious Men, and that was good. It was good, and business had never been better, but it was still a long way from being safe.

"I can see two faces that shouldn't be here," Bloody Anne said quietly, her voice raspy from years of shouting orders and the smoke of blasting powder. "The top of Fellmonger's Alley, you see them?"

I glanced casually that way as I waved to a shopkeeper I recognized. He was behind on his payments, that one, and from the look on his face I could see that he knew it. No one fell behind with their payments on my streets, not if they knew what was good for them. I was the new boss of the Wheels, and I needed everybody there to understand that.

"Aye," I said. "I see them, Bloody Anne."

One of them was a resin smoker and petty thief who I had kicked out of the Stink a year ago. The other I knew worked for Bloodhands. I had to force myself not to shudder when I thought of that name. He called himself Klaus Vhent in public these days, but he was Bloodhands and he was a nasty piece of work and no mistake. He had been Ma Aditi's second in the Gutcutters, but I knew he was more than that.

Much more.

The Gutcutters had been wiped out on my wedding day, but the Skanians very much hadn't, and more to the point neither had Bloodhands. That man who had called himself Ma Aditi's second in the Gutcutters was the Skanians' head man in Ellinburg. He was something like a Queen's Man himself back in Skania, far across the sea to the north, or at least he was working directly for someone who was. Worse than that, I knew he had the ear of the governor. He was a man who ruled his gang through simple fear, a man who commanded the loyalty of his men by holding a knife to the throats of their hostage children.

We might be done fighting, but that didn't mean we could afford to grow complacent.

I let my hands fall to the hilts of the Weeping Women as they hung heavy at my belt. They were a pair of beautifully crafted shortswords that I had looted from a dead colonel after the last battle of Abingon. I had named them Remorse and Mercy, and thinking about Bloodhands had made me very much want to stab someone with them.

I couldn't do that, though, not here. Not in front of people, not anymore I couldn't. I was a prince in Ellinburg, and princes have men who do that sort of thing for them. I shot Fat Luka a look.

He nodded and let his horse slow until he was riding behind the rest of us. He was still no horseman, but he was getting better at it. More to the point, he knew where Cutter was in the crowd, which was more than I did.

The man could be virtually invisible, when he wanted to be, but I knew Cutter was following us on foot. He was an unremarkable-looking fellow with a little less than forty years to him, lean and wiry and bearded like so many working men in the Wheels and the Stink. He was just another face in the crowd in his nondescript laborer's clothes.

Cutter was my brother Jochan's man, not mine; I still had no idea where Cutter had come from or what levers moved him. He had certain skills, though, skills I knew he hadn't learned in the army.

Luka rode up beside me again, and I looked at him and he gave me a short nod. That was done then, and there was no need to spare it another thought. Those two faces wouldn't be seen in the Wheels again. Or anywhere else, for that matter. That would make Bloodhands think twice about trying to spy on me on my own streets.

The spies aside, our ride out went well enough. The Wheels was mostly on its way to being rebuilt by then, and many of the factories were back in operation. Those factories paid their taxes to me now, not to the Gutcutters, as did every business on Dock Road. That was good. I had never thought to see the day when the Pious Men controlled so much territory. I was rich, richer than I'd ever been, and one of the most powerful men in Ellinburg. Those things pleased me a great deal.

Every business in the Wheels had paid their protection money to Ma Aditi for years, of course they had, but come my wedding day she hadn't been able to protect them at all. She had been too busy having her head cut off. That had been Cutter's work too. Afterward, when the Pious Men came calling, with coin to rebuild and promises of a better future, those businesses had fallen into my lap like so much ripe fruit.

Oh, how Governor Hauer hated that.

"Good turnout," Bloody Anne observed.

"Aye," I said, and I was unable to stop a smile of satisfaction from crossing my face. "It is."

"Everyone loves you, Tomas," my brother Jochan said, but there was something in his tone that made me give him a look.

He resented me, I knew that well enough, and more than that he resented Anne's place at my right hand. He still thought *he* should have been my second, for all that he was fundamentally unsuitable for the role.

"That they do," I said softly. "That they do."

I hadn't wanted to return home afterward, but then I usually didn't. Ailsa would be at home, after all, and I was in too good a mood to want to spoil it by seeing her. I went back to the Tanner's Arms with Anne and Luka instead. I would take the company of people I knew I could trust over that of a Queen's Man any day of the week. I didn't know where Jochan went; he just said he had something to do, and he gave his horse to Luka and headed off on his own. He should have had a bodyguard with him, of course, but Jochan hated that. I suspected that the thing he had to do was get blind drunk and start a fight. It usually was.

Still, we were back in the heart of the Stink by then, the original Pious Men streets, and I knew he wouldn't come to any harm. Someone else probably would, before the night was out, and tomorrow it would cost me silver to make it right with them. That happened too often these days, but Jochan was Jochan.

Cookpot met us in the stable yard and took the horses, a smile lighting up his round, sweaty face as he stroked my black mare's nose. Cookpot had been a soldier once, and a Pious Man for a little while, but life as a groom suited him better. He was hurt in the mind, where it doesn't show, hurt by the things he had seen and done, but the horses brought him some peace. I felt like I had owed him that much, at least, after what I had put him through.

The three of us went into the Tanner's through the back. Hari was behind the bar, still leaning on his stick but a lot stronger than he had been six months ago after he had taken the terrible wound that had nearly killed him. Black Billy was on the door, his heavy club hanging from his belt and his shirtsleeves rolled up to display dark-skinned arms that were almost as thick around as my legs. He grinned at me as we came in, and I gave him a nod across the crowded common room. Borys was there too, I noticed, playing dice with Mika. Borys was an older man, thoughtful and trustworthy, while Mika had a sharp intelligence to him that you'd never have guessed from looking at him.

They were good lads, all of them. They were my Pious Men, but before that we had been in the army together. We had fought together in Messia and then in the Hell that had been Abingon, and we had fought together again to reclaim my streets here in Ellinburg. I would have trusted any man of them with my life.

Hari lined up brandies on the bar for us, and Luka took his and went to talk with Mika and Borys. I picked up my glass and the bottle both. Bloody Anne and me took my usual table in the corner, the one no one else ever sat at, however busy the tavern was. Simple Sam saw to that, and he came and stood there now with his back to us and his thickly muscled arms folded in front of his barrel chest to say that we weren't to be disturbed. He was a slow lad but a faithful one, and the sheer size of him brooked no arguments.

"Did you see the bodies?" Anne asked me. "On our way back, I mean."

I nodded, and smiled with grim satisfaction. The two men had been sprawled at the end of Fellmonger's Alley with their throats slit and their blood sprayed up the wall behind them. That was what happened to spies, on my streets anyway. That would send a message to Bloodhands all right, and that message was a simple one.

Stay off my streets, you cunt.

I wondered if they had even seen him coming.

Cutter would be back at Slaughterhouse Narrow by now, at the boardinghouse he ran in my name. That place was nothing special, a cheap and run-down flophouse for traveling slaughtermen and the skinners and laborers who followed them, but he seemed to like it there well enough.

"What do you make of Cutter?" I asked Anne.

"Can I be honest with you about this?"

"You're my second and my best friend, Bloody Anne," I said, and I smiled at her. "I'd like to think you can be honest with me about anything."

She sucked her teeth for a moment, the long scar on her face puckering and drawing the corner of her mouth down into a twisted half-scowl.

"He gives me the fear," she admitted at last. "I know he's part of our crew, but . . ."

She took a swallow of her brandy.

"Go on," I said, after a moment. "Say what's on your mind. I won't take it ill."

"But he's *not*, is he?" she said. "He's your brother's man, and that's all he is. It's been a year and more and still he don't mix with the others. He doesn't go to Chandler's Narrow and he's never in here. He doesn't talk or joke or gamble or rough about like soldiers do. I know we aren't soldiers anymore, not exactly, but . . . you know what I mean, Tomas. No one even knows where he's from, or what he likes to do, or anything. The man hardly seems human."

I nodded slowly.

"Aye," I said. "He's been a Pious Man for over a year, and he's made no friends among the crew. Has anyone tried to befriend *him*?"

Anne frowned at that, as though the thought hadn't occurred to her.

"I don't know," she said at last. "Truth be told, I doubt it. He's not what you'd call likable."

He wasn't, at that.

"Aye, well," I said. "Perhaps you might put it about that someone should try."

"So long as it doesn't have to be me," Anne muttered.

I laughed and refilled our glasses.

"I wouldn't do that to you," I said, but I could see that she meant it.

There was something about Cutter that would make anyone uneasy, and I didn't like not knowing what it was.

TWO

I had to go home eventually. I rode, with Desh and Emil and Bernd as bodyguards. They were new lads, and while Emil was a veteran from some other regiment, the other two had been too young to be conscripted. None of them were Pious Men yet, but they were working out well enough. Desh especially showed promise. He was a young Alarian lad from Hull Patcher's Row who seemed prepared to do almost anything to earn a place at my table. That was the sort of man I wanted.

I let myself into my great house off Trader's Row, startling the footman who had obviously been dozing in his chair in the hall. Stefan was there too, but he definitely hadn't been asleep.

He lowered the crossbow he was holding and gave me a nod when I stepped into the hall.

"Evening, boss," he said.

He was a solid man, was Stefan, if an unimaginative one. He was a soldier right down to his bones and no mistake.

"All quiet?" I asked him.

He inspected the mechanism of his bow for a moment, not meeting my eyes.

"No one's bothered the house," he said.

I sighed.

"She's still up, then?"

"Aye, boss."

That wasn't what I wanted to hear. It was late by then, well after midnight, and I had hoped Ailsa would have retired for the night by the time I got back. It seemed I was going to be disappointed about that.

Ailsa. My wife.

I nodded and opened the parlor door. She called it the drawing room, and I knew I was supposed to do the same, but to my mind a parlor was a parlor however many chairs it held. I still hadn't discovered why she called it that, nor learned to draw either.

She was sitting by the fire with a lamp burning on the low table beside her chair and her embroidery hoop in her hands. Her smoothly powdered face remained expressionless until I had closed the door behind me.

"Where in the gods' names have you been?" she demanded.

"Good evening, my love," I said, and I couldn't keep the sarcasm out of my voice.

"Don't try my patience, Tomas."

I poured myself a brandy from one of the bottles on the side table and turned to face her with the heavy crystal glass in my hand.

"I told you we were riding out into the Wheels today," I said. "We did that, and then I went to the Tanner's for a drink."

"Your place is here," she snapped.

"And my friends are there."

Ailsa put down her embroidery and glared at me.

"Sit down," she said, "and I will try to explain this to you one more time. I am your wife. I know that I am your wife in name only and we care not one rotten fig for each other but *only we can know that*. Servants gossip, Tomas, and neighbors peep between their shutters, and it is well known that you are almost never here."

I pinched the bridge of my nose between my finger and thumb, idly wondering what a fig was. Something rotten, it seemed.

Ailsa was an aristocrat from Dannsburg, and I was the son of a bricklayer from the Stink. The longer our sham marriage went on, the more the distance between those two things became plain to me. I sighed and looked at her.

Ailsa, the Queen's Man.

Oh, yes, she was that all right. Ailsa was a knight, of a very specialized order of the knighthood that answered directly to the crown. She was a diplomat and a spy, a master of the false face, and she was a tactical genius. She had planned and arranged the bombing of the Wheels herself.

She was responsible for the deaths of over five hundred people on our wedding day, and those were just the ones I knew of.

If three people die in a fire it's hard news, and if ten die then folk call it a tragedy. But five hundred? There comes a point where it's just a number, where your mind can't accept the reality of what happened. Abingon had been like that. If she had done that then Our Lady only knew what else she had done before I met her. A murderous stranger, I had thought her that morning, and as I looked into her dark eyes I felt the truth of that.

"I am almost never here," I started quietly, "because I have a *fucking business to run*!"

I knew I shouldn't be shouting, not where the servants could hear us, but over the last six months she had worn my patience thinner than an old linen shirt. There had been a time when I had thought I was falling in love with Ailsa, but that had been before the Wheels. Now the distance between us seemed too great for that. The distance, and what she had done. Ailsa was concerned with politics and the crown's orders, not with business, with the Skanians and with what society thought of us. The Skanians were one thing, but as far as I could see society in Ellinburg consisted of Governor Hauer, who was a cunt, and a small collection of factory owners and guild masters and pointless minor aristocrats. I didn't give a fuck what any of them thought of me.

Ailsa ignored my outburst.

"Your business interests me where it concerns the Skanians," she said. "Otherwise, not at all."

"Cutter killed two of their spies this morning," I said.

"While you were there?"

"I'd ridden past by then, but aye, while I was there."

Ailsa hissed with irritation. "Distance yourself, I told you. You're a respectable businessman now, Tomas, or at least you must appear to be. You know as well as I do that Vhent has the governor's ear. How would it look to society if he were able to implicate you in any wrongdoing?"

I stared at her. Klaus Vhent was the name Bloodhands was using in public, and as she said it seemed he had got himself close to Governor Hauer. That implied the governor was taking Skanian coin. I knew that, and it concerned me greatly. Society didn't.

"For the Lady's sake—" I started, but she cut me off.

"We'll speak in the morning, when you have a clear head," Ailsa announced.

I thumped my glass down on the side table and glared at her. It was tempting to keep shouting at her, but whenever I did that she made me regret it one way or another. Besides, shouting at a woman who could order me hanged with a word wasn't something that I'd call wise. I drew a breath and forced myself to nod at her.

"Aye," I said. "We'll do that. I'm going to bed."

I left her to her embroidery and slowly climbed the stairs to the upper floor where our adjoining rooms stood at the end of the corridor. Adjoining rooms, I supposed that was something. At least no one expected me to lie down with my murderous lioness of a wife, and I was grateful for that. Sharing a house with her was trial enough, never mind a bed. I had always thought that owning half of Ellinburg and living in a big house off Trader's Row would have made me happy, and to an extent it had, but I had never stopped to consider who I might have to share that house with. Me, married to a Queen's Man? It was preposterous, unthinkable, and it had stayed that way right up until it had suddenly been forced upon me. I sighed and shook my head, and walked down the corridor past the room where Billy the Boy slept.

I tried to be quiet, but either I woke young Billy or he hadn't been sleeping anyway.

"Uncle Tomas?" he called out as I passed his door.

I paused, then opened the door and looked inside. The lad was in bed, but he was obviously wide awake, and the lamp on his nightstand was burning. There was a big leather-bound book facedown on the blankets that covered him, and a quill and ink beside the lamp.

"Hello, Billy. I'm sorry if I woke you," I said, although I plainly hadn't.

"I wasn't sleeping. I was working on my notes."

"Aye, well that's good," I said, "but a young lad like you needs his sleep."

"I don't sleep much," Billy said.

No, that didn't surprise me.

I had moved Billy in with us shortly after the wedding, as my adopted nephew. He called us Uncle and Auntie, but he was still the orphan boy I had found in the ruins after the sack of Messia, the boy our regiment had taken in. The boy who had learned the cunning and given Old Kurt the fear.

The boy who had torn a Skanian magician inside out with the power of his mind.

"Aye, well," I said, for want of anything better.

"I heard you and Auntie Ailsa fighting," he said.

"Fighting? No, not that. Just words, Billy, how husbands and wives have sometimes. It's nothing to worry about."

That wasn't strictly true, of course. I thought it very much *was* something to worry about, but that was nothing young Billy needed to hear.

"You should be friends," Billy said, his young face solemn and serious.

He had somewhere around thirteen or fourteen years to him by then, no one was really sure, but on occasion he spoke wisdom beyond his years.

"We are," I assured him.

"Everyone needs a friend," Billy went on. "Even Cutter."

I blinked at him.

Billy was a seer; I knew that. Billy was touched by the goddess, for all that Old Kurt insisted he was possessed by some devil from Hell. Billy was touched by Our Lady, and that made him holy, to my mind. Sometimes Billy saw things no one else could see, and when he said a thing would be so he was always right. Even so, it made me shiver to think he seemed to know what I had been talking to Anne about that evening, half the city away.

"What makes you say that, Billy?"

He shrugged.

"Cutter," Billy said again. "He's lonely. I'll be his friend."

If I had to choose a friend for my adopted nephew, a professional murderer more than twice his age wouldn't have been my choice. Billy had that tone in his voice, though, the way he sounded when he knew that a thing would be so. I looked at him.

"Are you sure about that, Billy?" I asked him. "I know you get on well with Hari and Black Billy and Desh, but Cutter . . . well, Cutter isn't like the other men in my crew."

"He isn't like Sir Eland, either," Billy said, and he sounded certain of that.

I nodded. Sir Eland liked young lads, that was no secret, but he had only tried it on with Billy once. Whatever Billy had done to him that night had been enough that he had left well alone after that.

"Well and good," I said, "but that doesn't mean he won't hurt you."

"He won't," Billy said. "Not for no reason."

I blinked at him, but he had picked up his book again by then, and taken up his pen. He bowed his head over his work, whatever it may have been, and it seemed that was to be the end of it. The pen scratched softly against the velum page.

Billy could write but he seemed unable to read any hand but his own, and I still couldn't understand how that came to be. Old Kurt had had no answer for it either, I remembered.

Touched by the goddess, I thought.

The boy's fucking possessed, Old Kurt had told me once.

I looked at Billy, sitting up in bed with the lamplight casting half his face in shadow, and wondered if perhaps we were both right.

"Good night, Billy," I said, and closed his bedroom door behind me.

THREE

The three of us sat down to breakfast together the next morning, an intimate family group in the smaller of our two dining rooms with only Salo our steward, Ailsa's lady's maid, two footmen, and a houseman to attend us. Being outnumbered by servants seemed ridiculous, to my mind, but then I wouldn't know how these things were supposed to be done in polite society.

"I'll go and visit Cutter today," Billy announced.

I was drinking a shallow bowl of steaming hot tea while the steward served my food. It was something made from smoked fish and eggs, so far as I could tell, and little grains that could have been anything. The tea at least was good, for all that it cost a queen's ransom even without the import tax that I didn't pay. I would have been happier with small beer and black bread or salt pork, but of course Ailsa wouldn't have heard of that at her table. That was for commoners and servants, apparently, and that meant I wasn't allowed it even though she plainly regarded me as both of those things.

"Take one of the footmen with you, and Stefan," I said.

"I don't need anyone," Billy said, and I supposed that was true enough.

"You'll do as you're told," Ailsa said. "You must never leave this house unguarded, Billy."

It seemed we were of a mind about that, if nothing else.

Billy shoved a forkful of fishy eggs into his mouth and scowled.

That was the way my brother found the three of us when one of the other footmen showed him into the small dining room.

"Fuck a nun, Tomas." He laughed. "What the fuck are you eating?"

"I have no idea," I said.

I tossed my fork down and turned to look at him. Jochan smelled of brandy, and he had a black eye and a scabby cut on his left cheek, and his knuckles were grazed and raw. I could see that I had been right about how he had spent his evening. I could feel Ailsa quietly simmering at his language, but I ignored that.

"Tea?" I asked him.

"Fuck off," he said good-naturedly, and pulled another chair up to the table.

"What's the lay of things?"

"Well enough," he said with a shrug. "There's been no noise from the Northern Sons about those couple of cunts yesterday, so there's that."

The Northern Sons, that was what the Skanians were calling their new operation in western Ellinburg. Bloodhands was their boss, I knew that much, but beyond that we had been hard-pressed to learn anything about them. Fat Luka had sent his spies into Sons territory, but more often than not they went out and didn't come back. With Bloodhands as their boss, that didn't surprise me.

I thought about what Cutter had done to the two spies in the Wheels yesterday. He had killed them, aye, but at least it had been quick. I doubted that Fat Luka's men had fared half so well in the hands of the Northern Sons. Rumor on the streets was that Bloodhands liked to flay people alive, and that that was how he had earned his name. I didn't want to think about that, though, not while I was eating. Or at all, truth be told.

"Brother-by-law, can I send for something for you?" Ailsa asked, her voice like cracked ice. "Salt pork and small beer, perhaps? I dare say there are both, in the servants' kitchen."

I knew she meant it as a cutting insult, but that was what Jochan had for breakfast every day, and he took her at her word.

"Aye, thanks," he said, without looking at her.

I would hear about this after he left, I knew.

"Billy's going to visit Cutter later," I said.

"What the fuck for?" my brother wanted to know.

I shrugged.

"He's lonely," Billy said.

Jochan paused and looked at the boy.

"Aye," he said after a moment, and he looked uncomfortable about it. "I'll allow that he might be, I suppose. I haven't . . . spent much time with him recently. He's an odd one and no mistake."

I frowned at that. I had never had the opportunity to speak to my brother about Cutter before, not without looking like I was prying into a past that perhaps didn't bear close inspection. All the same, that sounded like an opening.

"He is, at that," I said. "You never did tell me where you met him."

"Messia," Jochan said, and then the footman brought his pork and a mug of small beer and he busied himself with them, ending the conversation.

I made myself look at Ailsa, and I didn't like what I saw in her face.

"Can I go, Uncle Tomas?" Billy asked me. "I'll take Stefan and a footman if I have to."

"You have to," I said. "And aye, you can."

The lad jumped down from the table and hurried out of the room, calling Stefan's name. A few minutes later we heard them leave the house.

"You shouldn't let him leave the table before we have finished breakfasting," Ailsa said. "It's bad manners."

"If you're waiting for me to eat *that* you'll be here for fucking days," I said, waving at the cold fishy eggs on the plate in front of me.

Jochan snorted laughter, and I stole some of his pork and we both sniggered like the young boys we had once been. I felt close to my brother then, if only for a moment. That moment lasted right up until there was a great crash from the hall, followed by the sound of running men.

We were both on our feet in seconds. Ailsa disapproved of me wearing the Weeping Women in the house, so I was unarmed, and Jochan only had a dagger on him. He would have come with bodyguards of his own, of course, even if he didn't like it, but there was no sign of them now. A moment later the door of the small dining room flew open and six of the City Guard stormed in with bared steel in their hands.

"Tomas Piety," their sergeant growled, and pointed her blade at me. "We're taking you in."

I told Ailsa and Jochan that it was all right, that I was just going to see Grandfather.

That was what it was called, in street cant, when you were arrested but it wasn't bad. I hoped that was true. If it had been serious, if I was being taken in for real, surely they would have arrested Jochan as well, and probably Ailsa too. Going to see the widow, that was what it was called when it was serious. I don't know what would have happened if Governor Hauer had tried to take a Queen's Man to see the widow, even without knowing who she was, but I doubted that it would have been anything good.

I let them march me out of the house and into the warm summer's morning. Jochan's two bodyguards had been Borys and Emil, and they were outside, with another four guardsmen covering them with crossbows. It had been raining earlier, and now the cobbled streets around Trader's Row glistened wet under the light of a watery sun.

"What's this about?" I asked.

"This is about my orders to take you in," the sergeant said. "Now shut up."

I gave her a sideways look. I didn't know this one, and that concerned me. Most of the governor's crew, under his chief bullyboy Captain Rogan, were career guardsmen. I knew all the officers by sight, or so I thought, but I didn't know this one. If the governor was hiring new muscle, then I had to wonder who they were and where they had come from.

The guardsmen led me up Trader's Row to the governor's hall, and I didn't resist. It would have been pointless, with six armed and armored men around me and me in my doublet and shirtsleeves without so much as a pocketknife in my hand.

Oh, what will the neighbors think? I wondered, and smirked to myself. *Fancy going out in public without a coat.*

"I don't know what you're fucking smiling about," the sergeant growled. "Rogan wants you."

I nodded and held my peace. She had already told me more than she should have done, and that was good. Rogan wanted me, which meant I wasn't being flung straight into a cell. Rogan worked for the governor, but he was also a good customer of mine at the Golden Chains, and he owed me gambling money. The Golden Chains was the best and most exclusive gambling house in Ellinburg, and I owned it. He played a dangerous game, did Captain Rogan. I thought it would only be a matter of time until Hauer started questioning where his captain's loyalties lay.

They marched me across the cobbled road to the area of smooth flagstones in front of the governor's hall. There, another two uniformed guardsmen stood on duty outside the great iron front doors. The royal standard that flew from the roof of the building flapped sullenly in the wind, its bright red darkened by the earlier rain. I was ushered inside. The sergeant searched me before having me thrust into a small office off the main hall.

Captain Rogan was waiting for me, sitting behind a cheap desk with his big, hard hands resting on the scarred wood in front of him.

"Thank you, Sergeant Weaver," he said. "Dismissed."

"Morning," I said.

"Don't be cheeky with me, Piety," he said. "I told you I'd get you, and I have."

I wasn't in irons and his men hadn't arrested my family alongside me, so I very much doubted that. I looked at him, at his broken nose and the flecks of iron gray in his hair, and all I could see was the man who regularly lost large sums of money at my gaming tables.

"Have you?" I asked. "On what charge?"

"It's well known that you import poppy resin," Rogan said. "That's illegal."

"I'll allow that it is, Captain," I said. "However, I import nothing. I'm a city businessman, not a merchant. I have no ships, and no men to sail them."

"Your bloody Golden Chains is the heart of the poppy trade in Ellinburg," Rogan accused me.

"That it is," I agreed. "As you would well know, being there so often yourself."

"I don't smoke the fucking poppy," Rogan growled.

He didn't, at that. Captain Rogan was a hard man and a ruthless bully and he had his vices, but the poppy wasn't among them. Gambling was his weakness, and there he was weak indeed.

"I don't believe I said that you did. I don't recall saying that at all, Captain. Not yet."

"No one would believe that."

"Wouldn't they? That would rather depend on who agreed with my version of the story, to my mind."

Many of the richest and most respected members of Ellinburg society were customers of the Golden Chains, and some of them were greatly in my debt. Some were by now slaves to the resin they smoked as well, and they knew I controlled their supply of the drug. Addiction is a strong enough lever to move almost anyone, which was why Ailsa had been so insistent that I enter the poppy trade in the first place.

Rogan glared at me, but I had him and I could see that he knew it.

"You can argue it with Hauer," he said. "If you drag me into this . . ."

"I have no cause to do that," I said. "You play right by me, Captain, and honor our agreement, and I don't see that I ever will have."

Our agreement was based on bribery, pure and simple, and those bribes funded Rogan's gambling habit. He sucked his teeth for a moment and nodded.

"Our agreement stands," he said.

FOUR

Rogan took a small handbell out of his desk and rang it, and two guardsmen hurried into the cramped office. They led me back out into the hall, and Rogan got up and followed. I was taken to the governor's office through the servants' corridors and up a back stair, not the grand staircase that I had climbed when I had attended a ball there in the spring as the governor's guest. That message wasn't lost on me.

It was still short of midmorning so the governor was at least sober, although from the look of his face I suspected he was feeling the effects of the previous night's wine. He scowled up at me from behind his desk as Rogan pushed me down into the chair across from him.

"Thank you, Captain," Hauer said. "You may leave us."

I felt Rogan's hesitation. I was unarmed, but Governor Hauer was a poor specimen, physically. He didn't have many more years to him than I had myself, but he was fat and weak and unhealthy from too much rich living. I could have killed him with my bare hands if I'd had a mind to, and I could tell Rogan knew it.

"Is that wise, m'lord?"

"Get out," Hauer snapped at him.

I heard heavy footsteps, and then the door closed behind me as Rogan left the room.

"Governor," I said.

"Tomas Piety, here you are again," Hauer said.

"That I am, although I'm at a loss as to why."

"The poppy resin, as you well know," Hauer snapped.

"As I explained to the captain, I import nothing," I said. "What may get past your customs men at the docks is your problem, Governor. Trade within the city is fair game, as per the terms of our agreement and the taxes that I pay you."

Those things were both true, if unrelated. The poppy resin I sold at the Golden Chains was smuggled into the city by road from Dannsburg, by Ailsa's agents. If I could keep the governor's attention focused on the docks and the tea ships from Alaria, then that was good. I didn't approve of the poppy trade but it brought in a fortune, and once I had managed to convince Ailsa to keep it off the streets and confined to the idle nobility, I had just about managed to make my peace with it.

"Taxes are one thing, but this is too much, Piety."

I leaned across the desk and met the governor's stare.

"I pay you enough in bribes for you to overlook anything," I reminded him. "I'm overlooking some things myself, Governor, after all. Your association with Klaus Vhent, for one."

"Vhent is a businessman, the same as you," Hauer said, a slight flush creeping up from under the collar of his doublet. "He heads the Northern Sons, that's all."

"It seems to my mind that you're closer to the Sons than is healthy, Governor," I said.

"For the gods' sakes, Tomas, I am trying to keep the peace." Hauer sighed and slumped back in his chair. "Vhent was Ma Aditi's second, as you well know. When she . . . died, he set up his own operation. I have to keep an eye on him, you understand that."

"You told me something, last year," I reminded him. "You told me about these Skanians you were worried about. That they were people like the Queen's Men, you told me, in their own land. Are you sure you know who you're associating with?"

I thought that he probably did, but I couldn't prove it and I couldn't know for sure.

"You dare to speak to me of the Queen's Men?" he hissed.

This is why I'm really here, I thought. *This interview isn't about poppy resin. It never was.*

"The Queen's Men sought you out," he went on. "It seems to me that happened close enough to the carnage in the Wheels for there to be a connection."

"I had nothing to do with that," I said. "I was getting married on that terrible day, Governor, in front of Father Goodman and all my family and friends and half the Stink beside. I have explained that. At length."

"Yes, and isn't that convenient? On that one day in particular you have unshakable proof of where you were and who you were with."

I held the governor's stare and said nothing. He knew very well I had been behind the bombings, but he couldn't prove it, and to my mind he never would. Ailsa was no fool, I had to give her that much.

"How is your lady wife?" he asked suddenly.

I forced myself not to blink. He didn't know who Ailsa really was, I told myself. He *couldn't* know.

"Well enough."

"Where is she from, again?"

"Dannsburg," I said.

"She doesn't have the look of Dannsburg to her."

She didn't, at that. Ailsa was obviously of Alarian descent, but she was from a wealthy, aristocratic Dannsburg family nonetheless. That carried a lot of weight, out here in the provinces, and Hauer seemed to be going out of his way to cause offense.

"She's a lady of the Dannsburg court," I said. "A very *respectable* lady. You would do well to remember that."

Hauer met my flat stare and swallowed. He was close to crossing a line with me here, and I could tell he knew it. Ailsa was my wife, after all, painful sham though that may be. To openly disrespect her to my face would be a step too far. I wouldn't be able to let it pass if he did that.

"A lady of the court," he repeated, and I nodded slowly.

If anyone remembered there had been an Alarian barmaid working in one of my taverns last year, well, who was to say they were one and the same woman? The Ailsa I had married was nothing like the funny, flirty, common girl who had worked in the Tanner's Arms. She was a master of the false face, as I have written, and for all intents and purposes those were two totally different women.

None of my crew would say otherwise.

Not ever.

Hauer let me go after that, having no other option bar throwing me in the cells without charge. He couldn't do that without facing dire consequences, and he knew it. I had spent a night in the cells back in the winter, and when I had finally been released Bloody Anne had been waiting for me with some two hundred folk from my streets around her. A mob like that rioting on Trader's Row would have been disastrous for Hauer.

But it was Ailsa who was waiting for me that day, in our carriage with two of the footmen and Desh for muscle. Our house was barely ten minutes' walk from the governor's hall, but of course I was in my shirtsleeves and how would that have looked? I stepped up into the carriage with her and thumped on the roof to get the coachman moving.

"What happened?" she asked me.

I looked sideways at Desh and gave my head a tiny shake.

"I'm well," I said. "A misunderstanding about business, that's all."

She nodded and held her peace.

We stayed silent until we were back in our parlor or drawing room or whatever it was called and the door was closed behind us.

"Hauer knows," I said.

"He can't do."

I sighed and poured myself a brandy. I offered Ailsa one, but she shook her head.

"No, perhaps not," I allowed, "but he suspects *something*. He knows very well that what happened in the Wheels was my doing."

"Of course he does, he's not a complete idiot. The important thing is that he can't prove anything, so it doesn't matter."

"No, but he's still picking at it like a scab, and he's started asking questions about you," I said. "I don't like it."

"I don't like anything Governor Hauer does, but everything in its time. What of his association with the Skanians?"

"I brought it up, in a roundabout way," I said. "He knows who Vhent works for, I'm sure of it."

Ailsa nodded.

"I agree," she said, "and that will be his downfall. However much they're paying him, he must realize that Dannsburg will notice what he's doing eventually and send . . . well, someone like me, to put a stop to it. He clearly intends to make himself rich enough to flee the country before that happens. He's a fool if he thinks there is anywhere in the world he could run to that is beyond the reach of the Queen's Men, but that's beside the point. What he *doesn't* know is that I'm already here, and two steps ahead of him. I won't see Vhent rebuild the Skanian hold in Ellinburg, whatever it takes. Destroying the Gutcutters was only the first step, Tomas. These Northern Sons now control most of the west side of the city, and we need to drive them out. It's time to ready the knives."

I could only stare at her as the realization sank in.

She wanted more bloodshed.

Even after the Wheels, she still wanted more. I remembered how it had been at Messia, after the sack, the starving people living like animals among the ruins. I remembered Abingon, the fires and the choking dust, plague and the bloody flux. I remembered the screams of the wounded and the inhuman howls that came from the surgeons' tents loud enough to be heard even over the endless pounding of the cannon.

I felt cold then, cold to my bones.

Was my war never going to end?

FIVE

The next morning found me in the Tanner's Arms, sharing breakfast with Bloody Anne. She was living in my old room above the tavern by then, and the Tanner's was still the Pious Men's main seat of power. Ailsa wanted me to distance myself, so I tried to keep business out of our home as much as I could. In truth, that morning I had mostly wanted to distance myself from her.

Billy had spent most of the previous day with Cutter up at Slaughterhouse Narrow, and I could tell Ailsa was displeased about that. About that, and about my brother coming uninvited to breakfast, about me being arrested and about Hauer's suspicions and the Northern Sons and how they had taken over western Ellinburg, and more other things than I knew how to count. Once again we had ended the day with shouting, so the next morning I had made sure to be up and out of the house before I was subjected to another inedible breakfast.

I broke bread with Anne instead in the comfortable surroundings of the Tanner's, in the heart of the Stink. That was where I belonged, I knew that, however much money I had now. Not up on Trader's Row with the rich folk and their servants and their society manners. Here, among my own people, that was home.

"What's the lay of things?" I asked Anne. "In general, I mean."

She put down her mug of small beer and shrugged.

"A lot has changed, but a lot hasn't," she said. "There's still poverty down in the Wheels. We've got perhaps half the factories running again, but tensions are high."

I nodded. They would be. A lot of Wheelers had died in the bombings, leaving the workforce sorely depleted. With the lack of work in the Stink I had been filling jobs in the newly reopened factories with Stink men wherever I could. Folk from the Stink and folk from the Wheels don't get on, and they never have done. Wheelers and Stinkers, that was what they called each other, and there was no love between them.

"Aye," I said. "It's to be expected, but the Wheels is mine now. These are *all* my streets, from the south of the Stink all the way north to the docks, and the people need to get used to that and learn to work together."

Bloody Anne sucked her teeth, her long scar twisting the corner of her mouth into a scowl.

"It'll get ugly before it gets better," she said.

"Be that as it may. How're the men?"

"Well enough. Luka's doing everything he can to keep the streets happy, even with the horror stories folk are hearing from the west of the city. In a way, that helps us. The Northern Sons rule their streets through terror, so folk are hearing, and they know you don't. The worse the Sons are to their people, the better we look in comparison, and Fat Luka's been making the most of that. Will the Wencher is still turning a small fortune up at Chandler's Narrow, and you know how successful the Chains is. Everyone's well paid, so there's no discontent in the crew. Even Sir Eland is behaving himself."

"Aye," I said. "That's good. You're doing well, Anne."

She looked at me then, and I couldn't read her face.

"It's doing itself," she said. "I'm a soldier, not a businesswoman. I'm your second, aye, but this isn't what I know how to do. I thought . . . I thought perhaps your aunt might take more of a hand in the running of the business side of things."

"She'll have to, soon," I said. "Bloodhands and his Northern Sons need teaching a lesson, and that's *exactly* what you know how to do."

"We'll stop once Aditi is done, you told me," Bloody Anne said. "You said that we'd be a ruling garrison, not a fighting force. That's what we've been for the last six months, and business is the best I've ever seen it. That means it works, Tomas. Haven't we fought enough?"

"Have we?" I challenged her. "Have we, when there are still foreign witches in the city?"

I had used Anne's fear of witchcraft against her once before, to sway her to my way of thinking, and to my mind what had worked once would work again. Bloody Anne was my best friend and it was low of me to manipulate her like that, I knew, but sometimes when you lead you have to do things you might not be proud of. You have to know the levers that move a person and be prepared to use them, and I knew how to move Anne.

"They're with Bloodhands, then?"

"Yes, Anne, they are," I said.

That was only an educated guess, but magicians had been a big part of the Skanian strength when they had backed the Gutcutters and I couldn't see that it would be different now. Things would have been so much simpler, I thought, if I could have told Anne the truth. She had no great loyalty to the crown, I was sure, but if I could just have explained the lay of things to her the way Ailsa had explained them to me, then I was sure she would see the necessity of what I was doing. There were a number of things I wished I could have told Bloody Anne.

Ailsa wouldn't hear of it.

I had never got to the bottom of why but she didn't seem to have a high opinion of Anne, and I thought that was unwise of her. Be that as it may, she had sworn me to secrecy under the Queen's Warrant and I couldn't break that oath. An oath sworn under the warrant was as binding as one sworn to Her Majesty in person, Ailsa had explained to me. To break such an oath would be to declare yourself a traitor to the crown and to hang for it.

All Anne could do was nod. She didn't like it, I could see she didn't, but Anne wanted the Skanian magicians out of the city every bit as much as I did even if she didn't know who they really were.

"How's high society?" she asked me.

I snorted, and she smiled to say she was making mischief.

"Tell me this, Bloody Anne," I said. "Would you eat eggs mixed with fish and grit for breakfast?"

She laughed at that, as I had hoped, and the tension passed.

Truth be told, society had its merits, for all that Ailsa chafed me. The house off Trader's Row was comfortable, palatial in fact compared to what I was used to, and, as Anne had said, incomes were the best they had ever been. I had been thinking I might buy myself another racehorse, to replace the one that had been taken from me while I had been away at war. Owning a racehorse was a symbol of status, of course, and I had certain expectations to meet. The people of my streets saw me as their prince, and a prince looked and acted a certain way. He had certain interests, too, and the racetrack was one of those. Most of the common folk were keen gamblers, and to their minds the owners of the horses they wagered on were rich beyond their dreams. It had been one of the best days of my life, the day I had bought that horse.

I remembered my aunt telling me how it had been nobbled in a fixed race while I had been fighting in the south, and how Doc Cordin said it had broken a leg and they'd cut its throat. I hadn't let that pass. The Gutcutters had done that, or the Skanians had, and on my wedding day I had shown them what I thought of it. All the same I missed that fucking horse, and I wanted another one. More to the point, I wanted what it represented.

Respect, power, authority. Those are the levers that move me.

When I returned home I found that Ailsa had gone shopping with her lady's maid in tow, and taken faithful Borys with her as her bodyguard. Desh had the door, and he welcomed me home with a respectful nod.

"Morning, boss," he said.

"Aye," I said.

The young Alarian was a good lad, I thought. He couldn't have had more than seventeen or eighteen years to him and he wasn't a Pious Man, not yet, but he showed promise. He was from Hull Patcher's Row in the depths of the poorest part of the Stink, and he was just young enough to have missed being conscripted for the war. He had grown up on Pious Men streets, though, knowing who we were and what we did. When I had been recruiting new men he had been among the first to take my coin. I thought perhaps Desh might well have spent most of his life wanting to be a Pious Man.

"Where's Billy?" I asked him.

"In the kitchen, boss," he said.

I nodded and went in there. Billy the Boy was always hungry, as growing lads usually are, and he had worked hard to build a friendship with our undercook. She was a plump lass with maybe twenty years to her, and when I walked in she was kneading dough with her sleeves rolled up and flour to her elbows. Billy was sitting at the long kitchen table where the servants took their meals, a pastry in his hand and crumbs on his chin.

". . . do make me laugh, master Billy," she was saying. "And that Mr. Jochan so rough and handsome, and him from the same streets as me too! Oh, but a girl could—"

She stopped with a gasp when she saw me standing in the kitchen door.

"Don't mind me, Hanne," I said. "I'm just here for the lad. And one of those pastries, if there's one going."

Hanne blushed bright red, to be spoken to by the master of the house. Cook herself was nowhere to be seen and I supposed she was probably at the market with one of the housemen, buying fresh produce for our dinner.

"Oh, Mr. Piety sir, wouldn't you rather sit in the drawing room?" she asked.

"No, I really wouldn't," I said, and smiled to take the sting out of my words.

It was hot in the kitchen but it smelled good, and even though Ailsa was out I still wasn't easy with formality. I sat on the bench beside Billy and nodded my thanks as Hanne set a fresh pastry and a mug of beer down in front of me with her strong, floury hands. She seemed a good woman, I thought.

"I can put in a word, if you like," I said. "With my brother, I mean."

Hanne's blush deepened to the color of an overripe plum, and she giggled and stumbled over her words.

"Oh, no, Mr. Piety, don't bother him on my account. I'm sorry, and I didn't mean to speak above my station, as it were."

I held my peace to spare the poor lass any further embarrassment, and I took a swig of beer. Truth be told, I didn't even know if Jochan wanted a woman. He was rarely sober enough, to my mind, and when he was he seemed happy enough to visit the house on Chandler's Narrow. It came to me then that it had been nearly two years since *I* last lay with a woman, and the realization surprised me.

That had been during the war, of course, when I had been a priest in the army and had had my pick of the camp followers. Since coming back to Ellinburg I had been first too busy, then too enthralled by Ailsa, then too wary of her, and finally married to her in an unwanted and loveless union. I sighed and picked up my pastry, but I found my appetite had gone. I owned a stew, for Our Lady's sake; I could have a woman any time I wanted one. I didn't, though, not like that. Running whores was one thing; lying with them when you were their boss was quite another. That didn't seem right.

"Uncle Tomas?" Billy said, bringing me back to myself.

I looked at the lad.

"Aye?"

"Aren't you going to eat that?"

I smiled as I saw that Billy had finished his pastry and was now looking hopefully at mine. I didn't want it anymore, so I gave it to him and contented myself with beer instead.

There might be a lesson in that somewhere, I thought.

SIX

"You spent a lot of time with Cutter yesterday," I said.

Billy nodded and wiped crumbs from his chin with the back of his hand.

"Yes, Uncle Tomas."

"I'm surprised you found enough common ground with him to talk for so long," I said. "He's not a talkative man, so far as I've seen."

"He talks, when he wants to," Billy said. "He didn't have anyone to talk to, is all. He told me stories."

"Did he now?" There was something about Cutter that worried me, but I couldn't have rightly said what. Yes, he was a killer, but then so were most of my crew. So was I, for that matter. It was something more than that, something strange about the fellow. Even Bloody Anne admitted he gave her the fear, and that was a rare enough thing by itself. "What sort of stories, Billy?"

"He told me about when he was a boy, in Messia," Billy said. "That's where he's from too, like me."

I nodded slowly. I hadn't known that. Jochan said he'd met Cutter in Messia during the war and I had no reason to doubt him, but if that was his home then he should have been fighting for the enemy, not for us. Billy hadn't been, to be sure, but then he had only had twelve years to him at the time. He had been far too young to be conscripted, but Cutter hadn't.

"That's interesting," I said. "Did he talk about the war, at all?"

Billy shook his head. "No," he said. "No one really does, do they, Uncle Tomas?"

I had to allow that he was right about that.

"No," I admitted.

"Can I go and see him again tomorrow?"

I wasn't sure I wanted that to happen, but I couldn't think of a sensible reason why not, and young Billy was looking at me with a hopeful expression on his face that I was finding hard to refuse.

"Aye, well," I had to say at last, "I suppose there's no harm in it. Be sure and take someone with you again, though."

"I will," Billy said, and that was settled.

I got up and left him to pester Hanne for another pastry. I strolled into the parlor to get myself a brandy and found that Ailsa had returned from her shopping trip, and she had a visitor.

"Mr. Piety," Rosie said by way of greeting.

I nodded to her and poured myself a drink.

"What brings you here, Rosie?"

"Just visiting," she said.

That was unlikely, to my mind. Rosie was Bloody Anne's woman, a redhead in her early twenties who worked out of the Chandler's Narrow house, where she ruled the other girls with a firm hand. Even now she wore the bawd's knot proudly displayed on her shoulder in yellow cord. Anne didn't know it, but she was also Ailsa's contact in the Queen's Men. There was only one reason for Rosie to be calling on Ailsa, and that was if there was news from Dannsburg.

News, or orders.

Of course, I didn't get to find out what those orders might be. Rosie worked for Ailsa, not for me, at least where crown business was concerned. I had given my loyalty to the Queen's Men, but I wasn't one of them, or even really part of their network of spies. I was just a man Ailsa was using, I was under no illusions about that. She was my wife for convenience only, and her expression made it quite plain that I wasn't welcome to join their conversation.

I left the two of them to talk. I found Desh still in the hall with a crossbow propped beside his chair while he watched the door. He got up smart enough when he saw me, and all but saluted. Guard duty is the most boring thing there is, every soldier knows that, and I felt for him.

"How do you like the life?" I asked him, taking a sip of my brandy.

He gave me a respectful nod.

"Very well, thank you, Mr. Piety," he said.

He wasn't a Pious Man yet, but he had been with me a good while now. I knew little enough about him, for all that.

"Tell me about yourself, Desh," I said. "Do you have family? A special girl, maybe?"

He shook his head. "No one special," he said. "My parents and my sisters still live down on Hull Patcher's Row, but we don't see a lot of each other anymore."

"Family is important," I said.

"This isn't the life they'd have chosen for me, and that pains them," he admitted. "They'd have seen me work my hands raw on the boats until I was half crippled, just like they did. Honest work, they'd call that. A fool's errand is what I call it."

I smiled at that, and thought of how I had turned my back on bricklaying as a young man and become a businessman instead. There was something in Desh that reminded me of myself at that age. That might be a good thing, or it might not. He was ambitious, I could see that much, and ambition is always to be admired. To a point.

He was wearing a good coat, I saw. Not as expensive as those the Pious Men favored, of course, but cut in the same style and certainly richer than anything a lad from Hull Patcher's Row might ever expect to own. Status mattered to Desh, I could see that. That might well be the lever that moved him, and again there we weren't so very different.

"I agree with you about that, as you won't be surprised to learn," I told him, and showed him a smile. "There could be a future for you here, in the Pious Men."

"That's what I want, sir," he said. "That's all I've ever wanted, as far back as I can remember."

I nodded slowly. I had thought as much.

"Good," I said.

Rosie came out of the drawing room then, a thin cloak draped over her kirtle to hide the bawd's knot on her shoulder. Ailsa would never have wanted the neighbors to see a whore come calling at the house, not even a licensed one. Those who wore the knot were a good deal more respectable than unlicensed street scrubs, to be sure, but even so I knew that would never have done.

I found myself wondering what had happened to the sweet, funny, common girl called Ailsa who had come to work for me in the Tanner's Arms last year. The girl I had started to fall in love with.

She never existed, I reminded myself. *She was just a false face.*

That was true enough, but the thought pained me all the same.

I watched Rosie leave, then turned back to Desh.

"There's going to be work soon," I told him. "I was wondering if perhaps you'd like to do something more than guard a door. Would you?"

He straightened at once, a determined set to his jaw.

"I would, sir," he said.

"It might be harsh work, I won't lie to you about that, but harsh work is well rewarded."

He nodded. "I can do that."

He wasn't a veteran and I didn't know if he could, but there was only one way to find out.

SEVEN

I held a council of war that night at the Tanner's Arms.

We were in the back room where the men had used to sleep. Many of the lads had their own homes in the Stink by then, and those who didn't were content living out of one or the other of my boardinghouses. Only Anne, Hari, Sam, and Black Billy lived at the Tanner's now, and the big storeroom had been converted into my headquarters.

There was a long table and twelve chairs set up in the big windowless room, lit by half a dozen oil lamps stood along its length. I had the head of the table, with Bloody Anne in her place at my right hand and my brother at my left. Fat Luka was beside Anne, with Aunt Enaid opposite him at Jochan's side. Those were all I had summoned to this meeting, them and young Desh.

He sat nervously beside Fat Luka. Enaid was staring at him with her single eye, and I could tell it was making him uncomfortable.

"Why is this foreign boy here?" she said.

My aunt had been a soldier in the last war, and she made no pretense to being a lady. She had some sixty years to her, and she was one-eyed and half-crippled and blunt and rude and fucking a lad called Brak who was barely a third her age. No one would think she had been a nun, barely a year past, but then I doubted many would think me a priest, either.

"His name is Desh, and he's here because I invited him," I said.

"Why?" she demanded. "He's not a Pious Man. Barely old enough to shave, and he's off the tea ships at that."

"He's not off the tea ships; he's from Hull Patcher's Row," I said.

Aunt Enaid had a deep-seated dislike of Alarians, I knew, although I had no idea why. That hadn't gone well between us, when I married Ailsa. My aunt had taken that very ill indeed. All the same, it had given me an idea.

Desh looked somewhere between embarrassed and angry, hearing my aunt talk, but he held his peace about it, and that was wise of him. I could see he knew his place at this table. The lad was clearly no fool.

"He's a good man," Fat Luka said, "but I'd ask the same question. This table is for Pious Men."

"Aye, it is," I said. "It might be that Desh will be joining us at this table, someday. I wanted to introduce him to you all. We've work, and soon. Bloodhands and the Northern Sons need a good kicking. They hold Convent Street, and I want it. There's a lot of taxes to be taken from the warehouses along there, and it'll allow us to spread our streets across west from the docks and cap the north end of the city all the way to the racetrack. Desh is going to help us with that work, and then we'll see."

Luka nodded to say he understood.

"Pious Men are Ellinburg men," my aunt said.

I turned and glared at her.

"He's from fucking Hull Patcher's Row," I said again. "You could stand on the roof here and hit his da's front door with a thrown rock. Enough of that."

"I'm not from Ellinburg, nor a man," Bloody Anne said in the quiet, rasping tone she used when she was getting angry. "Do you question my place at this table?"

"I'll question who I like in my own city," Enaid growled. "He's a fucking tea monkey and you're a cunt-eater, and why should I sit with either of you?"

Anne was across the table faster than a blink, and one of her daggers hammered down into the wood barely half an inch from my aunt's hand.

"Enough," I said, in the voice that threatened harsh justice to come.

Anne glared into Enaid's eye for a moment, then finally wrenched her dagger back out of the table and regained her seat.

"I won't be spoken to like that," Anne said.

"No, you won't," I said. "You're my second, but I'm the boss here. If there's justice to be done at my table, then it's me who'll deal it. If anybody, and I mean *anybody*, disrespects my judgment like that again, then Lady help me I will fucking blind them. Is that absolutely understood?"

Enaid looked at me and then away.

"Yes, Tomas," she said.

"Aye, Tomas," my brother muttered.

"Yes, boss," said Fat Luka, and Desh echoed him with a tremor in his voice.

Anne gave me a short nod.

That was done, then.

"Good," I said. "I'll hear no more about that, and you mind that it doesn't leave this room. Desh, you can go and get a drink now. We've business to discuss."

He nodded and left us there, and to my mind he looked a sight less cocky than he had before the council had started. That was good. I had needed him to know what he would be getting into if he became a Pious Man, and who he would be sitting with at the table. He had been starting to think of himself as a big man, I had realized, so it was my job to show him that he wasn't. Not yet, anyway. I think he understood the lay of things in the Pious Men now and who was in charge.

The door closed behind him, and a moment later Jochan roared with laughter.

"Fuck a nun! If he still wants to join us after that then the boy's made of the right fucking stuff," he said.

Anne and Enaid grinned at each other across the table, obviously pleased with themselves and rightly so. Anne had told me once before that she was no actress, but she was wrong about that, to my mind. Between them they had made a fine job of the little mummer's show I had set them to perform for Desh.

"Exactly," I said. "He ain't a veteran but that's through no fault of his own, and he's just proved he knows when to sit still and keep his mouth shut. We'll put him to work on this, and if word doesn't spread of what he just saw then we'll see about his future."

"To work on what, exactly?" Enaid said. "And why are you so bloody keen on him, Tomas?"

"I'm planning some mischief, Auntie," I told her. "That's not your side of things, I know, but it means I'll want to take Anne away from the business and put her back into the sergeant's role. I need you to run things again for a while."

Enaid just nodded at that. She knew the Pious Men business inside out, after all.

"And the lad?"

"We lost a lot of good men this last year," I said. "We're enough, for now, but not if we mean to expand. And I *do* mean to expand, you mark me on that. All of you, you mark me. All of eastern Ellinburg belongs to the Pious Men, but all that means is there's half the city that doesn't, and I mean to change that. If I need to make a few of the hired lads up to this table, then that's what I'll do, and Desh is the most likely of them so far. Any questions?"

I stared around the table, meeting their eyes one by one. Anne was resigned, Luka calculating, Jochan eager. Only my aunt was unreadable, her one blue eye glittering in the light of the lamps.

"Where, and when?" my brother asked.

"The racetrack," I said. "There's a big meet on Coinsday, and I want us there. We're going to make a statement."

Coinsday was the day before Godsday, the day when working folk got paid their wages for the week. It was traditionally a day of drinking and gambling and excess. A man might give two thirds of his pay to his wife to keep their house but the rest was his, and he'd waste it as he saw fit. It was the busiest night of the week in the Tanner's Arms, and the busiest day at the track, too.

We were there shortly after noon, perhaps an hour before the first race of the day. The racetrack lay to the north and west of Trader's Row and the docks, just outside the northern city wall. I was with Jochan and Bloody Anne and Fat Luka, all of us dressed in fine clothes and out for a day at the races with Stefan and Borys and Simple Sam following as our bodyguards.

Away out in the crowd, shabbily dressed and inconspicuous but with daggers and other things hidden under their coats, were eight of the hired lads, including Desh. He had the command of them, and he had his orders.

We circulated, Anne and my brother and Fat Luka and me, exchanging nods and handshakes and pats on the shoulder with people we knew. The betting tents were open by then, and men were calling odds on the races to come. Men from the Northern Sons, I knew that much.

Ailsa had reminded me yet again before I left that I was to keep a distance between myself and the inevitable bloodshed, and she had sent me off with a stern reminder that I was to be back at the house by sundown. I fully intended to keep my distance that day—I was enjoying a day at the races with my friends, that was all. Besides, it was her who had wanted the fight taking to the Sons and their Skanian backers. That was what I was doing, to my mind.

We made our way to the betting tents, and now heads were turning in the crowd to follow us. We were known, all of us. Of course we were; that was half the point. We were dressed like lords and flanked by guards and everyone knew *exactly* who the Pious Men were.

I placed bets, seemingly at random, and my brother did the same. Today wasn't about silver, and it didn't much matter if we won or lost. Today was about steel, and there we *would* win. All the same, I only bet on horses that I knew weren't owned by the Northern Sons.

That done, we visited the tavern tents and circulated some more, drinking and making merry and being seen. Desh and his boys weren't visible in the crowd anymore, and that was good. Lady willing, they were about their business.

The time came for the first race, and we crowded to the rail with the common folk. They left a respectful space around us, and any who forgot to do that were sharply reminded by Borys and Stefan.

The track was a great oval of grass, with the winning post not a hundred yards from where we stood. The ground seemed to tremble as the horses pounded down the home straight, their riders bent low over their necks and whipping them into a frenzy. A horse called Glory's Dream had the lead, a horse owned by the Northern Sons and the clear favorite according to the odds. Glory's Dream led by two lengths, then by one length, then her front legs buckled and she crashed to the turf and pitched her rider head over heels out of the saddle and under the merciless hooves of the pursuing horses.

Clear Water galloped home, and I allowed myself a smile. I'd had ten marks on her at three to one.

There was shouting in the crowd, and men rushed onto the track to see to the fallen rider. He was alive but grievously hurt, and I doubted he would ride again.

Four races we watched that afternoon, and each time the horses owned by the Sons fell or collapsed or simply refused to start. By the time the day was done my purse was a good deal heavier than it had been, and the atmosphere at the track was turning ugly.

Desh had done well.

EIGHT

"They've been nobbled!" I heard a man shout, somewhere in the crowd.

There were angry rumbles of agreement from the men around him.

I could feel Simple Sam drawing closer to me, and Stefan had Anne's right while Borys minded Luka and my brother. I could see Desh and his crew now, in the distance near the stables. He had five men with him, where before he had had seven, but it was done.

"We should go," Anne rasped, close to me, and I nodded.

It was known that we had been there, and what had happened, and that was enough. I hadn't forgotten my own racehorse and I hadn't forgiven anyone for what had happened to it, and I had sent that message loud and clear to the Skanians.

Desh had done the work I had set him. His orders had been simple enough: break into the Sons' stables, kill their guards and drug their horses. Him and his boys had nobbled the Sons' horses like he had been told to, and if he had lost two men in the process, then he had seen hard fighting doing it. Truth be told, I had expected that, but the lad had stepped up and done what he was told and that was good.

We left without waiting for them, me and Anne and Luka in my carriage while the others rode. Desh and his remaining crew would slip out in ones and twos, mingling with the crowd in their shabby clothes until they could make their way back to the Tanner's Arms on foot.

"That went well enough," I said, once the carriage was under way.

"Desh lost two of his crew, unless I missed my count," Anne growled. "That's not well enough to me."

"They're just hired men, Anne," I said. "The weakest fall first, just like conscripts in the army, and they weren't anyone we knew. Our Lady welcomes them. They may have crossed the river, but Desh didn't and he did what I wanted him to do, and that's good."

She had no answer to that.

"The Sons aren't stupid, and most everyone saw us there," Fat Luka said.

"Aye, they saw us betting and drinking and standing at the rail, and if we were doing those things then we weren't anywhere near those horses, were we?" I pointed out.

"That's true enough," he admitted.

"Two men dead, and I don't see what we've achieved," Anne said.

"Little enough, save a pile of silver," I said, "but that was today. Today was about sending a message to the Sons, telling them I can hurt them if I want to. Telling them I *do* want to. They'll have half their boys guarding the track and their stables tonight, and that means they won't be guarding everywhere else half so well as they should be."

Anne nodded slowly, and her scar twisted as the corner of her mouth turned up in a smile. She might say she'd had enough of fighting, but I didn't think that was strictly true. Bloody Anne had earned her name at Abingon, and a hundred times over since then. She had been getting bored, I could tell that much, and the prospect of a raid was cheering her.

"Where do we hit them?"

"Convent Street," I said at once. "That runs west from the docks to the foot of the hill, and they've the bulk of their warehouses along there. I want them burned down."

"Aye, we can do that," she said. "I assume you're not joining us?"

"I wish I could," I said, and I realized that I meant it. Anne wasn't the only one who was growing tired of inactivity. "I have a society reception to host this evening."

Anne snorted.

"What fun. Leave it to me," she said.

I knew I could. Bloody Anne was the best second I could have asked for.

* * *

Ailsa was already dressed for the evening when I returned home. She was waiting in the parlor in a flowing gown of russet silk with her thick, glossy black hair pinned up between ivory combs.

"How were the races?" she asked me as I poured myself a brandy.

"Good," I said. I gave the footman a look, and he left the room and closed the door behind him to give us our privacy. "I gave the Skanians something to think on, and Lady willing they'll be thinking on it so hard they won't see the attack coming tonight."

"And you kept your distance?"

"Yes, Ailsa, I did," I said. "Princes don't lead from the front, I know."

"Mmmm," she said. "We may need to rethink that."

That made me look up. "How so?"

"There's a thing that needs doing, and I don't want to trust it to Anne or gods forbid to your brother."

Ailsa thought even less of Jochan than she did of Anne, and there at least I thought she was right. Jochan was rarely sober, and his battle shock was so deep-seated it could overtake him at a moment's notice, leading to sudden rages or incoherence and no way to predict it. He was my brother and I loved him, in my way, but I knew I couldn't rely on him.

"Tell me," I said.

"The common folk, the workers," she said. "How much attention do we pay them, truly? Are they just pieces on our game board?"

I blinked at her in confusion. I paid attention to *my* people, the folk from my streets who paid their taxes to me and showed me respect. A prince should do no less, to my mind. Other folk, folk from the west of the city, for example, no. No, I didn't pay them any mind.

"I have to get dressed for this fucking reception in a minute," I said. "Whatever you're working your way around to saying, say it now."

"Do you know how many cunning folk there are in this city?"

"No, of course not," I said. "Apart from our Billy I know Old Kurt, from the Wheels, but that's all. One person in ten thousand has it in them to learn the cunning, so they say, if that. Maybe he's the only one in Ellinburg."

"He isn't. Not at all he isn't. I need you to do something for me. You're recruiting men, and I support that, but I need you to focus on the cunning folk. Find out who they are. Find them, and bring them to our side. From what I hear there are a number of them at large in the city. Not openly, like your Old Kurt, but just getting on with their lives. I want them, and that means you're going to go out and get them."

When Ailsa said *I want* in that tone of voice, she always got what she wanted. One way or another she did. I frowned for a moment but nodded. This had something to do with Rosie's visit, I was sure. Whatever her reasons, this felt like orders from Dannsburg itself.

"I'll see what I can do," I said, and changed the subject. "I thought I might wear my priest's robes tonight."

"Gods, no," she said. "Save the religion for the common folk and the easily led. Tonight you must be the businessman. The valet has already laid suitable clothes out in your room for you. Now hurry up, they'll be here in an hour."

NINE

The grand dining room had been set for the occasion: the big formal room at the back of the house that we rarely used. I had the head of the long table, of course, and Ailsa its foot as custom and manners dictated. Our guests were seated between us. There were twelve of them in all, tedious factory owners and ridiculous minor aristocrats. And Governor Hauer, of course. He was seated at my right hand in the place of honor, although it was no secret that we weren't friends. It was less than a week since he'd had me arrested, after all.

The forms of society had to be obeyed, so Ailsa told me, and there had been no way for us to host this reception without inviting Hauer. I had known that, but I hadn't expected him to accept. Whether Ailsa had or not I really couldn't say, but I think it was what she had hoped for. Be that as it may, there he was sitting in my dining room, drinking my wine and filling his fat face with my roast goose and suckling pig.

Conversation at my end of the table was subdued, as might be expected. There wasn't a guest there who didn't know who I was and what I did, and many of them either paid me protection through their businesses or smoked my poppy resin at the Golden Chains, or both. Everyone was very polite and very guarded around me. At the other end of the table Ailsa was keeping up a lively conversation and acting the perfect hostess. She knew how to do this sort of thing, and I really didn't.

"Do you think this uncommon heat will last, Mr. Piety?" asked the lady seated to my left.

I couldn't remember her name, but I knew she owned a pair of mills in the Wheels that had recently been reopened. She had paid her taxes to Ma Aditi a year ago, and now she paid them to me.

"I hadn't given it much thought," I said.

She looked as though she expected me to say more, but how I was supposed to know the minds of the weather gods was beyond me. I was a priest of Our Lady of Eternal Sorrows, not the Stormlord, and men die in all weathers.

"I believe not, Madame Rainer," the fellow next to the governor said. "The ships' captains bring word of cooler weather at sea than of late."

This one at least I knew—Jon Lan Barkov, who seemed to do nothing in particular but who had a great deal of money all the same. He also had a great fondness for the poppy, and he was a regular at the Chains.

"That's good to know," I said, for want of anything better.

This pointless talk about nothing chafed me, as I dare say it did them. What they wanted to know, what they *all* wanted to know, was why I had been arrested and whether it was likely to affect them and their businesses. The governor's presence at my right hand was easing their minds about that some, as I suspected Ailsa had intended it to.

I labored through the meal until the sweet had been cleared away and the ladies were preparing to withdraw to the parlor. I would be expected to entertain the men at table with brandy and conversation, of course, but it looked like I might be spared that when a footman hurried into the room and bent to speak quietly in my ear.

"One of the governor's men is here, sir," he whispered. "An urgent message."

I nodded.

"Show him in," I said, and turned to Hauer. "It seems you have business that won't keep, Lord Governor."

Hauer frowned and turned in his chair. He was already drunk, I noticed.

"What?" he demanded of the nervous-looking messenger who was being admitted to the dining room.

The man whispered to the governor, whose flushed face darkened by the moment as he listened. Eventually he dismissed his man and got to his feet.

"I fear I must excuse myself," he said, fixing me with a steady glare even as he swayed slightly on his feet. "Something of an emergency has arisen."

"Oh?" I asked.

"Half of Convent Street is on fire, Piety," he growled.

He turned and stormed out of the room without even bidding Ailsa a good evening or thanking her for her hospitality, which even I knew was almost unforgivably rude. A shocked hush descended over the table at the governor's lack of manners, but Ailsa rescued the situation with her usual grace.

"Such terrible news," she said. "I completely understand the lord governor's haste to be about his urgent duties."

With those waters smoothed, she rose and ushered the ladies out with her, leaving me at the table with Lan Barkov and five other men I barely knew. I motioned to the nearest footman to pour brandies.

"It seems the uncommon heat will last tonight," I said. "On Convent Street, at least."

It was late by the time the last of our guests finally took themselves out of my house and off home to their beds. I had resorted to a game of cards to keep the men happy, and if one wasn't supposed to play cards at the dining table then I didn't care, nor did they seem to. They had all drunk a good deal of my brandy by then, and in their cups they had become even more tedious company than they had been while sober.

Still, I hadn't been drinking half so heavily as my guests had, and I had cleared a neat pile of silver from the card game by the time they left. That was small enough consolation for so dreary an evening, but the news from Convent Street pleased me. I had known I could rely on Anne.

"That went well, I thought," Ailsa said when I joined her in the drawing room.

Withdrawing room, I realized at last. That finally made sense and put my mind at rest that I'd not be asked to take up a sketching book after all.

It was a small matter, and one that made me feel something of a fool after the fact, but all the same it impressed further on me how much I didn't know about Ailsa's way of life. What things were called in polite company, how to entertain society guests and to make pointless conversation, all those things were still mysteries to me. I understood business, and tactics, and how to lead men. Those things were a sight more important, to my mind.

"Anne's crew did what we wanted," I said, "and while the governor was sat at my right hand, at that. There's no way I can be implicated."

"Yes," Ailsa said. "Yes, very good, but the other matter is more important now."

I frowned at that, and again I wondered exactly what orders she had received, and who had sent them.

"Aye, well," I said. "I'll have to talk to Fat Luka about it, if no one else. I don't know who these hidden cunning folk are, but I'll wager he can find out."

Ailsa didn't argue about that, which surprised me. She had more time for Luka than she did for Anne or my brother, I knew. Perhaps she sensed a kindred spirit, there. Had his life been different, I thought, Fat Luka might just have made a Queen's Man himself.

"Very well, and I know there's no point telling you to keep it from Anne, but no one else," she said. "Not unless you absolutely have to."

That seemed fair, so I nodded and left her to it. I had been drinking wine with the meal because you were supposed to but I don't care for wine, and I had had enough of brandy. I wandered through to the kitchen to draw myself a mug of beer from the big barrel that was kept there.

I found Jochan in there, with his britches round his ankles, vigorously fucking Hanne the undercook over the kitchen table.

He looked round as the door opened and grinned at me.

"Don't mind me," I said.

The poor lass went crimson with embarrassment, but Jochan wasn't showing any signs of stopping so I drew myself a tankard from the barrel and left them to it. Soldiers think little of that sort of thing. There's nowhere to be alone among the tents, after all. If a man wants to lie with a camp follower or a comrade, then that's his affair, but there's no use him expecting privacy while he does it.

I stood in the yard behind the house with my beer in my hand, content to just enjoy the cool of the summer night. Jochan joined me a few minutes later, still lacing his britches.

"I came calling an hour ago, but your man said you still had guests, and he put me in the kitchen to wait," he said. "Me and the lass got to talking, and that."

"Mostly that, from what I saw," I said, and he laughed.

"Aye, well," he said. "Some silver pennies got rid of the rest of your kitchen staff, and they were coins fucking well spent. I like a big lass, you know that."

He laughed again, and for a moment there it was almost like having my brother back.

"What word from Convent Street?" I asked him.

"Only six guards and we killed the fucking lot of them," he said, and there was a sudden savage light in his eyes. "Three warehouses are in ashes."

I nodded. The moment had passed, and now all I could see in Jochan's eyes was a reflection of the fires of Abingon.

"Aye," I said. "That's good work, well done."

There would be more of it to come, I knew.

Much more, and soon.

TEN

There was, at that. A great deal more.

As the summer heat broke and cold autumn winds began to gust down the streets of Ellinburg, my men continued to fight the hidden war against the Skanians in the alleys and factories of the city. Three months had passed, and the fighting had turned ugly. The raid on Convent Street might have gone well, but Bloodhands had wasted no time in striking back. The uneasy truce of the previous nine months was in the shithouse now and no mistake. This wasn't open warfare, not yet, but it was close to it. Too many men on both sides had been knifed behind taverns and dumped in alleyways, or simply found floating in the river.

I was seldom home now, but this time Ailsa had no complaints on the matter. Not now that I was being useful to her again, she didn't. Young Billy was away a lot too. He was still spending most of his days with Cutter at Slaughterhouse Narrow, and for all that I wasn't keen on the idea I was too busy to give it much thought. Not today he wasn't, though. Today I would need him.

Although I had kept myself away from the actual violence, I did the queen's bidding in secret. Fat Luka's spies and silver had turned up two cunning folk in the last couple of months, a pair of nondescript women who plied their trades of herb lore and midwifery in the west of the city.

Neither was wealthy, and when I offered to change that they came to my side willingly enough. Life on the streets controlled by the Skanians through their Northern Sons was harsh, I knew that, and Luka had used that fact to help talk them over to my side. That, and silver. Katrin the herbalist lived in the Stink now, where I had set her up with a small shop of her own.

Gerta the midwife had stayed in her house on the west side of the city, where she provided Luka with regular information on the movements of the Northern Sons and their murderous agents in exchange for his coin. Gerta especially played a dangerous game there, but she played it willingly enough. I heard from Fat Luka that she had personally witnessed children being taken away from their families by Bloodhands's agents, to be held hostage and guarantee the loyalty of their fathers. She had heard what happened to those children if Bloodhands decided someone had crossed him, too. Aye, winning Gerta to my side had been done easily enough. Ailsa was pleased, and that was good.

Now Luka had found another one, up in the docks this time.

Luka had arranged to bring her to the Tanner's Arms that afternoon for me to meet, and as with the other two, I had brought Billy the Boy to meet her with me. I know nothing of magic or the cunning or whatever you wanted to call it, but Billy had known almost at a glance that Gerta and Katrin both had the talent. I wanted him to look at this woman too before I offered her anything. She wouldn't have been the first fraud in search of silver that we had uncovered. There had been harsh justice for those as thought they could cheat me.

I was sitting at the head of the table in the back room of the Tanner's Arms, with Billy at my right hand. Only three of the lamps on the table were lit, keeping the room mostly in shadow. There was a knock at the door, and then Fat Luka opened it and stepped inside with a woman beside him.

"This is Mr. Tomas Piety," Luka told her. "Boss, this is goodwife Lisbeth Beck."

She attempted a shaky curtsey, and I gave her a short nod in return. Billy just sat staring at her in that intense way he had about him. She had perhaps thirty years to her, at a guess, with long, light brown hair bound up at the back of her head. Her kirtle and cloak had both seen better days, and she wore no jewelry. This one obviously wasn't wealthy either.

"Thank you, Luka, you can leave us," I said. "Lisbeth, take a seat."

Fat Luka stepped back out into the corridor and closed the door behind him, and Lisbeth Beck seated herself at the long table. She looked from me to Billy and back again, and cleared her throat.

"Thank you for coming," I said, although I was sure she wouldn't have been given a great deal of choice in the matter. "Do you know who I am?"

"I know," she said, and swallowed.

I nodded slowly. She was from the docks, and I had expected no less. The docks had belonged to the Headhunters before the war, but the Headhunters hadn't come home and we had. The docks belonged to the Pious Men now.

"Do you know why you're here?"

"I've got a little bit of the cunning in me, sir, I always have had," she said. "I know that's why I'm here."

I glanced at Billy. He nodded, but there was a frown on his face.

"What?" I asked him.

"More than a little bit," he said. "Much more."

I smiled at her, indulgent of her reticence. "Are you being shy with me, Lisbeth?"

"No, I am not," she said.

The lamp nearest to me exploded, throwing broken glass and burning oil in my face. I flung an arm up to protect my eyes just in time, yelling in shock and pain. Billy flew out of his seat and slammed back against the wall behind him. Some invisible force held him pinned there, the pressure crushing the breath from him. I lurched to my feet, struggling to free myself from my burning coat.

"Pious Men, to me!" I bellowed.

The woman, this Lisbeth or whoever she really was, shot a hard look at the door a moment before fists started to bang on it. It rattled in its frame but wouldn't open, and I swore on Our Lady's name as I realized that she was holding it closed with the cunning. I tore my coat off at last and hurled it at her, but she evaded it easily enough. Billy was thrashing and struggling against the wall now, his face starting to go blue as he was choked by the grip of whatever magic held him.

I cursed myself for falling out of the habit of wearing the Weeping

Women. That was Ailsa's influence, and it wasn't serving me well. Unarmed, trapped in the room, and facing what had to be a Skanian magician, I did the only thing I could think of.

I charged her.

Lisbeth spat in my face as I crashed into her and bore her to the floor, using the simple fact of my weight to force her off her feet. Sudden searing pain gripped me, making me scream like an animal. The ceiling hit me in the back a moment later and my vision swam as I stared helplessly down at the assassin. She kept me pinned to the ceiling with the sheer force of her magic, and she was still holding the door closed behind her and Billy against the wall as well, but it seemed that the effort of doing too many things at once meant that she had to choose between them.

She released Billy the Boy, and that was her mistake.

The lad fell to his knees on the floor, clutching his throat and gasping as Lisbeth got to her feet and stalked toward him. I heard a crash as someone in the corridor brought an axe down against the door. It shuddered in its frame, but that was a solid oak door and I knew they wouldn't get through it quickly.

One look at Billy told me they wouldn't have to.

Lisbeth reached into the bodice of her kirtle and her hand came out with a small dagger in it, but it was too late for her. Billy had his breath now, and the haunted look in his unblinking eyes told me the lad was once more among the ruins of Messia.

He was in Messia after the sack, where men had torn each other apart with their bare hands over half a loaf of stale bread. That was Billy's childhood, lived among those ruins, and he had survived it alone.

The sudden flash of power in his eyes gave me the fear and I've no shame in admitting that, but by then it was far too late to stop him and I couldn't truly say that I wanted to. With all that he'd been through, to my mind he was entitled to that rage, to that vengeance.

All the same, when he spoke his voice was flat and cold and utterly without anger or hurt or any emotion at all.

It was just like mine was, when I pronounced harsh justice.

"No," he said.

Lisbeth Beck exploded where she stood.

It's quite a thing, to see a human body explode. There's a great deal of blood in a body, after all. Her magic dissipated all at once, and the door flew open just as I found myself falling, splattered in blood, face-first onto the table. I hit with a bone-jarring impact and rolled onto the floor, taking two chairs over with me.

Jochan was standing in the doorway with his axe in his hand and his mouth open, staring into the room in disbelief. It was like an abattoir in there.

"What the fuck . . . ?" he whispered.

I looked at Billy and nodded my thanks to him before turning my eyes on my brother.

"Get me Fat Luka," I said. "Right now."

I had sent Billy away to rest and regained my seat at the head of the table by the time Luka came in, but I had made no attempt to wipe the blood off my face. My shirt was spattered with it too, and one sleeve was scorched from the burning lamp oil that had drenched my coat. I must have looked like some devil from Hell, to Luka's eyes.

He stared around the dimly lit room, at my still-smoldering coat and the huge spray of blood and torn meat and shattered bone that decorated the walls and floor and ceiling where Lisbeth Beck had been.

"How the fuck," I said, my voice falling into that special tone that promised harsh justice, the tone I shared with Billy the Boy, "did this happen?"

"Lady forgive me," Luka whispered.

His fat face had gone the color of curdled milk, as well it might. I had known Luka since we were boys in school together, and I knew he served me well. All the same, it would have felt like justice to kill Fat Luka, right then. He was fortunate, I think, that the Weeping Women were in a chest in my bedroom, half the city away.

Bloody Anne stepped into the room after Luka and closed the door behind her. There was a hard look on her face, and the blood and viscera on the floor and walls and above her head didn't seem to be bothering her at all.

"You brought this woman here, Luka," I said. "You stood her in front of me."

"As I brought the last two," he said. "Lady's sake, boss, you can't think . . . I wouldn't betray you, you have to know that!"

I *did* know that. I knew that, but I was angry, angrier than I like to allow myself to get. I could feel the cold devil inside me, awake and vengeful. I had nearly been assassinated, and in the very heart of my own streets at that. In the Tanner's Arms itself, where I should be untouchable. If it hadn't been for Billy the Boy I would be with Our Lady now, it was as simple as that.

I slammed the flat of my hand down on the table, and Fat Luka cringed. Bloody Anne put her hands on the hilts of her daggers, awaiting my judgment. I knew if I had given the word she would have killed Luka without a second thought.

"I want blood for this," I said, holding Fat Luka's wide-eyed gaze with a murderous glare that brooked no argument. The cold devil in me was awake, and I could tell that Luka knew it. "Not yours, before you piss your britches, but I promise you there will be harsh justice. No one does this to me. *No one!* You go out there, and you find whoever sent you to this goodwife Lisbeth Beck, and you bring them to me. You *will* do that, Fat Luka, and you will do it right fucking now. Is that clear?"

Luka swallowed and nodded. Anne took her hands off her daggers and stepped aside, and he hurried from the room.

I got to my feet and stared down at the table for a moment, breathing hard.

"Fuck!" I shouted.

I picked up the broken lamp and hurled it across the room in a fury. It smashed into the wall, and I clenched my fists until my knuckles ached. I could feel myself losing my way, as I had done before, could feel the shadow of the deeply buried battle shock gathering behind my eyes. In that moment, I understood my brother. I understood his need to find a fight of an evening. The need to hurt someone, anyone, to make the pain go away for a little while.

Bloody Anne knew what she was seeing, and she took a very careful step toward me.

She spoke quietly to me. I don't recall what she said, but she was talking and then I was sitting down again and she was sitting at my right hand, where she belonged. My second, always there to support me, always at my right hand. My shaking fists were on the table in front of me and they slowly opened as Anne just kept on talking, and then her hand was on mine and her callused fingers curled around my palm and squeezed gently, in a way that said she understood.

I came out of it then, whatever it had been, and I took a slow breath. I looked at her, met her eyes, and knew that words between us were unnecessary. She had been there, at Messia and at Abingon. There were no words needed, for that.

She understood, and that was enough.

"Brandy?" she said.

"Aye."

She went to get a bottle and two glasses, and we sat at the table together and drank, and waited.

When Fat Luka finally came back he was escorted in by Black Billy and my brother, and they were holding a man between them. He was no one, just some Ellinburg man. He was of average height and his hair was sandy and short and dirty, and it had been some days since he had last shaved. His lips were split and bloody, and one of his eyes was swollen shut. He was no one I knew, and that was good. That made it easier to do what had to be done. The battle shock might have left me, but the cold devil in my heart very much hadn't, and it demanded its due.

Bloody Anne put one of her daggers in my hand.

ELEVEN

It was late when I got home. I had washed the blood from my face and hands and hair in the kitchen at the Tanner's Arms, and Hari had lent me a clean shirt and a coat. We had wrapped Billy the Boy in one of Simple Sam's old cloaks to hide the bloodstains on his clothes. All the same, as soon as she saw me Ailsa knew something had happened. She was sitting in her chair by the hearth in our drawing room when I came in, but I could tell that she knew. She put her embroidery down and looked at me.

"Was there a raid?" she asked once I had chased the footman and her maid out of the room and closed the door behind them.

"An assassination attempt," I said. "A magician, posing as a dockside cunning woman. A Skanian, I can only assume."

"What happened?"

I shrugged. "She nearly killed me, then Billy killed her," I said. "Then I sent Fat Luka to bring me the man who introduced us to her, and I killed *him*. It's been a good day for killing."

"With your own hands?"

"Yes, Ailsa, with my own hands," I snapped at her. "They attacked me in my place of business. I'm a businessman and I'm a fucking soldier, and I *will not have it*!"

"No. Quite," she said. "I'm not pleased about this."

"Do you really fucking think that *I* am?"

Her brow furrowed in thought. "Were the City Guard involved?"

"No, of course not," I said. "The Pious Men don't shout for the Guard. My streets, my law. My justice."

"Hmmm," she said, and took up her embroidery hoop again. "We'll hear about this from Hauer nonetheless, you mark me."

"You think *he* was behind it?"

"No, this has to have been Skanian work—it has Vhent written all over it. But Vhent has the governor's ear, and I'll wager he will bend that ear the first chance he gets."

I sighed and poured myself a brandy.

"Aye, no doubt," I said.

I sank into the chair opposite her and sipped my drink, looking at her over the rim of my glass.

My wife.

My wife, the Queen's Man, who had just learned that there had been an attempt on my life a few short hours ago. She pushed the needle through her work and drew the thread after it, stitch after stitch after stitch. Some concern might have been nice, to my mind.

"Where's Billy?" she asked, after a moment.

"Upstairs, asleep," I said. "It took a lot out of him, fighting that magician. She was strong, I think, this one. Very strong."

"But Billy was stronger."

"Aye," I said.

No, there would be no concern from Ailsa. Not from the woman who had killed over five hundred people in a single afternoon and thought nothing of it, there wouldn't. Ailsa's concern was for the crown's orders, and never mind who got hurt in carrying them out.

I drank my brandy and stretched my feet out toward the fire, and realized I was still wearing Hari's shirt. It didn't matter. I was alive, and comfortable, and drinking expensive brandy in the parlor of the sort of house I could have only dreamed of when I was a lad making my way in life through the alleys of the Stink. If that had cost blood, then what of it?

Perhaps we weren't so very different, my wife and me. That was an interesting thought, but one for another day.

I felt myself dozing, the tension of the day draining out of my body as

I finally started to relax. I could hear the fire crackling in the grate, and the wind whistling through the eaves of the house as the night drew in outside. Ailsa's needle moved through her hoop, stitch after stitch after stitch.

A pounding on the front door made my eyes open. Time had passed, I didn't know how much, but Ailsa had turned up the wick of her lamp at some point. A moment later one of the footmen entered the room and presented me with a folded paper.

"A messenger has come to the house, sir," he said. "He is in the hall, awaiting a reply. Apparently it is urgent."

I blinked sleep from my eyes and took the offered paper, unfolded it, and scanned the hastily scrawled and no doubt drunken writing.

Piety,

Heard what happened. I will intervene.

There must be no more blood spilled between you and the Sons in reprisal.

Think of the peace!

Gv. Hauer

The peace, that was a fucking joke. There was no peace between the Northern Sons and the Pious Men, to my mind. Not anymore there wasn't.

I passed the note to Ailsa without comment, and she read it and then cast it idly into the fire. She cleared her throat.

"I believe we can agree, in principle," she said.

I felt the anger quicken in me before I caught the look in her eye and realized her deeper meaning. Ailsa was subtle and no mistake, and I had to admire that about her.

"Aye," I said. "Tell him that the response is in agreement."

The footman nodded and left the room.

No blood spilled in reprisal.

Very well.

There are a lot of ways to kill a man.

* * *

Two nights later I was in the west of the city with Borys and Jochan and Bloody Anne, along with Desh and five of the new hired lads who I had put under him. Desh was doing well as an underboss, and I didn't think it would be long now before he joined us at the table.

I was standing in a shadowy earthen courtyard behind an unlicensed brothel on the edge of Northern Sons territory, just off Convent Street where it met the docks. The Badger's Rest, that place was called, and it was a shithole. Inside, the five new lads were shoring up the doors we had broken down on our way in. While they did that, Borys was reassuring the women who worked there that life under the Pious Men would be better than what they were used to. No one wore the bawd's knot there, and they were dirty and underfed and scared, and a lot of them had bruises that spoke of the harsh treatment they had received. Nobody mistreated whores, not in my crew they didn't. Not since Grieg, anyway, and everyone remembered how that had ended for him.

In front of me in the courtyard was the brothel keeper, and a deep hole in the ground.

The man had around fifty years to him and he was big and fat and brutal looking, with a bald head and a great jut of unshaven jaw that bristled silver in the moonlight. He was of an age to have fought in the war before mine, in Captain Rogan and Aunt Enaid's war, and he had the look of a veteran about him. He had big, hard hands, that man, and from what I had heard most of the women inside had felt the backs of them on a daily basis.

Valter, his name was, and to my mind he was a cunt.

He was also a member of the Northern Sons and in the pay of the Skanians. There was a spade at his feet, and sweat on his face, and fresh blisters on his hands. He had been digging for the last two hours with Anne's crossbow trained on him.

"Get in," I said.

He looked at me like he thought I was mad.

"What the fuck are you talking about, Piety?" he said. "I'm not getting in no hole. I'm your prisoner, I understand that, but you'll ransom me back to Bloodhands and the game will go on."

"I'm not playing games," I said. "Get in."

"Fuck off," he said. "You're a businessman, same as I am. You know how this works."

"Aye, I know how this works," I said. "I own my streets and Bloodhands owns his, and we joust and skirmish around the edges, and sometimes bodies turn up in alleys. That's how this fucking works. But you send a foreign assassin into the heart of my business, to kill me with witchcraft? That's *not* how this works."

He swallowed and shook his head, but I thought he knew what I was talking about.

"I ain't getting in that fucking hole," he said.

Jochan took up the spade and hit him with it so hard his knees buckled and he fell to the ground, and then the kicking started.

I let my brother have his way until Valter was insensible, then I held up a hand to tell him it was enough. Together, we rolled him into the grave I had made him dig for himself and we began to fill it in.

I had promised Hauer that I would spill no blood in reprisal for the attempt on my life, and I am a man of my word. I'm a priest, after all.

I looked down into the hole in the ground, and I smiled as a clod of wet earth landed on Valter's unconscious face.

Not a drop of blood had been spilled.

TWELVE

I left Borys there to hold the stew, and Desh and a couple of his new lads to help him do it. A business once taken had to be held, or I knew I wouldn't keep it long. Borys was ideal for the job. He was older than the other men, as I have written, quiet and thoughtful and almost fatherly in his way. I hoped his presence there would go some way toward reassuring the women that life with the Pious Men in charge would be better than it had been under the Northern Sons.

The place was on the border between my territory and that belonging to the Sons, which was why I had picked it. That kept my supply lines strong, so Borys couldn't find himself cut off from help if he needed it. That was the way it was done, just like in the army.

Ailsa wasn't expecting me back that night, so I was free to return to the Tanner's Arms with Jochan and Bloody Anne and the rest of the new lads. They were quiet, those boys, and a couple of them had thoughtful looks on their faces that said they might be having second thoughts about working for me. I made a mental note to have Fat Luka keep an eye on those two.

This life wasn't for everyone, I knew that, and those lads especially were young. They weren't veterans, and perhaps they hadn't ever seen harsh work before. Bloody Anne was quiet too, though, and she had done harsh work more times than I knew how to count. I could tell there was something on her mind.

The Tanner's was a welcome sight. I clapped Black Billy on the arm as he held the door open for me, and smiled to see Hari already pouring brandies for us. The Tanner's was home, in a way that I thought the big house off Trader's Row could never be.

"Usual table, boss?" Billy asked me.

I shook my head.

"Not tonight," I said. "I'll be in the back."

Once we had our drinks I took Anne to one side and led her through to the back room.

"You have the look of a woman who wants to say something," I said, taking my seat at the table.

"Perhaps I do," Anne said. "Perhaps I shouldn't."

I frowned at that. She was still standing, I noticed, when normally she would have taken her seat at my right hand by then.

"You're my second, Bloody Anne, and you know I respect you. If you've thoughts, then I want to hear them."

"All right, then, I've thoughts," she said, and she sounded angry now. "We're rich, all of us. We control half the city. Yes, the Sons tried to have you killed, but who can blame them? We fucking started it, and we're still doing it now. If I was their boss, *I'd* want you dead too."

"What do you suggest I do, Bloody Anne?" I asked her. "Sit here and wait for the next assassin to come?"

"You lived alongside Ma Aditi and her Gutcutters for years before the war, so I'm told. What's wrong with a truce, like you had then? Why the fuck can't you draw up a border with the Sons and let well alone?"

I looked at her, and I held my peace for a long moment. I had known it would come to this, sooner or later. *I'm taking my businesses back*, that's what I had told my crew when I had led them home from war. Well, I had done that, and more besides. I had destroyed the Gutcutters and taken over the Wheels and the docks, and now here I was looking to the west of the city and the Northern Sons. I had no doubt that Anne wasn't the only member of the Pious Men to have noticed this, but it spoke well of her loyalty that she was voicing those concerns to me in private instead of spreading them among the men.

Of course, what I was really doing was following Ailsa's orders, orders from the Queen's Men. This wasn't about territory and taxes, and it never had been. It was about the Skanians and preventing the possibility of another war. I couldn't tell Anne the truth, though, and that pained me, but there was nothing to be done about it.

"I had a border with the Gutcutters, aye," I said. "For a long time, and look how that ended. Truces don't last, Bloody Anne, not ever. You only have to look at our country's history to see that. One war after another, with one neighbor or another. We've had enemies who were good and loyal friends barely a year before it came to the exchange of cannon between us. It's the same in business. We're strong now, and I'm capitalizing on that. If I make a peace instead, then well and good, but what happens afterward? What happens next year or the year after, if the Sons are stronger than us by then? They come down on us like all the devils in Hell, that's what happens. We die, and so do our families and everyone we love. Do you want to see Chandler's Narrow fall to Bloodhands?"

Anne gave me a long look. I knew she was in love with Rosie, and I thought those feelings might even be returned. Anne knew what would happen if the Sons took Chandler's Narrow.

"You're holding that over me?" she whispered at last.

"No, of course I'm not," I said. "I'm just pointing out the realities of how things work in Ellinburg. Because you asked."

"Aye," Anne said. "I did."

She turned and left the room then, leaving me sitting at the head of my table.

Alone.

"Your job is very important, Fat Luka," I told him the next morning. "My people need to know how well I govern them. It's your job to tell them, and to make sure they understand why my decisions are good ones."

Luka nodded.

"Is there a problem?" he said.

"There might be," I said.

I didn't want to name Bloody Anne to him. She was my second, not him, and I needed him to respect her. All the same, something had to be done, and soon.

"Oh?"

"The raid on that stew last night, the Badger's Rest," I said. "Some of the new lads looked a sight uncomfortable with what they saw, and maybe with what they did."

Luka nodded again and took a sip of his breakfast beer.

"They're young," he said. "Those of us who were at Abingon . . . well, it takes a lot to make us uncomfortable. Perhaps we forget that not everyone has seen what we have."

"Aye, perhaps," I said. "All the same, I want it put around the crew why we have to take down the Northern Sons. The *whole* crew. Everyone's got money now, and it might be that's making some of them complacent. Just because they're comfortable now doesn't mean the threat goes away. It doesn't make *Bloodhands* go away, or his skinning knife either. You understand that, don't you, Fat Luka?"

"Course, boss," he said. "Don't worry, I'll make sure everyone understands it."

"Everyone," I said again.

Luka just nodded. He was a good man, I knew that.

I got up and wandered through to the kitchen to find something to eat, and when I came back I looked round the common room. Black Billy gave me a nod, but I thought he looked like maybe he had something on his mind as well. He never said much, but he was no one's fool, wasn't Billy. I had been expecting this, as I have written, but now that I saw it starting to unfold in front of me I realized that perhaps I hadn't truly been prepared for it. Now I'd be depending on Luka to make it right and, while I knew I could do that, the thought made me uncomfortable. Fat Luka always supported me, always and without question, but that was still a lot of faith to be putting in a single man, whoever he was.

Nonetheless, it would have to keep for the moment. I needed to go home and face Ailsa, who had insisted we attend some pointless society function or other at Lan Barkov's house that afternoon. At least it wasn't another formal dinner, but it still meant mixing with a roomful of fools again when I had better things to do, and I didn't understand the need for it.

I rode home with three of the crew, their watchful eyes scanning the alleys and narrows for trouble as we passed. There shouldn't be any, not there in the Stink, but after the attempt on my life at the Tanner's I was taking no chances. Besides, it wouldn't do for Tomas Piety to be seen in the city without bodyguards. There were certain expectations to be met, after all.

I understood *that* sort of society well enough.

THIRTEEN

Governor Hauer was also attending Lan Barkov's afternoon reception, which I thought might prove interesting.

Once we were there he wasted no time in joining me by the drawing room windows, while the other guests made a show of admiring the ridiculous new painting of Lan Barkov that we were all supposed to be there to look at. The artist was standing alone in the corner nursing a glass of wine while Lan Barkov soaked up the praise of his peers as though he had done anything but sit on his fat arse while another man worked. That summed up the nobility quite neatly, to my mind.

"I am not impressed," Hauer murmured.

"I know little of art, I admit, but I'm not impressed either," I said. "It barely looks like him."

"Not by the stupid painting," Hauer hissed at me. "I mean by your antics last night."

"What of them?"

"Three days ago you made your promise to me. Is that how long your word is good for, Piety, three fucking days?"

I turned and looked at the governor. His face was flushed with wine despite the hour, I noticed, and his tight collar was digging into the fat of his sweaty neck.

"I am a man of my word, Governor," I said. "Spill no blood, you said. No blood was spilled."

Of course he knew what had happened. We had made little enough effort to disguise the mound of fresh-turned earth in the yard behind the Badger's Rest, and it's well known that whores gossip. That stew in particular, being cheap, was a favorite with the rank and file of the City Guard. He had heard, all right.

"You buried him alive!"

"That I did, but I never spilled his blood."

Hauer stared at me. "Do you honestly think that makes any difference to Vhent?"

"I honestly don't care," I said. "My promise was to you, not to him. I don't owe him the steam off my piss."

"Fuck you, Piety!"

Hauer turned and stormed off to replenish his wine, and I glared after him. If the terms of my agreement weren't to his liking, then that agreement was off the table. I considered the promise unmade, at that point.

I saw Ailsa looking at me across the crowded room. She raised one eyebrow a fraction, and I gave her a small nod to tell her that Hauer already knew what I had done. She had suspected as much, of course, but if anything I thought she cared even less for the governor's opinion than I did. I wondered how much longer her masters in Dannsburg would let Hauer remain in his position.

They're giving him the rope, I thought, *parceling it out one indulgence at a time until he has enough to hang himself with.*

She joined me by the window a moment later.

"A remarkable likeness, don't you think?" she said, loud enough to be overheard by those nearest to us.

"Remarkable," I said.

It was. Remarkably unlike its subject, to my mind. The artist had made Lan Barkov look tall and handsome, and he was neither of those things. Such flattery was the nature of the painter's trade, I supposed, but it amused me that the other guests either couldn't see that or felt they had to pretend otherwise.

"How did he take it?" she whispered.

"Very badly."

"I thought as much," she murmured, and then more loudly, "It's so warm in here, Tomas. Do you think perhaps we might take some air?"

Lan Barkov was at her side a moment later, all concern and flattery as he gestured urgently for one of his footmen to open the tall windows.

"Forgive me, Madame Piety," he said. "I fear, with so many people come to admire my portrait, the house is quite overheated even at this time of year."

I saw Hauer speaking urgently to someone I didn't know, could see the sweat rolling down his florid face.

"Indeed it is, Lan Barkov," I said. "Indeed it is."

By the time we were able to excuse ourselves and return home, Billy had come back from Slaughterhouse Narrow. He had been there almost every day for months now, and I still wasn't comfortable with that. I couldn't see that there was any real harm in it and Billy seemed happy enough, but something kept nagging at my mind.

I joined him in the kitchen where he was tucking into a pastry. Hanne blushed bright red when she saw me, as she had every time we met since the night in the summer when I had caught her and Jochan fucking. She was plumper than ever, and I wondered just how much of my food she ate when Cook wasn't looking.

I drew myself a mug of beer from the barrel and sat down at the table with Billy.

"How was your day?" I asked him.

He shrugged. He was getting that way about him that boys get come their thirteenth or fourteenth year, when it seems they can only talk to adults in shrugs and grunts. I had been the same at that age, and so had Jochan. I hoped that was all it was, anyway. If it was anything else making him withdrawn, something to do with Cutter, perhaps, then I wanted to know about it.

"Billy," I said, and paused until he looked at me. "Billy, I want you to promise me something. Will you do that?"

He shrugged again, then nodded. "Yes, Uncle Tomas," he said.

"I know he's your friend, and don't take this ill, but if Cutter . . . if

Cutter ever hurts you, or touches you in a way you don't want him to, you tell me straightaway. Promise me that, Billy."

"He won't do that," Billy said. "He's not like Sir Eland."

I remembered what my da had done to me, and to Jochan, and how it wasn't something you felt you could tell folk. I didn't want Billy feeling like that, the way that I had. I wouldn't have wished that on anyone.

"No, well. I hope he's not. I just want you to know that if he was, it wouldn't be your fault and there'd be no shame in it, so there'd be no reason to keep it from me. You understand?"

"Of course it wouldn't be my fault," Billy said. "Anyway, if he did, I'd hurt him."

I blinked in surprise. This was Billy the Boy I was talking to, I reminded myself, not just some lad. Billy the Boy, who could kill with his mind. Billy, who had survived alone in the ruins of Messia for Lady only knew how long before we found him. Of course Billy would kill him, if it came to it.

Just like I had killed Da.

"Aye," I said. "I suppose you would, at that."

"But he won't," Billy said again, and I could hear the certainty in his voice.

When Billy said a thing would happen it did, and I supposed the same was true if he said that a thing wouldn't. I hoped so, anyway.

"That's good," I said. "What do you do together all day, Billy? He must have run out of stories to tell you by now."

"Stuff," Billy said with another shrug. "I help around the boardinghouse, when there's work wants doing. Sometimes we play cards, or go climbing or stuff."

"Climbing? What do you climb?"

"The house," Billy said.

I blinked at him. "The what?"

"The boardinghouse," Billy said again. "The back wall, mostly, from the yard to the roof. There's good handholds in the stone. Coming down again is harder."

"Aye, I dare say it is," I said, and shook my head.

I really didn't know what was going on up at Slaughterhouse Narrow, but I didn't think I wanted Billy spending all his time with Cutter.

I took him to the Tanner's with me that night, to mix with some of the others for a change.

Jochan was in and still fairly sober, so I sat with him a while at my usual table in the corner. Billy had gone straight to the kitchen when we arrived, to see Hari and no doubt wheedle something to eat out of him. Simple Sam was guarding the table, and there was no one in earshot except my brother. I leaned closer to him anyway and voiced my concerns in quiet tones.

"Nah," Jochan said after I had finished. "Cutter ain't like that. He don't like boys, not in that way, nor women neither for that matter. Cutter don't . . . fuck it, that's his business. He can certainly climb a fucking wall, though; I've seen him do it. I don't reckon there's anything to worry on."

"Well, that's good," I said.

Jochan seemed to know a lot about what Cutter liked or didn't like, to my mind, but then he had known him longer than I had so I supposed that was fair.

I put it out of my mind.

"What are your thoughts about Desh?" I asked him. "I've a mind to make him up to the table."

Jochan frowned for a moment and took a drink, then nodded.

"Aye," he said. "Aye, I reckon it might be time. He's done well, and he held his peace through Enaid and Anne's little mummer's show back in the summer and he never told anyone about what he'd seen and heard at the table, so he passed that test. I reckon he's made of the right stuff."

I nodded. I thought so, too.

FOURTEEN

Come Godsday I held confession for the crew in the back room of the Tanner's Arms, seated at the head of the long table. That wasn't how a priest normally heard his confessions, to be sure, but then I wasn't a normal priest.

One by one they came to me to say their words, and it surprised me that Desh was among them. He knelt beside my chair and bowed his head.

"I wish to confess, Father," he said.

He had never come to me before, and I wondered if this was just an attempt to win my favor. I would take it ill, if I thought that was the case.

"Speak, in the name of Our Lady," I said.

"I led a raid, at the racetrack," he said, "and I did what I was supposed to, but . . ."

He tailed off, and I realized that no, this wasn't for my benefit. I could tell that he had something on his conscience. I sat and waited, giving him the time he needed to find his words. Every man in his own time and his own way, that was how I held confession.

"I had seven men under me," Desh went on at last. "Seven men who looked to me as their boss that day, to tell them what to do and to make it come out all right. When we was done, I had five men. Two of my crew died in the fighting in the stables, you remember, Father, and . . . and that's my fault, isn't it? That's been on my mind a lot, these past months.

I don't . . . I don't sleep well, thinking about that. I shouldn't have got them killed, Father."

He looked up at me, and the pain on his face told me that the guilt had been sitting heavily on his shoulders since that day in the summer. It was months ago now, and truth be told, I had all but forgotten about it, but it was plain that Desh hadn't. I had to remind myself that he was young, and he wasn't a veteran. He hadn't been at Abingon, where we had lost so many comrades that after a while all their faces blurred together into one and you found you couldn't remember their names anymore. This had been troubling him for a long time.

"You did the task that I set before you, and you led the men to do it, and that's important," I told him. "If you want to be followed, first you must lead. You lead men, but you don't own them. When the steel is drawn, every man's fate is in his own hands and those of Our Lady. Not yours."

"Aye," he whispered.

"It was their time to cross the river, and Our Lady forgives you," I said. "In Our Lady's name."

I doubted Our Lady much cared one way or the other, but it was what he needed to hear.

Desh looked up at me, and I could see the loyalty burning fiercely in his eyes.

"In Our Lady's name," he repeated, and that was done.

After I had heard confessions I put it about that there would be a meeting of the Pious Men that evening and that all my top table and all those others who could be spared were to be there. I told Desh he was to be there too, and why.

Come the evening we were all seated around the long table in the back room of the Tanner's, me with Bloody Anne at my right hand and Jochan at my left, with Aunt Enaid and Fat Luka and Sir Eland and the others. I had the Weeping Women buckled around my waist.

Anne had spoken to Desh beforehand, and now he was waiting awkwardly by the door while everyone stared at him. He was wearing his best coat and standing tall, but I could see the nervousness on his face. They were hard men and women around that table, and I could see

Desh's gaze move from Cutter to Mika to Sam to Stefan, as though looking for some sign of acceptance in their scarred faces and flinty stares.

"This is Desh, as you all know," I said. "He's served us this last year, and since the summer he's been an underboss among the hired lads. He's done well, to my mind, and I propose to give him a seat at this table as a full Pious Man. If anyone here gathered thinks otherwise, now would be the time to say so."

I looked around the table and for a moment I caught my aunt's eye, but she held her peace the same as the others and that pleased me. This was how we had done it before the war, with Alfread and Donnalt and others who had long since crossed the river. When I brought my crew back from Abingon and made them Pious Men there had been no time, and the ceremony would have meant nothing to them anyway, but Desh was Ellinburg born and bred and I knew that he'd been waiting half his life for this moment. I owed it to him to do things properly.

I nodded and got to my feet, pushing my chair back from the table. I looked at him and pointed to the chair.

"Sit," I said.

Desh cleared his throat and sat in my chair, and I drew Remorse and laid it on the table in front of him where the light of the lamps would make the steel shine. I took his left hand in mine and drew Mercy.

I cut his palm with the edge of the blade, then curled his hand into a fist in mine and squeezed it hard. His blood dripped onto the table in front of him, and he gritted his teeth but said nothing.

"Your blood on this table means we are now one family," I said. "I told you once that family is important, but now it's your life. If you would be a Pious Man you will live by the sword in front of you, in brotherhood with those here gathered, from this day forth until the day that you cross the river. Do you so swear?"

Desh nodded, looking a little pale but with a fervor that told me he meant it.

"I do so swear," he said.

I stood him up and took him by the shoulders, and then I embraced him and kissed him on both cheeks. Bloody Anne was next to welcome him into the family in her place as my second, then Jochan, then Aunt

Enaid, then Luka, and so on until each man around the table had embraced him and kissed his cheeks in brotherhood.

That was how Desh became a Pious Man at last.

I was sitting behind the desk in my study in the big house off Trader's Row, going through some papers of accounts. It was wet that morning and I was listening to the late-autumn rain pattering against my window and the crackle of the fire in the grate when a footman knocked at the door to tell me Desh was wanting me.

"Show him in," I said, and a minute later the lad was standing there dripping on my good Alarian carpet.

His coat was magnificent, better than many of mine, in fact, and I knew he must have spent a small fortune on it. Status mattered to Desh, as I have written. That was the lever that moved him, and now that he was finally a Pious Man at last he obviously wanted everyone to know it. I could understand that.

"Boss, can I have a word?" he asked me.

I waved him to one of the chairs opposite my desk, just the way Governor Hauer had when he had received me in his own study.

"What's on your mind?"

Desh cleared his throat, and he told me about a cunning man that he had found up on Rigger's Alley and how he had put our standing offer to him. This fellow, Desh told me, had flat refused him.

"I see," I said, when he had said his piece. "And why's that, then?"

"Well," Desh said, and he looked uncomfortable about it, "he didn't give me the time of day, boss, but that got me thinking about why not. I know I'm new and I know I'm young, but word's got around who I am and who I work for. I get respect on my patch, but not off this fucker I didn't. That made me angry, but it made me curious, too. So I asked some questions and I spent a bit of coin to get them answered, and it seems to me from what I heard that maybe the Northern Sons got to him first."

I'd put the lad in charge of a small area in the north of the Wheels, up near the docks where the rebuilding was still going on. Desh was doing well up there, so Luka told me, establishing his authority and getting respect. It seemed someone hadn't respected him enough, but at least he'd had the sense to come to me about it rather than trying to hide what an older man might have seen as an embarrassment.

"That's interesting," I said.

It was more than interesting. If the Sons were taking notice of the cunning folk too, then we had a problem, one that I needed to talk to Ailsa about. That was nothing Desh needed to hear, though.

"What do you want me to do, boss?"

I gave him a level look. He was a Pious Man now, and he needed to learn to think for himself.

"What do *you* think you should do?"

"We can't be disrespected on our own streets, and we can't let the Sons take our folk," Desh said, and he was right about that. "All the same, though, he's a cunning man. I don't . . . I don't know what he might do, if I took some lads up there and we went and kicked his door in."

Desh didn't want to get any more men killed, I knew that. That was something he'd need to harden up over, given time. All the same, though, he had the right of it for now.

"No, don't do that," I said. "You're right to be cautious around the cunning, and you were right to bring this to me. Well done. Give me this man's name and I'll deal with it."

Desh nodded, obviously relieved.

"Arndt, his name is," he told me. "He's got a little cooper's shop, up on Rigger's Alley like I said."

"Right," I said. "Well, that's good. You're doing well, Desh. I'm pleased."

I opened a drawer in my desk and took out a purse, and gave him five silver marks.

Desh looked at them in surprise before making them disappear into his pouch with a nod of thanks.

"Get yourself some more nice clothes," I said. "You deserve them."

Desh smiled at me and nodded.

He was a Pious Man now, and I knew that was all he had ever wanted in his life.

FIFTEEN

I had to tell Ailsa, of course. I'd like to say she took it well, but that would be a lie.

"This won't stand, Tomas," she told me once Desh had left. "My orders were very clear—the cunning folk join us, or they must be removed."

"Removed," I repeated. "If you mean killed, then say killed."

"Of course I mean killed," she snapped. "We are not children, Tomas, and this is not a child's game we play. The Skanian magicians are dangerous enough as it is without them recruiting new talent that rightfully belongs to the crown."

I frowned, trying to see how she worked that out.

"Our streets, our people, you mean?" I said at last.

"Exactly that, but on a larger scale," she said. "Subjects of the crown owe their loyalty to their country and to their queen; it's that simple. Anyone who would choose otherwise is a traitor and will be dealt with as such."

"How would this fellow even know?" I asked her. "He's chosen between one gang and another in the same city, to his mind, that's all. That might be betraying me, to an extent, but not the crown."

"I don't care," she said, her voice cold enough to make it clear that was to be an end to the discussion. "Remove him. At once."

I sighed. I had thought that would be her answer. The Queen's Men weren't renowned for their tolerance of differing opinions, after all.

"Aye, as you say," I said. "I'll need Billy, though. I don't know how strong this Arndt is, and I haven't forgotten what that Lisbeth nearly did to me at the Tanner's Arms."

"Quite," she said. "Billy is a valuable asset. Use him."

Billy was my adopted nephew, as far as I was concerned. He was as good as my son, not a fucking *asset*, but there it was. Ailsa knew what needed to be done and the best way to get it done, as she always did, and I couldn't argue with her on that.

"I will," I said, "but if he's going, then so am I."

Ailsa gave me a look for a moment, then nodded.

"Yes," she said. "I told you before that I don't want to trust the matter of the cunning folk to your underlings. You deal with it."

I had meant more that I wasn't sending a lad of barely fourteen off to the north of the Wheels to fight on my behalf without me, but Ailsa didn't see that. Still, if we ended up at the same answer through different lines of reasoning, then that was well and good, to my mind. The answer was the important thing, not the path to it.

"Aye," I said. "I'll arrange it."

"This won't keep, Tomas," she said. "He must be removed before the Sons can make use of him. You go tonight."

I met her stare for a moment, then nodded. That wasn't just my wife making my life hard because she could, in the way that wives sometimes do. That was a direct order from the Queen's Men, and I knew I had to obey it. I was in far too deep now to have any other option. I had taken the crown's money, dirty money, and that was bad enough. I had accepted their help, too, and there was no coming back from that. There was no coming back from what Ailsa had done on our wedding day. I sighed and went to get it done.

Billy was actually at home for once that day, and I went up to his room to find him.

He was sitting in the chair under his bedroom window with his big black book open on his lap and a quill in his hand. He was bent over his work, the pen scratching furiously across the velum as he wrote.

I knocked on the open door and stepped into the room, and he looked up at me with a blank expression on his face.

"Uncle Tomas," he said.

"Hello, Billy."

"I'll kill a man, tonight," he said.

I stared at him.

He knew. Somehow he already knew, and there was no fear or argument in his eyes. If this man Arndt had to die, then Billy and me would kill him, and I knew he would think nothing of it.

"Aye," I said after a moment. "I think we might have to. He's a cunning man, Billy, an Ellinburg man, but he ain't on our side. That means—"

"He has to die," Billy interrupted me, and there was no trace of emotion in his voice. "I know, Uncle Tomas. He will."

"Right," I said. "Right, well. That's good, I suppose."

No, Billy didn't need a reason or an explanation. Our Lady had told him what he would do, or at least *something* had, and he would do it.

The boy's fucking possessed.

I nodded again and left him to it. Sometimes Billy gave me the fear, as I have written, and I've no shame in admitting that this was one of those times.

I closed his bedroom door behind me and went back downstairs, and sent one of the housemen off into the rain to find Fat Luka and bring him to me. That done, I sat down in my study and poured myself a brandy, and for the first time in a long while I said a prayer. Our Lady of Eternal Sorrows doesn't answer prayers, I knew that much, but just that once I hoped perhaps She might at least listen to one.

By the time Luka arrived it was midafternoon and I was watching the sheeting rain through my study window. I told Luka what Desh had told me and that he was to set some of his spies to watching this Arndt's shop. If the man went out before we got there, then I wanted to know where he went and who he spoke to. It was only going to be Billy and me that night, and I didn't want to risk running into half a dozen of the Northern Sons creeping around down there in the Wheels with steel in their hands.

The Wheels were mine, yes, but the closer to the docks you went, the closer you got to Northern Sons territory on the west, and some of the borders were still a bit unclear. In the Stink the Sons could never have got an armed band near me, but down there it wasn't impossible.

No, it wasn't impossible at all.

We waited until well after dark, and then me and Billy the Boy headed out wearing nondescript clothes and patched old cloaks. It felt like old times then, like on the road from Messia, when we had been ahead of the main march of the army and had caught up with the enemy's baggage train. It had been raining then, too, and outnumbered as we had been, we'd raided under the cover of darkness and melted away into the night afterward like ghosts. Tonight would be like that, I knew.

At least, I hoped so. I'd have liked to have a couple of the other men with us just in case, but Ailsa insisted that anything to do with the cunning folk was crown business and was to be kept away from the Pious Men as much as possible.

"Are you all right, Billy?" I asked him as we slipped out of the alley we had been following through the Wheels and onto the top of Dock Road, beyond the blackened ruin of a tavern called the Stables. That filthy place would never be rebuilt, not while I was boss it wouldn't. Running whores was one thing, but the Stables had run *children*. Boys as young as six had been whored out of the Stables, until Billy and I had put a stop to it with fire and sword. Never again, not on my fucking streets.

He nodded.

"Yes, Uncle Tomas," he said.

I led him across the road and into another alley, our sodden hoods pulled up and the rain dripping from them as it lashed against the cobblestones and made puddles around our boots. I found Rigger's Alley at last, with only the light of a single lantern hanging from a rusty iron bracket on a street corner to guide us. I didn't know the north of the Wheels as well as I should, I had to admit, and in the dark and this weather it was hard to keep my bearings.

At last I spotted Luka's man, a scrawny type who was huddled in a doorway under a threadbare blanket with an old tin cup in front of him, pretending to be a beggar. Good that he was only pretending; his cup was half full of rainwater, but there were no coins in it.

"Pious, in Our Lady's name," I murmured to him as Billy and me joined him in his scant shelter.

"Mr. Piety," he whispered. "He's gone out, sir. Not far, just down the way to a sink called the Barrel o' Tar. Gone drinking like, I reckon. We've another man there, watching the door."

I nodded and dropped a silver mark into the man's cup, where it landed with a splash.

That wasn't what I had wanted to hear. I had wanted to find this Arndt at home, alone and well away from prying eyes, where Billy could keep his cunning under control and I could do what needed to be done in peace.

If he was out drinking, probably spending the coin the Northern Sons had given him, then he could be out half the night or more. If he went out the back with some street scrub and then down an alley and into Sons territory we might never see him again, and I could just imagine what Ailsa would have to say about that.

No, that wouldn't do at all. She had told me it wouldn't keep and that meant we were doing it tonight, wherever he was.

"We're going for a drink," I told Billy, and the lad just nodded.

Luka's man told us the way, and sure enough after a couple of turns there was the Barrel o' Tar. It was nothing but a door in a windowless wall, with a lantern and a faded sign over it and another beggar slumped in a doorway opposite. He had his head down and his hood pulled forward to keep the rain out of his face.

He looked up as we approached, and coughed.

"Pious," he muttered. "Pious, in Our Lady's name."

I stopped and pretended to take a piss in the next doorway, close enough to hear him over the rain.

"Well?"

"He's still in there, boss," the beggar said. "Might be he's with friends and might be not, I can't rightly say."

I grunted and tossed him a coin as well, then led young Billy across the street and through the low doorway into the Barrel o' Tar.

The smell of the sink tavern was vinegar and sweat and bad eggs, tallow smoke and vomit. If this was the best place he could afford to drink, then either our man Arndt had very simple tastes or the Sons hadn't paid him as much as I would have expected. The ceiling was low and the air thick with smoke from the fire and the candles and a few illicit resin pipes that burned in the shadows. There was no bar as such, just a trestle table set up in front of three barrels standing against the back wall and a fat, ugly woman standing behind it in a stained shift. The man lurking at the end of the table was fatter and uglier and had the look of her brother about him. He had a big wooden club at his belt with rusty nails hammered through it.

"Shit night," the woman observed as I approached her table, rain dripping from my cloak.

"Aye," I said. "Two mugs, if you please."

She drew two wooden tankards of beer for us from the barrel behind her and thumped them down on the table, and I passed her a copper. I wasn't paying more than that, and she made no argument about it. If anything I had probably overpaid, in a place like this.

Billy took one of the mugs and sipped it, and his face told me all I needed to know about the quality of the beer. He was looking around the room, a slight frown on his smooth young forehead. After a moment he tapped me on the arm.

"The far corner, Uncle Tomas," he murmured. "See the scrub on that man's lap? Mark the fellow beside her, with the sick down his shirt. That's him."

I just nodded. Billy could sense the cunning in someone, or perhaps he could actually see it somehow, I wouldn't know. That was how he had known Katrin and Gerta had been genuine and how he had uncovered the frauds we had found too.

"Aye, I mark him," I said. "Well done, Billy."

"He needs a piss," Billy said.

That made me blink, but if Billy could see one thing about a man then I supposed there was no reason he couldn't see another. The man looked drunk enough to just piss in his britches where he sat, to my mind, but Lady willing I was wrong about that. If he went out the back, then we had a chance.

I took a sip of my beer and wished I hadn't. It had an oily sheen on the top of it and a taste that told me it was a quarter river water. A minute later the man in the vomit-stained shirt lurched to his feet and staggered away from the bench he had been sitting on, almost knocking the scrub off her customer's lap. I thought they might actually be fucking, but it was too dark to tell for sure, and I wasn't sorry about that.

"If he goes out the back to piss we'll follow him," I murmured to Billy, and he nodded.

True enough our man stumbled across the room and ducked through the low doorway at the back, into the courtyard behind the sink where the shithouse would be. I put my mug down on the table and followed him, and I could feel Billy at my heels. I heard the fat brute behind me say something, but I couldn't catch what, and then something that sounded like his sister talking him out of it. That was wise of her.

A moment later we were in the dark, rain-lashed yard where our man was leaning against the side of the wooden shithouse with one hand and holding his cock in the other. He was taking an almighty piss onto the ground as though he had got as far as he could and that would have to do.

"Don't let him use the cunning," I whispered to Billy, and reached inside my cloak for the Weeping Women.

"No," Billy said, and my hand stilled.

I don't know why, but it did. I could feel the hilt of Remorse against the tips of my fingers, but I didn't move them. Something held me there, something that I would have bet a gold crown to a clipped copper was Billy's doing. I wasn't frozen and I knew I could have moved my hand if I had wanted to, but I no longer wanted to. That was worse, in a way, to think that he was doing something to my mind rather than my body. Being physically stopped by magic was one thing, I supposed, but having it in your head was quite another.

"I should do it," he said, and he walked toward the pissing man.

He reached under his own cloak, and then he was beside Arndt, pretending to be drunk himself.

"Need to piss," I heard Billy say.

Arndt swayed and looked at him.

"Fuckin' say wha', boy?" he said.

Billy turned and seemed to stroke the inside of the man's thigh with his hand, in the killing place. Dark blood sprayed across the mud of the yard. Arndt staggered and Billy's arm came up, and the dim light caught the edge of the blade concealed in his hand. He touched the side of Arndt's neck, just once, and more blood gushed and Arndt fell, and that was done.

My hand relaxed all at once and I gripped Remorse's hilt, but I didn't need her anymore. Billy came walking back to me as Arndt died in the mud and the rain and the piss behind him, and I saw that the lad had a small knife in his hand. He was holding it backward, to my mind, with his thumb against the top of the hilt and the bloody blade flat against the inside of his wrist. I had only ever seen one person hold a knife like that before.

"Who taught you that?" I asked him.

"Cutter," he said.

That was what I had been afraid of.

SIXTEEN

I awoke from a dream of the war, of the smoke and screams and the endless noise of the cannon. That nightmare was nothing new, but this time I had dreamed of Cutter, too, stalking through the bloody smoke with a dripping knife held backward in each hand. He had Billy the Boy at his side, and the lad's smile had been red murder. That was when I woke, with my blankets tangled around my legs in a sweaty mess and my heart pounding.

It was almost light outside my window, so I sat up and rubbed my hands through my hair, thinking it was high time I paid another visit to Ernst the barber. Thinking of anything I could, any nonsense that didn't matter, to take my mind away from the dream and from the memory of the previous night. Down the hall from my room Billy was asleep in his own bed, and I wondered what he dreamed of there.

Cutter was teaching him to kill, that much was obvious now. Why he was doing it was another matter, but it seemed that Billy had learned fast, the same way he had learned the cunning fast at Old Kurt's house. Billy had killed before, of course, many and more times, but killing an enemy in battle was one thing. Coming up to an innocent man in a tavern yard and opening his veins was something different, and it took different skills and a different way of thinking.

That sort of thing was what Cutter did best.

I remembered the previous year, and the army sappers that Ailsa had produced when I had needed them. Sappers are hard men, tunnelers and demolition experts. They had done some of the harshest work, at Abingon. It was men like them who undermined walls and set charges, fighting in the stifling confines of the tunnels. That was the stuff of nightmares. It had been those men who had delivered my wedding present from Ailsa.

Before the bombing of the Wheels I had sent those sappers out to cripple a factory, and I had sent Cutter with them. When they came back, I remembered, the sappers had walked softly around Cutter and kept a respectful distance from him that spoke of a quiet fear. When even sappers fear a man, I had thought at the time, that man is to be feared indeed. I wondered again who Cutter really was, and what he had been doing in Messia before the war, and how he had ended up in Jochan's crew.

It would keep for now, I told myself. It would keep.

I got up and took a piss into the pot, then got dressed and headed downstairs. It was early, but I could hear activity in the kitchen already. Cook would be baking the day's bread by then, of course, with Hanne's help. There might even be some ready if I was lucky.

"Oh, Mr. Piety sir, you did startle me," Cook said when I opened the door.

She was a sturdy woman with some fifty years to her, with red cheeks and big, strong hands from years of kneading dough and churning butter and turning spits. Hanne looked like a plump child beside her. Very plump indeed, to my mind.

"I woke early, that's all," I said. "Is there anything ready?"

Cook sat me down at the kitchen table and put some hot bread and a mug of small beer in front of me with a motherly smile. I barely remembered my own ma, who had died when I'd had only six years to me, but I hoped she had been something like Cook.

"My thanks," I said, and started to eat.

"I really don't feel well," I heard Hanne say a few minutes later, and then she was off and running out the back door into the yard behind the house.

She left the door swinging open behind her, and I could hear the sound of her retching outside. I frowned.

"Oh dear," Cook muttered to herself, giving her dough an extra hard thump as though Hanne's illness was somehow its fault. "Oh dear, oh dear."

I shrugged and finished my breakfast, then went up to my study and waited for Ailsa to rise.

She was up an hour or so later, and of course took her breakfast in the small dining room the way I was supposed to but usually didn't. I joined her there, and although I didn't want anything else to eat I took a bowl of tea to be polite.

"How was last night?" Ailsa asked casually, mindful of the small army of servants that it seemed to be impossible for her to eat without.

"Well enough," I said. "Wet."

"Did *you* get wet?" she asked me, and I took her meaning.

"No," I said, "but Billy did."

"It won't do him any harm," she said.

I wasn't sure about that, but this was neither the time or the place for us to have that conversation. It made me wonder, though, if this was why Billy had insisted on doing the work himself the previous night. Perhaps he knew Ailsa's mind on the matter and had wanted to help me keep my distance. If he had known that, then I wondered if he might know Ailsa's mind on other things, too, and that was an interesting thought.

That was something Billy and I needed to talk about.

Among other things.

That afternoon a messenger came to the house and brought me a note from Fat Luka that put all other concerns out of my mind. I sat behind my desk in the study and scanned it, trying to make sense of Luka's childish, barely schooled handwriting.

Boss,

> *Come to Tanner's if can, I need to stay here.*
> *Shit happening.*
> *New faces in town, need to talk.*

Luka

I frowned and crumpled the note in my hand, and tossed it into the fire. Luka wouldn't summon me like that unless it was important. He had more respect for me than that; I knew he did. He could even be in trouble, I realized, and unable to say what he meant.

Ten minutes later I had my coat and cloak on and was out of the house with the Weeping Women buckled around my waist. At least it was dry today, that was something, although the chill wind told me that autumn was almost done and winter was well on its way to Ellinburg. I had Stefan with me as well as the messenger whose name I didn't know, and we rode with haste down the road together while heads turned to watch us pass.

Even up there on Trader's Row most folk knew all too well who I was by then, and I got the feeling that some of them might think I was lowering the tone of the neighborhood by living there. I didn't care. They were nothing to me, these moneyed fools who thought they were better than everyone else. They could think what they liked, to my mind, so long as there was no open disrespect of me or my family. I knew very well what I thought of them.

We rode down into the Narrows and the Stink, through streets where people huddled into their cloaks against the wind and watched us go by with hooded eyes. There were more people than usual on the streets, and many of them were armed. I wondered why that was.

When we reached the Tanner's Arms I left my horse with the messenger and walked into the tavern with my cloak open over my swords and Stefan at my side.

Luka was sitting at a table in the middle of the room with Bloody Anne and Jochan around him, and Mika and Black Billy were standing near the bar. Both looked agitated and alert, and Billy was wearing his mail and sword in addition to the doorman's club that hung at his belt. There were no civilians in there at all, I noticed, and I could only assume someone had taken the decision to close to the public for the rest of the day.

"What is it?" I said, when they turned to look at me.

"There's news," Anne said, and Luka beckoned me to their table.

"Seems the Abingon garrison has been dissolved, about two months ago would be my guess," he said. "They've been trickling into the city all morning. They're all coming home. Everyone."

I nodded slowly, understanding.

After the war we had left a good-sized garrison at Abingon, and a lot of them had been Ellinburg men. Those officers with wealthy families in Dannsburg and the west had managed to get themselves and their men sent home early, by and large, and it had only been luck and our respective colonels' connections that had seen us and Ma Aditi's crew come home when we did.

"Who?" I asked.

"Everyone," Luka said again. "The Blue Bloods, the Alarian Kings, the Flower Girls, the Headhunters . . . everyone, boss."

"Right," I said. "Luka, I need you and your little spies to get on this right now. They'll be weak at the moment, and some of them did fealty to the Gutcutters before the war. The landscape here has changed while they've been down in the south, and we need to jump on them before the Northern Sons do. Most of them will find they've no territory to go home to and powerful people standing where they once stood. What I fucking *don't* want is any of them doing what I did when that happened to me, do you understand?"

"We don't need any more enemies," Anne said.

"Fucking right we don't," I said. "Spend gold, make promises, do whatever it takes. I want as many of these fuckers as possible calling me boss by the end of the week, do you understand me?"

"Aye," Luka said, and Jochan and Anne both nodded.

I'd never get all of them, of course, I knew that and truth be told, I didn't even really want them, but every minor gang I took was one the Northern Sons didn't have. A soldier in my camp was one who wasn't in theirs, and that was good.

"Get Desh back down from the Wheels and put him in front of the Alarian Kings," I said, pacing the room as I thought out loud. "They'll be more likely to listen to another brown face, I reckon, especially a richly dressed one. The right man for the right job, always. Anne, I'll want you to talk to the Flower Girls. It's the same principle, you understand?"

"They're women, then?" she asked, and again I had to remind myself that she had never set foot in Ellinburg before the war.

"Fuck, yes," Jochan said. "Every one of them. They started out as whores before some of them realized they could make more money with their knives than with their cunts. They're hard as fucking nails, the lot of them."

"Aye, that they are," I said, "but they ain't *you*, Bloody Anne. They'll listen to you, I reckon."

"What about the others?" Luka asked. "The Headhunters are just dock rats and we ought to be able to sweep them up with no bother now Aditi's gone, but I don't know what we can do about the Blue Bloods."

"No, that's in the shithouse," I had to admit. "Don't even try."

The Blue Bloods had been a medium-sized gang from the west of Ellinburg. Their streets were squarely in the middle of what was now Northern Sons territory and there would be no getting to them, I knew that. The best I could hope for was that they would fight Bloodhands rather than bend the knee and do fealty to him.

"Aye, well," Jochan said. "If we can take the other three . . . fuck me, Tomas, we'll be the biggest the Pious Men have ever been."

I nodded. We would be, I knew that.

If we were going to take down the Skanians, we would fucking need to be.

SEVENTEEN

I spent the next week all but living at the Tanner's Arms, returning home only to wash and change my clothes, and that only every second or third day. I worked at the head of the long table in the back room of the Tanner's, where spies and messengers could come and go freely without having to run the gauntlet of servants and neighbors as they would have had to do at the house off Trader's Row. Ailsa was fully supportive of the situation once I explained to her what had happened, and truth be told, I doubted that she missed me. I needed to take these soldiers before the Sons, and therefore the Skanians, did, and we both knew it.

On the fourth day Bloody Anne came to me, and she had two of our hired lads and a woman who I didn't know with her. The woman was whip-thin and hard faced, wearing a soldier's britches and coat under a cloak that had seen better days. Her hair was long but filthy and scraped back from her face, knotted behind her head with a bit of old rag. I could see she was missing half of her left ear.

"This is Florence Cooper," Anne told me. "She runs the Flower Girls."

"Tomas Piety," Florence said, by way of greeting. "I remember you from before."

"Aye, I dare say you do," I said. "How was your war?"

She shrugged and spat on the floor, and never mind that she was right in front of me. This one gave no fucks about anything, that was plain enough. Not at all she didn't, I could see that much and I could see that she wanted me to know it.

"I'm still here," she said. "Most of my girls, too. We volunteered and joined up to fight, but they set us to guarding the fucking baggage train and then to the garrison. Like women can't fucking fight in battles."

"Anne fought," I said.

"Aye, I'll allow that she did," Florence said. "Even back at the wagons we heard tell of the Bloody Sergeant. We heard how she ate men's balls with her breakfast beer, and that's most of the reason why I'm stood here now."

I gave Anne a look, but I held my peace. Tales can grow tall in the telling, all soldiers know that, and if Anne hadn't said anything to spoil that story then I couldn't say that I blamed her.

"But you *are* here, with the Bloody Sergeant and me," I said.

Florence spat again and scratched at a scabby patch on the back of her left wrist until it started to weep.

"I am," she admitted. "My crew did fealty to Ma Aditi and the Gutcutters before the war, you know that, and that made us enemies. Only now there ain't no Gutcutters, and word is that the devil Tomas Piety himself killed Aditi and fucked her corpse. So now I've got no streets and no boss and nowhere else to go but to follow the sergeant."

Cutter had killed Ma Aditi as far as I knew, and I hadn't even been there at the time. He had been the one who brought me her head, at least.

"That's the word, is it?" I said. "I assure you, I wouldn't have fucked Ma Aditi if she'd been the last woman in Ellinburg, alive or dead. And you *have* got somewhere to go, Florence Cooper. Back to your old streets, if you want them, and your crew with you. But those streets belong to the Pious Men now, not you and not the Gutcutters, and you mark me on that. You'll do your fealty to me from now on. Does that sound fair?"

Florence shrugged and looked sideways at Bloody Anne.

Anne gave her a short nod.

"Take it," she said. "It's better than dying."

"Aye, suppose it is," Florence said.

She turned back to me and set her jaw.

"Right you are, then," she said, "but I want my businesses back. My streets always paid their protection to me, and I'm not giving that up. I'll pay you a fifth for respect, like I used to pay Aditi, but I'm my own woman, not some fucking hired bitch. My whoring days are behind me, and they're fucking staying there. Does *that* sound fair, Mr. Piety?"

"A quarter," I said, "and if I call the knives your crew fight with mine, under my say-so."

Florence sighed, but she didn't have any choice and I could see that she knew it.

"Aye," she said at last. "That sounds like as fair as I'm going to get."

She spat in her hand and held it out to me, and I stood up and spat in mine and we shook on it, the old way, and that was done.

That was how the Flower Girls came to do their fealty to the Pious Men.

Nothing happened the next day, but the day after that a runner came to the Tanner's to say that Desh was dead.

He'd been found in an alley down in the Wheels, Fat Luka told me, his throat slashed open and his tongue cut out and placed in the wound like it was hanging out of his neck. The Elephant, the Alarian gangs called that, and it was an ugly thing. They had tucked a card with the sign of the Northern Sons into the pocket of his beautiful coat.

"Fuck," I said, when Luka brought me the news.

Desh had waited his whole life to become a Pious Man, and he had done that. He had achieved his dream, and he had lived to enjoy it for a matter of weeks. Pious Men got the finer things in life and they lived well, as I have written before, but not necessarily for very long. He hadn't even got the glorious death he had no doubt dreamed of. There was no blaze of glory for Desh, and no tales would be told of how he had died. No one sang songs of men ambushed and murdered in alleys.

I scrubbed a hand over my face and dragged in a breath.

Desh was dead.

Desh, who had reminded me so much of myself at his age. Desh, who was moved by status and respect, the same way I was.

Desh, who was barely eighteen.

Fuck!

He shouldn't have died, not yet and not like that. Not in some piss-sodden alley down in the Wheels with his tongue pulled out of his throat, making him look a mockery of a man. That wasn't right. That wasn't justice.

What the fuck was I going to tell his da?

"The Headhunters have come over, though," Luka said. "They're ours, now."

"What are there, six of them?" I barked at him. "I don't much fucking care, Fat Luka. Where's Desh, now?"

Luka swallowed and examined his boots for a moment.

"We, um, we didn't think his family would want to see him like that," he said eventually. "He's in the river."

"Lady's *sake*!" I shouted at him. "We can't even give them a fucking body to bury?"

I was on my feet then, and I realized my fists were clenched. I was over the fucking table before I knew it and I could feel it happening, could feel the battle shock coming down on me like thunderclouds and cannon and I didn't want to, but I couldn't fucking help it.

Do you understand me?

I couldn't fucking help it.

I hit Fat Luka, and I could hardly see him for the tears in my eyes, and I hit him again and again until he was on the floor. The door opened and Bloody Anne roared at me in her best sergeant's voice, and then she had me bent backward over the table and her scarred face was right in mine and she bellowed, *"Stop it!"*

So I did.

I don't know.

It just left me, as fast as it had come, and then my hand was hurting and my knuckles were bleeding and Fat Luka was crawling out of the room on his hands and knees leaving a trail of blood and snot on the floor behind him, and that was done.

"Lady's sake, Tomas," Anne hissed at me, and she kicked the door shut behind her. "Sit down."

I sat, and I started to come back to myself.

"I . . . I shouldn't have done that," I said, after a moment.

"No," Anne said. "No, you shouldn't, but there's no use telling me that. Tell *Luka* that, when you can face him again."

I sighed, the breath coming out shaky from a dry throat that felt too small for the air I needed.

"Aye," I said. "That was ill done of me, I know. Desh . . ."

"I heard," Anne said, and there was really nothing more to be said about that.

I could see the sorrow in her eyes, and of course she had lost people she cared about too. We all had; that was war.

And so was this.

"Right," I said, after a moment, when I had got myself back under control and managed to hide how badly my hands were shaking. "We've lost the Alarian Kings to the Sons, then, and perhaps the Blue Bloods too, but we've gained the Flower Girls and the Headhunters. The Headhunters are nothing but dockside thieves, but the Flower Girls are well worth having, and you're our tie to them. I've a mind to put you over Florence, to be her area boss. Can you do that for me, Bloody Anne?"

Anne gave me a short nod.

"I can do that," she said.

"Good," I said. "We'll need to step up security, now. It's going to get bad, now that the others are home. The regular army, such as it is, the career soldiers, they'll rally to the queen and the governor's law, and they'll hold to the peace. The rest of them, the gang members and the poor bloody conscripts, they'll follow whoever will fucking feed them. It'll get ugly in Ellinburg now, you mark me on that."

EIGHTEEN

I was right about that.

By the time full winter came, the streets were all but lawless. Violence and petty crimes were the worst I had ever seen them, and there had even been robberies up near Trader's Row. That would have been unthinkable a year ago, but it seemed that the City Guard was stretched to the breaking point.

I sent the Pious Men out in force.

These were my streets, and on my streets I'd have my law and my fucking justice.

Up by the docks I hanged a rapist, and the Guard said nothing of it.

Two men were caught trying to rob a shop under my protection, down in the Wheels. I had them dragged the mile and more length of Dock Road behind two galloping horses and then thrown in the river. The water was icy at that time of year, and no one saw them come out again.

A resin smoker who had mugged an old man in an alley up in the Narrows lost both his feet.

I caught a man running a whore who had barely nine years to her. Him I strangled with my own hands, while she watched and smiled and wept.

That was how I dealt justice on my streets.

My streets, my law.

The city might be going down the shithouse, but I kept an iron grip on my territory, and my people respected me for it. They paid me for protection and I saw that they got it. That was how this worked, to my mind. I was a prince in Ellinburg, and a prince looks after his people and he keeps the fucking peace.

On his own streets he does, anyway.

Ailsa had thoughts about that, of course, and they didn't always agree with mine. To her mind I should have been concentrating on the Northern Sons and the Skanians who backed them, but with how things were across the city that winter I reckoned Bloodhands had as much on his plate with his own streets as I had with mine, and there were no more hostilities between us.

The Flower Girls were doing well down in the Wheels, and after a couple of months I gave Florence Cooper the streets that Desh had been running for me as well. I took a quarter there, too, as we had agreed, while Anne watched over them as area boss.

I made things right with Fat Luka, too. I apologized for what I had done, and explained why I had done it, and I knew he understood. We spent a night in the Tanner's together drinking ourselves stupid and telling each other tall tales about our exploits growing up in the city, about places we had robbed and lasses we had fucked.

We had known each other since we had been in school, for Our Lady's sake, and we had been soldiers together. We had fought back to back in the choking dust of Abingon, and it took more than a beating to break a bond like that. We had known each other a long time, and if we had never really been friends before, then I think by the end of that night perhaps we were, and that was good.

I needed all the friends I could get.

Anne and Rosie were growing even closer, and Anne's new status and the income it brought her allowed her to lavish gifts on her woman like never before.

We were in the back of the Tanner's Arms one night, just Bloody Anne and me, with bottles of brandy and glasses and lamps on the long table in front of us, and Simple Sam standing guard outside the door to see that we were left alone. She had been giving me the week's news from the Wheels, which she now practically ran in my name with the Flower Girls under her, but that was done.

"I've other news," Anne said, and it was hard to tell in the light of the oil lamps but for a moment she almost looked shy. "If you want to hear it, that is. As a friend, I mean. It's not business."

"Of course I do," I said. "You're my best friend, Bloody Anne. Probably my *only* real friend, truth be told."

That was right enough. My marriage was a loveless sham. Jochan was my brother, but we had never been close as adults, and although I had made it right with Fat Luka, that friendship couldn't compare to the bond I had with Anne.

Anne was all I truly had in the world. Her and Billy, anyway.

"It's Rosie," Anne said, and she couldn't hide the smile that made her scar twitch along the length of her face. "I suppose it ain't a big thing, but . . . I'm not paying her no more. She . . . she said I didn't have to. She said she loved me, Tomas, and that she wanted to be with me of her own choice and not for coin."

I looked up and met her eyes, and I saw the shine of tears in them.

"That's good," I said. "I'm pleased for you, Anne."

"No one's ever said that to me, that they loved me, I mean. Not since my Maisy, and we weren't much more than children, so what did we know? Rosie . . . she's the one, Tomas. Do you understand me?"

"Aye," I said. "I do. I'm happy for you, Bloody Anne. Very happy."

She poured us both a glass then, and we drank together, in friendship and comradeship, but there was something I knew about her woman that she didn't.

Rosie was a spy and an agent of the crown, in the pay of the Queen's Men. I thought of my own wife, of Ailsa, and how she had done the things that she had done. A lioness, I had thought of her once, and how no sane man would want to lie down with her. I wondered if Anne's Rosie was so very different, when all was said and done.

I wished I could tell her, but of course that was out of the question. Sometimes, when you lead, there are hard truths you have to hold to yourself. I wondered what the captain had known, back in Abingon, and not been able to tell us. I wondered what burdens our colonel had borne, and told no one.

That was what it was, to be a boss.

All the same, I envied what Anne had. If she could be happy with her lioness, then couldn't I with mine?

I remembered what had happened in the Wheels, the destruction and the charred bodies that had been pulled out of it. Ailsa could be harsh and ruthless, yes, but then was I any different? Perhaps I had just drunk too much brandy that night, but when I thought back on the justice I had dealt over the last couple of months I decided that no, I probably wasn't.

It was just a matter of scale, that was all.

I had made my way back home to Trader's Row in the early hours, but the next morning I was up with the dawn as was my habit. I took my breakfast in the kitchen where it was warm and there was less fuss and ceremony attached to it than there would have been in the small dining room.

By then there was no hiding that Hanne was with child.

The girl had always been plump, but now her belly was heavy and pressing through her apron in a way that could only mean one thing. I thought she was perhaps five or six months along, not that I really knew much about that sort of thing.

It was Jochan's, obviously. I knew she was besotted with my little brother, and she wasn't likely to have lain with anyone else. I thought on that as I watched her kneading the dough for the day's bread, and I wondered what he would think of it. We would have to see, I supposed.

After my breakfast I found Ailsa, and we took tea together in the drawing room. I looked at her sitting there in her chair by the fire like a Dannsburg lady, in her fine woolen kirtle with her embroidery beside her.

My wife.

Yes, that was a sham, but I wondered if it truly had to be. I had taken ill against her over what had happened in the Wheels, aye, but I thought now that perhaps that had been wrong of me. I had played as much a part in that as she had, truth be told. It had been me who had demanded blasting weapons in the first place, for Our Lady's sake, and perhaps I had forgotten that. It's a thing that I do, sometimes, when I don't want to face a hard truth about myself. Some truths are best buried, pushed into the strongbox in the back of my mind until they can be forgotten. I'm not proud of it, but there it is.

I sat there and I looked at her, and I wondered if perhaps there might be a life to be made for us. If Anne and Rosie had made a go of it, then why shouldn't we?

I would have to make an effort, I knew, but I could do that and I intended to.

"Hanne's pregnant," I said, by way of conversation, and Ailsa nodded.

"Yes," she said. "Unmarried, too. It's not seemly."

"Aye, well," I said. "I'd bet good money that my brother is the father."

Ailsa looked up at me then, and I could see that was something that she hadn't known. Perhaps she *did* miss things, sometimes, if not often. It was good to be reassured that she was still human after all.

"I see," she said. "Does he know?"

"I doubt it; he's not been here for months," I said. "I'll tell him."

"What do you think he'll do about it?"

"I have no idea," I said. "I have to admit that I don't know my brother as well as I might. We weren't together in the war, and the fighting changed him. It did all of us, I know, but him more than most. Whatever he chooses to do, I'll see that Hanne and the child are well provided for."

Ailsa nodded and showed me the ghost of a smile.

"You're a decent man, Tomas," she said. "Deep down you are."

I wasn't quite sure how she meant that, but I would take it. One step at a time, that was how it was done.

That was how you built a trust in business, and it might be that was how you built a love, too.

NINETEEN

Jochan did the last thing I expected. He married her.

It wasn't a grand ceremony like Ailsa had arranged for us, just a quiet affair in the temple of the Harvest Maiden who Hanne held to. I was Jochan's Closest Man, and Cook stood with Hanne and her father, in her mother's place. Her ma was dead, apparently, and her da didn't look far off it himself. Perhaps it was just shock on his part, to see which family his daughter was marrying into. The poor fellow was gray of face and sweating in his cheap coat throughout the saying of the words. When it was done, Jochan took his now heavily pregnant bride in his arms and kissed her in front of everyone, and I led the cheer while Ailsa stood at my side, her arm in mine.

That was two months ago, and now Ellinburg was in the grip of a fierce winter cold. Hanne was confined to her bed with the pregnancy, in the house Jochan had bought for them in the Stink. I had long since hired another girl to replace her in the kitchens.

I was in the Tanner's Arms that night, drinking with Jochan and Bloody Anne and Fat Luka in the busy common room where the fire blazed and kept the chill of the snowy streets away. Simple Sam was standing with his back to us, watching the room and keeping unwanted folk away from my table like he was supposed to.

All seemed well, until a beggar came calling at the door.

The man had both legs off at the knee and horrible burns on his hands and face. He was sitting propped up in a wheeled handbarrow and being pushed by a skinny child who was obviously struggling with the weight of the thing. I saw Black Billy having words with the man at the door, his brow furrowed. After a moment he turned and beckoned to Sam, who went over to see the lay of things.

"The fuck is this?" Jochan muttered, his voice thick with drink.

I frowned over at the door, but Sam was coming back by then. He bent to speak to me.

"Man's asking to talk to you, boss," Sam said. "Him in the barrow, I mean."

"Is he now?" I asked. "And why's that?"

I didn't allow begging inside the Tanner's, it was bad for business, but if this fellow wanted to speak to me personally then I assumed he must have a reason for it. That, or big enough balls to have come asking me for coin, which as I didn't know him from an open grave would have been something of a misjudgment on his part.

Sam just shrugged. "He's asking for Mr. Piety, boss."

"Aye, well, I'm here," I said. "Tell Billy to let him in."

Sam nodded, and a moment later the child was struggling his way toward us behind the handbarrow while folk turned to stare. Sam went over to help, and then the man was wheeled up to our table. He looked like shit and he smelled of it too, and his threadbare coat had a dusting of snow on it.

He looked up at me, haunted eyes in a gaunt, ruined face, and I knew I was looking at a veteran. He had maybe thirty years to him if that, and his life was effectively already over.

"Mr. Piety," he said, the voice coming like windblown dust from his burned throat while the young lad behind his barrow stood silent.

"Do I know you?" I asked him. "From Abingon, perhaps?"

"I was there," the man said, "but I don't think we ever met. Different regiments, I suppose."

"Aye," I said, waiting for him to work his way around to his point.

"I survived Abingon," he said, "and I marched home on my own two feet with the other men from my streets. I went home to my wife and my son, this lad here who's now pushing my barrow. I went home to my little house in the Wheels, and then some cunt blew it up."

I swallowed.

"They blew up my house and the whole street with it, because it was near a factory," he went on. "They killed my wife. They took my legs and they left my son mute with the horror of seeing his ma die burning in front of him. He dragged me screaming and burned and broken to the cunning man to save my life, and he ain't said a word since. Do you take my meaning, Mr. Piety?"

I looked at the fellow in the barrow, and I found that I had no words to say to him.

"What's your name?" Jochan asked at last, and that broke the awful silence that had fallen over our table.

"Wainwright," the man said. "Yan Wainwright."

"Well, Mr. Wainwright," I said, once I found my voice again, "I'm sorry to hear your story. I'm sure we can find a coin for you."

The words were acid in my chest, but I knew I couldn't own to the bombing of the Wheels. Not to him and not to anyone else outside my family, not ever. Ailsa had gone to great lengths and enormous expense to ensure that that could never be laid at my door, and I couldn't do anything to endanger that.

Apparently Jochan felt differently.

"For the Lady's sake," he hissed at me, loud enough for all around the table to hear. "We did this to him, Tomas. We owe him more than a fucking coin!"

I gave my brother a look like murder, but it was lost on him. I could see the pain in Jochan's eyes, in the faraway look that he got sometimes, and I knew what he was seeing.

He was seeing the surgeons' tents again, back behind the lines at Abingon, was hearing the howls and wails of the maimed, the tortured, the burned. He was hearing the broken men like Yan Wainwright, men who would never truly live again whether they survived or not.

I wiped my mouth with the back of my hand, fighting the urge to vomit. Wainwright had me fixed with a look that said he was past caring what I did to him, that he'd just wanted to have his say to me at last before he died on the streets of starvation or the cold. My eyes were stinging fiercely, as though the air in the Tanner's were thick with the smoke of blasting powder.

"Aye," I said at last. "Aye, perhaps we do."

"I don't want your coin, Piety," Wainwright said. "I just wanted you to see what you've done."

"You don't want my coin," I repeated. "You'll take it, though. For your son."

I reached into my pouch and produced a gold crown, and put it on the table in front of him. Wainwright swallowed. A working man didn't earn a gold crown in a year in Ellinburg. At last he reached out and grabbed it, and clutched it tightly in his filthy, ruined hand.

He fixed me with a look, and then he very deliberately spat on the table in front of me.

Simple Sam moved to make something of that, but I held up a hand to tell him to be still. No one said anything while the mute boy turned his crippled father's handbarrow. He slowly wheeled him out of the Tanner's Arms and into the merciless cold, with my gold coin clutched in his hand.

Gold for blood, and what use was that?

Jochan took that hard.

Very hard, to my mind. I cared about the people I knew, whatever my aunt might think, but my brother cared about people he *didn't* know and that was a difference between us. That was what broke him in the end.

Of course, we had to have it out with the Alarian Kings eventually, for what they had done to Desh. Eventually came a week later, when we ambushed them in a snow-swept square between the Wheels and the territory west of there, south of Convent Street. There were ten of us, me and my brother and Bloody Anne included, and eight or nine of them. It was just another fight and I won't record the details of it here, save to say one thing.

The fighting was hard and the icy footing treacherous, and several of us ended up on the cobbles wrestling with our opponents with blades in hand. When it was done and the Pious Men were victorious, Jochan got to his feet and stood over the body of the man he had killed. He grinned at me. I looked at my brother, and I could see by the light of the moon that his mouth and chin and all the bottom part of his face was black and wet.

He was chewing.

My gaze fell to the corpse at his feet, and then I saw that its throat had been torn out as though by the teeth of a wild animal. Jochan just grinned at me and said nothing.

That was when I knew that my brother was gone.

Aunt Enaid was fully supporting me by then, I think having finally realized which side the bread was buttered on. She was the grand matriarch of the Pious Men now, and even Florence and her Flower Girls showed her respect. I could tell she liked that.

She liked it a good deal less when Anne and me brought Jochan to her door in the dead of night, him all blood around the mouth and grinning and still saying nothing.

"Oh, my poor foolish boy," Enaid said, standing there in the doorway in her nightshirt and staring at him in horror. "Oh, what have you done?"

"You know what he's done, Auntie," I said, and I could see in her face that she did. "He can't be at home, not now, not with his wife barely a week from giving birth."

"No," Enaid said. "No, you've the right of that, Tomas. Bring him in."

Enaid roused the maid, old Doc Cordin's granddaughter, from her bed and made her get dressed, then sent her off round to Jochan's house to be with Hanne in case the baby came early. Jochan was sitting in a chair in Enaid's parlor by then, staring into space with his chin glistening and sticky red with blood. Brak had joined us in the hall.

"Go back to bed, boy," I said to him. "This is family business."

He looked from me and Anne to Enaid and back, and cleared his throat.

"Do what he says, love," Enaid told him, and that was done.

I waited for young Brak to head back upstairs, then turned to look at my aunt. Brak was a good lad, and a Pious Man, but he wasn't blood family. Enaid was, and she was the one I trusted with this, not him.

"Can you take him in?" I asked.

Enaid sighed. "I'll have to, won't I?" she said. "I saw this before, in *my* war. Maybe he'll come back and maybe he won't, but until then he'll be dangerous. Too dangerous to be around his wife and a newborn, as you said. I can make up a bed in the coal cellar. There's bars on the window, and a strong door with a good lock."

I swallowed and nodded. I didn't want to think about my little brother locked away in a dark cage like an animal, but then I didn't want to think about what he had done that night, either.

"It's for the best, Tomas," Anne said gently, and I nodded.

She had the right of that, I knew she did.

But that didn't make it any easier.

TWENTY

I didn't sleep that night. I think the only thing that kept me from drinking myself into a stupor to forget it was thinking of Anne and of how she had been with me afterward. She had walked me back to my house, all the way up to Trader's Row, and all the way there she had spoken to me in a low, soothing voice that somehow kept the battle shock at bay and stopped me from murdering the first stranger I saw. I thought drink might go a way toward undoing her good work so I stayed away from it, but it wasn't easy.

"It's been a bad night," was all she said to Ailsa when she met us in the hall, and I don't remember much after that.

Ailsa had put me to bed, I supposed, or woken the valet and had him do it. Once there I lay awake, twisting in my sweaty blankets and trying to recall the sound of Anne's voice. Anything to not think about my brother's bloody face and the bits of human meat stuck between his teeth.

I got through the night somehow, and come the dawn I needed to see Bloody Anne. I had to tell her, I knew I did, and Lady take the Queen's Warrant or what Ailsa thought of it. I had to tell Anne what we were doing and why, that it wasn't just my greed that kept us fighting, my greed that had broken my brother's mind. She had a right to know, I told myself, but truth be told, I simply couldn't stand to have her think that of me an hour longer.

I knew where Anne would have gone after that night, and once I was up and dressed I went straight there, to the house on Chandler's Narrow.

Will the Wencher opened the door to me himself, and he nodded a greeting.

"Morning, boss," he said. "Anne told me you'd likely be by this morning."

Of course she had. Bloody Anne knew me better than I knew myself sometimes, or so it seemed to me. I doubt she'd been expecting me so early, though, and when Will showed me to Rosie's room the two of them were still abed.

Will knocked, then put his head around the door, and I heard Anne say something but I couldn't catch what. A moment later Will nodded and held the door open.

"She says to go in," he said, so I did.

Rosie's room was set up for whoring, as might be expected, with a big feather bed and a cheap gilt-framed mirror on the wall, lamps with shades of red glass and even a bit of old silk canopy hanging above the bed. It struck me as strange to see Bloody Anne in those surroundings, with her short hair and her scar, sitting up in that feather bed and wearing a linen nightshirt. Rosie was lying beside her, her red hair spread out on the pillow and framing her face. Her eyes were closed, but I didn't think she was asleep.

"Sorry," I said. "I can wait, if . . ."

Anne shook her head. "No, it's all right, Tomas," she said. "If you need to talk, I understand."

"I do," I said, "but not about what you think."

"Do you want me to go?" Rosie asked without opening her eyes, and there was no hint of sleep in her voice.

"No," I said, before Anne could reply. "No, Rosie, I don't. I've something to tell Bloody Anne this morning, something I should have told her a long time ago. I think you know what that is."

Rosie sat up at that and fixed me with a stare.

"Is that really wise, Mr. Piety?"

"I don't give a fuck if it's wise," I said. "I'm doing it."

"As you will, then," Rosie said.

She swung her bare feet out of bed and sat there in her thin shift, watching me. Anne looked from me to Rosie and back again in obvious confusion. I don't know what words she was expecting me to say, but I do know they weren't the words she got.

"What is it, Tomas?" she asked at last.

"There's something I have to tell you, something that Rosie already knows, but before I do I have to ask you to swear you won't tell another soul. Will you do that for me, Bloody Anne? Will you swear it on our friendship and our trust?"

"I swear," she said, and she looked worried now.

"My wife," I said quietly, "my Ailsa, is a Queen's Man. She's a knight, Anne, a knight and a spy and an agent of the crown, and my marriage is a sham for the sake of appearances. I've never shared a bed with her, and I never expect to. Ailsa has orders from the crown, to do with things in Ellinburg, and to carry out those orders she needed me, and she needed the Pious Men. Everything I've been doing almost for the last two years, everything the Pious Men have been doing, has been on Ailsa's orders. I work for Ailsa, Anne. I work for the Queen's Men."

Anne stared at me for a long, cold moment, her scar twisting as she clenched her jaw. I knew that look. I had seen Bloody Anne moved to anger before, and that was the look that usually came just before she rammed a dagger into someone. I had never thought to have that look turned on me, and in that moment I feared her.

"I thought I was working for you," she said at last, in a flat voice. "For you, my boss and my priest and my friend. The Queen's Men, Tomas? Haven't we done enough for the fucking queen? We went to Hell for this queen none of us has ever set eyes on, and some of us are still there. Cookpot, that man Wainwright, your own mad brother, even you, all broken by this queen you still want to serve. Tell me why, Tomas. Give me one good *fucking* reason why I should even listen, and not just bury my dagger in your neck and ride for the south."

She was pure furious, I could see that well enough, and my mouth went dry. I remembered what Ailsa had told me, about the Skanians and why I had to do what she said, but that conversation had been a long time ago and I had trouble finding the words now.

Rosie rescued me. I had expected her to hold her peace, to keep Anne's rage away from her, but I had to allow that she had more spine than that.

"This is vital work," she said, and now she turned and met Anne's startled gaze. "There are foreigners in the city, as you know. Magicians, and people who are their version of the Queen's Men. Men from Skania, who back Bloodhands and his Northern Sons. We are all but at war with Skania already, although this is a secret war that we fight, a war in the shadows, and it *has* to stay that way. We have to win this war while it remains a secret. The country won't stand another open conflict, not so soon after Abingon. We've neither the men nor the money for it, and if it comes to open battle *we will lose.* If it comes to open battle it will be Abingon all over again, but it will be *us* dying of plague and starvation while they smash *our* walls with cannon, not the other way around. You think you had it bad in Abingon, Anne? Just imagine what it was like to be on the other side. *That* is why Tomas does what he has been doing, and why it is vital that he continues to do so. In secret, do you understand?"

Anne could only stare at her woman, her throat working as she swallowed.

"We," she said at last. "You keep saying 'we,' Rosie."

"Aye," Rosie said, and her chin lifted slightly as she spoke. "I'm not a Queen's Man, but I work for them. I've lied to you about some things, I'll admit that, but no more than I had to."

Anne's jaw clenched again.

"What else?" she demanded. "What else have you lied to me about, Rosie?"

"I truly do love you," Rosie said. "That was no lie."

I reached for the door handle behind me, opened the door, and slipped out of the room. That was a matter between them, and it wasn't a conversation I needed to overhear.

I heard Anne's voice as I closed the door behind me, raised in hurt and anger, but my hearing had been damaged by cannon in the war and I didn't catch her words. I sighed and went to sit in the parlor and wait.

Perhaps an hour or more later Anne came and joined me there, and she was dressed now but her hair was messed up more than it had been and she had a slight smile on her face. I didn't think the two of them had spent the whole time arguing, and that at least was good.

"So," she said, before I could speak. "Now you're a spy and a killer for the queen, then."

"Aye, among other things," I said. "But consider this—it's not murder when the queen does it. If I kill you, it's murder. If the queen has you killed, it's called justice. That's just the lay of things, and I know which side of it I'd rather be on. I'm still a businessman, that hasn't changed, and I'm still a priest too, but sometimes I have to do things in the interest of the crown. You understand why, don't you, Anne?"

She sighed and looked at her boots.

"I do," she said. "I do now that Rosie's shouted some sense into me, about that and about doubting her. She . . . I think she really *does* love me, Tomas."

"I think so too," I said.

I reached for her hand, but Anne moved away and looked at me.

"Just answer me this," she said. "We're fighting a secret war to stop an open war, and we blew up the Wheels and killed Lady only knows how many people to do it. How does violence prevent violence, Tomas? How does that work?"

I shook my head. I had no words to answer that.

"Truth be told, I don't know," I said. "They say in the temple that sometimes a man has to balance two evils in his hands, and choose the lighter one. Perhaps that's what this is. I hope so anyway, but I can't make you any promises. I'm not a general, Anne; I never have been. I'm just a fucking soldier, and I do what I'm told."

Anne nodded, but her expression was unreadable and I knew that hadn't been the answer she was looking for.

When I left Chandler's Narrow I went into the Wheels alone. That was madness, I knew, but I did it anyway. It had been just over a week since Yan Wainwright had come to the Tanner's Arms, crippled and burned and pushed in a handbarrow by a son sent mute by the horror of what I had done. I had to find him.

I survived Abingon, he had told me. *I went home to my little house in the Wheels, and then some cunt blew it up.* Aye, he knew I was responsible for the bombings, of course he did. Half the fucking city knew that, for all that no one could prove it. But that wasn't the point.

He knew, and so did I.

I walked the streets of the Wheels alone and unguarded, calling into workshops and taverns and inns, asking where I might find Yan Wainwright. I got no answer.

"That burned beggar with no legs, Mr. Piety?" a smith said to me at last. "You won't be finding him; he's dead. Drowned in the river he was, and most like by his own hand. Poor bastard."

I stared at the smith, a lean, bearded fellow standing there in the ruddy glow of his workshop with a hammer in his hand like an illumination of the Forge Father from some old book in the temple.

"What about his boy?"

The smith just shrugged. "That I couldn't say, sir."

I left him to his work and went back out into the cold, heartless street. I had thought at the time that Wainwright had the look of a man who'd had enough, who just wanted to have his say to me before he died. It seemed I had been right about that.

I drew my cloak around me against the freezing wind and I walked, paying no mind to where I went. Eventually my feet took me down the alley that led to Old Kurt's door. There was a rat nailed to it, as was his custom, and it didn't look more than a day or two old. I raised a fist and knocked, and the door opened before I had the chance to call out the words.

"Piety," Old Kurt said, and there was neither welcome nor friendship in his voice.

"Can I talk to you?" I asked him.

The old man spat on the cobbles beside my boot, his seamed and creased lips working as he thought on it for a moment. He must have had eighty years to him at least, but his eyes were still bright with a sharp intellect.

"Aye," he said at last. "Might be I've a thing or two to say to you, in return."

I nodded and let him lead me into his parlor, a cramped and filthy room filled with junk that he claimed was treasure. That sword that hung over the fireplace had once belonged to a king, or so he said. The skull on the windowsill with its temple bashed in had supposedly belonged to the same king. I had believed it, too, when I had been a lad.

The boy was there, sitting on the low stool by the fire where my own Billy had used to sit when Old Kurt was teaching him the cunning. Yan Wainwright's son turned and looked at me, and turned away.

"That's Wainwright's boy," I said to Kurt.

"That it is," Kurt said, and waved me to another stool while he took the room's only chair. "You knew his father, then?"

I told Old Kurt how Wainwright had come to me in the Tanner's Arms a week ago, and what he had said. The old man just nodded, and I realized he already knew.

"It was hate kept him alive, I reckon," Kurt told me. "The lad here brought him to me in a barrow after what happened. He was shrieking and burned, with his legs crushed to pulp by a falling timber. I took the ruin of his legs off with an axe and closed him up with the cunning, but still he should have died. Hate kept him going. Hate for those who took his world away."

"You might have the right of that," I had to admit.

"Boy turned up here two days ago," Kurt went on, "and I knew that his da was dead. I weren't surprised. I'd already heard how he came to see you, to say his piece. He were done after that, I reckon, nothing left in him. Drowned himself, the way I heard it."

"I heard the same."

Kurt ignored me and continued.

"But the boy come to me and he had a gold crown in his hand to give me, and for that I took him in. He don't speak no more but maybe that'll change, in time, and I'll teach him if he's got the spark to learn. If he ain't, well, I'll raise him anyway. I wonder how a boy like this came to have a gold crown, Tomas Piety. I wonder if perhaps that's guilt money, for what someone might have done."

I looked at the old man, and I remembered that he heard confession the same as me and every other priest in the city. He shouldn't, to my mind, as he was no priest, but he did all the same and I realized he was waiting to hear one now.

I shouldn't have done it, I knew that. That was twice in one day I had broken Ailsa's trust, first to Bloody Anne and now to Old Kurt, but I said my confession to him that morning. I left Ailsa out of it, of course, and I never mentioned the crown, but I owned to the bombing of the Wheels and that was enough.

When I was done the old man just looked at me, and he said no words of forgiveness.

"Well, that's something half the city already knew," he said, and he spat into the fire to show me what he thought of it. "Tell me this, Tomas, while you're in the mood for confessing your many and varied sins—what happens to those cunning folk who don't join you when they're told to? What happened to Arndt the cooper, from Rigger's Alley?"

"You don't need to worry about that," I said. "I've known you a long time, Old Kurt, and you taught Billy the Boy as well as you were able. I won't come knocking on your door with my offer."

"That ain't what I fucking asked," he hissed at me. "Arndt was found dead in the yard behind the Barrel o' Tar and you know it. 'Join or die,' is that the lay of things?"

"What if it is?" I snapped at him. "I confessed to you, and Lady only knows why I did that, but you stay out of my head. If I find out you used the cunning on me to make me talk I'll fucking gut you, Old Kurt."

He laughed, a horrible sound that was thick with phlegm and malice.

"I'd like to see you try," he said. "Now get the fuck out of my house."

TWENTY-ONE

It was late when I finally got home, and I was frozen and hungry. I found Ailsa waiting for me, and she was in a cold fury.

"You told Anne," she said, as soon as we were alone together in the drawing room.

I looked at her and I realized that yes, of course Rosie would have sent a runner as soon as Anne was gone, or perhaps she had even come herself. Rosie's loyalty was first and foremost to Ailsa. Or perhaps it was to Anne by now, I wasn't sure about that, but it certainly wasn't to me.

"Aye, I did," I said.

"You broke an oath sworn to me under the Queen's Warrant. I could have you hanged as a traitor for that."

I poured myself a brandy and stood close to the hearth as I drank it, soaking up warmth from the fire and the spirit both.

"I know," I said.

"So why, pray tell, did you do it?"

I turned to look at Ailsa, at the lioness. I didn't think she'd truly have me hanged and lose everything she had gained in Ellinburg, not now, but I wouldn't have bet on it. I knew I had to try to make her understand.

"What we're doing here," I started, "I know it's important, Ailsa, and I know why we're doing it, but we're ruining people all the same. My brother finally lost his mind last night, do you understand that? He ate human flesh, and he maybe lost his soul for it. Only the gods can say. We killed hundreds of folk, down in the Wheels, and . . . Anne's my second. She has to support me, in everything I do, otherwise the Pious Men will tear themselves apart and we'll have nothing. She's spent all this time thinking I've been doing it just for me, destroying lives to line my purse, and I *know* her, Ailsa. That wasn't sitting well with her and it wasn't going to do, not for much longer it wasn't. She had to hear the truth of things eventually or I'd have lost her."

Ailsa looked into the fire for a long moment, and she sighed.

"Perhaps you're right," she said at last. "Perhaps. It's done now, and nothing more to be said on it save for this—*do not do it again!*"

"No," I said. I thought on what I had told Old Kurt that afternoon, and decided it was best to keep that to myself. I hadn't mentioned the crown to him so it was none of Ailsa's business, to my mind. "No, I won't."

"You had *better* not," she said, her voice cracking like a whip in the empty room. "Now, there's news."

"Oh? What news?"

"From Dannsburg."

I nodded. News from Dannsburg meant orders, most likely, and urgent ones at that. I pitied the rider who had braved the West Road in the snows. I refilled my glass and waited.

"These cunning women you have recruited," she said. "I assume you still know where they both are?"

I nodded. There was Katrin the herbalist, in her shop in the Stink, and Gerta the midwife out in the west of the city who passed notes to Luka's spies.

"Of course I do."

"Good," she said. "They're to go to the capital. I will arrange a wagon and guards, and laborers to clear the road, but they have to go and they have to be on the road by Queensday at the latest."

I blinked at her. "In this weather? And besides, that's only three days away. These women have lives, and jobs, and Gerta has a family. I can't just—"

"I don't care," Ailsa said, cutting me off. "They have to be rounded up and put on that wagon, and that's all there is to it."

"Why?"

She fixed me with a look.

"Because my orders say so," she snapped. "And you need to find more of them. We've only recruited two, and stopped one other from joining the Skanians. That's not good enough."

"Maybe that's all there is," I said. "Them and Old Kurt, and he's no use to anyone. The cunning is a rare thing, Ailsa."

"Is it? The Skanians have magicians enough to make me think otherwise."

"You've got a whole fucking house of magicians, in Dannsburg," I pointed out.

"That's different," she said, although I couldn't see how.

That made me think of something, though, some memory I couldn't quite grasp. Something Old Kurt had said to me once, perhaps.

The look on her face told me that the time for questioning her was over. I sighed and nodded. If it had to be done, then it did, I supposed, although I couldn't think what the two women would make of it, and I said as much.

"Tell them it's an adventure," she said. "Tell them it's an honor, or their duty to you and the Pious Men, or even to the queen. You can tell them anything you like, but you *will* make it happen, Tomas."

"Aye, right you are," I said.

Fat Luka would make it happen, I knew that. He could sell water to a drowning man, could Fat Luka, and I knew he'd think of something. Failing that we would pay them, and failing *that* we would force them.

That was how business was done, in Ellinburg.

Three days later Katrin and Gerta were on a wagon on the West Road, headed for Dannsburg.

When the Queen's Men say jump, you jump.

Governor Hauer had told me that once, and he'd had the right of it. Still, when I gave Fat Luka the same orders he had jumped just as high for me, so that was well and good.

The day after that Cook came to tell me she'd had word that Hanne had birthed a baby girl and was asking for her husband. I just nodded and thanked her. What I was going to do with that I had no idea. Jochan was still locked in Aunt Enaid's coal cellar, too dangerous to be allowed near a newborn, or anyone else for that matter.

The weather that day was foul, and it matched my mood. Rain and hail whipped almost sideways outside the windows, bad enough that Billy the Boy hadn't made his usual journey to Slaughterhouse Narrow to train with Cutter. Instead he was haunting the house like an ill-tempered ghost, sullen and withdrawn the way boys of that age get when their hands are idle.

"What's wrong, lad?" I asked him when I finally caught him in my study, stealing a glass of my brandy. "Oh, drink if you want it, there's plenty. But don't let Ailsa see you drunk in the house or it's me who'll get the sharp side of her tongue."

I earned a smile for that, and Billy almost looked like his old self again.

"Something's not right, Uncle Tomas," he told me.

I frowned at that, and I topped the lad's glass up and got one for myself as well. I waved him into a chair and took the seat behind my desk, and I looked at him.

"Is Our Lady speaking to you?" I asked him.

"I don't know," Billy confessed, "and that's part of what's not right. There's something . . . I don't *know*."

He looked sullen again then, and I didn't want that.

"Is it something now, or something to come?" I prompted him.

Billy was a seer, as I have written, and that must have been a heavy burden to carry on shoulders so young.

"Both, I think," Billy said, "but they might be different things."

"Right," I said, and took a sip of brandy. "Well, the captain always said that today matters more than tomorrow, for we may not live to see tomorrow. What do you think is wrong right now, Billy?"

"Old Kurt," he said at once. He looked surprised to be saying it, like he hadn't known what he was about to say until the words fell out of his mouth. Perhaps he hadn't, at that. "Old Kurt's sore at you, Uncle Tomas. He'll make trouble later."

"Aye, I'll allow that might well be the lay of it," I said. "We had words a few days ago, me and Kurt, and I don't know that we parted friends."

Billy nodded, and he looked relieved to have got that part of it right at least.

"It's more than that, though," he said. "Not today or tomorrow, but yesterday."

"Really yesterday, do you mean? Or . . . before."

"Before," he said, and I knew he meant the war.

It's a thing that has to be understood, that the war broke a lot of strong men. It had broken Cookpot and Jochan, and it had almost broken me, and we were grown men and Jochan and me at least were no strangers to violence even before we were conscripted. When we had found Billy, in the ruins of Messia, he had been a child. An orphan child living wild in the devastation like an animal, killing to survive. A child who joined our regiment, and then went through the Hell of Abingon with the rest of us. A child who was touched by a goddess or possessed by a devil or maybe both, and who could truly say which was the truth of that?

I loved Billy, in my way, but I'll admit that he scared me, too.

"Aye," I said. "It's a hard thing, Billy, I know that. If you want to talk to me about the war, then I hope you know that you can."

"I know," Billy said, but he said no more about it.

"Well," I said, and took another drink. "That's up to you, of course."

"I don't want to go, but I know that I will," he said suddenly.

I blinked at him.

"Go where, Billy?"

"Dannsburg," he said.

"You don't have to go to Dannsburg," I assured him. "I know Katrin and Gerta did, but that's different. They're cunning folk, aye, but you're my . . . my nephew, Billy. You don't have to go."

"I do, and it'll be bad," he said, his voice dropping to a hoarse whisper. "That's the tomorrow. You'll see."

PART TWO

TWENTY-TWO

Spring finally came to Ellinburg after one of the hardest winters in memory.

Even the midwinter festival had been a subdued affair, with not enough food or work to go around among the common folk. Ailsa and I had marked the occasion by enduring a joyless midwinter ball at Governor Hauer's invitation. But the real highlight of the season had been the day I signed the papers of law that made Billy officially my son.

My adopted son, to be sure, but I would take what Our Lady offered and be thankful for it. After that day in my study when Billy had got drunk on my brandy and told me his fears for the future, I had resolved to protect him the best way I could. His name was Piety now, and in Ellinburg that was the strongest shield that I could offer.

To be sure, that name hadn't saved my brother from his own madness. His daughter was three months old now and still he hadn't seen her, or even thought to ask if she had been born alive. He remained confined to Aunt Enaid's cellar, and the city was the safer for it. That had been hard to explain to Hanne, and she had wept once she finally grasped my meaning, but eventually even she had come to see that it was in the best interests of the child that she held so close to her ample bosom.

That was done, then, and no more to be said about it. I hired maids to look after Hanne and to help her with the baby, and I put guards on her house. She was my sister-by-law now, after all, and I wouldn't see her go without or come into harm's way. Family is important, as I had once told young Desh. Perhaps one day her husband could come back to her, but until then she was still a Piety and that gave her a certain status in Ellinburg.

The winter snows melted away eventually and the West Road became passable again, and a rider came to our house.

"There's word from Dannsburg," Ailsa told me that evening. "We are summoned to the capital, Tomas."

I remembered Billy's words to me in the winter, his fears for the future, and I swallowed.

"Us and Billy," I said, and I knew I was right.

"Yes," she said, a slight frown creasing her perfectly powdered brow. "Yes, that's right. Were you listening at the door while I spoke to the messenger?"

"No, of course not," I said.

I told her what Billy had told me, that brandy afternoon.

"Interesting," she said, in a soft voice that perhaps I hadn't been supposed to catch. "Yes, he may well be what they seek."

"What?"

Ailsa turned and looked at me, and her dark eyes were pitiless.

"Nothing," she said. "You need to consider this carefully, Tomas. We will be away a good long time, I suspect. The business must continue to run without you."

"Aye," I said. "Bloody Anne's my second, she'll take over the business. Fat Luka can—"

"I would prefer that Luka came with us," Ailsa interrupted, in a tone that made her preference an instruction.

I blinked at her. "What the fuck for?"

"He's a clever man, and he's devious and he knows how to find things out," Ailsa said. "Dannsburg is . . . not like Ellinburg. I think he'll be useful to us there."

"You're a fucking Queen's Man," I snapped at her. "Don't you know everything that happens in the capital?"

"If we did there would be no crime and no sedition," she said. "Of course we don't know *everything*, just almost all of it. Luka will be useful, and he is coming with us."

That sounded like that was the end of it, then, but something was bothering me all the same. Ailsa was right; Fat Luka *was* a clever man. Too clever, perhaps. He was devious, too, as she had said.

If we were going to Dannsburg on crown business, and I couldn't think that it was anything else, then perhaps Luka might find his way to working that out for himself, in time. Still, I thought, that wasn't my problem. If Ailsa trusted him, then well and good. I had thought before that perhaps she sensed a kindred spirit in him, and it might be that I had been right about that. That wasn't my concern, though. My only concern was how best to keep the Pious Men going without me.

"Right," I said. "Well, Anne's still in charge here. My aunt will have to step up again, and Mika too. He's a clever lad, and it's probably time I gave him some more responsibility anyway. I'll—"

"I don't actually care, Tomas," she said, cutting me off. "Arrange your men how you see fit; just see that you lose no ground to Vhent and the Skanians while we're away. That's the only thing that really matters."

Dannsburg is maybe a week's ride from Ellinburg for a messenger, if the weather is fair. That's if you pack a saddlebag and bedroll, get on a horse and point it down the West Road, and sleep under a hedge wherever you stop each night. Of course, it wasn't going to be that simple.

Traveling with Ailsa meant carriages and wagons, servants and guards, and stopping at an inn every night to sleep in real beds. It meant her and Billy and me in one carriage and Fat Luka and Salo, our steward, and Ailsa's fucking lady's maid in another with a wagon for the baggage and five men ahorse as guards. It meant making five miles a day if we were lucky instead of the twenty with ease that a lone rider could have made, and it resulted in my patience wearing very thin indeed.

The whole point of money is to make life easier, to my mind, but it seemed Ailsa thought differently about that. Almost the complete opposite, in fact. Money in the way people of society manners had it seemed designed to make life as difficult as fucking possible, as far as I could see, and that made no sense to me.

Our caravan crawled through the mining country in the hills to the west of Ellinburg, then into the open farmland beyond it. There was nothing to do but sit there and watch plowmen toil endlessly up and down their fields, or to attempt to count the heads of sheep and cattle until I fell asleep on the bench.

Sometime near the end of the second week of travel, when we had again stopped at a village inn for the night with hours of daylight still left to us, I lost patience with the whole business.

"It'll be high summer before we reach Dannsburg at this pace," I complained to Ailsa. "I've seen cannon moved faster than this."

"I am in no hurry," she said. "I have been summoned, but not by those for whom I must make haste. I have sent word ahead that I am on my way, now let them wait on my pleasure. That sends a message, in itself, and every extra day that I take only serves to reinforce that message."

I had no idea who or what she was talking about, so there was little enough I could say to that. This was how society folk fought their battles, I had come to realize: not with blades but with insults disguised as courtesy. It was a whole different world to mine, I knew that much.

Eventually, after well over a month of travel and tedium, the road crested a hill and in the distance I saw the walls of Dannsburg at last. Banners flew everywhere, the queen's white rose rippling across an endless field of red. This was the capital, then. This was Dannsburg, the city of the Rose Throne.

This was Ailsa's home, and I couldn't shake the feeling that I might not be welcome here.

TWENTY-THREE

Things worked differently in Dannsburg.

That much was plain enough even before we passed the walls. The City Guard here wore heavy plate half-armor, with red surcoats emblazoned with the white rose of the royal house. There was a long line of people waiting to enter the city, and it was plain that those without coin to pay the gate tax were being turned away. Old women, barefoot children, crippled men—if they couldn't pay they were refused, and driven off with the butts of spears if need be.

Those who had coin were allowed through the gates, but grudgingly all the same. From what I could see the amount of the tax appeared to vary depending on the mood of the guard and the desperation of the plaintiff.

"What are they running from?" I asked Ailsa as we sat in our carriage behind a line of wagons.

"Starvation, I imagine," she said. "The winter was even harder in the west, and many farmers will have gone hungry, but the granaries and storehouses of Dannsburg could withstand siege for two years and more. There is food in the city, and that draws people like flies."

"I see."

There was food in the city, but only for those who could pay. A prince looks after his people, but it seemed that perhaps a queen did not.

An armored man rode down the line of those waiting to enter the city, a Guard captain by the look of him, and he reined up in front of our carriage. He exchanged a word with one of our men, and then his face was at the window.

"Sorry to keep you waiting, m'lord," he said to me. "Shouldn't be too much longer."

"It shouldn't be *any* longer," Ailsa said, her voice sharp enough to cut glass.

"No, m'lady," he said. "My apologies. I'll see to it."

Ailsa sat back in her seat and turned away, dismissing him with a cold indifference that said she expected no less.

A moment later I heard shouting, and then armored guards were beating people out of our way with cries of "Make way, make way!"

"I don't think there's any need—" I started, but Ailsa gave me a look that silenced me.

"If we had sat and waited patiently it would have looked conspicuous," she whispered. "The nobility don't behave like that, not here."

"I see," I said again.

There was a jolt as the carriage started moving again. Salo must have already paid whatever was asked, I could only assume, as we weren't stopped at the gates. That or nobles weren't expected to pay at all, which wouldn't have much surprised me. Our two carriages rumbled through the gatehouse tunnel under the massive city wall, the baggage wagon creaking along behind us, and then we were in Dannsburg itself.

The cobbled street was wide and busy, and one of our guards had to ride ahead to clear people out of our way. I saw carts and wagons and folk afoot, and guardsmen. I saw a great many guardsmen, distinctive in their red surcoats. Something seemed to be missing, too, but I couldn't have said what.

"A lot of guards," I observed.

"They keep the queen's peace," Ailsa said.

"I'm sure they do."

They looked tough, those guards, well armed and obviously well drilled and well disciplined. The City Guard in Ellinburg were little more than another gang, just a bigger and better-armed one, but this lot looked like proper soldiers. It seemed to me that doing business in Dannsburg might be a sight harder than I was used to, although as far as I knew that wasn't what I was there for. Truth be told, I still had no idea *why* we were there. Ailsa had refused to be drawn on the subject through all of our long, tortuous progress here, and young Billy had sunk into a state of silent dread the closer to the city we got, and refused to talk at all.

"Where are we going, anyway?" I asked her. "There's a lot of us to try and get into a city inn."

"My house," she said, and that surprised me.

"You've got a house, here?"

"Yes, of course I have," she said. "Did you suppose that I lived on the streets before I came to Ellinburg? I am a lady of the court, Tomas. Of course I have a house."

I must admit I hadn't really given it any thought, but I supposed that she would have. Again I remembered that I knew practically nothing about this woman who I called my wife.

"And am I to be your husband here?"

She shot a pointed look at Billy and kicked me under the seat, but the lad had his eyes closed and seemed to be asleep.

"Of course, my love," she said, and I couldn't miss the acid in her tone. "I will be very pleased to introduce you to society."

I had a feeling I wasn't going to enjoy that.

"Of course," I repeated, and turned my attention back to the window of the carriage.

This part of the city at least was grand enough, all built of stone and with statues and fountains in the squares. It didn't stink like Ellinburg did, either. Lines of neatly clipped trees ran down the middle of some of the wider roads and cast pleasant shade in the spring sunshine. A massive castle loomed on a hill in the distance, red banners fluttering from its heights, and beyond it to the north I could see the soaring spires of a great temple. Every building that wasn't obviously residential seemed to be flying the royal flag, and it seemed to my eye that the city was a sea of shifting red and white.

Billy had his eyes open by then, and he had obviously noticed the same thing.

"There are so many flags, Mama," he said.

It still made me smile, to hear him call Ailsa that. He had started with Ma, but Ailsa had informed him that was common and told him the correct way to address us. I was Papa now instead of Uncle Tomas, not Da. Ailsa seemed to have quite taken to her new role as his adopted mother, and that pleased me a great deal.

"They show allegiance to the queen, my dear," Ailsa said.

"It's quite the show," I said.

"It is best, in Dannsburg," she murmured, "to show allegiance to the queen. Openly, and often."

That made me frown. The royal standard flew in Ellinburg, of course, over the governor's hall, but only there. How much allegiance did one woman need to be shown? I supposed royalty needed to be shown respect in the same way that a businessman did, although obviously on a far greater scale. A man could have enough of banners quite quickly in a place like this, I thought.

Ailsa's house was much like the one we had in Ellinburg, although larger and set back from the street with walls around it and guards on the gates. It's good to have guards, to my mind, but only if you know and trust them. I had no idea who these men were, and that troubled me.

They opened the gates for us and admitted the carriages and the wagon into a spacious area of grass in front of the house. I frowned as two more armed men came out of the house and started toward us.

"Do these people all work for you?" I asked her quietly.

"For my friends," she said, and that was exactly what I had been afraid of.

These were Queen's Men, then, or their soldiers anyway. It occurred to me that I had never thought to question Ailsa's rank within the Queen's Men, if they even had such a notion, but this was how I had always imagined a colonel's house might be.

One of the house guards made to open the door of the carriage then, and he found one of *my* guards between it and him before he could complete the action. My man was still ahorse, and he had a hand on the hilt of his sword.

"Peace, Oliver," I said. "We're among friends here."

I hoped that was true, but I wasn't completely sure.

I looked over Oliver's horse and saw yet another man at the door of the house, a loaded crossbow raised to his shoulder.

"Oh, for the gods' sakes," Ailsa snapped. "Brandt, stand back. Oliver, don't be a fool. This is my house, and I am mistress here. You both disgrace yourselves in front of my lord husband."

I thought this Brandt fellow might injure himself, what with how fast he bowed to her. He seemed to be in charge of her household guards, from what I could see.

Oliver reached down from his horse to open the carriage door, and I climbed out onto the churned-up grass and offered my hand to my lady wife. Ailsa stepped gracefully down beside me and Billy jumped down after her, staring around him with his eyes wide.

"This house is safe, Papa," he said after a moment.

That was good to hear, especially coming from Billy. When he knew a thing was so, then it was so, and I was past arguing with that or doubting him. I no longer even cared whether he got that knowledge from Our Lady or from some devil in Hell. I would take what help I was given and be grateful for it.

"Yes, Billy, it is," I said, for the benefit of the men around me. "This is our house, just like the one in Ellinburg."

"Exactly," Ailsa said, and she gave me a nod of approval to say I had handled that well.

Fat Luka and Salo were out of their own carriage now and looking around them. Luka had a thoughtful look on his face as he took in the sight of the household guards, and right then I found I was glad to have him with me despite my earlier misgivings. He was wondering the same things I had been, I knew—who these men were and how much we could trust them. Ailsa's lady's maid was sitting waiting patiently for one of them to give her a hand down, which neither of them thought to do.

I went over to Luka while Salo started to supervise the unloading of the baggage wagon. Eventually the maid climbed down by herself with a pinched look of annoyance on her face.

"Well, Tomas," Luka said, scratching his belly through his fine doublet, "this is Dannsburg, then."

"Aye," I said. "It seems that it is. Don't wander off exploring just yet—I'll need to speak to you in private as soon as we have the chance."

That chance was a good while coming. Everything in Ailsa's house was even more formal than it was back in Ellinburg, which chafed me raw. No, I wasn't supposed to go into the kitchen; that wouldn't have been seemly. Yes, of course I could have a drink, but that meant ringing a bell that summoned a footman who sent a houseboy to the kitchen to pester an undercook to draw me a mug of beer from the barrel and give it to him to bring back to the footman to give to me, when I would quite happily have just gone and got the fucking thing myself. What the point was I had no idea, but the result was that I was thirsty and in short temper by the time I finally got it. Perhaps this sort of nonsense was why nobles always seemed to be angry about something.

Ailsa's steward was fucking insufferable. He was a tall, thin man with perhaps sixty years to him. He had elegantly styled gray hair and he thought far too much of himself, to my mind. I wondered if he hadn't perhaps been playing lord of the house while she had been in Ellinburg these last two years. His name was Aliyev, and he and Salo hated each other on sight.

Aliyev ran the house his own way, it soon became clear, and he quite plainly did not want another steward there. My men were assigned to servants' quarters without consultation. It wasn't until he tried to put Luka in a servant's garret that I had to speak to him.

"This man is my friend and my guest, not a servant," I told Aliyev. "He'll be treated as such and put in a guest room."

Aliyev looked at me, and his nose crinkled ever so slightly as though he could smell something bad and was trying to pretend that he couldn't. It was my voice; I knew it was. My accent is strongly Ellinburg, nothing at all like Ailsa's cut-crystal Dannsburg tones. He thought I was some common oik from the provinces who had no class and no business being his mistress's husband, that much was plain enough.

I didn't care for it.

"I see, sir," he said.

He did as he was told, that was something, but the man's manner all but dripped disrespect onto the polished wooden floor beneath him. He gave orders to a pair of housemen to install Luka in a guest room, and he turned away from me without another word or so much as a nod, as though he was dismissing me.

I wasn't having that. This needed sorting immediately, so everyone understood how things were going to work from now on.

"Aliyev," I said, my voice falling into the flat tone that meant harsh justice wasn't far away.

He turned back to me with a look of thinly veiled disgust at the way I pronounced his name.

"Sir?"

"Show me the wine cellar," I said. "Right now."

He cleared his throat and led me down a corridor, and then through a low door and down a flight of steps under the house. I had only been guessing that there *was* a wine cellar, but of course there was. It was dark down there, with only the single lamp Aliyev was carrying to light the low, vaulted chamber and its rows and rows of dusty bottles. He put the lamp down on a shelf and turned to face me, his gaze expressionless.

I had him by the throat a moment later.

TWENTY-FOUR

"Aliyev seems to respect you as my husband, which pleases me," Ailsa said, later that evening when we were sitting in the drawing room together. I had already chased the servants out so we could talk in peace, and young Billy was in bed.

"Aye," I said. "I think we understand each other."

She gave me a look over the rim of her glass that said she knew exactly what I must have done.

"And there I was thinking he might make trouble," she said, and the corner of her mouth curled into a wry smile.

"I'm boss here, not him," I said. "I think he grasps that now."

"As long as you both understand that *I* am in charge here, that suits me well enough," she said. "You are my husband and the staff need to treat you as such, but this is *my* house, Tomas."

"Aye, I know," I said. "How many of your household know who you really are?"

"All of them know I am a lady of court," she said. "Brandt works for the same people I do and he knows my business, but that's all. He has charge of the house guard, and they answer to him."

"Well, they'll have to work alongside my lads," I said. "I'm not trusting everything to men I don't know."

"They'll work something out between them," she said. "Dogs always do."

"My men aren't dogs."

She waved a dismissive hand. "You know what I mean. What *did* you do to Aliyev, by the way?"

"What dogs do," I snapped at her, and to my surprise she laughed.

"Yes, I suppose I asked for that," she said. "You have to understand, Tomas, this isn't going to be like Ellinburg. Here in Dannsburg I'm afraid everyone of consequence knows me, and no one knows you at all. That reputation you depend on simply does not exist here."

That was what I had thought too, but I'd soon change that.

Once Ailsa had finished her glass of wine and retired to her room for the night, I sent a houseman to bring Fat Luka to me. He settled awkwardly in the drawing room, and I put a glass of brandy in his hand.

"Tell me your thoughts," I said.

"How do you mean, Tomas?"

"You don't miss anything, Fat Luka, I know that. That's what I pay you for. We've been here half a day; tell me what you think."

"I don't like it," Luka said, after a moment. "There's too many City Guard, and too many fucking flags, and this house is protected harder than the Golden Chains. There's something a bit funny here, but I don't know what it is."

"That's what you're going to find out for me," I told him. "Take a bag of silver, and Oliver and Emil for muscle, and go have a night out. Find the rough part of the city; there must be one. Find *our* streets, here. Grease some palms and start figuring out how this city works."

"Aye, right, boss," Luka said.

Now that there was work to be done he had gone back to calling me boss, I noticed, not Tomas. We might have found a friendship of sorts, but business would always come first with us and that was only right. He drained his brandy and stood up, and gave me a look like he had something on his mind.

"What is it?" I asked him.

"Nothing," Luka said eventually. "Night, boss."

"Oh, fuck it," I said as he turned away. "I'll come with you."

Luka grinned like that was what he had been wanting to hear, and I went upstairs to open the traveling chests that had been brought up to my bedroom. My room adjoined Ailsa's, the same as it did in Ellinburg, but here there wasn't even a connecting door. That suited me fine; I had no desire for her to hear me getting ready to go out. No doubt she would find out about it anyway, but by then it would be done and nothing she could do to stop me.

Ten minutes later I met Fat Luka in the grand hall, and now I had a well-made but plain cloak on over my fine coat, and the Weeping Women buckled around my waist. Luka was similarly dressed and he had a short-sword and dagger at his belt as well, and Emil and Oliver both wore the plain russet of servants over their weapons.

Getting out of the house was half the battle, of course, between Ailsa's men on the door and more of them on the gate, but as her lord husband I could come and go as I pleased. If it had just been Luka and the men, I realized, perhaps the answer might have been different. Even so, I thought as we walked down the street and took a turn at random, I suspected Ailsa had already been told that we had gone off into the city.

Still, she hadn't said I couldn't, and she surely knew I wouldn't have paid her any mind even if she had. Ailsa was a Queen's Man and my wife, but she wasn't my boss, not to my mind she wasn't. Not in Ellinburg, and not here in this strange city she called home either.

Luka and I had plenty of silver in our purses and I even had a couple of gold crowns for emergencies, and we were both armed and had two bodyguards with us. Dannsburg held no terrors for us that night.

Truth be told, this part of the city was very fine, all high buildings of pale stone. There were lanterns lit every twenty yards or so, hanging on iron hooks from the walls of the houses. That was no use to me. I was sick to my throat of society and manners and servants and how things were supposed to be done. I wanted to find my sort of people, the people who knew how things were *really* done.

I thought Ailsa was actually that sort of person too, but she moved behind such a thick blind of society manners and secrecy and sheer money that it was impossible to tell. The Queen's Men got things done, I knew that much, but exactly how remained a mystery to me.

After we had walked another couple of streets and seen nothing to interest us I heard shouting in the distance, and that was a lot more promising. We headed that way. The sounds led us down a narrower but still well-to-do street, and here there were smart inns and the closed shops of expensive tailors and glovers and milliners. There were a group of City Guard there as well, and they were kicking the living shit out of a pair of beggars.

These were the first beggars I had seen since we had arrived in the city, and I realized that was what had seemed to be missing. It's a funny thing, how you grow so accustomed to the sight of street people that you almost don't see them until they're not there, and you wonder what's wrong.

"Oi!" I called out, striding toward the Guard with my three men behind me. "What's the problem here?"

One of the guardsmen turned to face me, obviously the boss of them, and he looked me up and down. I could see him taking in the high-gloss polish of my boots and the fine cut of my coat under my open cloak. I wasn't known here, no, but money is known everywhere and I quite clearly had plenty of that.

"Vagrancy is a crime, m'lord," the guardsman growled, and I knew it was only my fine clothes and a fear of who I might be that prevented him from giving me a taste of what the beggars had got.

"Then find them somewhere to go," I said. "Hitting them won't make them stop existing."

The guardsman snorted. "Get caught three times and they'll stop existing all right, you mark my words. Three offenses and they'll hang. M'lord."

"I see," I said.

That seemed harsh, but they were no one I knew and I was in a strange city where they did things their own way. That was their business, to my mind.

We walked on, and we found what we were looking for eventually.

A river ran through Dannsburg, and it was soon clear that the far bank was what might be called the wrong side of the city, as far as most folk were concerned. Dannsburg wasn't industrial in the way that Ellinburg was and the river itself looked reasonably clean, but the streets on the far side of the stone bridge we crossed were anything but. Where there had been lanterns on the walls before, now there was oppressive darkness, broken only by the occasional smoking torch or red lamps in alcoves above the doors of what were obviously brothels.

"Here we are," Fat Luka muttered to himself, and I knew what he meant.

This was home, to my mind, but of course here in Dannsburg it was nothing of the sort. Here it would be home to someone *like* me, I could only assume, but these weren't my streets. This wasn't the Stink and I wasn't known here, and I knew I had to remember that.

We found a tavern and went in, nodding respectfully to the hulking brute on the door as we passed. Of course, I wasn't really dressed for a place like this, not when I didn't own it anyway, and I could feel the stares following me as I walked slowly into the room with Fat Luka and our two men behind me.

There was a young man with perhaps sixteen years to him sitting at a table with a mug of beer by his hand and three upturned shells on the scarred wood in front of him. I knew that game, and so did every lad in the Stink.

"Find the pea, m'lord," he called out. "Only a silver penny a bet, and five to one."

"I won a whole mark off him not ten minutes ago, m'lord," said his shill in the crowd, right on cue. "Ever so easy, it is. You've just got to keep your eye on the shell he puts the pea under, and you can't lose."

I turned and fixed them both with a stare.

"Don't take me for a cunt," I said. "I was running that game when you were still sucking on your ma's tit. Who's the boss in these parts?"

The shell boy coughed into his beer and looked up at me, and I could see in his face that he had realized I was a businessman and not the easy mark he had taken me for.

"Mr. Grachyev's the boss," he said quietly, "but he don't come in here. You want to talk business, you might want to speak to Leonov, over at the bar."

I nodded my thanks to him and went that way, where three large and unwelcoming men were standing around a fellow wearing a decent-looking coat.

"You'll be Leonov," I said to the man in the coat. "My name is Tomas Piety."

"Nice for you," Leonov said. "You sound like the east."

"Ellinburg," I agreed. "The Pious Men."

Leonov nodded slowly. "Might be I've heard of you," he said. "What the fuck are you doing here, and with only three men behind you?"

"Nothing uncivil," I assured him. "I'm visiting Dannsburg, that's all, and I'm looking to make some friends while I'm here. The right sort of friends, you understand me?"

"Aye," Leonov said after a moment. "Perhaps."

"This is Fat Luka," I said, introducing him. "Luka handles my diplomatic interests, as you might say. I'd be obliged if you and him between you could broker a meeting between me and Mr. Grachyev."

I could see that each recognized something of a kindred spirit in the other. Luka and Leonov shook hands, and Luka's hand had a silver mark in it.

"Right," Leonov said, after a moment. "We can do that."

That was how I started to do business in Dannsburg.

TWENTY-FIVE

The next morning I had to answer to Ailsa, of course. She was not well pleased, to speak lightly of it, but then I had never supposed that she would be.

"You can't *do* that, Tomas," she hissed at me over breakfast that morning.

We were seated in a small dining room that was half again the size of the one we had at home in Ellinburg. At least the size of the room meant that the servants who lined the walls were too far away to hear what we were saying. I supposed that was something.

"I can't what, go out for a drink with my friend Luka? And why's that, Ailsa?"

"Go south of the river," she said. "*No one* of quality in Dannsburg goes south of the river, wasn't that plain to see with your own eyes?"

"Aye, and that's why I went there," I said. "That's my part of the city, Ailsa, right there. Anyway, no need to trouble yourself over it. I had a drink and a very pleasant conversation with a man I have some things in common with, that's all. If Fat Luka does his job, then in a week or two I might be having a sit-down with his boss, to get to know each other as it were, but if it makes you happy I can invite him here instead."

Ailsa gave me a look like daggers, but I could tell she knew I was just making mischief with her. Even I wasn't so uneducated as to know that receiving this Mr. Grachyev at Ailsa's house was out of the question.

"Yes," she sighed, after a moment. "Yes, there might be some use to it, and these are your sort of people. The right man for the right job, isn't that what you always say? You're definitely the right man for mixing with scum like those."

She meant to insult me, I knew, but I didn't care and for the simple reason that she was right. These *were* my sort of people, not the society fools she kept trying to introduce me to. I would never be one of them and they would never accept me, and we both knew it. Still, it seemed that wasn't going to keep her from trying.

"We have an engagement this afternoon," she said. "Word has already spread that I have returned home, and invitations are starting to come in."

"What sort of engagement?"

"A bear bait," she said. "Lord Lan Yetrov has had a bear pit built at his house. He very much enjoys the sport."

"Why the fuck would I want to watch that?"

"You don't have to watch it if you don't care for it, but you *do* have to mingle and be seen. There will already be a great deal of gossip about this mysterious new husband I have brought home with me from the east. People need to see you and become . . . accustomed to you."

"Why?" I asked. "What the fuck does it matter what these people think of me?"

"One day it might matter a great deal," she said, and then she lifted the small silver bell beside her on the table and rang for more tea.

Apparently that was the end of the conversation. So that was to be my afternoon then, watching some poor bloody bear having dogs set on it for the entertainment of fools.

So far I had to say I didn't care for Dannsburg.

Jochan had thought my house in Ellinburg was a palace, the first time he saw it. Truth be told, at the time so had I, and I could only think how this Lord Lan Yetrov would have laughed at that.

Lan Yetrov's house was three times the size even of Ailsa's, with high walls around the extensive gardens and armed guards in his house livery on the gate. Our carriage rattled past them, and we stepped down outside the imposing stone building. Servants directed our coachman toward the stable block where the carriages of those other guests who had already arrived were lined up.

We were ushered inside the house by waiting footmen. They served us wine in tall goblets, and little things to eat that I neither wanted nor enjoyed. The hall was huge. Where the gallery in my house in Ellinburg was wooden with a finely carved staircase that I had thought so grand, here everything was marble and polished stone and gilded metal. Two huge stairs swept up to the second-floor gallery where musicians played for the entertainment of those gathered below.

Ailsa and I were dressed well, richly in truth, but even Ailsa was outshone by the gowns of many of the ladies present. This was true society, I realized, Dannsburg society. This was the royal city, after all, and many of those present were probably courtiers. The man nearest me, a gray-haired fellow in a black silk brocade coat and sash of cloth-of-gold, could have been a duke for all I knew. This assembly put all the fools in Ellinburg to shame.

"We must greet our host," Ailsa said out of the corner of her mouth. "Let me take the lead."

I nodded and followed her as she threaded her way across the room, exchanging smiles and courtesies with people she knew along the way. Ailsa knew a great deal of people there, I soon came to realize, and I started to understand how this worked.

She was a Queen's Man, a diplomat and a spy and a killer, and yet placed so highly in society that I heard her address a countess by her given name. Oh yes, Ailsa was a weapon indeed in the crown's arsenal, I realized, but a weapon that was better placed to turn inward than anywhere else. It seemed to me that a good part of the work of the Queen's Men involved watching the queen's own subjects.

"My dear Lord Lan Yetrov," Ailsa said at last, greeting an overly dressed young man who was leaning possessively close to a woman who wore a queen's ransom in diamonds around her throat. "I must thank you for your gracious invitation. Please allow me to present my husband, Father Tomas Piety."

The man turned to us with a smile on his face.

"Charmed," he said. "A priest, you say?"

"Aye, I'm that," I said, "and a businessman too. Pleased to meet you."

The smile curdled on his face when he heard me speak.

"You are from . . . is that *Ellinburg*, I hear in your voice?"

"Aye."

"And are you looking forward to the entertainment?"

This was where I was supposed to tell him a flattering lie, I knew, but fuck that. I already didn't like him, and I could tell he felt the same way about me.

"I don't much care for cruelty for its own sake," I said. "Cruelty should have a purpose to it, to my mind."

"It's only sport," he said. "It doesn't hurt anyone, does it?"

I thought the bear might have a different opinion about that.

"Doesn't it?"

"You don't care for sport, Father Piety?" asked the woman with the diamonds. Lady Lan Yetrov, I assumed.

I looked at this Dannsburg couple and found I didn't care for *them* at all. I had never seen a bear bait before, although cockfighting took place often enough in Ellinburg. I didn't much care for that, either. People in their position should have known better, but what would I know? I was just a commoner with a common accent, after all.

"I like sport well enough," I said. "I used to own a racehorse before the war, back in Ellinburg."

"A *racehorse*?" she said, her lip curling with evident disdain. "How very . . . provincial."

"Delightful," Lan Yetrov said, in a tone that meant the exact opposite. "My dear Lady Ailsa, you must tell me sometime how in the world this happened."

He laughed at that and turned away to continue his conversation elsewhere. I clenched my teeth but let Ailsa lead me back into the crowd.

"You mustn't take it personally," she whispered as she let a footman exchange her empty wineglass for a full one.

"How else am I to take it? These people know what I am, Ailsa."

"No, they don't," she said. "They may think they do, but you are a respected priest and successful businessman and a high-ranking member of Ellinburg society, as my friends are very busy telling everyone. It will take time, that's all. Do you honestly think someone like Jon Lan Barkov would be welcomed any more warmly by this company?"

I couldn't say I had given that fool or his idiot painting any thought since we were in his house, but now that she raised the matter I supposed perhaps she had a point. The provinces were simply beneath the notice of these people. All the same, I thought he would fare better than me.

"At least he's got a Lan in his name," I muttered.

"That's beside the point," she said. "He has no real breeding and not quite enough money to make up for it, and no worthwhile pursuits whatsoever. You are a priest and a man of influence in business, and those things at least are respectable."

"As pastimes, maybe," I said. "How many of these here have worked a day in their lives, truly?"

"Don't start," Ailsa hissed at me. "Drink your wine and try to look amused."

I didn't feel amused, and I felt a lot less so when a bell rang and the steward announced that the entertainment was ready to begin, if the company would please make their way to the bear pit in the informal garden.

The bear pit was quite the construction, I had to allow. It was a walled circle some thirty feet across, surrounded by raised wooden tiers of seating for the spectators. Ailsa and I took our places with the other fools, the warm spring sun on our faces and the babble of excited conversation in our ears. Lan Yetrov and his wife were already seated in their private box.

The bear was a fearsome-looking thing. It was already in the pit, chained by one leg to a stake close to the far wall from where we sat. Bear baiting was a popular sport among all social classes, I knew that, but I found nothing to entertain me in seeing animals rip each other apart. I had seen enough of that in Abingon to last me a lifetime.

"The old bear looks tired," the man beside me remarked.

I glanced at him and saw a young fellow with maybe twenty-five or so years to him. He was wearing a dark red coat of a military cut, and he had the customary bristling side whiskers of a cavalry officer. He looked to my mind as though he might be slightly less of a fool than most of his peers.

"Aye, well, wouldn't you?" I replied.

The man chuckled.

"Most likely it has no teeth and its claws have been pulled," he said. "I'll bet on the dogs, I think."

"I'll take that bet," I said, to goad him as much as anything else. "A tired old soldier is a soldier still, and those dogs will be nothing but arrogant pups."

His eyes flashed at that, and I could tell he had taken my meaning.

"Oh, so it's like that, is it?" He laughed. "Well, I'll take your gold as happily as anyone else's. I can have my man wash the Ellinburg off it later."

I could have taken that as an insult, but I thought he meant it in the good-natured way of soldier's talk, so I let it pass. I had to admit I hadn't realized we'd be betting for gold and not silver, but it was done now and no backing down unless I wanted to look an utter fool.

"A crown on the bear, then," I said. "My name is Father Tomas Piety, by the way."

"Major Bakrylov, pleasure to meet you," he said. "A crown it is."

We shook on it, and I could feel the swordsman's calluses on his palm. Perhaps he wasn't such a pup, after all.

Lan Yetrov very much enjoyed bear baiting, Ailsa had told me, and bears were expensive and not easily come by so I doubted that he would pull their teeth and claws just to see them slaughtered by dogs, which were cheap and plentiful. I hoped I had the right of that.

The babble of conversation died away when Lan Yetrov rose to his feet in his box and waved a red silk pocket square in his hand like a fool.

"Bring in the dogs!" he shouted, and got a muted cheer from the assembled members of society.

A gate rumbled up and three dogs burst into the pit. They were big mastiffs, two black and one brown, and all of them solid and muscular. Each one was muzzled and had a handler behind it holding tight to a sturdy leash.

"The brown one will still be standing by the end," the major said. "Look at the size of him!"

The bear chose that moment to rear up on its hind legs.

"Look at the size of the fucking bear," I said, and he had no answer to that.

Then the dog handlers removed the muzzles from their charges, and loud barking echoed around the pit. The dogs strained at their tethers, eager to begin. Lan Yetrov let his ridiculous pocket square fall from his fingers, and the dog handlers let their beasts off the leash.

The big brown dog charged at once and leaped in an attempt to seize the bear by the throat, a savage growl coming from it as its jaws opened. The bear swung a massive paw and roared, and the dog spun away in a spray of blood to crash into the wall of the pit.

No, Lan Yetrov hadn't had his prize bear's claws pulled, or its teeth either. I hadn't thought so. The bout was fierce and bloody, and the pit became a mess of clawing, howling, roaring fury. I'll not record the details here for I found that the affair sickened me, but suffice it to say that I had been right to bet on the bear.

I relieved Major Bakrylov of a gold crown, and he just laughed as he handed it over.

"Well played, Piety, old chap," he said, as though it were no amount of money at all. "That's one for the tired old soldiers, eh? Abingon, I assume?"

"Aye," I said, and we nodded to one another in comradeship.

I saw bets being settled all around the makeshift arena. Men came into the pit and dragged the dogs out with long billhooks, and that was done.

It seemed a brief enough entertainment to have brought so many people here, even those who might actually have found it entertaining.

I made to rise, but Ailsa put a hand on my arm.

"Be still," she said. "The main event is about to start."

That made me frown. I had thought the bear bait *was* the main event, but it seemed I had been wrong about that. Perhaps I had simply misunderstood some subtlety that a Dannsburg noble would have seen plainly.

Once the dog handlers were clear of the pit, another gate opened and a naked man was shoved into the open space. His body glistened with something that looked and smelled like an awful mixture of blood and fish and honey. He fell to his knees in front of Lan Yetrov, and I saw that he was pleading. Behind him the bear was growling and pulling at its chain, slobber visible at the sides of its mouth.

"Please, m'lord!" the kneeling man begged. "Please!"

"Some of you," Lan Yetrov said, his voice carrying across the crowd, "may remember my former friend Salan Anishin. He owes me a great deal of money over a failed and foolish business venture, but rather than pay his debts like an honorable man he attempted to flee the city with his family. Of course, I had already posted a warrant with the Guard and he was arrested at the city gates and thrown into debtor's prison to await the queen's pleasure. However, I took pity on him. I bought his debt, and therefore with it, of course, his life."

I stared at the groveling man and at the bear. It took no degree of cleverness to see how this would end.

"I want to make it very clear," our host announced, "what happens to those who cross the house of Lan Yetrov. Release the bear."

A handler reached down over the wall of the pit with some implement on the end of a long pole, and a moment later the chain fell away from the bear's leg. The beast was bleeding from its encounter with the dogs but now it seemed to become maddened as it caught the scent. It took a step toward the poor bastard in the pit with it, its nose twitching and ropes of slobber running from its jaws.

It snarled.

"Please!" Anishin screamed.

The bear roared and charged, and blood exploded up the walls of the pit. A gasp went up from the crowd, followed by vigorous applause.

Those were the times we lived in.

TWENTY-SIX

We were able to leave Lan Yetrov's house shortly after that, for which I was grateful. He was a cunt, to my mind, and the sooner I got away from him the less chance there was of me telling him so in front of half of Dannsburg society. That wouldn't have been wise, I knew, but it was tempting all the same.

"I know you didn't care for the entertainment, Tomas," Ailsa said to me in the carriage on the way back to her house, "but on the whole you did well. Major Bakrylov will remember you, certainly, if only because he'll want to win his money back."

"The fellow with the whiskers who I had the bet with?" I asked. I had already forgotten his name by then, but again I had to remind myself that Ailsa seemed to know each and every one of these people. "Aye, he seemed less of a shit than the rest of them, I'll allow that."

"He's a good officer and a decorated war hero," Ailsa said. "He was with the Queen's Own Fifth, at Abingon. When their colonel fell in battle, he assumed command of the regiment and stormed the west gate with barely six hundred men."

I remembered hearing of that, back in the war. He'd had barely six hundred men *after* he had taken the west gate, to be sure. When he gave the order to charge, he'd had over three thousand.

That was what made a war hero in Dannsburg, it seemed.

"Aye," I said, and left it there.

Even if Ailsa had understood, I knew she wouldn't have cared. She hadn't been there, and no one who hadn't been there could truly understand what Abingon had been like. How could they? There was nothing to compare it to, nothing at all. Aye, you might see violence in the streets, be it robberies or territory disputes between crews, or even the City Guard brutalizing the homeless, but there was nothing that could prepare you for something like Abingon.

It was Hell, pure and simple.

I remembered the roar of the cannon, the choking smoke and the unnatural darkness it brought with it. I saw flames leaping from fallen buildings, and bodies so tormented by the plague they barely looked human anymore. I saw the broken, burned, ruined people dragging themselves like living corpses through a sea of the dead, screaming as they came . . .

Ailsa's hand gripped my arm so tightly it was almost painful, and she brought me back to myself before I tipped over the edge into the darkness.

"It's all right, Tomas," she said softly, and in that moment I could almost have believed she truly cared for me. "Breathe with me, deep and slow. Deep, and slow."

I sagged back against the bench of the carriage and breathed with her, and it began to pass. I wondered if I would ever truly be free of the battle shock. Truth be told, I doubted it. To be free of it would be to forget, and I didn't see how I could do that. That would feel like a betrayal, of myself and of all those I had fought beside. I wondered if it was like this for my brother, or if he felt something different when it came over him. What had he felt that night, that had moved him to tear a man's throat out with his teeth and eat it?

"Breathe with me, Tomas," Ailsa said again, her voice soothing as the carriage jolted over the cobbles. "Just breathe. Just . . . breathe . . ."

"Aye, I'm well," I said at last. "I'm well, and I thank you."

Ailsa understood battle shock, I had to allow. I wondered why that was and who she might have worked with during the war. It wasn't impossible that she *had* been there, for all I knew. The Queen's Men were knights, after all. Not the armored sort who fronted the charge of heavy cavalry, no, but knights nonetheless.

There was more than one sort of hero in a war, I knew that much.

We were left alone for the next few days, thank the Lady, with no further society engagements, and Ailsa took the time to arrange for a tutor for Billy. He was a thin, birdlike man called Fischer who we installed in a servant's room on the top floor of the house. I tasked him with teaching the lad to read and write properly, if nothing else, and his figures as well if he could. Billy wasn't happy about it, and I remembered I hadn't much cared for schooling either, but then few lads do at that age.

On the morning of my sixth day in Dannsburg, Fat Luka came to me and said that a meeting with Grachyev had been arranged.

"You'll sit down at the Bountiful Harvest tonight," he told me over tea in the drawing room. "It's an inn, a fancy one about half a mile from here. He owns it."

"I wanted neutral territory," I said.

"Well, there ain't much of that," Luka told me. "There's only one crew doing business in Dannsburg, and Grachyev runs it."

"What, in the whole fucking city?"

"Aye, boss, that seems to be the lay of things," Luka said. "He's a big man, is Grachyev."

I remembered what Governor Hauer had told me the year before last, about the men the Skanians had sent to take over Ellinburg during the war. *Men from country towns by and large, and a few billy-big-bollocks they've brought up from Dannsburg to stiffen them.* I wondered if those billy-big-bollocks had been Grachyev's men. That might be interesting, if it was so.

"I see," I said. "So he owns Dannsburg, does he?"

"No, boss, he doesn't," Luka said. "I've done a lot of talking these last few days and I've greased a lot of palms, and I've had to be fucking careful about it too. The *queen* owns this city, make no mistake about that. Their City Guard ain't like ours. They're not for bribing, from what I hear, not over the big stuff anyway, and there's no getting them to look the other way when they've got the bit between their teeth. There's watchers everywhere and everyone seems to be informing on everyone else, and it all goes back to the crown through one channel or another. How Grachyev manages to do business at all is a mystery to me."

"That's very interesting, Fat Luka," I said. "Right, tonight then. I'll want you with me, of course. What have you and Leonov agreed about guards?"

"We agreed no weapons and no guards, but that's horseshit and we all know it. Grachyev doesn't know you and he owns the inn, so half the customers will probably be his men. I can't see a way around it, in truth."

"No, perhaps not," I said. "Right, well, get Emil and Oliver and the other three over there this afternoon and have them wait for us. I'll stand them dinner at the inn as long as they don't drink too much. I need *someone* there, in case it all goes to the whores."

"Aye, boss," Luka said. "That'll leave no one here, though."

He was right, I knew. I had only brought five men with me from Ellinburg, not counting the steward or Luka himself. And Billy, of course. All the same, this might have been Ailsa's house but I was Ailsa's husband and her household guard seemed to respect that. I suspected that Brandt at least had been told the lay of things between Ailsa and me, or close enough anyway.

"Right, I'll tell you what we'll do," I said. "Have one of the men stay here just in case, but we'll bring Billy the Boy with us. With you and me, I mean, not with the men."

Luka frowned at that.

"How's Grachyev going to take you bringing a lad barely old enough to shave to a sit-down? I don't think we want to offend him, boss."

"It's fine," I said. "Billy is my son now. I'm teaching him how business is done, that's all. Grachyev will understand that."

"Aye, well he might," Luka allowed, "but he might not. Still, as you say, boss."

I nodded and Luka went off to speak to the men, leaving me alone in the drawing room. I wondered what sort of man this Grachyev was. From what Luka had told me it seemed impossible that he was doing business in Dannsburg without paying off someone, but if it wasn't the Guard, then who?

I passed the rest of the day wondering about that, and after a light supper that I didn't really want I went out in my carriage with Luka and Billy the Boy. The Bountiful Harvest was barely half a mile from the house, as Luka had said, but arriving on foot would have made us look poor and I couldn't have that. I understood well enough how that sort of game was played.

We were all unarmed, as per the agreement Luka had made with Leonov, but of course we had Billy with us so I wasn't overly concerned on that score. Billy was more of a weapon than any sensible number of men with swords could hope to be. It pained me to think of the lad in those terms, but there it was.

The Bountiful Harvest was very respectable, as all the inns in this part of the city appeared to be, and the man on the door was courteous and unobtrusive but all the same I could tell he had the look about him. There was a cudgel at his belt like all doormen wore, but although his coat was well cut I thought I could see the shape of a sheathed dagger strapped to his forearm underneath it. He had old scars on his hands, too, and those looked like they had been hard earned. After a while you learn to spot the signs of a man who lives the life.

Luka spoke to him and palmed him a silver penny, and we were shown in and ushered straight through to a private dining room at the back. I could see my boys at a couple of tables as we walked through the common room, spread out in the crowd as was wise. Of course I paid them no mind, nor did they greet me or so much as look up when we entered. Emil knew what he was about, and he was the boss of them that night.

The private dining room was paneled in dark oak and lit with lamps, and had a single long table with glasses and brandy bottles on it. Leonov was sitting at that table, with two older men who I didn't know. He stood up when we entered, and I nodded a greeting to him.

"Mr. Piety," he said, "I'm glad we have managed to arrange this meeting so swiftly, and to everyone's satisfaction."

I wasn't sure that meeting in a place that was actually owned by Grachyev was entirely to my satisfaction, but as Luka had said there wasn't much to be done about that.

"Thank you for taking the time to sit down with me," I said, addressing the two older men. I had no idea which one was Grachyev, and I didn't want to risk giving offense. "It's my sincerest hope that we can forge bonds of friendship between Dannsburg and Ellinburg tonight."

"I too share that hope," said the younger of the two. "I am Grachyev."

He had some fifty or more years to him, and he was heavily built and dark haired with a pockmarked face. He wore a red silk doublet under a black coat, and a large gold ring with a black stone on the third finger of his right hand.

"And I am Tomas Piety, head of the Pious Men," I said. "This is Luka, who works for me, and my son, Billy."

Grachyev smiled indulgently at Billy and ignored Luka completely.

"My second, Iagin," he said, nodding to the man beside him.

This one had closer to sixty years, with thinning gray hair and a heavy white mustache that all but covered his mouth. He wore a doublet of thick black leather worked in a pattern of vines and thorns.

"A pleasure, Mr. Piety," Iagin said. "Will you take brandy?"

The form of these rare meetings between bosses who had no bad blood between them was very simple. You sat down together and looked each other in the eye and spoke pleasantries, and if neither gave offense to the other then usually a trust could begin to be formed. A fragile one, to be sure, ready to be broken by the first wrong word, but we were all businessmen and we understood each other.

We drank together and discussed business in a way that involved neither of us actually telling the other anything in any great detail, but allowed each to get a feel for the other's interests. Grachyev, I learned, dealt mainly in taverns and inns and brothels, public baths and tailors' shops, and the protection he could take from them rather than in industry or smuggling. That struck me as strange at first. Still, across a whole city the size of Dannsburg I supposed that was a good deal of businesses, and he obviously did well for himself.

I told him about Ellinburg, and about tanneries and factories, about the Golden Chains and the poppy trade, and he listened and nodded. He allowed that he too dealt in the poppy through some of his brothels and bathhouses, and that made sense. There were areas where we could help each other, we both agreed, and that was good.

It wasn't until the meeting was almost over that I actually learned something useful. Grachyev had left by then, on his way to some other meeting apparently, and Luka and Billy had gone through to the common room now that we were all friends. I was alone with Iagin in the dining room, where we were finishing the second bottle of brandy between us. That I had been left with Grachyev's second wasn't lost on me, I'll admit, but I didn't take it ill. I was in his city, after all, not he in mine, and he didn't owe me anything.

Iagin was polite enough, and I could tell he understood how things worked. He understood a little more than I expected, in fact.

"We have a mutual friend, Mr. Piety," he said as he topped up my glass.

"Oh? Who's that then?"

"Your lady wife," he said.

I looked at him, trying to work out if he was being disrespectful.

"In what way?"

"We both work for the same person," he said.

It took me a moment, but I stared at him as the cold realization sank in.

Iagin was a Queen's Man.

TWENTY-SEVEN

It all made sense.

That was how Grachyev managed to do business in Dannsburg and how he was the only businessman running a crew in the whole city. Business in Dannsburg was done with the consent of the Queen's Men, I realized, or it wasn't done at all. His businesses in the city were taverns and inns, tailors and baths and stews, all the places where folk might speak unguardedly and be heard. Grachyev's crew were listeners for the crown.

"I see," I said. "That's very interesting, Iagin. What do you know about me?"

"Everything," he said. "Assume we know everything, and you'll never be caught out in a lie that might hang you."

Ailsa had said something similar to me once before, shortly after we had first met. I nodded.

"I see," I said again. "Does Grachyev know?"

"No, of course not," Iagin said. "We don't trust him quite as much as Ailsa appears to trust you. He thinks he's a gangster, not a spy. He's not a stupid man, but he is a vain one, and something of a fantasist. That makes him easy to manipulate."

I swallowed my brandy and put the glass back down on the table in front of me.

"And what do you want from me?"

"Ailsa will tell you what we want, when we want it," he said. "Until then, just do as she tells you. Oh, and Tomas?"

"Aye?"

"Don't bring your insane pet magician to any more meetings."

"He's my fucking son," I snapped.

"No, he isn't," Iagin said. "I know *exactly* what he is, and he's not welcome. Now, it's time you left."

"Aye," I said, and gave him a hard glare. "I think it fucking is."

Before I fucking stab you, I thought, but I didn't say it.

Iagin just smiled at that and got to his feet. Trying to intimidate a Queen's Man was a fool's errand, and I should have known better. Too much brandy and not enough thought before speaking—I wouldn't make that mistake again. He opened the door and went ahead of me, exposing his back to show me how little he thought of my hard looks. I wasn't even armed, for the Lady's sake.

We returned to the common room, where Luka and Billy were waiting with Emil and Oliver and the others. I kept my expression carefully blank, not wanting to betray that I had just made myself look a fool. At least Iagin had the grace not to mention it in front of my men. That, or he simply didn't care enough about me to offer insult, which I thought was more likely.

I was glad to leave the Bountiful Harvest, truth be told. Grachyev had struck me as a decent enough fellow, but Iagin was a snake in man's clothes. He was far more how I had always expected a Queen's Man to be than Ailsa was.

It was late by the time the carriage brought us back to Ailsa's house, but once I had sent Billy up to bed I found her waiting up for me in the drawing room with her embroidery in her hands and a glass of wine on the low table beside her chair.

"How was your meeting?" she asked when I came in.

I chased the footman and her lady's maid out of the room with a glare, and ignored her until the door was closed behind them and I had poured myself a large brandy from one of the many bottles on the side table. Then I turned to face her.

"What was the fucking point?" I demanded. "What was the point of me meeting with Grachyev when you already control his business?"

"I don't control his business," Ailsa said. "Iagin does, as you appear to have discovered. Did he tell you himself?"

"Aye, he did," I said. "You're both in the same crew, aren't you? Both Queen's Men, I mean?"

"We are," Ailsa allowed, "but it's not quite that simple. Nothing ever is, in Dannsburg. There are factions, Tomas, even within the Queen's Men."

"And what about the Dannsburg men that Governor Hauer told me had been brought up to strengthen the Skanians' raw recruits while we were all away at war? They didn't dare recruit Ellinburg men so their lads were country yokels, most of them, and some hard boys from down here to stiffen them. Billy-big-bollocks, he called them. Were they Grachyev's? Was that your crew's doing?"

"No, obviously that wasn't us," she said. "They may have been Grachyev's thugs once, bought off by Skanian agents, but of course the Queen's Men had no hand in that. Why in the gods' names would we?"

I sighed. No, of course they hadn't. I was getting myself confused, that was all, tying my head up in knots with conspiracies and politics and other things I barely even understood enough to put names to them.

"No, of course not," I said. "It's late, that's all, and I'm tired."

"You're drunk," Ailsa corrected me. "Why did you take Billy with you tonight?"

"I wasn't allowed weapons or guards at this meeting," I said, "and a few men in the common room would have been little enough use if Grachyev had meant me ill. Billy, though, Billy is weapon and guard both."

Ailsa nodded.

"He is," she agreed. "I'm glad you see that."

"He's our fucking son," I said. "I shouldn't think of him that way."

"He *is* our son and I love him as much as you do, but be realistic, Tomas," she said. "The right man for the right job, that's what you always say, and Billy is the right man for any number of jobs. Especially now."

I thought of the training that Cutter had apparently been giving him, and it pained me that I had to agree with her. Partly, at least.

"He's not a man, though, he's just a lad," I said, for all that he was legally of age. "Fourteen at the most, as far as anyone can tell."

"How old were you when you killed your first man, Tomas?"

I thought of my da, dead by my hand when I'd had only twelve years to me.

"That was different," I said.

"No, it wasn't," she said. "Billy killed before you ever met him; he must have done. A child alone in the ruins of Messia, how else do you think he survived? And then there was Abingon, of course, and everything that has come after it."

"I know," I said, and drained my brandy. "I know, but that doesn't make it right."

"Does it have to? It makes it the right man for the right job, that's all. Billy is part of this family now; he knows what that means."

I sighed and looked at her, at my wife sitting by the hearth with her embroidery in her hand. The lioness. Everything she had said was true, I knew that.

I knew that, but that didn't mean I liked it.

Ailsa spent the next couple of days out of the house alone, staying overnight to visit friends, she said, and two nights after that we had the dubious pleasure of attending a function at court. A minor function, Ailsa assured me, which meant that at least the queen herself wouldn't be in attendance. I supposed that was good, even if nothing else about it was. I had absolutely no desire to meet the queen, and had she even known I existed I was sure the feeling would have been mutual.

The Princess Crown Royal was hosting the evening, Ailsa explained to me: the queen's heir. She was a girl of eleven, apparently, so I doubted she would be doing a great deal of hosting by herself.

"Tell me again what the point of this is?" I said, as we climbed into the carriage.

"In all honesty very little, but it's an invitation to court so we *have* to go," Ailsa said. "No one turns down a royal invitation, lest people begin to ask why. Besides, I told you that you need to mingle and be seen, and this is another opportunity to do it."

I sighed. We had two footmen with us and four of Ailsa's household guard to see us safely through streets that were heavily patrolled by the City Guard anyway, but she had forbidden me from bringing any of my men or even Fat Luka with me.

She had *forbidden* me.

I took that ill, I have to confess, but there was little enough I could do about it save to have Emil and two of the men follow us on foot and keep an eye out for trouble. That I had done. They wouldn't get past the castle gates, I knew, but even that was better than placing myself completely in the hands of my wife and the Queen's Men.

After ten minutes it came to me that we were going the wrong way. The castle was away to the left of us now, and our carriage showed no signs of turning. Eventually the street widened and there were more trees and far more City Guard in evidence, and then I saw a high wall and the top of what I could only assume was a real palace.

It was simply preposterous. I had never seen a building so large in my life save for the great citadel of Abingon, and by the time we had finally fought our way to that through the burning streets our cannon had all but smashed it to rubble.

The palace of Dannsburg was vast. It was colonnaded and marbled and gilded and with hundreds of windows in its walls, all in the new style with square panes of glass instead of the leaded diamonds of older buildings. It would be impossible to defend, and it was utterly ridiculous.

Huge banners flew from the heights, ten or more of them at least. They seemed the color of blood in the evening light, until the breeze caught them and made the white roses dance.

"I had thought that the queen lived in the castle," I admitted.

Ailsa smiled.

"The castle is home to the City Guard and the army high command," she said. "Castles are cold and uncomfortable places, and Her Majesty much enjoys comfort."

"I'm sure she does," I said.

Her Majesty was a fool, to my mind. With war brewing yet again, she dwelled in this iced cake of a building when there was a stout fortress barely two miles away? Threats of war brought assassins long before they brought soldiers. I was no general but even I knew that, and if she put that much faith in her city walls and the Guard then I had no words to say about it. I looked at Ailsa and saw the small smile still playing around the corners of her mouth.

Of course, Her Majesty had her Queen's Men too, and perhaps that gave her another type of protection that I still didn't fully understand. There was too much about Dannsburg that I still didn't understand, and that didn't sit well with me.

Could people like Iagin and my lioness truly do the work of fortress walls?

I had to allow that I wouldn't have bet against it.

TWENTY-EIGHT

Court was worse than I could ever have imagined.

To begin with it wasn't so different to how our visit to Lan Yetrov's house had been. There were heavily guarded gates to pass, then hordes of footmen outside the palace, and rows of parked carriages and an abundance of fuss and ceremony and wine. The hall we were shown into was probably one of the smaller ones, but it was still vast, easily twice the size of Lan Yetrov's. I couldn't even imagine what the grand great hall used for state receptions must have looked like. Here, gilded chandeliers hung on long chains from an impossibly high ceiling, and musicians played everywhere, lute and pipe and fiddle all blending together under the muted hubbub of a hundred or more conversations.

A herald was gradually admitting guests into a ballroom, announcing them in a loud voice as they passed, while the rest of us milled around with wineglasses in our hands.

"Lord and Lady Lan Andronikov," he announced, ushering in a couple in early middle age.

I saw Ailsa turn to watch as they entered the ballroom.

"Do you know them?" I asked her.

"Of course I do," she murmured. "The Lady is a personal friend of mine. *Very* fond of the poppy, I'm afraid. She starts to sweat after a few hours without a pipe, tremble after six, and beg after ten. By the time we got to fourteen I could have made her do absolutely anything. Her husband managed to avoid the war by taking a position on the governing council. He is a weakling and a coward and he's said some extremely unwise things recently, but he's very, *very* rich."

"These things are good to know," I said, and Ailsa showed me a small smile.

I was beginning to appreciate her skills and her knowledge more and more with each day that passed in Dannsburg. I think that pleased her.

"General Garin of the Queen's Own Cavalry," the herald pronounced, admitting a potbellied man with sixty or so years to him. He was wearing a crimson coat and hugely bristling white side whiskers, and he swayed as he walked.

"What about him?"

"Can't even get out of bed in the morning without a glass of brandy first," Ailsa said, keeping her voice too low to be overheard. "It takes him three before breakfast to stop shaking. He gets through two bottles a day, without fail."

It was quite remarkable, I supposed, that we had won the war at all with men like him in charge. I wondered how many plans had gone awry, how many attacks had failed and how many men had died, because that cunt was drunk.

"The Duke of Samarind and his paramour, Gidia of Alassai."

"She's only ten years old," Ailsa said. "And yes, he is bedding her."

That made my stomach clench with revulsion, and I glared at the Duke of Samarind's velvet-cloaked back until he was out of sight. I wondered how it would feel to kill a duke, and if they died the same as lesser men. I remembered the man I had strangled back in Ellinburg in the winter, and I thought that they probably did.

"The Lord Lan Yetrov."

"Well, you know him. It appears his wife is indisposed again."

I wondered what she meant by that, but I put it down to some gossip I hadn't heard. Of course I remembered him well enough, and his bear pit and his idea of how debt collection worked. I knew more than enough about him.

"Major Bakrylov, of the Queen's Own Fifth."

I smiled a little at that, and the memory of the gold crown I had won from him at Lan Yetrov's bear bait. The thought of betting with gold still made my head spin a little, I had to admit, but it seemed that was how things were done in the moneyed circles of Dannsburg high society. The major had seemed like a decent fellow, at least, and among this company that was quite some achievement.

"The Lord Chief Judiciar, Dieter Vogel."

"He's *very* dangerous," Ailsa said, dropping her voice so low I could barely hear her for all that her head was almost on my shoulder. "I'll introduce you later, but you've to show him the utmost respect."

"Why's that, then?"

"Officially, he's the Lord Chief Judiciar," she whispered, her lips so close to my ear that I could feel the warm flutter of her breath against my skin. "Unofficially, he is also the Provost Marshal of the Queen's Men. He's my boss."

I nodded in understanding. Everyone answers to someone, after all, even a Queen's Man.

Eventually it was our turn, and a footman ushered us through those still waiting until we were in front of the herald.

"The Lady Ailsa and Mr. Tomas Piety?" he asked us, glancing down at the papers in his hand.

"Father Tomas," I corrected him, thinking on what Ailsa had said to me a few days before about how being a priest was a respectable occupation. "I'm a priest."

The herald consulted his papers again and sniffed.

"A *military* priest, Mr. Piety," he said. "You have attended no seminary that the crown is aware of, nor have you in all likelihood actually been ordained. Even the professional classes have their standards, after all."

"I—" I started, but he interrupted me to introduce us to the ballroom.

"The Lady Ailsa and Mr. Tomas Piety," he proclaimed.

I resisted the urge to stab him, but only just.

Ailsa pulled me through the doorway and away from the herald, and I saw the ballroom in all its splendor. Massive gilded mirrors hung on every wall, reflecting back the light of the chandeliers and making the already huge room look ten times the size it was. The floor was marble and it gleamed with polish, slippery underfoot. Footmen circulated everywhere in their bright red royal livery with the white rose sewn over their hearts, with silver trays in their hands bearing glasses of wine and plates of strange delicacies.

"What even is this?" I asked Ailsa, as I chewed a thin piece of bread with some sort of salty black stuff on it.

"Fish eggs," she said, and I almost spat it out on the floor in front of me.

"Is it possible to get a brandy?"

"This is the royal palace." Ailsa smiled. "It is possible to get absolutely anything here."

She caught a footman's eye and exchanged a few words with him, and less than a minute later I was drinking the best brandy I had ever tasted in my life.

We circulated, or truth be told, Ailsa did. I followed her around exchanging empty words with people I didn't know and didn't care to know, but that was no more than I had been expecting. I managed a brief conversation with Major Bakrylov, at least, which lifted my spirits somewhat. He really wasn't a bad fellow at all. It was well enough until I found myself face-to-face with Lord Lan Yetrov.

"Ah, the provincial priest," he said, and the look on his face was a sneer by anyone's definition. "Who in the gods' names let *you* in?"

"Aye, that's me," I said, making no attempt to hide the Ellinburg in my accent. "And you're the man who likes to set bears on people."

"Oh, I do declare we have offended the good priest's holy sensibilities." He laughed, far too loudly for my liking.

"You've offended my fucking *human* sensibilities," I said, and I leaned close enough that I knew no one else could have heard us. "You, *my lord*, are a cunt."

Lan Yetrov took a step backward then and he glared at me, but I saw him checking to make sure for himself that we couldn't have been overheard.

"I should see you in the dueling circle for that, Piety," he snarled.

"Oh, that would be my greatest pleasure," I said. "I was at war for three long years. I was at Messia, and at Abingon, and I came home to tell of it. I've killed more men than you've ever fucking met, you prick."

He paled slightly and turned away. No one had heard us, so he had no obligation to protect his honor. I knew that, and in truth I was glad of it. I could almost certainly have killed this arsehole in a duel, but what would that have proved? That I was a violent thug from Ellinburg, that was all, and that was the very thing Ailsa had been working so hard to play down.

No, I wouldn't be dueling in public with Lan Yetrov, or anyone else for that matter, not if I could help it. There was simply no point. I realized that was exactly how Iagin had regarded me and my empty glares at the Bountiful Harvest. I had learned a lesson that night, and I wouldn't forget it. So long as Lan Yetrov knew the lay of things and who was boss that was enough, to my mind.

That was how I did business, in Dannsburg or anywhere else.

The night wore on forever.

The Princess Crown Royal was brought out in an enormous gown of sapphire-studded silk that had probably cost more than a working man made in his whole lifetime. The thing almost certainly weighed more than she did, and I thought that the weight of the skirt hoops against her tiny hips must have been agony. She was a child doll with thick paint and powder on her face, and her hair teased up into an impossible confection of gold and diamonds that I suspected hurt even more than the gown did.

The princess regarded the room with a studied indifference that spoke of the many layers of tutors and guards and officials between her and the real world outside the palace walls. I didn't at all care for the Princess Crown Royal, but I couldn't help but feel sorry for the little girl inside her.

After she had been seen she was taken away again by the swarm of nuns and tutors who had presented her, and the ball went on. As Ailsa had warned me, there seemed to be little point to this occasion. This was how the royal house entertained its most noble subjects, I could only assume, with pointless parties and the opportunity to worship its offspring for brief moments, and even those from afar.

"I should introduce you to Vogel," Ailsa murmured, sometime after the third hour of tedium had passed. "Be respectful, Tomas. I mean it."

I let her lead me around the edge of the floor, where a complicated dance was under way. It seemed to involve ranks of people facing each other, all of whom knew every step and turn and change of partner by heart. I had no idea how to dance, and I was glad that Ailsa knew that. If she had forced me to attempt it I would have made an utter fool of myself.

We slipped around the dancers to a place where a tall, lean, white-haired man in an immaculate coat was standing with a crystal goblet in his hand.

"My Lord Judiciar, it's such a pleasure to see you again," Ailsa said. "Please allow me to present my husband, Father Tomas Piety of Ellinburg."

This law lord who was apparently also in charge of the Queen's Men turned to face me, and I've no shame in admitting that I felt cold down to my highly polished boots. Dieter Vogel, his name was, or so the herald had said anyway. I had no way of knowing if that was true, of course, but I could tell *what* this man was just by looking at him. There was something in his eyes that gave it away, something that seemed utterly without a soul.

He reminded me of Cutter, in a way, but so much more so. I doubted that even Cutter could have met this man's eyes for long.

Dieter Vogel was Ailsa's boss in the Queen's Men, and from what I had seen it seemed to me that Ailsa ranked at least equivalent to a colonel. That made Vogel their general, then. The workings of the Queen's Men remained a mystery to me, I have to admit, and I wasn't too sure what Provost Marshal actually meant, but it took no degree of cleverness to work out that Vogel was the top boss of that crew.

"Lord Vogel," I said, and I could only hope that was the right way to address him.

He showed me a thin smile.

"So you're Tomas Piety," he said. "I've heard your name."

"Aye," I said. "That doesn't surprise me. You hear everything, so I'm told."

Vogel chuckled at that and raised his glass to me a fraction.

"You've the right of that, Father Piety," he murmured. "I hear *absolutely* everything."

I raised my glass to him in response, and I knew we had an understanding between us.

He knew who I was, all right, and that I knew who *he* really was, or that I had a fair idea at least. It showed a degree of trust, that he allowed that, but I knew he would only have to say a word in the right ear and I would simply disappear one night and never be seen again.

Do what your father says or the Queen's Men will come and take you away.

I suppressed a shudder. I remembered my ma saying that to me, when I was very little, to frighten me into doing what I was told. I wondered what she would have made of this.

Look at me, Ma, I thought. *Made it, Ma, top of the world. I'm at the queen's court, and I'm having a drink with the devil himself.*

No, I didn't know what she would have made of that at all.

TWENTY-NINE

Three days later a messenger came to the house in the morning and brought me a letter from Bloody Anne. Truth be told, I suspected it was Rosie's hand I was reading; the script was beautiful, and as far as I knew Anne couldn't read or write at all, as most soldiers couldn't. She didn't turn her phrases like that, either.

My dearest Tomas,

I hope this letter finds you well, and that the weather where you are is pleasing. I am sad to say there has been sickness near our house these last few weeks, though that will come as no surprise, I am sure. We have suffered some illness, but there have been no deaths within the family and all close relatives are as well as can be expected.

The weather in the city continues to be unpleasant. Our friend seems to be without sufficient coats for everyone, but I have hopes that I can keep us dry by my own efforts nonetheless.

Your brother has been taking the air these last few days, on the advice of your aunt, and seems much pleased with his wife and daughter. He spends so much time at temple that I believe he may follow your path into the priesthood, and wonder how you would take that news?

I do hope to see you again before very long.

Your loving little sister,
Anne

I read the letter three times before I sifted the meaning out of Rosie's phrases. Such letters were designed to be unhelpful to anyone who might intercept them on the road, I understood that, but this was a strange mixture of street cant and how I could only assume the Queen's Men spoke to each other.

"Little sister" was how any female second would end a message to her boss, that was familiar enough, and "sickness" meant violence and "illness" meant casualties. So she'd been fighting the Northern Sons, but no one who mattered had been killed, although "as well as can be expected" sounded as though she might have some wounded to deal with.

The business about weather and coats confounded me for a moment, I have to admit, but I took it to mean that there was still unrest in the city and the governor was struggling to contain it. It sounded like Aunt Enaid had decided it was safe to let Jochan out of her cellar, too, and that was good, but what the bit about the temple was supposed to mean I had no idea.

In the end I showed the note to Ailsa, and it seemed that part meant nothing to her either.

"It's no code of ours," Ailsa said after she had scanned the letter. "Perhaps she means it plain, that your brother has taken up religion."

"I'd be fucking surprised," I said. "Still, with the state of him before we left I suppose anything's possible."

It had been almost two months since I had left Ellinburg, after all, and Jochan was so unstable that a lot could have changed in that time. I wondered if that was a good thing or not, and eventually decided that I had no idea.

The news was a week old at best, and there was nothing I could do about it from Dannsburg anyway. I sat and penned a hasty reply for the messenger who was still waiting in the hall, following Rosie's example on the way things should be phrased.

My dear little sister,

Good to hear that you and the family are well. I know you'll do all you can to keep the sickness from our door, and tend to those who may be suffering from illness. Everyone here is healthy, and the weather appears to be fine, although it is difficult to tell in foreign climes. If the weather worsens at home, don't expect our friend to bring coats. Keep our people dry as best you can, and let the rest drown if need be.

Take my aunt's advice on my brother, she knows him better than any, but be wary of his mood if the weather worsens.

I will return when I can, but I can't say as yet when that may be.

Your loving big brother,
Tomas

That done I read back over the two letters, and I had to admit that Rosie's hand put mine to shame. Still, it was readable and that would have to do. I folded and sealed the note, and gave it to the messenger with instructions to deliver it to the lady who had written to me. That would be Rosie, I was sure. I suspected this man was yet another of the network of agents who worked for the Queen's Men, whether they knew that they did or not.

Once the messenger was on his way I rejoined Ailsa in the drawing room.

"Can I ask you something?" I said.

"You can ask," she said. "Whether I give an answer will depend on what the question is."

We were alone, the servants having grasped by then that I didn't like having them in the room with me unless they were actually wanted for something.

"How many of you are there? Queen's Men, I mean."

Ailsa took a sip of her morning tea and looked at me over the rim of the bowl, obviously deciding whether to answer me at all.

"I have absolutely no idea," she said, after a moment. "It would rather depend on your definition."

"Of what?"

"Of what a Queen's Man actually is. I have the Queen's Warrant, and of course Iagin does too. The Queen's Warrant grants absolute royal authority to the bearer, and I assure you those are not given out lightly. The Queen's Men as you think of them, people like me and Iagin, are few in number. Those who work for us, though, they are many. Some of them know who they work for, like Rosie, and some, like Grachyev, do not. The eyes and ears and knives of the Queen's Men are everywhere, but those who carry the warrant are very few. How many, I honestly don't know."

"You're not like the army, then, with a chain of command?"

"No, not at all," she said. "I report directly to the Provost Marshal, and my support staff and agents are my own affair and report only to me. I have no idea who Iagin's listeners and knives are, beyond Grachyev's organization, any more than he knows mine."

"Why the fuck not? That just sounds like making life hard for yourselves for the fun of it, when you could be organized so that you worked together."

"Oh, there's no fun in it, I assure you," she said. "We are not the army, Tomas. This way, if I were to be captured and put to the question by our enemies, as my predecessor in Ellinburg was, I could give away no more than my own staff. I couldn't betray another Queen's Man whatever they did to me, because I simply wouldn't know the answers to their questions. No torment could make me give up a secret that I do not know. That's how this works, because those are the realities we face."

I nodded in understanding. Those were the times we lived in, as she said.

It seemed to me that each true Queen's Man was like the boss of their own independent crew, then, each answering to the same overboss but knowing little if anything of each other's businesses. That was either very clever or extremely foolish, and I wasn't sure which.

Either way, it made Ailsa a very brave woman.

To face the question was one thing, but to know that you had no possible escape from it was quite another. Everyone thinks they can resist torture, and everyone is wrong. Perhaps they can hold out for a little while, but that's all. Almost anything can be endured for a little while, when you know there'll be an end to it; every soldier knows that. I had seen things in Abingon that told me that was true. But when you know there *won't* be an end, that was another matter. Everyone breaks eventually, in the right hands, and spills their secrets to make the torment stop. But if you truly don't know the answers to their questions, then where can you go, other than shrieking down to Hell?

The thought made me shiver. I had seen men put to the question, and I've no shame in admitting that it wasn't something I would have been prepared to face with half her bravery.

The lioness was made of stone and iron, make no mistake about it.

"Right, well," I said at last, and got to my feet.

"Oh, before you go, we've received an invitation," Ailsa said.

"For the Lady's sake, not another fucking ball."

"No," she said. "This one is rather different. It's from my parents."

I blinked at her. Neither of her parents had come to our wedding and I hadn't known for sure that they were even still alive, for all that she had said they were. This was the first I'd heard of them since we arrived in Dannsburg.

"I see."

"I'm not sure that you do," she said, and I sighed and sat down again. "How's that then?"

"My family are Alarian, obviously. They are very wealthy and very traditional."

"Is that why they didn't come to the wedding?" I asked her.

"No, they didn't come to the wedding because I didn't tell them about the wedding, but now that I am back in Dannsburg they have of course heard that I've brought a husband back with me, and so now you must be presented to them. I'm sorry about this, Tomas, truly I am, but manners demand it."

I looked at her, at her big dark eyes and the thick, glossy black hair that framed her flawlessly powdered face. She looked every inch the Alarian princess, and I couldn't imagine I was remotely what her parents would have wanted in a son-by-law. I sighed.

"They're going to fucking hate me, aren't they?"

"Yes," she said.

The invitation had been for two days' time, and Ailsa had spent those days drilling me like a raw recruit on the basics of Alarian manners. I had a feeling she wasn't looking forward to this afternoon's visit any more than I was, but now we were finally in the carriage on our way to her parents' house and she was still lecturing me.

We had left Billy behind with his tutor, of course, so it was just the two of us and a pair of footmen sitting up top with the carriage driver, and three guards on horseback. Apparently it would go ill enough that Ailsa had married a man who wasn't Alarian, never mind that she had also adopted a son with him. Telling them about Billy was going to have to wait for fairer weather.

"Now remember, they call me Chandari and you're to do the same in their hearing," she said yet again as the carriage rolled down a broad avenue. "They never did accept that I took a western name when I came of age. And be respectful, Tomas, *especially* to my mother. In Alarian households the wife is always in charge."

I looked sideways at Ailsa and smiled. That piece of news hadn't surprised me one little bit the first three times she had told me, either.

"I know," I said.

"All you need to say to her after 'hello' is 'yes, Madame Shapoor,'" she went on. "My father may speak to you, but Mother will be furious with me that I didn't marry an Alarian man, and even more furious that she wasn't invited to the wedding that she wouldn't have approved of, nonsensical as that sounds. And remember, they have absolutely no idea what I do and it *has* to stay that way. I'm just a courtier, as far as they know."

"I know," I said again. "We've been over and over this. Just tell me what your father does and I'm sure I can find some sort of common ground with him. You never did tell me that."

"What? Oh, he's retired, they both are. I'm a good deal older than I look, don't forget, and my parents are not young. Before that he was a merchant trader, with a fleet of ships that sailed the tea route from Alaria. He found it better for business to base himself here in Dannsburg, where I was born. Tomas, you will be respectful, won't you?"

I looked at her again, sitting there on the bench beside me and twisting her elegant silk shawl in her hands. It came to me then that this terrible and murderous Queen's Man who was prepared to face torture with no possible avenue of escape, this lioness of stone and iron, was actually nervous about seeing her own parents.

"Yes, of course I will," I said, and put a hand on hers for a moment.

I had only meant it to be reassuring, but to my surprise she gripped my hand and gave me a smile that actually looked genuine.

"Thank you," she said. "I don't know why their approval still matters to me, but it does. This is . . . important to me, Tomas."

"I know," I said. "I'll do my best."

THIRTY

The house was old, but very grand for all that. Ivy crawled elegantly over the front of the building and the windows were still in the old style, with small leaded diamonds of glass. The high wall around the property looked strong and well maintained, and liveried guards met our carriage at the gates.

It seemed to me that all the rich folk of Dannsburg spent a good deal on their personal security despite the almost constant presence of the City Guard, and I found myself wondering why that was.

Ailsa took a deep breath as the carriage drew up outside an imposing front door of heavy black oak. The door opened and a gray-haired man I took to be the steward came down the steps. He waited with his hands clasped in front of him while our footman opened the carriage door and handed Ailsa down. I followed and watched our guards being firmly directed toward the stables along with our carriage driver.

Ailsa smiled.

"Masha, you haven't changed a bit," she said.

"Nor you, Miss Shapoor," the elderly steward replied. "You never do."

"Well, I'm Madame Piety now, so that's a change," Ailsa said. "This is my husband, Father Tomas Piety."

I nodded to the steward, who gave me a very precise bow. I recognized it from Ailsa's teaching over the last couple of days. That was the bow to be used when unsure of another's station, apparently, and I wasn't quite sure how to take that.

"Masha is my parents' steward, and he was my tutor when I was a young girl in this house," Ailsa said. "He helped to make me the woman I am today."

"Then I owe you my most sincere thanks," I said, and that got a slight smile from the old fellow at least.

He led us into the house, where footmen were waiting in the hall, but no one had trays of wine or strange food for us today. One of them opened a door, and we were shown into a large drawing room. An elderly Alarian couple who I could only assume were Ailsa's parents stood waiting for us in the middle of a huge, richly colored carpet. Both were very formally dressed, as were we.

"Mother, Father," Ailsa said, dropping them a low curtsey. "May I present my husband, Father Tomas Piety of Ellinburg."

I bowed low to her father, as she had taught me, and lower still to her mother. Her father returned my bow, a short movement that I recognized as the bow appropriate for the respect due to a junior family member. Ailsa had told me it would be a good sign if he did that, so that pleased me.

Her mother didn't move or so much as acknowledge me, and I had been warned that that would not be a good thing.

"A pleasure to meet you at last, Tomas," Mr. Shapoor said.

He had some seventy or more years to him, I thought. He wore his longish white hair pulled back from his brow in a severe topknot, and he sported a magnificent white beard with a curling mustache that covered half his face. He was dressed in the Dannsburg style, in a fine doublet and coat not unlike my own.

Madame Shapoor was younger, perhaps sixty or so, and dressed in a flowing gown of loose red and gold silk cut in the Alarian style. She was a handsome woman, but her expression was stern and her stare hostile.

"The honor is mine, Mr. Shapoor," I assured him, reciting the lines that Ailsa had given me. "Madame Shapoor, I can only apologize that it has taken so long for us to meet."

She ignored me completely.

"Chandari," she said, her voice accented and sharp. "Who is this white man whom I do not know?"

"As I say, Mother, this is Tomas. My husband."

Madame Shapoor sniffed and turned her back. She stood looking out a window, her shoulders stiff with indignation.

"Your mother is offended that we received no invitation to your wedding, Chandari," her father said.

So was he, I could tell, but she was obviously the boss of him and that meant he got to blame her for the general atmosphere in the room.

"I'm sorry, Papa," Ailsa said. "We met in Ellinburg, and we married there. You know how the roads are. Messengers are waylaid, and letters go astray."

Both those things were true, of course, although totally irrelevant. That wasn't my affair, though, and she could tell them what she liked so long as we both sang the same song.

"I know," he said at last. "I know you would never disrespect your family like that on purpose."

He knew very little about his own daughter, to my mind, but that wasn't my affair either.

"Thank you, Papa," Ailsa said.

Mr. Shapoor's bearded face split open in a wide smile.

"We'll say no more about it, then," he said. "Come, come, I wish to know my new son-by-law. Come into my study, Tomas, and we will talk like gentlemen while my wife and daughter clear the air between them."

I realized he didn't want to be in the middle of that any more than I did, and I found myself warming to him already.

"My thanks," I said. "I would like that very much, Father-by-law."

Ailsa gave me an approving nod, but there was an appeal in her eyes that said *please don't fuck this up*. I followed her father out of the drawing room and into the hall, where a footman closed the door behind us.

"Custom dictates that I should offer you tea," Mr. Shapoor said as we walked across the hall to his study, "but it is after noon and already I feel I know you better than that."

Another footman opened the study door for us, and Mr. Shapoor dismissed him before he could follow us in. Once we were inside and alone together he turned and grinned at me.

"Brandy," he said. "You look to me like a man who enjoys brandy."

"That I do," I confessed, and his smile widened.

"So do I," he said. "Sit, sit. Be comfortable in my house, Tomas."

The carpet in the room was so fine I felt I shouldn't be walking on it with my boots on but he was, so I supposed it didn't matter. I took a chair and watched him open a finely carved cupboard that contained glasses and a good number of bottles. He poured for us both, and then took a chair opposite me rather than the one behind his large and imposing desk. Again, I took that as a good sign.

We drank together, and that in itself is often the first step toward building a trust. The brandy was excellent, and I told him so.

"I enjoy brandy," he said. "My wife does not approve, so I drink in my study where she does not have to see what I do and be offended by it. That is often the way, isn't it?"

I allowed that it was, but I knew he was feeling me out all the same. He wanted to assure himself that I was fit to be married to his daughter; of course he did. I understood that, and I respected it.

"We must be mindful of our wives' feelings in these things," I ventured.

"Always," he said, and changed the subject. "You are a priest, I understand. Tell me, Tomas, how does a priest make his way in this world?"

How can you afford to keep my daughter? That was what he was asking me. Ailsa had drilled me well over the last couple of days, and to my mind she knew her father a good deal better than he knew her.

"I am a priest, as you say, ordained while I was on campaign with the army. Before that I was a successful businessman in Ellinburg, and I remain so today. You were a merchant trader yourself, so Chandari tells me?"

He laughed.

"Oh, come," he said. "I thank you, but you call her Ailsa and I know that. Her mother will appreciate that gesture, but you do not need to pretend with me. Ailsa is the name she has chosen, and I must get used to it."

"As you will, Father-by-law."

"You have the right of it, though," he said. "I ran ships and I traded tea, and other things. I know business. Tell me of *your* business."

His eyes narrowed slightly as he looked at me, and I wondered if we might be working our way around the edges of something here.

"I own a number of businesses in Ellinburg," I told him, picking my words carefully. "Various interests that bring in a substantial income. I own inns and taverns and gaming houses, and I have an interest in a number of . . . vassal businesses, as you might say, such as factories and tanneries and forges. Those I don't own, as such, but they pay me a consideration for protection and respect."

Mr. Shapoor laughed then, and drained his brandy.

"Oh, Tomas, oh my son-by-law," he said. "You do not know me yet, I realize, but I am no fool. How do you think a simple Alarian merchant makes this much money, in Dannsburg? Not by being a fool he doesn't, oh no. Let us speak plainly to one another, as two businessmen should. I was a pirate and a smuggler, and you are a gangster. Those are the hard facts of it. Neither of our wives will ever own to those things, but they are true nonetheless."

He laughed again and refilled my glass. Perhaps Ailsa didn't know her father half so well as she thought she did, after all.

"That's about the lay of things, aye," I said.

Mr. Shapoor leaned forward to touch his glass to mine in a gesture of camaraderie.

"Welcome to the family," he said.

I spent quite some time with Ailsa's father that afternoon, drinking his brandy and swapping stories of business and bloodshed. He told me tales of piracy on the high seas, many of them obviously grown very tall in the telling. He told me of smuggling poppy resin in the holds of tea ships coming west, and of brandy in those same ships on their return journeys to Alaria.

He was the sort of man I wished my own da had been, and I think we found a closeness that day. We could hear occasional shouting coming from the drawing room, even with two closed doors and the width of the large hall between us, but we both pretended that we couldn't. That was between Ailsa and her mother, to my mind, and it seemed that her father thought the same.

Sometime after we had finished the first bottle he told me to call him Sasura. That was an Alarian word, and from what Ailsa had told me it was like calling someone Da, but when it was your wife's father and not your own. It was sort of their way of saying father-by-law but more intimate than that, more like you were actually part of the family by blood and not just by marriage. Ailsa had told me that yesterday, but she had said it was highly unlikely that I would ever be invited to address her father that way. I felt honored that he had allowed me to do so, and so soon.

"Tell me something, Sasura," I asked him, when the conversation had turned away from business and moved on to the realities of living life in the capital city, "why is it that the wealthy of Dannsburg seem so concerned with security when there are City Guard everywhere? Every house I've been to has strong walls around it and household guards on the gates. Ours is no different, but I've seen virtually no crime since I've been in the city. What is everyone so scared of?"

Mr. Shapoor smiled and shook his head.

"It is not crime that we fear," he said, lowering his voice even though we were in his own study in his own house. "Dannsburg is like a barrel of powder, just waiting for a spark to set it off. Everyone informs on everyone else, and everyone is watched. Everyone waits for the day that the City Guard come for them, or may the Many-Headed God prevent it, the Queen's Men themselves."

I thought of Ailsa, in the other room being yelled at by her mother, but I put that thought aside.

"The people seem happy enough," I said. "Compared to how folk are in Ellinburg, they do, anyway."

"Of course they do; they never know who is watching," he said, and now he leaned so close I could feel his mustache tickling my ear as he whispered to me, as though fearful of his own footmen overhearing his words through the closed door. "The queen herself led a full military triumph through the city when victory in the south was announced, and the cheers all but reached heaven itself. Everyone rejoiced in the streets, and do you know why? There were agents of the crown spread throughout the crowd to lead those cheers, and Queen's Men to note the names of any who did not join in. In Dannsburg, you show respect to the crown. You show your love for the queen publicly and loudly and often, or you disappear and are never seen again."

THIRTY-ONE

I had to allow I was somewhat drunk when we finally left Ailsa's parents' house. It was early evening by then and I had spent the whole afternoon with her father in his study. By Our Lady, that old pirate could drink.

We had originally been supposed to be staying for dinner, but it seemed that negotiations between Ailsa and her mother had broken down sometime around when Sasura and me were halfway through the second bottle. Shortly after that a footman had tapped discreetly on the study door and informed me that my lady wife was awaiting me with the carriage. I left my new father-by-law smiling sleepily to himself in a chair by the hearth in his study and allowed Masha to show me to my carriage. My mother-by-law didn't come out of the drawing room to bid me farewell, and I was quite grateful for that.

I stumbled across the lawn and let Masha help me haul myself up into the carriage.

The look on Ailsa's face was indescribable.

"You are *drunk*!" she hissed at me as the carriage started to move.

"Aye," I had to allow, "perhaps I am, but I was very respectful and I didn't fuck it up. About two hours ago he welcomed me to the family, and told me to call him Sasura."

Ailsa blinked at me in surprise.

"Really? Don't lie to me about this, Tomas, I mean it."

"Truly," I said, and grinned at her. "Your old da can fucking drink, though."

Ailsa put a hand to her brow and drew a breath, and I had a feeling she was fighting the urge to stab me.

"I'm sure he can," she said, after a moment. "And my mother can *fucking* shout. It was a disaster, Tomas. She will never forgive me for this."

I didn't know what to say to that. Ailsa never swore, and I confess it threw me for a moment.

"Your da took to me well enough, so there's that," I said at last. "Maybe he can talk her round."

Ailsa made a dismissive noise and shook her head. "I hardly think so," she said. "He's a retired merchant and a secret drunk whose secret is known by everyone. My mother has no respect for him at all."

That seemed a shame, to my mind, and I felt an absurd urge to defend him. I was very drunk, as she had said.

"He's a good man," I said. "He's a fucking businessman, same as I am."

"He was a respectable merchant," Ailsa snapped at me. "He is *nothing* like you."

I snorted laughter. "Merchant, smuggler, pirate. Same fucking thing."

She stared at me, and it suddenly came to me through the haze of brandy that perhaps that had been an unwise thing to say. Perhaps she truly didn't know, or more likely she did and had convinced herself it wasn't true, or if it was that it should never be mentioned.

"I beg your pardon?"

"Lady's sake," I muttered. "I'm sorry. I don't mean any disrespect to your father. He's a good man, as I said, and he showed me a kindness today and welcomed me into your family. We found some common ground over brandy, and perhaps even the beginnings of a friendship. That's all I mean. I'm sorry it didn't go well with you and your ma, truly I am."

Ailsa sighed then and put her hand on mine. That surprised me a good deal, I have to allow.

"Thank you," she said. "Perhaps that's what was needed, a son-by-law that my feckless father can get drunk with before the sun has even set.

He will probably love you forever now, Tomas, whatever my mother says. That's good, but I don't think she will ever accept you."

I couldn't see why it mattered whether she did or not, but it obviously mattered to Ailsa so I gave her hand a squeeze before she took it away.

"I have an aunt who has her prejudices, too," I said. "I know it's not the same, but I'm a little way toward understanding."

"Yes, well," Ailsa said, and turned away to stare out the carriage window.

It seemed that would be the end of it, then.

I retired early that evening, and even so the next morning I still felt the worse for drink. Sasura's brandy had been fiercely strong, and I doubted the old rogue had paid a copper in tax on a whole barrel of the stuff. Ailsa's father and I had a good deal in common, to my mind, but for some reason it pained me to see the way that her conversation with her mother had obviously upset her.

That was ridiculous and I knew it. The lioness was made of stone and iron, after all. Ailsa had caused hundreds of people to be killed, for the Lady's sake; what did I care what her mother thought of her? I really had no answer for that, but enough brandy can make a man's thoughts turn in strange directions.

I stood at the nightstand in my bedroom and bathed my face in cold water from the basin until I felt somewhat more myself, and then took a very long piss into the pot. Today was another day, and Lady willing, Ailsa's mother was done with and wasn't going to become my problem.

Truth be told, I was far more interested in the other thing Sasura had told me.

You show your love for the queen publicly and loudly and often, or you disappear and are never seen again.

He had quite obviously been concerned about someone hearing him say it, too, even his own servants. It was plain enough to see that Dannsburg was like no other place I had ever been.

Once I was shaved and dressed I went in search of Fat Luka and led him out into the gardens behind the house for a morning stroll. When I was absolutely sure there was no one within listening distance I told him what Sasura had told me. Luka nodded slowly.

"I've been hearing the same sorts of things, like I told you before the sit-down with Grachyev, but that was from our type of folk," he said. "If the nobles feel the same way, then that really is interesting. It seems to me that our queen rules almost like a businessman would."

He gave me a sidelong look then, and I recalled the day I had given him his own particular job within the Pious Men. *I want you to watch the men,* I had told him. *I want you to listen to their talk over dice, and when they're in their cups. If anyone starts disagreeing with me or questioning my orders, I want you to explain to them why they're wrong. Then I'll want to hear about it, and who said what.*

Perhaps he had a point, I had to allow. I didn't operate any different. All the same, I ran a business across half a provincial city, and that was one thing. Surely you couldn't run a whole fucking country like that.

Perhaps you could; I wouldn't know.

THIRTY-TWO

The matter of Ailsa's father wasn't mentioned again, and it was quite clear that it was to stay that way. That was her affair, of course, and none of my business, but I hoped to see the old rogue again before we left Dannsburg. When that might be I had no idea.

Ailsa still had yet to tell me why we were even in Dannsburg, and when she told me a few days later that she had accepted yet another invitation to yet another formal dinner that evening I found my patience wearing thin.

"What is it *this* time?"

"Don't snap at me, Tomas, it's impolite and I don't care for it," she said.

"And I don't care for society functions."

"I know that," she said. "You would actually be surprised how many invitations I have declined, to spare you, but we have to attend this one. It's from Lord Vogel."

She was right, I *was* surprised. I had never supposed Ailsa gave a fuck how I felt about these things, truth be told, and I found the notion that perhaps she might to be strangely pleasing. All the same, that name drove any further thoughts on the subject out of my head.

"Vogel? The . . ." I groped for his official title. "Lord Chief Judiciar, isn't he?"

"Yes," she said. "Absolutely."

We were in the drawing room with two footmen in attendance and Ailsa's lady's maid sitting demurely on a stool in front of her, holding a skein of yarn for her while she worked at some needlecraft or other. Billy was curled up beside her on the settle with his head nestled on her shoulder, like any good son with his ma. Speaking plainly was obviously out of the question.

"I remember meeting him, at the Princess Crown Royal's reception," I said. "We're honored."

I remembered Vogel all right. He was the Provost Marshal of the Queen's Men whatever other titles he might hold, and I could see that there would be no way to decline *that* invitation.

"We are," she said, and fixed me with a look that said to speak of something else in front of Billy and the servants.

Anything else.

"It's warm today," I said, feeling something of a fool. Empty conversation still didn't come easily to me, but I was working at it. "I wonder if the weather might break soon."

A ghost of a smile touched Ailsa's lips as she responded in kind, making the sort of idle chatter that seemed to be expected of society people. She looked pleased all the same, and that was good even if nothing else was.

My desire to sit down at table with Lord Vogel was simply nonexistent, but she was right. There was no getting out of it, especially as it was probably the whole reason for this interminable trip. There was still something I didn't understand, though, and I needed to before that evening's dinner.

A while after Billy had returned to his studies and Ailsa had retired to dress for dinner, I followed her upstairs and knocked on her bedroom door. Her lady's maid admitted me, and Ailsa turned with a curious look on her face. She was already dressed, of course, otherwise I would never have been let in, but the maid was obviously partway through arranging her hair.

"Could we have a moment?" I asked her.

She nodded and dismissed the maid with a wave of her hand, and I closed the door behind the departing girl.

"Can we talk freely in here?" I asked.

"Of course," Ailsa said, and frowned. "My servants don't listen at doors, Tomas."

"Your father thinks his do," I said.

She sighed. "Yes, well, his quite possibly do but that's beside the point. What do you want?"

"I want to know what the fuck is going on," I said. "You dragged me and Billy all the way to Dannsburg, and I've hardly seen the lad since that tutor of his arrived, this man Fischer. We're finally meeting with your boss, but that could have happened on the first day we were here. Instead we've sat and done nothing for weeks while Bloody Anne is fighting a fucking street war back home without me. And another thing—you said you'd been summoned but not by anyone you had to hurry for, or something like that. Surely you'd have to hurry for Vogel, so if he didn't summon you, then who the fuck did?"

"Ah," Ailsa said. "You seem to be working it out."

"Working *what* out? There's something here I don't understand."

"There are a lot of things you don't understand," she said. "Vogel didn't summon me, you're right about that. The house of magicians did."

I blinked at her in confusion.

"What? Does that mean they know who you are?"

"They knew there was a Queen's Man working in Ellinburg," she said, "but only because Vogel had to tell them as much when they first approached him. The instructions to recruit the local cunning folk and send them here to Dannsburg came from the house of magicians. That request was made directly to Vogel in the queen's name, so he *had* to grant it, and he ordered me to make it happen."

"Which we did, well and good," I said. "That doesn't tell me what they want you for."

"They don't particularly; they want Billy."

I stared at her. If they were interested in the cunning folk, then they would be all the more interested in Billy, I had to allow, but that still didn't make sense.

"So why haven't they come to see him, or had us go there?"

"Oh, but they have," she said. "Billy's tutor *is* a magician. He's studying him."

I didn't like the sound of that, but just then something else occurred to me.

"If they didn't know who the Queen's Man in Ellinburg was, then how the fuck did they know about us and Billy?"

"That is an extremely good question," Ailsa said, and I saw the flinty look in her eyes. "Someone has been talking."

We got in the carriage shortly before sundown.

"Does Lord Vogel live far away?" I asked her as the carriage rolled through the gates and out onto the street.

"I have absolutely no idea," Ailsa said. "He does his formal entertaining at the house of law, as befits his position."

That felt like one of the many things that I should have known, something anyone of society would have known without making a fool of himself by asking.

"Of course he does," I said, trying not to sound bitter. "Who are the other guests, do we know?"

Ailsa showed me a rare smile.

"You're beginning to ask the right questions," she said, and she looked pleased in the way that a dog trainer might the first time her hound learns to sit on command. "We will be joined by Lord and Lady Lan Andronikov; Major Bakrylov, you'll be pleased to hear; Lord and Lady Lan Yetrov, which I'm sure you won't; and Lady Reiter. Tell me what you know of these people."

I felt like a boy in school again, being tested by the tutor.

"Bakrylov's all right, for an officer," I said. "He can lose a bet and joke about it afterward anyway, which is more than a lot of men can. Lan Andronikov's the really rich one who squirmed out of being conscripted, and his wife is the poppy addict. Lan Yetrov is the cunt with the bear. I don't know anything about his wife, and I've never even heard of the last one."

"There seems to be very little about Lady Lan Yetrov *to* know, despite my best efforts to find something," Ailsa said. "She is a pointless, insipid little social climber who married far too far above herself purely for the money, and is now rumored to be deeply regretting it. Well done, by the way."

It irritated me how pleased I was, to hear her say that. I wasn't a fucking performing dog.

"Who's the other one, then? This Lady Reiter."

Ailsa smiled again. "She's very minor nobility, the third daughter of a baron who never amounted to anything in life and left a mountain of debt in death. Technically she's a courtier by virtue of her birth, but due to having inherited absolutely nothing she is now in fact a courte*san*, which is another way of saying 'very expensive whore.' She often accompanies Major Bakrylov to social occasions, to even the numbers."

I snorted laughter.

"I see," I said. "Bakrylov's not married, then?"

"No," Ailsa said, and left it at that.

"We're still not an even number," I pointed out. "Doesn't Vogel have a wife?"

"He always hosts alone," she said, "and his table is always an odd number with a vacant place setting laid at the foot. I don't know precisely why, but it's not something I would advise asking him about."

No, I thought, remembering the soulless look in Vogel's eyes. That probably wouldn't be at all wise.

THIRTY-THREE

The house of law was an imposing building by any standard. It reminded me of the governor's hall in Ellinburg, except it was probably three if not four times the size. The City Guard were very much in evidence outside, the light of the setting sun gleaming from their polished half-armor and the points of their spears. A huge royal standard flew from the stone heights of the building, cracking in the rising wind.

"You were right," Ailsa said as we were handed down from our carriage by hard-faced footmen who were quite obviously more than that. "I think the weather may be about to change."

"Aye," I said, and found myself wondering which way she meant that.

I was starting to sink deeper into Ailsa's world of intrigue and politics, and I didn't care for it. All the same, there was something brewing that night. I could feel it the same way I could feel when a sit-down was about to go bad and come to knives. This whole business with the house of magicians didn't feel right to me, and to my mind Vogel was as close to a devil walking as I ever wanted to meet.

I would have paid a great deal of money right then to be back in Ellinburg, in the Tanner's Arms with Bloody Anne and Jochan at the table with me, with brandy in front of us and careless soldier's talk on our lips.

No, I thought, my brother was a madman who had torn out a man's throat with his teeth and eaten it, and Bloody Anne was fighting a running street war in my name while I attended dinner with the head of the

Queen's Men. I could feel the distance between me and my crew growing, until it felt like a great chasm separated us. I didn't want that, but right then I couldn't see my way clear of it.

Ailsa took my arm as I stepped down from the carriage beside her, and together we were ushered up the stone steps of the great building and through the towering iron doors. The wearing of swords was in fashion in Dannsburg since the war ended, but all weapons were forbidden within the house of law, so I was unarmed. As the great doors closed behind us I felt the lack of the Weeping Women quite keenly. The hall within was marble, the floor echoing our steps back to us as we followed the attendant footmen up a sweeping flight of stairs to a formal reception room.

I had no idea what the room should be called, but it was somewhere between a drawing room and a hall, and it seemed to have been designed to provide the least comfort possible. There were chairs, but they were arranged around the walls in formal lines, useless for conversation, and the four other guests who had already arrived were standing in two clearly distinct pairs as they sipped wine from tall glasses.

A footman served us as we entered, and we each took a glass. I could see Major Bakrylov standing close to the huge fireplace, looking very bored. Beside him was an extremely beautiful woman with some twenty-five years to her who I took to be this Lady Reiter that Ailsa had told me about in the carriage.

The Lan Yetrovs were already there too, and I had no desire to talk to them. I saw Lord Lan Yetrov look my way, and I could tell from the curl of his lip that he had remembered what I had said to him at the court reception. Lan Yetrov hated me, I knew, and the feeling was entirely mutual.

"Talk to the major," Ailsa murmured to me. "I'll take the Lan Yetrovs."

I nodded my thanks to her and strolled toward the fireplace with the untouched glass in my hand.

"Major Bakrylov, a pleasure to see you again," I said, and realized I actually meant it.

Bakrylov showed me a grin that said he was genuinely pleased to see me, too.

"Piety, thank the gods," he said. "I was beginning to despair of seeing a friendly face this evening."

"Aye, well," I said. "Us tired old soldiers have to stick together."

"Absolutely!" he said, with a degree of enthusiasm that rather surprised me.

I glanced sideways at his companion, who he still hadn't introduced, and he took my meaning. Our Lady save me, I was beginning to speak the language of these people.

"Allow me to introduce the Lady Reiter," he said. "M'lady, this is Father Tomas Piety. We were at Abingon together."

That wasn't strictly true, of course, at least not the way he made it sound, but I let it be. We had both been at Abingon, that was true enough. Bakrylov had been a major who had got the best part of a regiment slaughtered in the process of becoming a war hero, while I had just been a company priest. Our paths would never have crossed in the war; priests and majors simply didn't move in the same circles. Still, that was past and done, and no use raising it now. Bakrylov seemed a good man aside from that, and I was sure he wouldn't have had the faintest idea why a simple conscript like me might possibly take ill against him for his wartime actions. He had just been rude to his companion, though, presenting her to me rather than the other way around as etiquette dictated. *Very expensive whore,* I remembered Ailsa saying, but that in itself should be no reason for rudeness. I wondered whether it was deliberate, or if he simply regarded her as a thing he had rented for the evening rather than a person. It wouldn't have surprised me, in Dannsburg.

"Charmed," Lady Reiter said, turning a smile on me that managed to be warm, welcoming, promising, avaricious, and utterly ruthless all at once.

I bowed over her extended hand as manners dictated, and indicated toward Ailsa, as was only wise under the circumstances.

"You know my wife, of course," I said.

"Of course," Lady Reiter said, and all the warmth, welcome, and promise fell out of her smile at once.

That left her only avarice and ruthlessness, her true face, but at least we both knew the lay of things between us and that was good.

"Have you seen our host yet?" I asked Bakrylov.

He smiled.

"Lord Vogel is famous for keeping his guests waiting," he said. "Privilege of being the Lord Chief Judiciar, I suppose."

"I suppose so," I said. "It must be otherwise a very joyless occupation."

Bakrylov laughed at that, more than it warranted to my mind, and clapped me on the shoulder.

"It really is good to see you again," he said. "You must find a way to let me try to win that crown back off you later. After dinner, perhaps?"

"I'm sure we'll think of something," I said, but just then the final pair of guests arrived and we turned to greet them.

Lord and Lady Lan Andronikov were much as I remembered them from the court reception—he had perhaps forty-five years to him, was weak-chinned and overdressed even in this company. His wife blinked vaguely around her as though unsure of where she was, the pupils visibly too large in her eyes.

"Ah, the brave and noble Lan Andronikovs," Major Bakrylov said, and offered them possibly the least sincere bow I had ever seen in my life.

I knew very well what a hotheaded young officer such as Bakrylov made of conscription-dodgers like Lan Andronikov, and it was plain that the older man did as well. He visibly flushed at the major's mockery and turned away as he took a glass from a footman's tray. I'm no courtier like Ailsa and I never will be, but it was plain enough even to my eye that Vogel seemed to have selected from all of Dannsburg society the dinner guests he could be most assured would hate each other. Why a man would choose to do that I wasn't sure, but I had a suspicion.

This sort of thing was Fat Luka's bread and beer, of course, and I wished then that I had him there with me that night. Even without his counsel, it seemed to me that people who violently dislike each other are more likely to fall to hard words than those who get along, and when hard words are spoken, truths come out that otherwise would stay buried in polite company.

Dieter Vogel was a subtle man, I realized. Subtle, and very, very dangerous.

Dinner itself was a strained affair, as might be expected. Lord Vogel had finally joined us just before his steward sounded a gong and opened the doors that led into a formal dining room. There we had been seated according to a plan of particular cruelty.

Lan Yetrov was seated at Vogel's right hand, which put him to my left, and I had Lady Lan Andronikov to my right, and neither of those things were to my liking. Ailsa was on the other side of the table, at Vogel's left hand, with Major Bakrylov, Lord Lan Andronikov, and Lady Lan Yetrov beside her, the last opposite Lady Reiter, who was on my side of the table.

I sipped my soup and considered Vogel's seating plan in the way that Ailsa had taught me. He had put Lan Yetrov in the place of honor, no doubt to spite Lan Andronikov, and sat me beside him to annoy both of us. Ailsa had his left hand, which further insulted Lan Andronikov, and he had seated the man opposite his own wife where he had no choice but to see the state of her. Also, he was next to the major, who clearly loathed him. Lady Lan Yetrov, the social climber who had married for money, was seated by the vacant foot of the table opposite the fancy whore, which spoke for itself.

The only good thing to be found was that I had the major opposite me, which was no doubt intended to cause dissent over what had happened at Abingon. In fairness, it probably would have done if we hadn't already found the beginnings of an unlikely friendship over our wager at Lan Yetrov's house. I found a new depth of appreciation for just how unpleasant Vogel was, but what this really told me was that Lord Lan Andronikov's days were numbered.

He's said some extremely unwise things recently, Ailsa had told me at the court reception. I thought those things might be on their way to catching up with him, however rich he was.

I wondered if he could see it too.

The soup bowls were cleared away and the fish course brought out, and Lan Yetrov continued to bray self-importantly at Lord Vogel while Ailsa engaged the rest of the table in light conversation about nothing. I met Bakrylov's eye over the table, and he winked at me in a way that said he too could see exactly what was happening. I ate my herb-crusted pike in silence until I was distracted by a low moan from my right.

"Are you well, my lady?" I asked, turning to Lady Lan Andronikov.

She had a sheen of sweat on her powdered brow, I noticed, and her hand trembled slightly as she raised her glass.

"Quite well, thank you, Father Piety," she said, but her tongue darted over her dry lips like a nervous animal as she spoke.

We had barely been in the house of law for three hours by then, and already the woman was looking in quite some need. I'd had no idea that poppy addiction could get so bad, but of course none of the addicts I had encountered in the Stink had had anything like her money to devote to their vices. I chanced a look across the table at her husband but he was intent on his food, and obviously choosing not to see what was quite literally right in front of him.

After the fish was done a troupe of minstrels entered the room, their lutes and pipes in their hands. They played for our entertainment for what seemed to me a very long time. The music was nothing I knew, far from the bawdy marching songs and soldier's laments that I was familiar with. When it was over at last I joined in the polite applause around the table with little enthusiasm and hoped they wouldn't come back. The music of society people, it seemed, was no more to my taste than any of the rest of it.

Finally it was time for the meat course, roast suckling pig and minted lamb and a number of crispy capons. Lord Vogel kept a good kitchen, I had to allow, for all that it didn't seem to be designed for the pleasure of his guests. At the foot of the table, either side of the strangely vacant place setting, Lady Reiter and Lady Lan Yetrov were ignoring each other in sullen silence. Lord Lan Yetrov was still trying to ingratiate himself with our host, while Ailsa chattered amiably to the major and Lord Lan Andronikov about the politics of war, which of course caused the pair's simmering hatred of each other to threaten to boil over at any minute. The meat course went on for a very long time.

I ate in silence, watching and learning.

There was an artistry to this sort of social manipulation, I came to realize, and Ailsa and Vogel were quite obviously allies in what they did. Once the meat was done a singer entered the room, accompanied by a lone piper, and I realized we were to have yet more entertainment inflicted on us. She had a good voice, I'll give her that, but her song was both very, very long and sung in a foreign language that I didn't know. When it was over at last and the singer had left the dining room, Lady Lan Andronikov made to rise.

"I wonder if I might be briefly excused," she said, and I could see that her legs were quivering slightly beneath her magnificent gown.

"Absolutely not," Vogel said, without so much as looking up. "My pastry chef is about to bring out his masterpiece. I would hate for you to offend him."

Lady Lan Andronikov sagged back into her seat beside me and drained her wine in a long, shuddering swallow that spoke of growing desperation. She managed to knock the empty glass over with her trembling hand as she set it down.

"For the gods' sakes," her husband hissed at her across the table, his voice unexpectedly loud as both Ailsa and Vogel stopped their conversations at exactly the right moment.

Lan Andronikov turned red with embarrassment, and his wife stifled a sob.

The sweet was brought out during a moment of awful silence, and then Ailsa resumed her chatter as though nothing had happened. At one point while we were eating I saw Vogel break off his conversation with Lan Yetrov while the other man was in midsentence and lean over to whisper something in Ailsa's ear. She just gave a short nod in return, and whatever that had been about it was obviously done.

By the time the sweet was finally cleared away we had been in the house of law for some six hours or more and Lady Lan Andronikov had developed the frantic look of a trapped rabbit. It was late by then, well after midnight, and when Vogel finally announced that the ladies should withdraw from the table I thought she might weep with gratitude.

Ailsa rose and led the other three women from the room, her hand firm on Lady Lan Andronikov's shaking arm.

"Come to the red drawing room with me, my dear," I heard her say as they passed. "Perhaps I may be able to find you something that might help your discomfort."

Could and might and possibly, I thought. Such were the promises of the Queen's Men.

That left me in the dining room with Vogel, Major Bakrylov, Lan Andronikov, and Lan Yetrov. Vogel gestured to a footman, and the long drapes at the end of the room were drawn back and tall windows opened to give us access to a wide terrace where brandy was being served under the stars. I accepted a glass and strolled outside into the warm summer night with the major beside me.

"Thank the gods that's over," he murmured in my ear.

"Aye," I said. "Not the easiest evening I've sat through."

We were at the far end of the terrace, away from the other men, when Major Bakrylov put his hand on my arse and leaned close as though he meant to kiss me.

"Come upstairs with me," he whispered. I coughed and took a step backward, more surprised than anything else. "Oh come, Piety, us tired old soldiers have to stick together, remember? You can't tell me you never did, in the tents at least."

"I never did," I said.

He snorted and drained his brandy with a practiced flick of his wrist. "I suppose it's because you're a priest, is it?"

I shook my head. "No, it's not that. Our Lady doesn't much care who we lie with, so long as both are willing. I mean no offense; I just don't like men in that way, that's all."

"Ah well," he said, and smiled. "My mistake. You don't know what you're missing, old boy."

He sauntered off inside then, and I saw that apart from a couple of footmen I was alone on the terrace with Lan Yetrov and Lord Vogel.

It came to me that perhaps I should have gone upstairs with the major after all.

THIRTY-FOUR

"Are you ready to apologize for your insult, Piety?" Lan Yetrov demanded, striding toward me across the terrace with his hand instinctively reaching for the sword he wasn't wearing.

Behind him, Lord Vogel stood watching us with a glass in his hand. His face was expressionless, unreadable.

"And what insult might that be, my lord Lan Yetrov?"

"You know very well what!"

His face was flushed with wine, with money and arrogance and Vogel's favor, and I very much wanted to put my fist through it. I wouldn't do that, though, any more than I had agreed to meet him in the dueling circle when he had tried to call me out at court. He simply wasn't worth my while.

"I'm afraid not," I said. "You seem to have slipped my mind."

"You *fucker,*" he hissed. "You ignorant lout! This is *war*, Piety!"

"No, it isn't," I said. "War is cannon, and corpses. This is a fool talking to me when I'd much rather he fucked off."

He grabbed me by the front of my doublet and leaned very close to me, his lips drawn back from his teeth in spluttering fury. I've killed men for less, but with the Provost Marshal of the Queen's Men standing not ten feet away and Ailsa nowhere in sight I didn't know how far I could take this. I could bear insults, if I had to.

"I promise you, you wretched, common little provincial oik, I will see the end of you," Lan Yetrov snarled in my face. "I will see the end of you, and then I will have my *special* way with your dirty, up-jumped tea monkey wife until her arse is bleeding, do you underst—"

I slammed my knee up into his balls so hard it was a wonder they didn't come out of his mouth. I've never been as good with my fists as Jochan was, but then you don't have to be, not if you fight dirty enough.

Lan Yetrov hit the floor like a sack of turnips dropped from a tower. He sucked in a single, hideous wheeze of breath before he vomited his entire dinner and several bottles' worth of wine onto the fine marble tiles in front of him.

I stamped on his guts once, twice, three times, then booted him in the side of the head. The last kick threw him over onto his back and knocked him out, and that was done. I could bear insults to *myself* if I had to, but I wasn't hearing talk like that about Ailsa.

"That took you longer than I expected," Vogel said, and there was no hint of emotion in his voice.

"My apologies, Lord Vogel," I said, "but I won't hear my wife spoken about like that."

"Quite," he said, and now he showed me a thin smile like the edge of a razor.

He turned to the footmen standing impassively behind him.

"Lord Lan Yetrov has made a drunken disgrace of himself and passed out on my terrace," he said. "Take him to his carriage, round up his whore of a wife, and throw them both out. I won't have drunkenness in the house of law."

"Sir," one of the footmen said.

He sounded like a soldier, to my mind. He and his fellow took Lan Yetrov by the armpits and dragged him off the terrace and back through the dining room. They had both just stood there and watched me kick the piss out of the man, but the Lord Chief Judiciar said he was drunk so that was how it was and that was how it would stay.

Vogel turned back to me, and now we were truly alone on the terrace.

"Did you understand this evening, Mr. Piety?"

I shrugged.

"Some of it," I said. "Probably not all of it."

"Tell me what you saw."

"Lan Andronikov's in disgrace, that was plain enough," I said. "His wife's a ruin of addiction, but I don't think that's much of a secret. Lan Yetrov is attempting to climb the social ladder, and he's making a horse's arse of it. Lady Reiter's a fancy whore and that's no secret at all."

"And the major?"

I shrugged. "He may or may not like men, but that's beside the point. Either he's a fool, which I doubt, or he was trying to get me away from you before this happened, or to distract me so I didn't notice something else. I suspect it was the last and if so then it worked, and that means he's one of your crew."

"Hmmm," Vogel said. "Ailsa was right, you're not an idiot."

"Who am I talking to?" I asked quietly. "The Lord Chief Judiciar or the Provost Marshal?"

"Which do you think? This is the house of law, after all."

"And that could mean either thing," I said. "Is this where policies of law are decided and taxes set?"

"No," he said. "That happens at court, between the queen's advisers and the governing council."

"So what do you do here then, in this house of law?" I asked, although by then I was certain I knew the answer.

"I ask questions, Mr. Piety, and I see that they are answered."

I met his razor smile, and I nodded. I knew what sort of man this was. I had seen men put to the question before and I remembered asking questions myself, after the attack on the Chandler's Narrow house. I remembered how I had got my answers to those questions. We understood each other, or so I thought at the time.

"This is the home of the Queen's Men, then," I said.

"Among other things," he allowed.

I picked up a bottle of brandy from the tray the footman had left standing on a bench, and refilled my glass. Vogel hadn't touched his, I noticed.

"You've gone to some trouble to get me alone tonight. Is this about the Skanians?"

"Not tonight," he said. "This is an entirely different matter, one of personal importance to me."

"What, then?"

"You're to do something for me, Piety," he said. "Directly for me. Ailsa does not need to know, unless you wish her to. Tell her if you will, or don't. I will leave that to your judgment."

I blinked at that.

"And what's that, then?"

"This boy of yours, this Billy. I understand you have taken him as a son. I believe that the magicians will want to keep him, and I do not want that to happen. I oppose anything that the magicians want. In truth I wish someone would rid me of them, and that cursed university, too." He paused for a moment to take a very small sip of his drink. "That aside, your boy is too useful a talent to allow them to dissect him as well. You have my personal permission to prevent that. Do what you need to do. Iagin will provide men and supplies from Grachyev's criminal organization, if they are required, and the Guard will look the other way if they have to, but *ensure* that you take the boy back to Ellinburg with you."

"*Dissect* him?" I managed to say.

I thought of the tutor, this magician who called himself Fischer, the one Ailsa had brought into our house, and I felt cold down to my boots. That wasn't happening. By Our Lady's name, that was not going to happen to my Billy.

Vogel shrugged.

"Or whatever it is they may do this time. Oh, you weren't expecting those cunning women you sent to us *back*, were you? I do hope that you weren't."

I swallowed, feeling suddenly sick. Had I sent Katrin and Gerta to their deaths, in the house of magicians? Or perhaps here, somewhere in the bowels of the house of law, where questions were asked in the screaming darkness.

I drained my brandy and poured another, taking a step backward as I did so to look through the tall windows into the dining room. The major was sitting alone at the table, idly shuffling a deck of cards.

It came to me then that one of our party was missing.

"What happened to Lan Andronikov?" I asked.

Dieter Vogel's soulless eyes didn't so much as flicker as they met mine. "Who?"

I didn't dare speak to Ailsa in the carriage on our way home, with our footmen too close for comfort. Once we were back in the house I all but dragged her into the drawing room despite the late hour and slammed the door in the servants' faces.

"Lan Andronikov disappeared tonight, right while I was talking to your fucking boss," I whispered. "You had his wife; what happened to her?"

"Oh, I let her have her pipe eventually," Ailsa said. "The poor thing was crying for it by then, and she knew what she'd done. She betrayed him herself, you know."

I remembered those couple of days Ailsa had spent out of the house alone, visiting friends, and her words from the court reception came back to me.

By the time we got to fourteen I could have made her do absolutely anything. . . . He's said some extremely unwise things recently.

"You made her betray him, didn't you?"

"Yes," she said. "He was spreading sedition, Tomas. It's my job to uncover that sort of thing and see that it is stopped."

"So now her husband's murdered over dinner at Vogel's word, is that the lay of things?"

"Yes, Tomas, it is," Ailsa snapped at me. "That is *exactly* the lay of things, in Dannsburg. We do not have executions here, not for traitors. There are no heroic ends, no ritual or grandeur to it. We make no martyrs and we leave nothing for others to aspire to, nothing to be emulated. They just disappear and are forgotten. Lan Yetrov's wife was marched out of the drawing room while we were in there, by the way. What did *you* do to her husband, while we're on the subject?"

I sighed and poured myself a brandy.

"He deserved it," I said.

"I'm not disagreeing with that; I asked you what you did."

"I gave him a kicking," I admitted, "and he got off lightly, to my mind. And that's another thing—when were you intending to tell me what happened to Katrin and Gerta?"

"Who?"

"Don't *fucking* give me that!" I shouted at her. "I don't give a fuck about Lan Andronikov, but those two women were my people, Pious Men people. I sent them here for your bastard magicians to talk to, not for them to cut up to see what was inside!"

"Ah," Ailsa said. "I see Vogel took you into his confidence. That surprises me."

Tell her if you will, or don't. I will leave that to your judgment. Vogel was testing me, I could see that much even if I didn't have the faintest idea why he was doing it, but that was a question for another day. Of course I was fucking telling her, and I was sure that in itself was part of the test.

I suspected that everything was.

"Aye, he did. Would it *surprise* you to learn that these cunts want to do the same thing to our Billy? I'm not having it, Ailsa, I mean it. Vogel said to stop them, and I will. First thing tomorrow morning that fucking tutor's out in the street for a start, you hear me?"

"*Vogel* said to stop them?" she repeated, her brow furrowing in thought. "That's interesting. I wonder why."

That was another good question, I had to allow.

"He said Billy was too useful to waste, or something like that, and that I could get men from Grachyev's crew if I needed them. Billy's my son and I won't see him hurt, but I don't understand why Vogel cares about him."

"He doesn't," Ailsa said. "Vogel doesn't care about anyone, but this must mean he thinks Billy will be useful at some point in the future. The house of law can't move openly against the house of magicians, of course, as both houses serve the crown. This is precisely why we have people like Grachyev—people like *you,* for that matter—to do this sort of thing when it needs doing."

"I see," I said. "This is like the fucking Wheels all over again, isn't it? If businessmen do a thing, then who can say that the Queen's Men were behind it, and if they get killed doing it, then who's to care?"

"It's called plausible deniability, Tomas," she said. "It's *very* useful."

Her smile was like a razor, just like Vogel's had been.

THIRTY-FIVE

The next morning I roused Billy from his bed before the sun had fully risen. I had only been abed myself a few hours and I was tired and feeling the effects of the previous night, but I needed the lad up and awake before I spoke to this tutor of his. He was a magician, so Ailsa had told me, and I wasn't facing one of those without a magician of my own at my side. Or my swords, for that matter. I was wearing the Weeping Women buckled over my shirt when I woke the lad, and I knew that wasn't lost on him.

"What is it, Papa?" Billy asked me.

He sat up in his blankets and rubbed sleep from his eyes.

"Your tutor, Mr. Fischer," I said. "Has he ever hurt you, Billy?"

"No," Billy said. "Why would he?"

"I don't know. What has he been teaching you?"

"Reading mostly, and my 'rithmetic and that," the lad said. "He doesn't teach much—he asks me questions, more than anything else."

"What sort of questions?"

"About the cunning. About how it works, and where it comes from, and how I do it, and about Our Lady. He's writing a book, he says. For the university."

No, he fucking isn't.

"I see," I said. "I want you to listen to me now; this is important. Mr.

Fischer isn't who he says he is. He's a magician, and I didn't know that when we hired him, but I do now and I'm throwing him out. I need you to help me with that, in case he tries to do magic at me. Can you do that for me, Billy?"

"Yes, Papa," Billy said, without hesitation. "I don't like him anyway."

"Good lad."

I waited while Billy got dressed, then led him up the servants' stair to the top floor of the house where the small garret rooms were. I kicked Fischer's door open without knocking.

The man was stood at his nightstand, naked apart from his small-clothes, scraping at his narrow, pointed chin with a razor. He was thin and pale, and his bare back was a mess of old, faded scars that looked like they had been left by a whip.

"Oi," I said. "I want a word."

He turned and looked at me, and at Billy beside me, the razor dripping in his hand.

"Mr. Piety? Billy? What . . . what is this?"

"This is me knowing who you are and who sent you," I said. "This is me throwing you out of my fucking house. Try any of your magic on me and you'll have Billy here to answer to."

"Mr. Piety, please, I can—"

"I mean it," I said. "Pack your shit and fuck off, right now."

"He won't," Billy said, in that way he had when he knew a thing was so. "He doesn't dare."

"He'd fucking better."

But Billy was right, of course.

When Billy said a thing would be so he was always right. Fischer looked from me to the door to Billy and back again, his eyes wide with panic. I put my hand on the hilt of Remorse and glared at him.

"Get out, or I'll gut you," I promised him.

Fischer took a stumbling step backward, and then he slashed the glittering razor across his own throat in one savage sweep.

"Fuck!" I shouted, but it was too late.

Blood jetted across the wall and the mirror and the nightstand, and darkened the water in the basin. Fischer sagged to his knees before collapsing to the bare floorboards in a bubbling, dying heap.

"In Our Lady's name," I whispered.

"I told you, Papa," Billy said.

"Aye," I had to allow, trying to keep the tremble out of my voice. "Aye, you did. Why, Billy? Why didn't he dare?"

"He was more scared of them than he was of you or of dying."

"Who? Who was he more scared of, the magicians?"

The lad just shrugged and looked down at his tutor, watching the lifeblood run from his ruined neck and pool on the floor around him.

I sighed and looked around the small, cramped garret room. There was nothing there to tell me anything. A few spare clothes, some simple teaching books of the kind we had used when I had been in school myself, and that was all. I walked over to the bed, and on impulse I picked up the pillow and looked beneath it.

There was another book hidden there, a slim volume of the sort that you could buy unprinted to write in yourself. I picked it up and flicked through the pages of spidery handwriting to the last entry.

Boy appears to have a talent unknown to us, but whether goddess-given, demonic, or of internal origin remains to be seen. Cannot operate here in family home. Am given to understand by my learned colleagues that vivisection of the previous subjects proved inconclusive.

Recommend extreme caution in this instance. Prone to starting fires. Propensity for physical violence also worrying, although whether product of training, wartime trauma, or familial surroundings unclear. A deeply troubled and worrying young man.

I confess, I fear him.

I closed the book and looked at Billy, standing across the room from me with the bloody corpse of his tutor on the floor between us.

"Billy," I said, "did you ever set fire to anything in front of Mr. Fischer?"

Billy looked at his boots for a moment, then shrugged in the way that boys of that age do.

"Suppose," he said. "Might have done. Nothing big, though."

"Did you ever hurt *him*?"

"I threatened him with harsh justice once, Papa," Billy said. "He kept on about wanting to cut me so he could look at my blood through a seeing glass, so I showed him my knives and said I'd fucking cut *him* if he tried it. I never *really* hurt him, though. He was a coward, so I didn't have to."

"Aye, well," I said. "That's good, Billy. Well done, lad."

The boy had picked up more from me than I had thought, I had to allow. I wasn't quite sure how to feel about that. Part of me was proud, that he'd stood up for himself, but part of me wondered how much of that had come from me and how much from Cutter.

A deeply troubled and worrying young man.

I found I had to agree with the late Mr. Fischer about that.

"He took his own life," I said to Ailsa, for the third time. "One slash of the razor and he was done. There wasn't much I could do about that."

"A magician dead in my home, and they know which house I work for," she said, pacing the drawing room like a caged lioness. "What am I supposed to do with this, Tomas?"

"He's not dead in your home. I kicked him out this morning at first light, and you and Luka and a number of your guards will have seen me do it," I said. "If he never made it back to the house of magicians across the dangerous streets of the city, then that's a failing to lie at the door of the City Guard."

"He is lying dead upstairs," she hissed at me.

"He soon won't be," I said. "I know how to do this shit, trust me. You just make sure that your guards know what they saw and when."

There was a knock at the door then, and a footman entered and presented me with a sealed letter.

"This came to the house, sir," he said. "The messenger wore no livery, but I recognized him as one of Lord Lan Yetrov's men."

I nodded my thanks and took it, and dismissed the footman as I broke the seal. I had hoped Lan Yetrov would just take his kicking like a soldier and learn to leave me alone, but of course he was no soldier. I could tell his mood from the furious slash of his handwriting across the expensive paper.

Piety,

You crossed a line last night, you pitiful oik.

I will end you!

Fleeing the city will do you no good. I have friends in Ellinburg, powerful ones who bear you no love and will do my bidding. You cannot escape my reach.

Die!

The note was unsigned, which was probably his idea of subtlety. I shook my head and showed it to Ailsa. Her brow furrowed as she read.

"Do you think he's talking about Hauer or Vhent?" I asked her.

"Hauer, almost certainly," she said. "Either way, it's not good news. I wish you had restrained yourself last night, Tomas. This is a complication we do not need."

"You didn't hear what he fucking said," I muttered. "Never mind him. I'll take care of it. Right now we need that body gone."

Ailsa tossed Lan Yetrov's letter into the cold grate where it belonged. "Yes, we really do."

I took a moment to pen and seal a note, then opened the door of the drawing room and told the waiting footman to fetch Fat Luka to me. When he arrived I told him the lay of things.

"Get a runner over to that Leonov fellow from south of the river," I said, and handed him the note. "Give him this, and have him get it to Iagin. Have him send a coal wagon here too, or a dray cart or whatever they've got. Something that looks like it's coming to make a delivery to the house. When they've done that they can take something wet away with them and lose it for me, you understand?"

Luka nodded.

"Aye, boss," he said, "but this will cost us. I don't see that they owe us any favors."

"If he argues tell him Iagin has already agreed to it and mention my name. There won't be a problem."

I had Vogel's personal promise that Iagin would help me against the magicians, after all, and I was going to fucking use it. For that and anything else I could get out of him.

"Right you are, boss," Luka said.

"Another thing," I said. "Once your runner's on his way, I want you to do something for me yourself. The sort of thing you're good at."

"What's that?"

"Find a way to get a message to Lady Lan Yetrov, a private one. Ask her how she'd like to be a very rich widow, and see if she wants to talk to me."

Luka just nodded at that. He was a good man, was Fat Luka, and I knew I could trust him.

He turned and left the room, and Ailsa raised her eyebrows at me.

"*Lady* Lan Yetrov?"

"You told me she only married him for his money, and from what he said last night I have reason to suspect he's pure misery to share a bed with," I said.

"Hmmm, there have been rumors," she said, "and Lady Lan Yetrov is frequently indisposed. Perhaps you have something, there."

"Aye well, it seems to me that a man who's cruel in one way is likely to be cruel in others. Be that as it may, I'm going to get that cunt before he gets me, simple as that. I do *not* need more trouble with Hauer. This is just business now, Ailsa, and I know how to do business."

"I hope you do," she said.

"If Leonov is halfway competent he can lose a body without anyone knowing where it came from, even in this fucking city," I said. "It's not hard, and he must know someone who keeps pigs. I kicked Fischer out in front of half your household guard, and I don't know where he went. That's the story, and that's how it's staying. If they complain about it, we'll accuse these magicians of putting a spy in our house and see how they take that."

"They will suspect I knew who he was when I took him in," she said.

"Know it, or suspect it?"

"Well, they can't admit to knowing it, you fool," she said. "Not officially, as they don't *officially* know who I am."

"Exactly," I said. "Fuck them then, we'll bluff it out. Give it a few days for him to be missed, then you show them *officially* who you are and we'll see what they can fucking do about it then."

Ailsa gave me an appraising look. She was a master at these intrigues, of course, and in her eyes I was only a blunt street thug. Me applying some street thinking to her way of doing things seemed to have thrown her.

"They will know we're lying," she said, and then paused for a moment to think about it. "But of course we know they're lying as well and they *know* we do so . . . yes. Yes, that actually works. That's a stalemate that gives no one the upper hand. Your business politics aren't so very different to mine after all, Tomas."

I shrugged. "It gets the job done."

"Hmmm," she said. "It had better."

THIRTY-SIX

I was right; there hadn't been any problems with Leonov. Vogel had obviously sent word to Iagin, which was no more than I expected, and it seemed that that same word had already been passed down to his street operatives as I had hoped. Once the dray cart had been and gone and taken the evidence away with it that was done, and best forgotten.

That was how business was done, the same way it was in Ellinburg.

Another messenger came that day, bearing a new letter from Bloody Anne. With the way the roads were I had no way of knowing if she would have received my reply to the last one by the time she wrote it, but it seemed things had taken an ill turn at home.

My dearest Tomas,

It pains me to have to write to you again so soon but I find I have to bear hard news. The sickness has reached our doors, and more and more of our extended family are suffering from illness. It seems our friend is not the friend we had thought. There have been no deaths within the close family, but many more distant relations are sadly lamented.

The weather in the city has become intolerable, although your brother has been stalwart in spreading the sickness among those with whom we are not friends.

Please tell me you will return soon; your dear aunt and I miss you so very much.

Your loving little sister,
Anne

Things in Ellinburg were fast going to the whores then, that was what she was telling me. The governor had quite plainly turned his back on law and order, although it sounded like Jochan was leading a counter-attack against the Northern Sons and their Skanian backers. If things were that bad at home, then I knew there was no way I could risk Lan Yetrov making even more trouble for us with Hauer. I couldn't help Anne fight the Skanians from Dannsburg, but there was one thing I *could* do, and it was plain what that was.

Lan Yetrov had to die.

We stayed low for a couple of days after that, until Fat Luka came to me and said that the maid he had found and bribed in Lan Yetrov's household had got my message to the lady of the house. She was willing to talk.

I had thought she might be.

It was a gamble, of course, but most things in this life are. If she was truly loyal to Lan Yetrov, which I doubted, then she would betray me and there would be hard times ahead. If, on the other hand, she was a woman both grasping for money and at the same time sick of being raped up the arse by her cruel cunt of a husband, then this could be a mutually beneficial arrangement.

"She'll meet you," Luka said, "but she can't be seen here, and obviously you can't go to her house without her husband hearing of it. There are inns and taverns, of course, but inns and taverns are full of eyes and ears. Everyone in this fucking city is watching everyone else. We could ask Grachyev to arrange something, but—"

But then Vogel would hear of it. I didn't think I wanted that, not yet.

"No, no, fuck that, this isn't Grachyev's affair and I'm into him for one favor as it is. We need some real neutral ground for this, outside of prying eyes. Give me a moment."

I pulled paper and quill and ink from the writing desk and scratched a note.

My esteemed Sasura,

This will sound strange, but I assure you the matter is purely business and there is no impropriety toward your daughter. I need to meet privately with a woman on neutral ground, and I wonder if I could beg the use of your house for an hour? I would welcome your presence at our meeting, for your advice and guidance.

Your most respectful son-by-law,
Tomas

I folded and sealed the paper and passed it to Fat Luka.

"Get that to Ailsa's father," I said.

Luka blinked at me, but he had the sense not to say anything.

That was how I got an old pirate back into the life.

A day later I received a note from Ailsa's father.

My beloved son-by-law,

I believe you are leading me back astray in my old age, and I think that I like it. Arrange your meeting for my house this Queensday afternoon, when I know my wife will be out with her friends. She need not and must not know of this.

With my greatest regards,
Your sasura

I had no idea where Ailsa's mother went on Queensday afternoons, but that was perfect. My mother-by-law hated me, after all, and she was hardly likely to accept me receiving a married woman at her house.

Sasura, on the other hand, quite clearly understood when business was just business.

Come that Queensday afternoon I was sitting in his study drinking his brandy with him when a footman showed Lady Lan Yetrov in. She looked cowed and broken, and she lacked the skill with paint and powder to completely hide the black eye she was sporting. She walked with difficulty too, I noted, and when she sat it was with a wince of pain. Lan Yetrov had obviously taken his rage at me out on her, which only made me hate him all the more.

"My Lady Lan Yetrov," I said, "I thank you for coming. It's no secret that your husband and I are not friends."

She laughed, a strangely brittle sound in the comfortable quiet of Sasura's study.

"Your man had the disgusting temerity to suggest that I might enjoy being a widow," she said. "I can scarce believe the disrespect you have shown to my husband and me."

Her tone was full of righteous indignation, but she had come to see me all the same.

She wanted rid of that cunt and she wanted his money, that was plain enough, but she was sat in front of a man she didn't know and I could see that she was picking her words with great care.

"That you might," I said. "You would be wealthy, and free, and with time you might finally heal from what he's been doing to you."

"I love my husband," Lady Lan Yetrov said, but there was a dead and despairing look in her eyes as she spoke.

Ailsa's father leaned forward and put a reassuring hand over hers.

"I am very old," he said, when she tried to pull away. "I do not want to fuck you. I'm too old for that, so listen to me. No one in this room is a listener for the crown or a friend to your husband. No one here will tell your husband what you say of him. Tomas is my son-by-law, and he has a reason to want you to be free. You don't need to know what that reason is; you just need to tell us some things, and we will help you."

"What things?" she asked, and there was no mistaking the quiver of hope in her voice. "What could you possibly want to know from me?"

"Just simple things," I said. "Who the captain of your household guard is and what levers move him. Who we need to bribe to get access to your estate at night. Who keeps your husband's prize bear, that sort of thing."

Lady Lan Yetrov looked at us both for a long time, my father-by-law and me. Then she started to talk, and I to listen.

She told me everything I needed to know, everything that I needed to tell Luka and Leonov in order to ensure that the wheels of revenge could begin to turn. Eventually it was done, and Lady Lan Yetrov accepted a small glass of brandy. Her hands were trembling, I noticed, and there were tears on her cheeks. Whether they were tears of guilt and remorse or of relief and joy, I really couldn't have said.

Truth be told, I didn't really care.

THIRTY-SEVEN

With that in motion, it was high time we visited the house of magicians. Ailsa was already waiting for me, on the morning of the appointed day.

"How does this work?" I asked her, when I came down the stairs and met her in the hall, still buttoning my coat. "Do we need to make an appointment or something?"

"Absolutely not," she said. "They will see me, and they will especially want to see Billy."

"They're not keeping him," I said at once. "I found Fischer's journal, remember, and he was talking about how his crew cut Katrin and Gerta open to study them. Billy doesn't leave our fucking *sight* in that place, you hear me?"

"Tomas, do you honestly think I would let that happen to my Billy?"

I looked at her, at my lioness, and I found that I had no answer to give her. I most sincerely hoped not, of course I did, but was I really sure about it? I had to allow that I had a place in my heart for Ailsa, but I couldn't let myself forget who and what she was. Her and Billy had grown close, yes, but if Vogel had ordered her to hand the lad over to the magicians she still might just have done it. I wouldn't like to bet either way on that.

We were both dressed in finery as befitted our station in Dannsburg, but all the same I buckled the Weeping Women over my coat. I refused to hear any argument about that. These fuckers had magic, or so they said, and I didn't, but I had good steel and the skill to use it. I wasn't walking into their nest of vipers without at least some way to defend myself. I was fortunate that the wearing of swords was back in fashion in Dannsburg, so at least no one would make too much fuss about it. The house of magicians wasn't the house of law, after all, and they couldn't forbid it. The fact that mine were real weapons and not dress blades would hopefully not be noticed.

"Aye, well," I said at last. "You can't blame me for worrying about the lad."

"No, of course I can't," she said. "He's every bit as much my son as he is yours, and I worry for him too. The house of magicians is . . . a strange place."

"In what way?"

I had a suspicion about the house of magicians but precious few facts to go on. I could still turn out to be wrong, and that was worrying me.

I'm not afraid of what I can see, of what I can fight. If I can fight it, then perhaps I can kill it, however long the odds might be. I'm afraid of the things that I *can't* see. Disease, and magic; those, I fear.

"Oh, don't sound so scared; there's no magic about it," she said. "It's just a building, very similar to the house of law, in fact. The things that go on there, though, those are different. Magicians scry the stars and they practice alchemy, and some say they have terrible powers and they call up demons from Hell and make pacts with them."

"And what about you? Do you say those things?"

"I really don't know," Ailsa said. "I don't know whether I believe in demons."

"Nor do I," I said. "Priest I may be, but that's a matter for mystics and I'm not that. I know one thing I *do* believe in, though, and that's evil men. I very strongly believe in them, and I think we're about to meet some."

"Perhaps we are," Ailsa allowed. "Human vivisection is an ugly thing."

That was putting it lightly, to my mind, but I wondered if it was really so very different to the way that questions were asked in the house of law. Was cutting people open to study what was inside them any worse than putting them to the question? That was a philosophical question, I supposed, and this was no time for philosophy.

"Aye, well," I said. "Is Billy ready?"

"Yes, Papa," he said from behind me.

I didn't startle, and I pride myself on that, but I hadn't heard him come down the stairs and I had no idea how long the lad had been there. Cutter's training had changed Billy, I realized. He moved like the knifeman now, silent and purposeful. If he'd had the mind to he could have cut my throat before I knew anything was wrong.

"Right, well and good," I said. "Let's get this fucking done, then."

The three of us rode our carriage across Dannsburg to the house of magicians, with two footmen on the carriage itself and three of Ailsa's household guard around us on horseback. The place lay in the northern reach of the city, near the university and the great library. As we arrived, I saw it was constructed much like the house of law as Ailsa had said, although as well as the royal standard on the roof there was another banner flying. This one was dark blue, with a single seven-pointed star picked out on it in white. It was the only other banner I had seen since I had been in Dannsburg, and it said a lot about the power of the house of magicians that they could fly their own colors within that sea of red.

Two guards flanked the massive double doors, both in full plate armor and closed great helms, and wearing dark blue surcoats with the same white star sewn on them. They had halberds in their hands and long, heavy war swords hanging from their belts.

"Who the fuck are they?" I asked as the carriage drew up outside.

"Guard of the Magi," Ailsa said. "The private army of the house of magicians. They're just soldiers like any others, but they like to pretend they're something special because of who they work for. There are considerably more of them than we are comfortable with."

"They must be fucking hot in all that lot," I muttered, as I climbed out of the carriage into the summer sun and handed Ailsa down after me. "Guard of the sweaty, maybe."

She smiled at that and smoothed her skirts while Billy jumped down after us.

"I'll do the talking," she murmured, and approached the overly armored guards with an easy confidence that told them she was court nobility born and bred.

"I am the Lady Ailsa Piety," she told them, "and these are my husband and my son. We are expected within."

"No, you're not," one of the guards said, his voice muffled by his cumbersome helmet. "No one is, today."

Ailsa reached into her purse and produced the thick piece of folded leather that contained the seal of the Queen's Warrant. She held it up and showed it to the guardsman.

"I really am," she said.

The man snapped to attention so hard he almost dropped his halberd.

"Ma'am," he said.

A moment later the doors were open and we were being ushered inside. It seemed that even the Guard of the Magi had a healthy respect for the Queen's Men, and that was good. All the same, it surprised me that she showed the warrant so openly.

But then this was Dannsburg, I had to remind myself, and things were done differently here. The Queen's Men didn't even officially exist, everyone knew that, but of course everyone also knew very well that they did. What had she called it?

Plausible deniability, that was it.

And who would be such a fool, in a city where everyone informed on everyone else, to go spreading tales of the Queen's Men and who had said what, and when? No, that wasn't going to happen. People had disappeared for less, I was sure.

Dannsburg, as I have written, was not like Ellinburg.

Not one little bit it wasn't.

Still, that was a thought for another day. The hall within the house of magicians was much what I had come to expect in Dannsburg, high-ceilinged and galleried and all of polished marble and gilded wrought iron. A man hurried out of an antechamber to greet us, his velvet livery all blue and white and bearing the seven-pointed star of the house of magicians over his heart.

"Lady Piety, such an honor," he said, bowing obsequiously to us both. "Father Piety, young master Billy. Welcome, welcome to the house of magicians."

The heavy double doors thumped closed behind us, and I heard a lock turn. I had to allow that I didn't feel very fucking welcome.

Ailsa again produced the Queen's Warrant and showed it to him.

"Go away, and bring me somebody who matters," she said.

The liveried nobody visibly paled as he looked at the warrant in her hand.

"Yes, ma'am," he said.

He scurried away and down a corridor, leaving us standing alone in the great echoing hall.

"Shouldn't there be some footmen or something?" I whispered to Ailsa. "I don't think I've ever been this alone in Dannsburg."

"This is the house of magicians," she replied, speaking quietly out of the side of her mouth. "They find it difficult to retain servants."

I couldn't imagine why.

After a few minutes the man in livery returned, from upstairs this time, and now he had what I assumed to be an actual magician with him. The magician descended the great marble stair with the attendant behind him, his long, flowing blue robes trailing down the polished stone steps after him. He was short and plump and pale of face, and he wore his black hair cropped close to his skull and his beard long and oiled and luxurious against his chest. I could see the toes of dainty, pointed velvet slippers poking out from under his robe with each step he took.

I hated him on sight.

"Lady Piety, Father Piety," the flunky said, "allow me to present the learned magus Absolom Greuv."

"A pleasure, Magus," Ailsa said, in a tone that meant the exact opposite.

She dipped him a curtsey so small I could barely see it, and I could tell that wasn't lost on him.

"Lady Piety," he said. "I see you have finally seen fit to answer our summons."

"The roads are slow at this time of year," Ailsa said, although they weren't.

"I'm sure they are," he said.

It seemed no one was going to bring up the spy that the magicians had had in our house for the last month and more, then, or ask what had become of him. That was good. I knew we could win the game of "who officially knows what" if we had to, but it would be better if it wasn't played at all, to my mind. It seemed that Fischer had been expendable, as far as the house of magicians was concerned. I remembered the whip scars on his back, and I wasn't overly surprised about that. It seemed that magicians were not benign masters.

We were still standing in the hall without drinks in our hands, and from what I had learned of how hospitality worked in Dannsburg, that seemed to me like it might be deliberately rude. I looked at this magus who still hadn't so much as acknowledged me, and then looked at Billy.

"Are you thirsty, lad?" I asked him.

"Yes, Papa," Billy said.

"Aye," I said, and if perhaps my tone was somewhat blunt, then I am a blunt man, and I make no apology for that. "So am I."

"Forgive me, where are my manners?" the magician said.

Up your arse, I thought, but I didn't say it.

He led us through into a reception room that wasn't much more comfortable than the hall had been, but after the evening I had spent at the house of law I had been expecting that. We were served sweet, cloying wine in tall glasses by a footman wearing the livery of the house and a sneer of disdain.

I already hated this place, and I would have done even if I hadn't known what they had done to Katrin and Gerta.

I wasn't going to forgive them for that, and I very much doubted that Billy was either.

"Ah, young Billy, what a magician you will make," Greuv said, peering at the lad over his glass in a way that I really didn't care for. "I am given to understand that you have already received a little rudimentary training from some primitive in Ellinburg."

Billy turned and looked a question at me.

"He's learned the cunning, aye," I said. "What of it?"

"He may have some *un*learning to do," Greuv said. "We will see that he unlearns, and then we will teach him correctly."

"No, I don't fucking think so," I said.

I felt Ailsa stiffen at my side, but I ignored her and stared the magician down. I was preparing to make a gamble here, a very big one, based on no more than a suspicion and a memory of a conversation I'd had with Old Kurt the cunning man, two years past. I offered up a silent prayer to Our Lady that I was right.

If not, we wouldn't get out of there alive.

THIRTY-EIGHT

"Mr. Piety, you seem to have misunderstood the purpose of your visit," the magus said, his voice turning cold. "You were instructed to deliver the boy to us, and you have done that. You may now leave the house of magicians, and preferably leave Dannsburg altogether. Good day."

"Why the fuck," I said, letting my voice fall into a flat tone, "should I listen to you?"

"Do you presume to question the power of the house of magicians?"

I could hear the contempt dripping from his voice as he looked down his nose at me, contempt for my accent and for my profession and my fucking *presumption*. I didn't care for it, so I threw the dice and I made my gamble.

"What makes you so special that you think you can give me orders?" I asked him. "What is it that you think you know?"

Greuv took a step toward me and looked into my eyes with a piercing gaze.

"The Magi know many things," he hissed. "I know you have seen horror and lost beloved comrades. I know you have done violence and will do yet more violence. I know that the violence you have done haunts your dreams and wakes you in the darkness, sweating with night terrors. I see into your heart, Tomas Piety. I can see into your very *soul*."

He knew I was a veteran and a businessman, that was all that meant, and those things were no secret. Many veterans had battle shock too, so that was no more than a fairly safe guess. That wasn't magic; that was just getting the measure of a man. I could do that as well as he could, and I was starting to think that I had the measure of *him*.

I prayed once more to Our Lady that I was right, that this wouldn't be the gamble that finally sent me across the river. The need to swallow was very strong, but I forced myself to hold his eyes with a steady glare.

Don't back down, I told myself. *Never fucking back down.*

I wouldn't, not ever. Not for this cunt and not for anyone else either. If I was wrong, then I knew I was about to damn us all, but I *never* back down in front of a bully.

"Well done, you've asked some questions about me," I said. "You know what *I* see? I see a prick in a dress who's pretending to be clever. I see a murderer who cut up two of my people for the fucking fun of it, and who thinks I'm going to let him do the same to my son. I see a fucking fool."

"Tomas," Ailsa cautioned me. "Be very careful."

The magus shook his head slowly.

"I cannot expect a cheap criminal like you to understand the mysteries, Piety, but *you*? You, a Queen's Man? You know *exactly* what we can do."

"Actually I don't," Ailsa said, and I thought that perhaps she had grasped the nature of my gamble. Ailsa was nobody's fool, after all. "I only know what you *say* you can do. I agree with my husband. You can't have Billy."

The magus's face flushed red with fury above his ridiculous beard, but I met his glare and held it.

"Show me some fucking magic," I said.

"I can summon the Gorgon of the Deep Hells if you push me!" Greuv bellowed at me. "I can bring forth horrors that would flay the hide from your bones with a look!"

"No, you can't," Billy said.

I turned and looked at the lad. He was staring intently at the magus, I saw, and his mouth was curling into a smile.

"How dare you, brat?" the magus snarled, and then he took two sudden, stumbling steps backward and sat down hard in a chair as Billy pushed him over with his mind.

"You're not a real magician," Billy said. "You've got no spark at all."

Lady be praised, I was right!

"Is that so?" I asked, and I drew Remorse.

Magus Greuv stared at me with open hatred. "You dare to threaten—"

"Aye, I do," I said. "Now, we're leaving and we're taking Billy with us, and you, my *lord magus*, can't fucking stop us. Billy, keep him in that chair until we've gone."

"Guard!" Greuv bellowed. "Guard, to me!"

The doors crashed open and four of the heavily armored Guard of the Magi stormed into the room with swords drawn. Mercy was in my other hand a moment later, and I moved to put myself between them and Ailsa. I was facing four trained soldiers in full armor with war swords in their hands, and me in a coat with just a pair of shortswords. I didn't stand a fucking chance and I knew it.

I heard movement behind me, and then a strangled scream.

"Put up your swords!" Greuv ordered, his voice coming out in a choked wheeze.

I turned to see Billy behind the magus's chair with an arm wrapped tightly around his neck and one of his wicked little knives at the side of his throat, pressing dangerously hard into the killing place. Ailsa was just standing to one side with her hands folded in front of her and an unreadable look on her face.

"How would you like me to cut you open and look at *your* blood?" Billy asked him. "I think I'd like to see *all* of it."

Billy twisted his arm around Greuv's throat in a way that gave the magus no option but to stand. He was a short man, as I have written, and he and Billy were much of a height. Billy kept the knife pressed into his neck, drawing a thin trickle of blood and seeming always on the brink of plunging through skin and flesh and opening the great vessel that would have meant almost instant death. His other hand was somewhere under the magus's ear, the knuckle of his thumb pressing into a soft place that was obviously causing Greuv a great deal of pain.

"We're leaving now," I told the Guard of the Magi, "and I suggest you stand aside if you want your master to live. Bring him to the carriage with us, Billy."

Billy nodded and applied the tiniest pressure with the knuckle of his thumb, enough to make Greuv gasp and stagger in the direction Billy wanted him to go. I faced down the Guard of the Magi as we passed between them, my swords in my hands and my glare meeting their faceless steel helms. They stood back as Billy forced Greuv between them, but I could feel the hatred coming off them like a living thing. Ailsa followed, a small smile on her lips now as we returned to the main hall.

When we reached the heavy doors there were another four armored guards waiting for us, with naked steel in their hands. I could sense their indecision as they saw Greuv helpless in Billy's grip.

"I have the Queen's Warrant," Ailsa said to the air in the hall. "I am leaving now, and my family are leaving with me. This never happened. I was never here. Do you understand?"

"Yes, ma'am," said a muffled voice from within one of the great helms, and then the doors were opened for us.

Billy waited until we were outside before he let go of Greuv. The magus fled back to his guards as Billy climbed up into the carriage with us. Then the lad turned back to stare into the hall, and he had a fierce look on his face.

"I liked Katrin," he said. "She was kind to me."

His fists clenched suddenly at his sides, and all the breath hissed out of him at once.

The learned magus Absolom Greuv fell to his knees and pitched forward in a tide of blood and slime as he vomited his own reeking intestines across the marble floor.

"How did you know?" Ailsa asked me as the carriage rattled hurriedly away from the house of magicians.

Billy was dozing on the bench beside Ailsa, his face pale from his exertions. She had a protective arm around his shoulders, holding him close to her.

"I didn't, not for sure, but I suspected and I took a gamble on it."

"A *very* large gamble," she said, and the sharpness in her tone was unmistakable.

"Aye," I allowed, "but I was right. It was something Old Kurt told me when I first took Billy to him for training, about how high magic and the cunning are different things. He told me the cunning was sorcery, about doing real things in the real world, and about how the magicians look down on that as beneath them. And they didn't go to war neither, saying war magic was beneath them too. When a man sneers at something and looks down on it, that means he doesn't understand it, and maybe that he fears it too. That got me thinking perhaps high magic is nothing but stars and mathematics and talking, and those things are no magic at all."

"Suppose you had been wrong? Suppose he *had* called up a demon against us—what then?"

"Aye, well," I said. "It was a gamble, like I said."

Ailsa looked as though she was wondering very seriously whether to stab me.

"The Magi have no magic," she murmured instead, thinking aloud now, "but the Skanian magicians very much have."

"That's true enough," I said. "I reckon they're cunning folk, like ours, only the Skanians don't call them that and they treat them a sight better. Now your magicians are trying to study the cunning and learn how to do what they can't, to fight the Skanians."

"To keep their grip on power and remain relevant, more likely," Ailsa said. "The house of magicians is a major political force in Dannsburg, and they won't surrender that power lightly."

"That's why Vogel wants rid of them," I said.

"He can't move against them, I told you that. That's not our problem, anyway. We need to return to Ellinburg as quickly as possible."

"Not until I've settled things with Lan Yetrov."

"Are you mad?" Ailsa demanded. "We need to return to Ellinburg with what we know and recruit as many cunning folk as can possibly be found. If the Skanians come in force and we can't rely on the magicians, then we shall need every single one of them."

"Aye, I know that, and I want to go home as much as you do, but I've unfinished business here. The last thing we need is that arsehole making trouble for us with Hauer. From what Anne said, things are bad enough at home as it is. I can't risk it, Ailsa."

Our time in Dannsburg was finally drawing to a close, but before we left the city I wanted blood.

And I was going to have it.

THIRTY-NINE

Ailsa urged me to make haste at least, but I didn't think that would be a problem.

As I had hoped, Iagin had put Leonov and his entire crew at my disposal. Of course that meant now Vogel knew what I was about, but I didn't think it mattered anymore. The death of the learned magus Absolom Greuv would have pleased him enormously, I was sure, so to my mind he owed me this one indulgence. If he had thought differently, then I was sure I would have heard about it, but no word came from the house of law, and that was good.

While Luka and Leonov made their plans, it seemed there was one more thing to do.

"I shall have to say good-bye to my parents before we leave," Ailsa told me. "I . . . I need to try again. I'm sorry, Tomas."

"No, I understand," I said. "But that will need to be soon. It won't take Leonov long to get things moving with Lan Yetrov, and once the thing is done I think we'll need to leave the city in something of a hurry."

Ailsa nodded. She was sitting in the drawing room, with Billy perched on the stool at her feet. He was holding her yarn for her as she worked at her needlecraft, the way her maid sometimes did. They looked like a real mother and son, and the sight pleased me greatly. Ailsa and I still might not have found the closeness I was beginning to wish for, but that at least was a good start. One step at a time, that was how it was done.

"I agree," she said. "I've arranged for us to visit them this afternoon."

"Can I come, Mama?" Billy asked her. "I've never had a grandma before."

"I'm sorry, my love," Ailsa said. "I don't think that would be a very good idea. Not this time, anyway."

Billy looked saddened by that, but Ailsa put down her needles and pulled him into a hug that made it right with him at once. I smiled and went to change my clothes in readiness for our afternoon visit.

Masha met our carriage that afternoon as he had done before, and this time the elderly steward's bow welcomed me as a family member rather than a stranger. I could only assume Sasura had spoken to him in advance. As before, we were shown into the grand old house, where a footman was waiting to usher Ailsa into the drawing room and her mother's presence. Another was holding open the door of Sasura's study for me, and it was plain how this was going to work. Ailsa took a deep breath and squeezed my hand unexpectedly, then turned away. I watched the drawing room door swing shut behind her.

Sasura was waiting for me in his study, and he waved the footman out. My father-by-law turned to me then, and his bearded face split open in a welcoming grin.

"Ah, Tomas, it is good to see you again, my son-by-law," he said.

"You too, Sasura," I said, and gave him a respectful bow.

"Enough of that." He laughed, and pulled me into a firm embrace. "Come come, let us drink brandy while Chandari and her mother once more raise the roof of my house."

"I hope it doesn't come to that again," I said, although in truth I suspected that it would.

I didn't know Madame Shapoor, but she had birthed a lioness. I couldn't think she was likely to be much different herself, and I thought the chances of either of them backing down were extremely thin.

Sasura poured drinks for us both and we settled into comfortable chairs. He raised his glass to me, and his eyes narrowed as he looked at me over the rim.

"So, Tomas," he said. "The thing that we discussed with the lady, here in my study. Will she get her wish?"

How would you like to be a very rich widow? That was what I had asked Lady Lan Yetrov. *You would be wealthy, and free, and with time you might finally heal.*

She had told us everything we wanted to know, my Sasura and me, and now Fat Luka and Leonov were using that information to put my plans into place.

"She will," I said.

Sasura chuckled into his brandy.

"I love you, my son-by-law," he said, "but I think you are a very dangerous man."

He had the right of that, I thought.

Sadly Ailsa fared no better with her mother than she had before, and our visit to her parents' house was a brief one. I bade Sasura a fond farewell, as I knew I wasn't likely to see him again.

Once the thing was done we would be leaving Dannsburg, and with all haste.

Two nights later I was in a very respectable inn close to the Lan Yetrov house, with Fat Luka, Oliver, and Emil from my crew. The inn belonged to Mr. Grachyev, as most public establishments in Dannsburg seemed to, and we met Leonov and six of his boys there in a private dining room.

"Iagin sends his regards," Leonov said as he gave my arm a friendly squeeze.

Iagin, I noted, not Mr. Grachyev. I wondered if perhaps this Leonov was better connected than he had let on before. It wasn't impossible that he knew who Iagin really worked for, I realized. In Dannsburg everyone seemed to have secrets and webs of hidden connections, and of course Grachyev was nothing but a figurehead. This was Iagin's crew in all but name, and Lord Vogel's in truth. That gave me pause, I have to allow. Did I even really still run the Pious Men, or was Ailsa working me like a puppet in the same way Iagin worked Grachyev?

No, I told myself, she wasn't that close to Pious Men business. She and Iagin had different ways of doing things, that was all.

"Thank you for coming," I said, and Leonov nodded.

"Wouldn't miss it," he said. He showed me a grin. "We've no more love for that prick than you have."

"Aye, good."

I wondered who he meant when he said *we*—his crew, or Iagin and the Queen's Men. It didn't matter. We were doing this; that was the important thing.

"Right, listen," Fat Luka said, and we gathered around him in the private room at the back of the inn. "I've bought off the captain of the household guard and his three top lads. The gates are unlocked and Lady willing so is the front door, and everyone we could get rid of for the night has been *got* rid of. There'll still be a few guards but not many, and two of the footmen belong to me now."

"What about the pitmaster?" I asked.

That was very important to me.

Luka gave me a look. He didn't like this part of my plan, I knew he didn't, but that was nothing I cared about. He didn't have to like it, so long as he did it. I had a point to make that night, and I was going to fucking make it whatever he or anyone else thought.

"Aye," he said at last. "That's done."

"And the wife's out of the way?"

"That I don't know," Luka admitted. "She's been told, but I never got no answer."

"Right," I said. "Well, be that as it may, then. Gentlemen, we have work to do."

Shortly after midnight, we left the inn.

It was only a short walk to the unlocked front gates of Lan Yetrov's estate. We stole across the darkened grounds as quietly as we could, until a patrolling guard rounded the corner of the house and saw us. He opened his mouth to raise the hue and cry, but Leonov threw back his cloak and raised a crossbow to his shoulder. The string thumped as he pressed the lever, and a bolt flowered in the man's throat, dropping him to the grass with a choking gurgle. That was a mighty fine shot, I had to allow, one that I doubted even Bloody Anne could have pulled off in the dark. Again, I wondered exactly who Leonov was.

Then we were across the front yard and Luka had his hand on the door of the house itself. It was unlocked, as he had hoped, and he eased it open with his other hand held up to tell the rest of us to keep quiet.

I heard him whisper something, and then the door was open and we were being ushered into the great hall by a nervous-looking footman. One of the two Luka had bought, then.

"M'lord is abed," he whispered. "He left m'lady's chamber perhaps an hour ago."

It pained me that she was still there, but that part had always been a gamble. From what I knew of Lan Yetrov, I hadn't been at all sure that she would have managed to get away from him even for one night. It seemed I had been right about that.

"Guards?" Luka asked.

The footman shrugged. "There's one outside," he said, although there wasn't anymore. "Two more in the house, but I don't know exactly where. Klim's at the pit, like you told us."

The other footman we had bought was out of the house then, like he was supposed to be. I turned to the crew and gave them a nod.

"This one stays with me," I said. "Kill anyone else you see except the wife and Lan Yetrov himself. That fucker is mine."

I waited in the hall with Fat Luka and the footman as Leonov and his men and mine spread out through the house. I wanted to tear Lan Yetrov out of his bed with my own hands, but that wasn't how this sort of thing should be done. This was about more than just the threat of what influence he might have with Hauer, I had to admit to myself. This wasn't even business now; this was personal.

He had threatened my wife, and I wasn't letting *that* pass.

I wouldn't lower myself to go after him in person, though, much as I wanted to. No, he would be brought to me.

He might be a lord, but I needed him to understand that I was a fucking prince.

I heard the thud of another crossbow from somewhere else in the house, and a brief clash of steel followed by a wet, choking death rattle. Leonov and his boys knew what they were about, and Emil and Oliver were both stout lads. Emil had been at Messia, and this sort of work was his bread and beer.

I turned to the footman and gave him a look.

"Take us to the pit," I said.

He nodded and led Fat Luka and me down a long corridor and into a room that overlooked the formal gardens behind the house. There was a guard dead on the floor in there, a crossbow bolt sticking out of his chest, but whoever had done it had already moved on. Leonov's boys knew what they were about, all right. The footman opened a door and we stepped outside onto a neatly raked gravel path between two clipped ornamental hedges.

The bear pit itself was in the informal garden behind the tortured lines of the formal part. Our footman opened a door for us and handed us off to his fellow, the one he had called Klim.

"You've done well," I said to him, and gave him another silver mark on top of whatever Luka had already paid him. "Now fuck off, and don't come back before dawn."

He took his coin and fled.

Klim led Fat Luka and me up the stair to Lan Yetrov's private box, the best seats in the house. He produced lamps and lit them, and I saw there was even a cupboard stocked with drinks. I sat down to wait with a glass of Lan Yetrov's brandy in my hand, and Fat Luka looming behind my chair. After a few minutes Klim coughed beside me.

"The Lady Lan Yetrov, sir," he announced.

I looked around in surprise.

She was standing at the entrance to the private box, a thickly embroidered velvet cloak wrapped around her over a silk and lace nightdress that must have cost more money than a working man saw in a month. She wore no paint or powder at that time of the night, and I saw that she had a split lip and a long yellow bruise on the side of her face below her fading black eye.

"My Lady Lan Yetrov," I said. "I hadn't thought to find you here tonight. You were supposed to be elsewhere."

"I tried," she said. Her voice sounded hoarse, and as she stepped into the light of the lamps I saw the livid red marks around her throat where he had obviously been choking her while he took his pleasure. "I said I needed to visit my sick mother, but he wouldn't hear of it. He told me my place is with him, always, bought and paid for. So tonight my place is with him. Bought, and paid for."

I looked at her, at the broken, vengeful hatred in her eyes, and I nodded.

"As you will," I said. "Will you sit with me?"

"I don't think I can," she said, and a small sob escaped her lips.

My hands curled into fists at my sides. If I had had any doubts about this, any thoughts at all that perhaps I had overreacted to Lan Yetrov's threats against Ailsa, then now they were gone. Fuck what he may or may not be able to make Hauer do; that was long since past being the point. Lan Yetrov was the sort of man I hate, pure and simple. I didn't know his wife and I didn't owe her anything, but that wasn't the point anymore.

He had hurt her, and now he wanted to hurt Ailsa.

I remembered Grieg, from my old crew, Grieg who had liked to hit whores. I remembered how I had made it right with Grieg, after he said his confession to me, and how my crew had made it right with him with their boots. You didn't hit women, not unless they were armed and they were trying to kill you. You didn't hit whores, and you most *definitely* didn't hit your own fucking wife. Anyone who needed that explained to him wasn't someone I knew how to talk to in a civil fashion.

Vengeance is mine, sayeth Our Lady, and I am Her priest.

"I see," I said.

We waited, Lady Lan Yetrov and Fat Luka and me, with Klim the footman watching the door. It didn't take long. Perhaps five minutes later one of the gates to the pit was hauled open and Leonov strode in. He was dragging Lord Lan Yetrov behind him, in his nightshirt and stumbling along on the end of a length of rope tied around his neck.

It was somewhere around the second hour of the morning by then. The moon was bright in a cloudless sky, but Leonov's men had brought more lanterns anyway. A great deal of lanterns. By the time they were done it was almost as bright as day in the circle of the pit. Leonov forced Lan Yetrov down onto his knees in front of me.

He stared up at me, squinting in the light and obviously trying to make sense of what he was seeing.

"Piety? Is that you?" he said. "Leonora? Leonora, what the *fuck* is going on?"

Lady Lan Yetrov took a breath as though to speak, then swallowed and said nothing.

I sat there in Lan Yetrov's own chair with a glass of his brandy in my hand, and I looked down at him, on his knees in the bear pit.

"Piety?" he asked again, and I could hear the mounting terror in his voice. "You're supposed to be a priest, man! What do you think you're doing?"

"I'm putting the fear of the gods back into religion," I said. "Do you fear the gods, Lan Yetrov? Do you fear Our Lady?"

"This is a fucking outrage!" he blustered, lurching back to his feet as anger overtook him. "You filthy oik! I'll bury you! I'll—"

Leonov hit him in the back of the head with the hilt of a shortsword to shut him up. He sagged to his knees again, swaying with the force of the blow.

"No," I said, "you won't. Is the pitmaster ready?"

Leonov nodded and waved at one of his lads, and a moment later a fellow in a leather apron came out of another gate. He had a big wooden bucket in his hand. He approached Lan Yetrov, and he dumped the contents of that bucket over his head, soaking him with it. I could smell it even from where I sat, a vile mixture of blood and fish and honey.

"No!" Lan Yetrov pleaded. "No, Piety, for the love of the gods, man!"

"It's only sport," I said. "You told me that yourself, once. It doesn't hurt anyone, does it? Do you remember telling me that, Lan Yetrov?"

"Please, I'm begging you!"

"I tell you what," I said, "I'll make a deal with you. I'll give you a chance, how does that sound?"

"Anything!"

Leonov had left the pit now, the gate safely shut behind him, and the pitmaster was about his business.

"We'll ask your wife," I said, and it seemed to me that the fool actually looked relieved.

Could one man truly be so fucking stupid, so blind? I turned to her, standing beside me because she was too torn and bloodied and in pain to be able to sit.

"Lady Lan Yetrov," I said to her, "your husband has insulted me and he has insulted my wife and threatened grievous and indecent harm to her person, but those things are nothing to what he has done to you. The judgment is yours."

Lady Lan Yetrov looked down at her husband, and a smile spread across her bruised face until her split lip opened up again and a trickle of blood ran over her teeth.

"Release the bear," she said.

"Leonora, *no*!" Lan Yetrov screamed.

The pitmaster hauled a rope and a gate rumbled open, and then the bear was in the pit with Lan Yetrov. It shambled forward on all fours, its head lifting as it took the scent.

"Don't you care for sport?" I asked him

"I take it back! I apologize, for everything!"

"It's far too late for that," I said, echoing his own words regarding the debtor Salan Anishin. "I want to make it very clear what happens to those who cross the Pious Men."

If he recognized his own words thrown back at him he gave no sign of it. He was too far gone to terror by then, I think.

"Piety, *please*!" he begged. "For the love of the gods, man!"

The bear snarled and charged, slaver running from its jaws.

"I only hold to one god, and Our Lady has no love," I said.

I turned away then, but I heard the wet splatter of blood hitting the wall of the pit.

Beside me, the Lady Leonora Lan Yetrov was smiling.

PART THREE

FORTY

I was standing on Cobbler's Row, looking at Katrin's shop while the keen autumn wind whipped my cloak around my legs. It had rained that morning, hard and bitter.

"Board it up," I said at last. "She won't be coming back."

"Yes, Mr. Piety," the carpenter muttered.

He was keeping his head down and staying out of my way, and that was wise of him.

"I'm sorry, Tomas," Anne said.

"Aye," I said. "So am I."

I turned away and spat into the gutter in disgust. This was where trusting orders from the Queen's Men had got me. Two innocent women had died, and in ways I didn't even want to think about. I remembered Katrin's face and how she had smiled with joy the first time she had stepped into her new little shop. She had been living and plying her trade of herbalist out of a single damp room in the west of the city when Fat Luka's spies had found her, barely scraping a living for herself. She had been overjoyed to take my coin when it was offered and move over to the Stink, but I dare say she hadn't wanted to die screaming for it.

Lady take the house of magicians, they'd get no one else from me and I didn't care *who* ordered it. Vogel could go fuck himself if he thought *that* was ever happening again.

Anne put her hand on my shoulder for a moment and I turned and looked at her. She seemed older somehow, weary in a way that she hadn't since the war. I had been away a third of the year and more, and all that time Anne had been boss of the Pious Men in my place. She had done well, I had to allow. Very well indeed, in fact, but she was a soldier at heart, not a businesswoman. All the same, the time she had spent running the Wheels for me had trained her well in how this was done. She had two of the Flower Girls with her now, flanking her like bodyguards.

Coming back to Ellinburg had been strange. After Dannsburg, the city seemed smaller than I remembered it, and I had almost forgotten how bad it smelled. It had been good to see Anne again, though, and Mika and Black Billy and Borys and Simple Sam and the others.

I had seen Jochan too, and I still wasn't quite sure *how* that had been.

As Anne had told me in her letter, Jochan had taken up religion. That was well and good in itself, I supposed, but Jochan had taken up religion in the way that Lady Lan Andronikov had taken up the poppy. He clung to it like a desperate man. From what I heard he spent most of his waking hours in the Great Temple now, and for all that Hanne was pleased that he had been allowed to see her and the baby, I had been able to tell from my brief visit to her that she was worried about him.

I turned my back as the hammering started, the carpenter and his lad boarding up the window and door of Katrin's deserted shop. The sign would come down later, and it would be like she had never been there. Like she had never lived at all.

I didn't need to see that.

She had been a spinster, with her parents dead and both her brothers lost in the war. There was no one left to mourn for Katrin, save for me.

Gerta the midwife had had a family, a husband and two young children of her own, and that was worse. I had been to see her man the day before, braving Sons territory under heavy guard to offer my condolences and enough silver to go some small way toward an apology for what had happened.

There had been an accident on the road, I had told him, an overturned wagon and nothing anyone could have done. It had been quick, I said, and she didn't suffer. I didn't think he had believed me, but it was better than him hearing the truth. All the same, silver couldn't return his wife to him nor give those children their mother back. This is harsh work we do, as I have written, and most of those who join us understand that. I thought that Gerta had understood it too, when she first took Fat Luka's coin and started passing him secrets from those streets, but that didn't mean that her family had.

"Lady's sake," I sighed, lifting my face into the wind to dry the tears in my eyes.

"Want a drink?" Anne asked me, and I nodded.

We walked back to the Tanner's Arms together, with Simple Sam and Borys and Anne's two hard-faced women around us. Going out without guards was impossible now, after the summer Bloody Anne had been through.

Black Billy gave me a nod as he held the door open for us, and I clapped him on the shoulder as I passed. He had a long scar on one cheek that hadn't been there before. The summer had been bloody indeed, from what I heard, and everyone had done their part.

Those were the times we lived in.

"How bad was it, truly?" I asked Anne, once we were alone in the back room of the Tanner's.

"Bad enough," she said. "We lost the Badger's Rest again, that stew we took off Convent Street. Borys did his best but it was just too far into Sons territory for us to hold it. Three of the hired lads died that night, but, thank the Lady, Borys made it out safe. He's took it hard, though. Hasn't really been himself since then. He's worried what happened to his girls, I reckon. Perhaps you might speak to him, when you get the chance."

I nodded and poured us both another brandy from the bottle on the long table that filled most of the room. Borys was a good man, older than most of the others, a big, thoughtful fellow who said little but who knew what he was doing. He had been good for the girls at the Rest too, I knew that much, fatherly and kind in a way that I thought none of them had ever experienced before. I would have been grieved by his death. That stew hadn't been important really, not compared to everything else, but a loss was a loss all the same.

"What else is gone?"

"I held the rest of it," Anne said, and I could hear a note of pride in her voice as she spoke. "We had hard fighting up in the docks but the Headhunters rallied when I called the knives, and Florence Cooper and her Flower Girls fought like devils to hold their streets. Your brother took the war back to the Northern Sons, and we gave as good as we fucking got on the western flank. He's a mad bugger, Tomas, but fuck can he fight. I wouldn't want to go against him, and I don't say that lightly of any man. He's had the battle shock bad, because of it, but Borys is good with him. Helps keep him calm, you understand what I mean? I put Sir Eland back in charge of the Golden Chains, too, and he's done well up there. Held it like a fortress, he has, like a real fucking knight would have done. After he repelled the first attack and left fifteen of the enemy dead, the Sons haven't dared even come near the place again. I might not be an officer, but you give me a position to hold and I'll fucking hold it, you can mark me on that."

I was impressed, truly.

"Well done," I said. "I mean it, Anne."

That pride in her voice was well earned, to my mind. She nodded her thanks and picked up her glass.

"Aye, well, it's not so different to the army when the blades come out."

That it wasn't, I had to allow.

Anne hadn't been an officer, no, but she was a fucking good sergeant and when it came right down to the close work I knew which I'd rather have beside me. All the same, I thought she might be moving past that now. Anne had made command decisions while I had been away, and good ones at that. She had it in her to truly lead men, I realized then, but that was a thought for another day.

"Where were the Guard in all this?"

"The fucking who?" Anne growled. "They might as well not exist, not on our streets anyway. They keep the peace around Trader's Row, of course, and by and large they keep it in the west of the city too. The Blue Bloods are all but wiped out now, and those as still live have bent the knee and joined the Sons. They didn't have any choice, in the end. Bloodhands captured their boss, and . . . and he fucking flayed him alive, Tomas. The Sons hanged what was left of him from the west gate, red and wet for all to see, and the Guard said nothing of it. The Sons fucking own the west side of Ellinburg now, all of it. The Guard had a hand in that, you mark me."

I didn't like that, not one little bit. I remembered back in the winter, how I had thought Hauer was doing all he could to keep the peace with the men he had. I had respected him for that, for all that I didn't care for him.

It seemed that had changed, as Anne had said in her second letter.

"Does it seem to you, Bloody Anne, that the Guard might be taking sides?"

"Aye, it fucking does," she said. "Hauer stands with the Northern Sons now, I'd bet gold on it."

I nodded. That was what I thought, too.

"Aye, well," I said. "We're the Pious Men; we don't need the fucking Guard to fight our battles for us."

I stood up then and clasped Anne's hand.

"Thank you," I said. "I couldn't want for a better second, or a better friend."

Anne cleared her throat and examined her boots, and I left the room before I embarrassed her any more. Bloody Anne wasn't one to boast, I knew that, and it was clear my praise was starting to make her feel uncomfortable.

I went to find Borys instead, and I sat at a table in the common room with him. The other lads made themselves scarce, obviously seeing that I wanted a word with him in private.

"About the Badger's Rest," I said. "I don't want you to feel bad about what happened, Borys."

"There were twenty of them," he said, "and just me and three lads. I tried, but . . . it was run or die, in the end. Perhaps I should have—"

"No," I interrupted him. "The place was lost, and you'd be no use to me dead. There's no shame in it."

Borys looked away then, and I thought there were tears in his eyes. He certainly *looked* ashamed, and that pained me. Borys was a good man.

He was worried about his girls, no doubt, as Anne had said.

"The lasses will be all right," I said. "They got by before, under the Sons. They can do it again, until we take the place back. For a little while they can."

Anything can be endured for a little while, every soldier knows that.

"Aye," Borys said, and wiped his eyes on the back of his sleeve. "You're right, boss."

"Tell me something," I said, as much to change the subject as anything else. "I'd value your opinion."

Borys was a thoughtful man, as I have written, and old enough to have learned how the world worked.

"What's that?"

"The Guard," I said. "Do you reckon the Sons have bought them?"

He looked at me for a long moment, and then he nodded.

"I do," he said. "I think they've been bought, and sooner or later I think they'll come for us."

I said as much to Ailsa that night, back in our house off Trader's Row while she sat by the fire in the drawing room and worked at her embroidery.

It was good to be home, in the house that had finally begun to feel like it was mine at last. Salo had sent a fast rider ahead of our journey home and made sure everything was prepared for us, of course, and when we had finally made it back to the city all our staff were waiting for us. I had been so pleased to see Cook's round, red face that I actually kissed her on the cheek, which made her turn redder than ever and set the housemaids to giggling.

It was good to be home with Ailsa, truth be told. We had made faster time on the return trip but still it had taken us several weeks, and without the pressures of Dannsburg hanging over us I liked to think we had grown somewhat closer during that time. She was good company when she wanted to be, and it had been a pleasant journey.

The house itself didn't seem half so big or so grand as it had done before I had been to Dannsburg, and I had to wonder how the last few months had changed me. I was an Ellinburg man through and through, and the place was certainly grander than a bricklayer's son had any right to ever expect to live in.

This was my home, I knew, not those great walled mansions of the capital. Of course, less than a year before I'd have sworn that the Stink was my home and I didn't belong in a place like this. It's strange how fast a man can grow accustomed to a thing.

"That's interesting," Ailsa said, in a tone that told me she wasn't at all surprised.

"Aye, it is," I said. "If Hauer's finally turned his fucking coat and sided with the Skanians then it's very interesting indeed. More to the point, what are you going to do about it?"

She showed me a thin smile then, the razor smile of the lioness.

"Wait," she said. "Hauer will hang himself eventually, given enough rope, and we have been passing great coils of that rope to him for quite some time now. Right now I am more concerned with finding those cunning folk, and with who betrayed our secrets to the house of magicians. Someone in your organization can't be trusted."

"Aye," I said, although it made my heart heavy to say it. I sighed. "I know that."

If they didn't know who the Queen's Man in Ellinburg was, then how the fuck did they know about us and Billy?

I remembered asking Ailsa that, back in Dannsburg. As she had told me then, there was only one way they *could* have known.

Someone has been talking.

There was a traitor in my crew, and I meant to find them.

I would find them, and then there would be harsh justice.

FORTY-ONE

The next day I called on my aunt. Jochan was still living with her and not with his wife and infant daughter, although he was no longer confined to the coal cellar. He spent time with Hanne and the baby, as I have written, but only under Enaid's supervision and only with two armed men attending her at all times.

My brother was better than he had been, but he wasn't healed in the mind and that was plain enough to see. Jochan had a faraway look about him now, like he was always staring into the distance even when he stood right in front of me. I didn't know what to make of that, but I doubted it was anything good.

He's a mad bugger, Tomas.

Anne had said that, and I thought she was right.

"What do you make of him?" I asked Aunt Enaid.

I was sitting in her parlor with her, and she had sent Jochan off to the kitchen with Borys and Stefan to find themselves beer and something to eat. I had brought Borys with me quite deliberately, in the hope that his reassuring presence and level head might do my brother some good. Jochan had gone with my lads meekly enough, I had to allow, but again I doubted that was a good thing. The Jochan I knew wasn't a meek man.

Enaid shook her head. "It's battle shock," she said. "The very bad kind."

"Aye, I know that. Will he get better?"

"Oh, how in the gods' names do I know?" she snapped at me. "He's forever at temple, maybe that will help."

I sighed, and looked into the fire. Kneeling in the temple doesn't make you godly any more than standing in a stable makes you a horse, to my mind. Still, if it helped, then who was I to judge? Hanne held to the Harvest Maiden, I knew that, but of course Jochan had been kneeling before the shrine of Our Lady. He was a soldier, and she was a goddess for soldiers and no mistake.

"Auntie, can I ask you something?" I said.

I still wasn't meeting her eye, and I could tell she thought that was queer.

"Of course you can, that's what your fat old aunt's here for."

I sighed, watching the flames dance in the grate.

Someone has been talking.

I should have gone to Bloody Anne with this, I knew I should. She was my second, not Enaid, but my aunt was real blood family and she was the one person I could absolutely guarantee wasn't the traitor. I knew Anne wasn't either, of course I did, but if I had put this before her then I would have made her feel small for not having seen it herself while she had been in charge, and I didn't want that. Anne was a soldier, as I have written, and politics and betrayals weren't her stock-in-trade. My aunt, on the other hand, knew how business worked in a way that Anne probably never would.

"There's someone in the crew I can't trust, and I don't know who it is," I said at last. "Someone has been talking, to the governor's men or to agents of the crown, and that talk made its way to Dannsburg ahead of us. Someone told them a secret I wanted kept, about Billy, and he could have died over it. I want to know who that was."

Enaid sucked her teeth for a moment and said nothing.

"Are you absolutely sure about that?" she asked eventually.

"Aye," I said. "I fucking am."

She nodded and spat into the fire.

"Well, there's men in your crew you barely know, even now. Men you made up to the table in a hurry, and I know why you had to do that and I'm not criticizing, but perhaps now it's time to take a good long look at them all. That arse-fucking pretend knight who Anne's got running the Chains, do you trust him?"

I sighed. I hadn't done for a long while, no, but last year he had changed that. Last year Sir Eland had brought me the head of a man who had tried to buy him. When I clapped him on the shoulder and thanked him for his loyalty he had almost wept with gratitude, to have finally found a place in the world where he belonged. For all his faults, I knew Sir Eland wasn't the traitor.

"Aye, I do," I said. "I didn't, but then he gave me a reason to and now I do."

"Well and good," my aunt said. "For what it's worth, so do I. So long as he keeps his fucking hands off my Brak he's all right by me."

I couldn't help but smile at that. Truth be told, Brak was probably too old to interest Sir Eland anyway. I very much doubted Brak was the one either; Enaid would have murdered him long before I got my hands on him. It wasn't Fat Luka, obviously. Since that night we had spent reliving our wild youths together in the Tanner's, and the time we had spent in Dannsburg, we had become firm friends. I knew I could trust Fat Luka with anything, and calm, faithful Borys too. Nor could I imagine it being Mika or Simple Sam or Black Billy. They were uncomplicated men and I understood them and what levers moved them, but I knew I had one man in my crew who I didn't understand at all. One who had spent more time with my Billy than I was comfortable with, at that.

"There's Cutter," I said.

"Aye, there is."

She said nothing more, just sat there looking at me while I thought it through in my own time. She was nobody's fool, wasn't Aunt Enaid, not by a long way she wasn't.

"What do you make of him?" I asked her.

She spat into the fire again and was silent for a long moment.

"It was Messia he came from, wasn't it?"

"Aye, what of it?"

"He was in Jochan's crew in the war, Tomas, but in case it escaped your fucking notice Messia was on the other side of the matter. How is it that he wasn't fighting for them?"

I had to allow I had wondered that as well.

"I don't know," I admitted.

"It seems to me," my aunt said, "that a man who turned his coat once might do it again."

I didn't like it, but I thought she might be right about that.

"Aye, perhaps," I said. "Perhaps I need to speak to Cutter."

"I think perhaps you fucking do."

I got up then and gave her a respectful nod. I tried to remember the last time I had hugged my aunt, and found that I couldn't. She had all but raised Jochan and me after I had killed Da, but of course she knew nothing of that and Lady willing she never would. I loved her, in my way, but she wasn't my ma.

"Thank you," I said, and turned to leave her parlor.

"Tomas," she said, and something in her voice held me.

"What?"

"You know the Rite of the Betrayer, don't you?"

I paused for a moment. That was an old thing, an old Ellinburg gang custom. I had never had cause to use it nor even to see it done, but I knew what it was. Every businessman in Ellinburg knew what that was.

"Aye," I said after a moment. "I know it."

"Then you'll know it's a fucking ugly thing," she said. "Be sure, Tomas. Be very sure indeed, before you call a Pious Man a traitor."

I wasn't sure, but I had suspicions enough to have Cutter brought to me in the back room of the Tanner's Arms the next day. I had never managed to work out which levers moved Cutter, but it seemed that perhaps someone else had. Hauer, maybe, or some agent of the house of magicians.

Bloody Anne was with me, and Luka and Billy the Boy and Jochan too. Anne and Luka were on my side of the matter, but I knew Jochan and Billy were Cutter's friends, or at least the closest thing he had to any. He wasn't proven guilty yet, so to my mind it was only right that he had people there who might speak for him. That was how I did justice.

Sam and Borys brought Cutter into the room, both of them looking stern and keeping quiet the way they were supposed to. Cutter had been dragged out of the house on Slaughterhouse Narrow just after dawn and he was in his shirtsleeves, and I had seen to it that his knives had been taken off him. I looked at the confusion on his lean, bearded face and I wondered if I had the right of this after all. Cutter could act as well as any mummer, though, I knew that, and I wasn't going to let an expression fool me.

"Cutter," I said from my seat at the head of the table. "I've some questions for you. You'll answer them, if you're wise."

The man just shrugged, and I saw him shoot Jochan a look. My brother was seated at my left hand, opposite Anne, and he stared at his man with that way he had about him now, as though he was looking a thousand yards behind where Cutter stood.

"Do what my brother says," he said.

"What is it?" Cutter asked, and there was an edge to his voice as he looked at Jochan that I didn't know how to read.

"Someone," I said, "told some people about young Billy. Someone passed information outside our family. Someone nearly got Billy killed, in Dannsburg. Someone can't be *fucking* trusted."

"Not me," Cutter said, and he shook his head to make his point. Again, his eyes were on Jochan as he spoke.

"Who are you, really?" I demanded, and that brought his attention around to me at last. "A soldier who should have been on the other fucking side and wasn't. A professional murderer. Why should I—"

"It wasn't him," Jochan interrupted me.

I turned and looked at my brother then. He was still staring, but I knew he was aware of what was happening in that room and of what *would* happen if this went against Cutter.

"And how's that, then?" I asked him.

"I know Cutter," he said, and he cleared his throat. "It wasn't him."

"Well, I *don't* fucking know him, and I think it was."

"You're wrong, Papa," Billy said.

The lad put his hand on my arm then in a way that he had never done before, and when I looked at him I saw the utter conviction on his face. This was Billy the Seer talking, I realized. Billy who was never wrong when he knew a thing. All the same, I wasn't sure that was enough. There was always a first time for being wrong.

"Can I say something?" Cutter asked, his voice quiet but carrying in the sudden hush.

"Aye," I said.

"I'll talk," he said. He paused to swallow, but I didn't think it was with fear. "I'll say my confession to you, Father, although I never did before. But only to you."

I frowned. Cutter wasn't a religious man, so far as I knew, and of all my crew he was the only one, save Billy the Boy, who had never knelt to me to say confession. Cutter was death walking, and now that he was accused he wanted to speak to me alone. Even unarmed as he was, I thought that might not be wise.

"Not alone," I said. "You and me and one other of those here, but I'll let you choose who."

That seemed fair, to my mind, and apparently Cutter agreed about that.

"Jochan, then," he said.

I nodded.

"Aye, as you will."

I sent the others out of the room, even Bloody Anne, leaving just me and Jochan and Cutter in the back room of the Tanner's Arms. There was something in my brother's face then that I wasn't sure I understood.

Cutter took a step forward and knelt before me, which was something he had never done before.

"I wish to confess, Father," he said, and now his voice was very quiet.

I looked down at Cutter, kneeling on the floor at my feet. Perhaps now I might finally learn what I needed to know about him.

Everyone has a lever that moves them, and everyone has their weakness, too. If you can't find the lever to move someone, then you find the weakness, and you take hold of it, and you squeeze until they break.

It was time to find Cutter's weakness.

"Speak, in Our Lady's name," I said.

FORTY-TWO

Cutter hung his head, and then his shoulders seemed to slump as though under a great weight. Beside me, Jochan cleared his throat again, but he said nothing.

"I'll say my confession to you," Cutter said softly. "I never have before, for what fucking priest could ever understand me? But to you I will, for you hold to another god than the ones I know, and you are more devil than priest. We ain't so very different, you and me."

The gods of Messia were certainly different to those I knew: cruel gods who demanded cruel sacrifices. They had told us that in the army when we were marching there to lay siege to the city. Messia was an evil place, we were told, where dark things were done in the names of their dark gods. That was what they had told us in the army, simple phrases for simple men. I wondered what the soldiers of Messia had been told about us, and whether it had been any more true.

"Is that so?"

Cutter looked up at me then, and I saw the corner of his mouth turn up in a rare smile under the thickness of his beard.

"Aye, it is," and there was a weary resignation in his voice now as he spoke. "I was born in Messia, and you're wondering how it is that I weren't in *their* army. I know that. Sooner or later I knew you'd work your way around to that. Your brother knows why, but he ain't never said."

"That I haven't," Jochan said quietly. "I promised you back then that I never would, and I haven't."

"Aye," Cutter said, and he sighed. "Well, here it is, Father. I doubt you ever saw Messia before the war, did you? Well, it weren't like it is here, but it weren't like they told you in the army, neither. We have different gods in Messia and they're no darker than any others, but the priests ran the city with their own laws and their own justice, and that justice was dark enough for any man. You have to follow the gods in Messia, or you find yourself swinging on the end of a rope. You have to be *seen* to follow the gods, and for a long time I did, but I ain't what you might call godly. Not in the way they'd have it, anyway. Do you understand me?"

In Dannsburg, you show respect to the crown. You show your love for the queen publicly and loudly and often.

I remembered Ailsa's father telling me that, and I wondered if there was so much difference between us after all.

"I worked for the priesthood since I was a lad. It was them that had me trained, them as taught me how to kill. That was what I did. I killed people for the priests. People they said needed killing, and I never questioned them on that. Sacred Blades they called us, those who did that, and I never questioned them. Right up to the day when I had to.

"I weren't in the army because I was in prison. I was in a special sort of prison, the sort where they don't dare conscript the inmates on account of we was too dangerous to be trusted with weapons. I was three weeks away from execution when the walls came down, just waiting my turn to hang. When the city fell and your lot was sacking it, your brother's crew broke open that prison to see what was inside. Well, *I* was inside, me and the other men they called too mad to be let out even to fight."

Cutter didn't seem mad, to my mind. Cold and ruthless, aye, but he was sane enough.

"Why?"

"I was in there for heresy and murder," he said. "They'd wanted me to kill a man I was close with, a man I maybe even loved, and I said fuck that. I said fuck that and they threatened me so I killed a priest and burned a temple, and in Messia that's enough to have you called mad and be treated as such before you swing. My man still died, but not by my hand."

He went quiet then, as though he couldn't quite find his words, and there was a silence until my brother spoke for him.

"When we got down there, into the deep cells, there was only Cutter," he said. "Cutter, and corpses. It seemed the guards had unlocked the cells before they ran away, and I don't know why. Maybe they thought the prisoners would do for us, but Cutter had already seen that that wouldn't happen. He had a . . . what was it now? I can't remember."

"A bit of glass," Cutter said. "A little bit of glass that I'd been hoarding in my cell against the day that I'd need it. I'd been planning to do myself with it, truth be told, before they could hang me. Never quite got around to it. But when those cell doors opened and I heard the others moving about outside I knew I couldn't let them be free, and I knew what needed to be done. Here's where I held it."

He held out his right hand to me and opened it to show me a thick, ridged scar that ran all the length of his palm.

"Some of the men in those cells had raped children," he went on, "and some of them had fucking eaten people, and I was supposed to be as mad as them. I done those cunts so they couldn't hurt no one else, Father, and when your brother came looking I knelt down for him and then I told him what I'd done."

"And I said good fucking work," Jochan said. "I said that, and I brought him out of those filthy fucking cells where they put the human animals, because Cutter ain't no animal. He'd killed folk, aye, but then who hasn't? Who *fucking* hasn't? He's no baby-eater, Tomas, and he's no traitor either. I . . . I fucking swear he ain't."

My brother was crying, I realized, and then he reached out his hand and Cutter rested his bearded cheek against it.

"I swore to love Jochan forever, for that," Cutter whispered, "and I meant it. I'm no traitor."

You can't tell me you never did, in the tents at least.

Major Bakrylov had said that to me, back in Dannsburg. I never did, but it seemed to me then that perhaps my brother had. That was his business, his and Cutter's, but it made me think of something else.

"And you never touched Billy?" I asked him.

"I like *men*, not boys," Cutter said. "I like . . . I *love* your brother."

He swallowed and looked away.

"Don't speak of that," Jochan whispered. "It's enough, Yoseph. He believes you."

I nodded slowly. I did, at that.

Cutter put his head in Jochan's lap, and he wept.

I got quietly to my feet and left the room, and walked out into the corridor where Bloody Anne and Fat Luka were waiting for me.

"It wasn't Cutter," I said.

I put it about that over the next few days I would have every member of the Pious Men and every vassal gang under my control brought before Billy the Boy and myself, and questioned. Even Bloody Anne, even the Headhunters and the Flower Girls and the hired men. Even my aunt.

Everyone.

These were superstitious men and women, simple soldiers in the main, and they all knew what Billy the Boy could do. Or at least they thought they did, and that was good.

Of course Billy didn't know who the traitor was, any more than I did. He didn't know, and he wouldn't unless Our Lady or whatever the fuck it was that spoke to him or through him chose to tell him, but the others didn't know that.

It was enough.

Bloody Anne went first, to show the others there was nothing to fear in it, and Florence Cooper was right behind her. Those two I knew I could trust, of course, and Sir Eland and Fat Luka and Black Billy who went after them, too. Simple Sam went next, then the Headhunters went one after another, and then Florence's crew of hard-faced women. After that was Stefan and then Emil, and then it was to be Borys.

When Borys's turn came he was nowhere to be found, and I knew my trap had worked.

Borys had run rather than face Billy's questions, and that said he was guilty as loud as if he had been shouting it in the street.

I couldn't fucking believe it. Steady, faithful Borys. Borys with his reassuring presence and his level head, who could calm even my mad brother. Borys who had been like a father to those women at the Badger's Rest. *Borys* had been the one to betray me?

I felt like I'd been punched in the fucking guts.

No one knew where he had gone, but that didn't worry me any.

I sent Cutter after him.

Hunting men was Cutter's bread and beer. He had been made to own to painful truths that I thought he would rather have kept buried, because of what Borys had done. Cutter would bring Borys to me wherever he had gone, I had absolutely no doubts about that at all.

"And then what will you do?" Ailsa asked me that evening, after I was done telling her the lay of things.

I poured myself a brandy from the bottle on the side table in our drawing room and turned to face her.

"I'll make a fucking example of him," I said. "No one betrays the Pious Men and gets away with it, and I intend to make that very clear indeed. There's a thing in Ellinburg called the Rite of the Betrayer. It's an old gang thing, an ugly thing. I've never had to do it before, but I know how it's done."

Ailsa looked up from her needlework then, and she showed me her razor smile.

"Oh, so do I."

FORTY-THREE

However angry I was about Borys, there was still work that needed doing. I wanted the Badger's Rest back, for one thing, that stew up near the docks. We needed to find some more cunning folk too, and I had Fat Luka working on that already, which left me free to think on the other matter. Now that I knew that Borys had been the one to betray me to the magicians, it seemed somewhat suspicious that his had been the only business Anne had lost in the summer, and even more so that he had been the only survivor of the fighting. If Borys had taken a bribe from one man, then to my mind it was likely he'd taken another from someone else, and sold that place back to Bloodhands and the Northern Sons. Faithful Borys, who I had thought was like a father to those women, had sold them back to a man who liked to skin people alive, and he'd had the sheer fucking balls to pretend to be ashamed afterward.

Cunt.

I wasn't going to let that pass, or leave those poor women at the mercy of Bloodhands and his flaying knife. I knew *exactly* how to make that right.

"The Sons treat their scrubs like dirt," I told Florence Cooper that evening, in the common room of the Tanner's Arms after I'd had a runner go fetch her down from the Wheels. "They ain't licensed and none of them wear the bawd's knot there, so they think they've nowhere else to go but the street. Might be they're right about that, but that's no excuse.

I don't hold with beating whores, but the last man the Sons had running that place very much did. I doubt the new one's any better."

I could see the hard anger in Florence's eyes. She had been a whore once, I knew, her and most of her Flower Girls with her, and I doubted she had ever worn the knot either. She knew all too well what life must be like for those women, and I knew what she thought of that.

Once you learn the levers that move a person, you can make them do anything.

"I'll run that place for you and I'll fucking hold it this time, if you let me and my crew take it back," Florence said.

That was what I had wanted to hear.

"Aye," I said. "I'll take a quarter, as before, but if you can take the Badger's Rest back then it's yours to run."

Florence gave me a short nod.

"Oh, I'll take it back, you mark me, Tomas Piety," she said, and that was done.

She went on her way after that, and I looked out of the window and saw that it was already dark outside. Simple Sam was looming in front of my table as was his habit, his thick arms crossed in front of him in a way that said I wasn't to be disturbed. That didn't apply to Anne, of course, and she came and joined me a moment later with a glass of brandy in each hand.

"What did she say?"

"Aye, she'll do it," I said. "Keen to, by the sounds of her. I thought she might be."

"It'll be bloody," she warned. "Florence has no love for whoremongers, and if any of those women have so much as a bruise on them she's like to have whoever's in charge burned alive."

"Well and good." I took the offered drink and sipped it while she sat. "He'll be no one we know, so fuck him."

"I'm sorry," Anne said, after a moment. "I just didn't see it. He seemed so . . . solid, I suppose. Borys was always the reliable one, the calm one, you understand what I mean? When we burned the Stables, he was the one who brought those boys out and saw them safely back here. He was . . . he seemed a good man."

I nodded. I knew exactly what she meant.

"Aye, he did," I said. "He wouldn't have been my guess either, and I wouldn't have seen it any more than you did. I don't think ill of you for it, Anne."

"Appreciate it," she said, and gave me a short nod.

"I thought I'd stop by the Golden Chains on my way home, see the lay of things," I said. "Want to come?"

Anne had no love for Sir Eland, I knew that, but to my mind that was something she needed to get past. I wanted real peace between them, not just the uneasy truce they seemed to have brokered over the summer. Besides, as gambling house and poppy den both, the Chains was one of my most profitable businesses. I didn't care for the poppy trade so I seldom went there, but after being away for so long I knew it wouldn't hurt to look in and see that all was well.

"Aye, I can do that," she said after a moment. "Give me a minute to get my good coat."

She went upstairs to the room above the Tanner's where she lived, and I sat and finished my brandy while I waited for her to come back. After a moment I reached out and tapped Sam on the arm.

"We're going to the Chains, me and Anne," I told him. "You're coming, you and a couple of the new lads. Go pick some."

Sam nodded, looking both pleased and surprised to be given a decision to make all by himself. He was a slow lad, but he knew fighting, and he knew who was any good at it and who wasn't. He'd pick well, I was sure.

Truth be told, I was starting to get low on men. Actual Pious Men, that is; I had more than enough hired lads, but that wasn't the same thing. The almost constant violence of the last two years had worn my original crew of twenty down to barely half their number, and now I had lost Borys as well and I was no longer sure how much I could count on my brother, either. I wondered whether it might be time to think about making Emil up to the table, but that only got me thinking about Desh and what had happened to him, and I didn't want that.

Perhaps I should move some lads about, I thought. I still had Black Billy on the door of the Tanner's, for one thing, and that was a job any number of the hired men could have done. It was *Billy's* job, though, and I knew he liked it and took it seriously. I wondered how he'd take being replaced, but I supposed that would depend on what I gave him instead. He was a good man, was Billy, and I couldn't help but think he was wasted where he was.

I was still turning that over in my head when Bloody Anne came back downstairs wearing a magnificent black brocade coat and her daggers at her belt. Sam had rounded up three men as guards for us by then, and the six of us headed out into the late-autumn night together.

Sam took the point with two of his men flanking Anne and me and the other as rearguard, just like a colonel's personal bodyguard in the army. It seemed like it came second nature to everyone, and I wondered just how bad the fighting had really been over the summer months. It wouldn't have surprised me at all to discover that Anne had been understating what she had done to hold my streets for me. Bloody Anne wasn't one to boast, I knew that, and the summer had been hard in Ellinburg.

I didn't know it then, but the winter to come would be harder still.

There were five lads on the door at the Chains, the way it was supposed to be, and all of them were mailed and well armed under their cloaks. We were treated like royalty there, as well we should be. I owned the Golden Chains, and to my mind that meant I owned everyone in it.

Once we were inside I looked around the main gaming room, at the busy tables and the richly dressed customers, at the liveried footmen and the thickness of poppy smoke in the air, and I liked what I saw. There was someone else there too, a lad of maybe seventeen years with longish fair hair and overly tight britches.

Sir Eland liked lads, everyone knew that, but he didn't seem to like any one lad in particular and he got bored easily. I hadn't seen this one before, but that didn't mean much.

"Is he treating you all right?" I heard Anne ask him as I walked past.

The lad shrugged.

"He's rich," he said. "Anyway, he's a knight."

He's no fucking knight, I thought, but that wasn't anything that needed saying out loud.

I left Anne to play cards and went and found Sir Eland. He was lounging at the back of the main gaming hall in a splendid knightly doublet embroidered with his false arms, the three towers and griffin rampant that he claimed were his own.

"Evening, boss," he said, straightening up when he saw me. "Everything good?"

"Aye," I said, blinking against the cloying sweetness of poppy smoke. "Just looking in."

I seldom went to the Chains, and I thought Eland was surprised to see me there. I hadn't sent word ahead so he hadn't known I was coming, but all the same I was pleased with how I found the place. It was busy, and the card tables were mostly full even relatively early in the night as it was. Security was in good order, too, and that was the most important thing. Sir Eland might have been a false knight, but he ran a good operation, I had to allow, and he gave the place a bit of fake class.

"Right you are," he said, and waved to a footman who hurried over with a brandy for me.

I sipped it and looked at Eland's doublet over the rim of the glass.

"Does it never bother you," I said, "that one day someone might recognize those arms you stole and think you're someone else?"

Sir Eland just smirked at that. "I never stole these arms," he said. "I might be a false knight, but I'm not a fool. I fucking made them up, and I paid some village woman to paint them on my shield all those years ago. Then I stole a warhorse and managed to change regiments in the confusion at Messia. I started calling myself Sir, and no one ever questioned it until I ended up in your crew."

That surprised me. I hadn't thought Sir Eland to be that imaginative, truth be told.

"Aye, well, it worked well enough," I said. "Keep it up. Having a knight on my crew is good for business."

Eland nodded, but he put his hand on my arm before I could turn away.

"Can I ask you something?" he said.

"Aye, if you want."

"Did you think it was me? The traitor, I mean."

I took another drink while I put my answer together in my head.

"No," I said at last. "No, Eland, I didn't. A year or so ago I would have done and I won't lie to you about that, but not now."

"What changed?"

"I never trusted you in the war, and I never trusted you all the way back to Ellinburg, nor in the days that followed, and that was because you never gave me a reason to. I don't trust folk first and wait to be disappointed; that's a fool's errand and no mistake. I trust no fucker who hasn't earned it, do you understand?"

"Aye," he said.

"Well, that's how it was," I said, "and that's how it would have stayed if you'd never given me a reason to, but you did. You showed me the sort of man you really are. First when you brought me the head of the cunt who tried to buy you, and again when you held Chandler's Narrow alone against the attack, when you nearly died to protect those women. No, Eland, I didn't think it was you."

"Thank you," he said, and I could see in his face that he meant it.

That meant a lot to him, I could tell, to finally hear me say it. Trust, that was the lever that moved Sir Eland the false knight.

FORTY-FOUR

I was thinking it was time to be on my way home when the back door of the gaming room opened, the one that led out to the shithouse in the courtyard, and Captain Rogan of the Guard walked in. He strolled straight back to the table he had been playing at before nature had called him away, and he never looked around him as he went. I knew he hadn't seen me standing at the back of the room with Sir Eland, and that was good.

I crossed the room and put a hand on Rogan's broad, heavy shoulder.

"Good evening, Captain," I said, letting my voice go flat in that way that I knew he recognized.

He didn't startle, although he hadn't known I was there until I touched him, and I give him credit for that.

"Piety," he said, turning slowly to look up at me standing behind his chair. "It's rare to see you in here."

"I fucking own the place," I said, as much for the benefit of the other players at the table as anything else. Rogan knew that, of course, but I didn't know all of his company and I thought some were guests from outside the city and perhaps they didn't. "I come in when I please."

"Aye, course you do," he said.

Captain Rogan and me had something of what you might call a complicated relationship. He worked for Governor Hauer, and he didn't like me and he didn't trust me, but he liked gambling and he liked the Golden Chains. He liked gambling very much indeed, and that was the lever that moved him. He also took a good deal off me in taxes, to keep the eyes of his guardsmen away from Pious Men business.

"I want a little word," I said.

Rogan tossed his cards facedown on the table and got up, and I led him to a quiet corner of the room.

"What's this about?" he asked, wiping a meaty hand across his lips in a way that gave away his nerves.

Rogan was a hard man and a bully, but in here without his uniformed thugs around him he was just another customer in a place where I could easily call on fifteen blades if I needed them. He knew that.

"Tell me about the summer, Captain," I said. "Tell me where the Guard were and who they were fighting. More to the point, tell me why they weren't where they fucking *weren't.*"

I could still remember what Bloody Anne had told me, about how the City Guard had seemed to be concentrating their efforts to keep the peace in the west of the city where the Northern Sons ran the streets, and how they had let the Stink and the Wheels fend for themselves while they were doing it.

They might as well not exist, not on our streets anyway, Anne had told me. *The Blue Bloods are all but wiped out now, and those as still live have bent the knee and joined the Sons . . . The Guard had a hand in that, you mark me.*

I wanted to hear what Captain Rogan had to say about that.

"I have my orders, and I follow them," Rogan said, but I could see something in his face that told me he wasn't entirely comfortable with what those orders had been.

He didn't like me, no, but then I dare say he didn't like Bloodhands either. The thing that has to be understood about Captain Rogan is that he was a soldier, before all else. Oh, he took bribes and he had his vices, and gambling was chief among them, but I didn't think he was truly a corrupt man. Rogan had fought in the last war, in Aunt Enaid's war, and like so many old soldiers he still carried a piece of that war around with him in his heart. It was buried deep perhaps, aye, but it was there.

I was aware of Bloody Anne coming up behind Rogan with her hands on the hilts of her daggers, her card game abandoned and one eyebrow raised to ask the obvious question. If I had nodded, I knew Anne would have killed him right there in front of everyone and fuck what anyone thought of it.

Bloody Anne was the best second a man could have asked for and no mistake, but I knew Captain Rogan still had his honor, somewhere deep inside him.

"Aye, you were following orders," I said, and I put a hand on his shoulder and leaned close enough to be sure no one else could hear us even as I held up the other to tell Anne to be still. "I understand that, Captain, but let me put something to you. If you ever get orders you don't feel you can follow with a clear heart, you come and talk to me about them before you do something you might regret. Will you promise me that?"

"I . . . I'll think on it," Rogan said, and I supposed I couldn't ask for more than that.

Two days later a runner came to the Tanner's to tell me that Cutter was back at Slaughterhouse Narrow and that he had something for me. My brother and I went up there together with a few of the lads as a bodyguard, but we left the hired men out in the narrow and only the two of us went inside.

I hadn't seen the inside of the boardinghouse on Slaughterhouse Narrow for a long time, and I was surprised by how clean and tidy it was. Cutter obviously ran a tight ship, I was pleased to see. He was waiting for us in the main room, with a look of grim satisfaction on his bearded face.

"I hear you've brought me a gift, Cutter," I said.

"Told you I would," Cutter said. "No one gets away from me. No one."

I cleared my throat. Cutter was enough to put the fear into anyone, as I have written, and I've no shame in admitting that included me.

"Aye, well done," I said.

"Where is he, then?" Jochan asked, and there was an eagerness in his voice that I didn't like.

I looked at my brother, and he was staring at Cutter in that way he had about him now, like he was always looking into the distance. His hand was on his axe and his fingers were moving like he was stroking it, like he couldn't wait to use it on someone. I wondered if he even knew he was doing it.

"In the cellar," Cutter said. "I'll show you."

He led us through a door and down a flight of narrow stone steps, into a damp space lit by a single lamp. There were things down there that surprised me and a thing that didn't.

He had targets set up along the wall for practicing the throwing of knives and hatchets, and big canvas bags stuffed with wool and sawdust for punching, like we'd had in the army. There were other things, too, things that I couldn't put names to. I saw frames made of wood, with blades sticking out of them at strange angles and padded leather places that I could only guess you were supposed to hit. There were big jars full of sand, canvas sacks stuffed so full of iron filings they were like rock, even a couple of small cannonballs. This was where he had been training Billy, I assumed, and that was all well and good even if I didn't know what half of it was for. It was the other thing that interested me, the thing in the corner.

The cage.

It was only about two feet high and maybe four square, made of narrowly spaced iron bars and bolted securely to the wall and the floor. It was the sort of cage that folk who went in for cockfighting kept their prize birds in, and I could only assume that had been what the previous owner of the house had used it for, but Cutter had found a new use for it.

I walked over to that corner and looked down through the bars to where Borys was huddled on the floor in the confined space, naked and bleeding from a number of cuts and abrasions. He'd had more than one vicious beating, by the looks of him, and that was good.

"He was out west," Cutter said, "trying to hide in one of the mining camps. He didn't hide well enough, though. No one ever does."

I nodded slowly. That didn't surprise me any. I didn't think many men had ever escaped Cutter, not once he'd set his eye on them. Whatever else he might be, Cutter was a trained, professional murderer. A Sacred Blade, he had called himself, and I knew he took pride in his work and I respected that.

"Well done," I said.

Jochan growled and took out his axe.

"I'll do it," he said. "In Our Lady's name."

I held up a hand to tell him to be still.

"Tonight," I said. "Not now."

I leaned over the cage and I looked down at Borys, and I spat on him.

That evening all the Pious Men gathered in the back room of the Tanner's Arms, and took their places around the table in uneasy silence. I could have cut that silence with a knife as they filed into the room one after another, all wearing the fine coats they had bought for themselves with Pious Men money.

It's a thing I've noticed about people, and that I've written of before; no one wanted to live near a tannery, no, but they might well enjoy the money from one. In the same way, my Pious Men liked the money they made from the sort of business we did, but perhaps they didn't always want to face the harsh realities of what that meant.

Well, tonight they would fucking face it.

I had made Billy the Boy stay back at the house with Ailsa. He was part a Pious Man and he part wasn't, but either way he was too young to take part in this. I knew he had probably seen worse in the war but that wasn't the point, and there Ailsa and me had been of one mind whether he liked it or not. He could sulk about it all he wanted but he wasn't there, and that was good.

Everyone else was, though. I had the Flower Girls and the Headhunters minding the businesses just for that one night so all the Pious Men could be there at the table together. The Tanner's was closed to the public that night, and so was the Chains.

That was how important this was.

Some of them, Fat Luka and Jochan, who were Ellinburg born, I suspected they already knew what they were going to see before they came into that room.

I knew fucking well that my aunt did.

She had known *exactly* what she was going to see, and there I didn't disappoint her. I had even included Cookpot, just for this one night, and he was an Ellinburg man too. He wasn't a Pious Man anymore and I knew he didn't want to be there, but he had known Borys before and he needed to stand witness and do his part, the same as the others.

Some, like Mika and Sir Eland, well, they could think for themselves and if they hadn't known quite how it was going to be, then I was sure they had formed a fair idea in their minds of what to expect.

Simple Sam and Hari and Will the Wencher, Black Billy and Brak and Stefan, they had just stared in shocked silence, and had said nothing.

Borys was nailed to the table.

Earlier in the day I'd had Bloody Anne and Cutter bring him down to the Tanner's from the house on Slaughterhouse Narrow in the back of a cart, gagged and bound hand and foot inside a big sack. They had held him down, and I had personally hammered a great roofing spike through each of his wrists and ankles and deep into the wood below. He was pinned there like an exotic butterfly in a gentleman's collection of curiosities. By the time the Pious Men gathered, he had been there for some hours.

All the Pious Men were seated now, around that table that was dark with Borys's blood and piss, and him mewling pitifully between them like a wounded animal caught in a trap.

In front of each place I had set a dagger.

No one spoke until I had taken my seat at the head of the table, the Weeping Women hanging heavy at my sides.

"We're a family," I said, and I looked around the table as I spoke and I met each of their eyes in turn, and no one looked away. "Each of us here, man or woman, is a Pious Man. That's a bond between us, a bond either of blood or of trust and comradeship forged in the fires of war. That's not a thing to be taken lightly. We're family, and we're comrades, and we stand by each other until the very last breath. That's what it means, to be a Pious Man. That's how this fucking *works*. Does anyone disagree on that?"

Again I looked around the table, and no one spoke. Borys made some noise into the ball of rags that Cutter had stuffed into his mouth and tied tight with a length of cord to keep him quiet, but no one paid him any mind. It was clear to everyone there gathered which way the wind was blowing that night. No one challenged me, and that was wise of them.

"Well and good," I said, after the silence had stretched almost to the breaking point. "Those of you who are from Ellinburg will have heard of the Rite of the Betrayer, and those who ain't ought to have got the general idea by now, but if anyone's feeling slow tonight this is how it is.

Borys betrayed us. Borys sold Billy the Boy to people you don't even want to fucking think about, and he sold our stew on Convent Street back to the Sons, too. Borys is a traitor. Borys took your trust, and the comradeship you forged together in the war, and he pissed on it. That's what you mean to him. *Nothing*. Nothing but something to be pissed on, for silver. For that, for silver, we pay him back in steel. That's how this is done, in Ellinburg."

Anne went first, as my second. She stood and took up the dagger I had set before her place and she rammed it into Borys's forearm just below the elbow, pinning him tighter to the wood. He screamed through his gag, but he'd get no mercy that night. Not after what he had done and the words I had said he wouldn't.

Jochan went next and he took Borys's left calf, striking with such ferocity that he shattered the shinbone. After him went my aunt, and there was no hint of pity in her single eye as she struck. Then each man around the table took his turn, each avoiding the killing places. Even Cookpot took his turn, for all that I knew he didn't want to, and I could see the deeply buried battle shock in his eyes as he rammed his blade through Borys's left biceps with a snarl of rage.

The final blow was to be mine, and for that he would have to wait.

When it was done, Borys barely looked human. He had fourteen daggers in him by then, all told, each one pinning him hard to the long table beneath him and blood flowing in rivers, but none of them in a killing place. Not quite.

I stood over him, and in place of a dagger I drew Remorse from her sheath.

"This is Remorse, Borys," I told him. "On my other hip is Mercy. One might earn you the other, if you're lucky. Tell me what you have to say."

I nodded at Cutter then, and he used one of his evil little knives to slice the cord that held Borys's gag. Borys choked and retched and spat the wad of sodden, rancid cloth out of his mouth at last.

"You're worse than them," he croaked, working his mouth to try to get enough spit into it to speak clearly. The pain must have been indescribable by then, but still somehow he managed to form words. "The governor's corrupt and the magicians are scheming, but you're fucking *worse*. The . . .

dear gods . . . lesser of two evils, they told me, and I hold to that. Since we came back from the war you've . . . killed more men than the plague did. You're the . . . Lady save me . . . worst of all the choices, Piety. You're a fucking devil."

"If you had concerns, you should have laid them before me," I said. "You went against the family. You betrayed us all."

Borys was dying, I could see that, but he managed one last defiance. "Fuck . . . your family!"

Remorse came down so hard she split his fucking head in two.

FORTY-FIVE

It was three months since I had said the Rite of the Betrayer over Borys, and a harsh winter was then upon us.

There was no invitation to the governor's midwinter ball that year, and it seemed society in Ellinburg was doing its very best to shun us. That was no loss, but I knew Ailsa was displeased by it. Trade at the Golden Chains had all but dried up as well, and that I *did* take ill. Some of my wealthy customers still sent their servants to my door to buy the poppy resin their masters couldn't live without anymore, but few folk now came to play cards at my tables. That was Hauer's influence at work, I knew, all of it was. Even Rogan had stopped coming to the Chains, and that could only be because he had been ordered to.

I spent more time at home with Ailsa than I had been used to, and I found that I liked it. She could be very pleasant company when she wanted to be, as I have written, and with fewer pressures of society to worry about she had grown a little less formal. She was a good mother to Billy, too, and the lad clearly adored her. In some ways I felt as though we were coming together as a husband and wife at last, and I liked that, too.

Not in every way we weren't, I'll allow, but to my mind emotional closeness between two people is a good deal more important than fucking is. I was rich and powerful and I could lie with a woman any time I wanted to, but I found that I didn't want to. I wanted to spend my time with Ailsa, not with some courtesan like Lady Reiter back in Dannsburg, who I didn't know and felt nothing for. I had even got a kiss on the cheek that morning after breakfast, before I went to wait for Fat Luka in my study. A dutiful one for appearances' sake in front of the servants, perhaps, but a kiss nonetheless. I liked that.

I liked that a great deal.

"Morning, boss," Luka said when he arrived at my house on Trader's Row that day. "You look in a good mood."

"Aye, well perhaps I am," I said as I showed him into my study.

I was happy with Ailsa, truth be told, and with the family we had made with Billy. With the exception of the Chains, business was good. Taxes from my streets and workshops and factories were coming in on time as they should be, and Chandler's Narrow was a gold mine. The Badger's Rest on Convent Street was doing well enough too, under Florence Cooper and her Flower Girls. She had taken it back and she had held it, as she had promised me she would, and I took my quarter for respect and left her to run it as she saw fit.

I sat down behind my desk and waved Luka into a chair across from me.

"What have you got for me?" I asked him. "This is important now, Luka."

"Aye, I know it is," he said, "but cunning folk don't grow on fucking trees. There's been two in three months, and I think that really is all of them now."

Billy had tested them both, I knew, with Luka there to put the terms of my deal to them. After what had happened with the assassin who called herself Lisbeth Beck I hadn't sat down with any more of them in person. I don't believe in making the same mistake twice.

"Perhaps it is," I had to allow, "and it's time I met them, now we're sure of them. Who are they?"

"A man and a young lass," Luka said. "Matthias Wolf, he calls himself, but if that's his real name then I'm a priestess of the Harvest Maiden. He's an outsider, only been in the city for a couple of months, if that. He thinks a lot of himself, but Billy says he's genuine, and he took the deal willingly enough. She just goes by Mina, don't seem to have a family name. Or a family, that I can find, for all that she can't have more than sixteen years to her. Young Billy's taken a shine to her and no mistake."

I smiled at that. It would do him good to find a lass close to his own age, I thought.

"Aye, I dare say he has. You've brought them to the Tanner's, then?"

Luka nodded. We'd had this meeting arranged for the last week or more. It had been planned that I would sit down with the cunning folk today unless Luka found any more of them in the meantime. It seemed that he hadn't, and that didn't surprise me. If there were only these two left to be found, then I would take that and be grateful for it. As I had told Ailsa, it's said only one person in ten thousand has it in them to learn the cunning, if that. I was surprised Luka had turned up as many as he had, truth be told.

"Right, then," I said, and got to my feet. "Let's go and see the lay of things."

We rode to the Tanner's wrapped in heavy cloaks against the cold rain, with six armed lads around us. We hadn't had trouble with the Sons since Florence took the Badger's Rest back, but that was only because we hadn't given them the opportunity to make any. No one went out alone anymore, and none of my top table rode with less than three bodyguards.

Those were the times we lived in.

We left the horses with Cookpot in his stables and went into the Tanner's Arms through the back way. Billy the Boy was sitting at a table with a tall young lass with long fair hair, him sitting up very straight and talking at her in a way that told me loud and clear that he was boasting about something or other. I just hoped he knew what he could talk about outside the family and what he couldn't. Mika was sitting at another table, Mika who I knew was a lot cleverer than he looked, and he had a man with him that I didn't know.

He thinks a lot of himself, Luka had said, and I could see now what he had meant. This fellow had his head shaved bald and shiny, and he wore a great thick black mustache, waxed to make it curl upward at the ends. He was dressed head to toe all in black, with a wide-brimmed black hat on the table beside his mug of beer. He looked something of a fool, but then cunning folk are sometimes strange in more ways than one.

"That's Wolf, sitting with Mika," Luka said.

"I guessed," I said. "Billy looks happy."

Luka smirked. "Told you."

"Aye, you did."

I walked into the room then, and Black Billy gave me a nod from the door while Hari poured brandy for us against the morning chill. I took the offered glass, and me and Fat Luka went through into the back room, where Bloody Anne was already waiting for me in her place at the long table.

"Go and get Billy the Boy," I told Luka, "and bring this man Wolf in here."

Luka nodded, and went.

"You sure about this?" Anne asked me. "After last time . . ."

"Aye, I know," I said. "I'm being careful. Billy's seen them both already, and he'll be here with us. If either of them tries anything it'll go hard on them."

Luka came back then with Billy and Matthias Wolf, and he closed the door behind them to leave us alone. I looked up at the man in black with his curling mustache and his shiny head and gave him a nod.

"My name is Tomas Piety," I said. "This here is my second, Bloody Anne, and you've met Billy. I understand Luka has already explained the lay of things to you."

"That he has," Wolf said, and he sat down at the table without waiting to be asked. He placed his ridiculous hat in front of him, and he grinned at me. "I am a cunning man, and you're recruiting cunning men. This is good for us both."

His accent spoke of the south somewhere, but I couldn't quite place where. Near the east coast, perhaps.

"What did you do before you came to Ellinburg?" I asked him.

"I was an entertainer with a traveling menagerie," he said. "I performed conjuring tricks on a stage, and we called it magic. What better place to hide the cunning than in plain sight, where all will assume it merely clever mummery?"

I had to allow he had a point there, and it wasn't something that had ever crossed my mind before. The next time a menagerie came to Ellinburg it would be worth looking at, I thought.

"You understand I'm recruiting cunning folk to fight other magicians, not to hide rabbits and do fucking card tricks?"

"No man fights like Matthias Wolf," he said, and flashed me his grin again. "You will find that I can do that."

I had already found him deeply irritating, truth be told, but I wasn't in a position to be choosy.

"I hope you can," I said.

I looked at Billy, and he nodded.

"He can, Papa. He can call fires, at least. I saw him do it."

"That's good," Bloody Anne said.

It was.

"Aye, that's good," I said at last, if somewhat reluctantly, and I took three marks out of my pouch and tossed them across the table to him. "Welcome to the crew. You can room for free at Slaughterhouse Narrow, but you'll stay out of Cutter's way if you're wise."

The man grinned again and swept the coins smoothly into his hand and out of sight. He rose then, and flourished a bow that involved waving his hat about like a fool. I've never cared for performing folk, I have to admit.

He left then, and Bloody Anne snorted laughter.

"Prancing idiot," she muttered, and there we were of one mind.

A few minutes later Luka showed the girl in, and again he closed the door behind her. Billy sat up straighter at once, I noticed, and I thought he might be feeling conscious that she was an inch or so taller than him.

"Papa, this is Mina," he said, as though that wasn't obvious. "She's very strong."

"Aye," I said, as the girl stood there with her hands clasped in front of her woolen kirtle. "Take a seat, Mina. I see you and Billy have already been talking, and that's good. I'm his da."

Mina nodded and looked at Anne.

"And are you his ma?"

Billy sniggered at that. "Anne's no one's ma," he said.

"Watch your manners," I snapped at him.

I knew he was only showing off for the lass, but I didn't care for his tone and I wasn't having it. I was his da now, and that meant something to me.

"Sorry," he muttered, sounding sullen in the way that only a lad in his teen years can.

"This is Bloody Anne," I told Mina. "She's a soldier, and my second in the Pious Men."

"And I'm joining the Pious Men, am I?"

"Not exactly," I said. "That's a special thing, like a family. Most of the men in that tavern aren't actually Pious Men, but they work for me like you've agreed to. You'll work for the Pious Men, but you won't be one, at least not any time soon. Do you understand that, Mina?"

She nodded, and looked up at me through the long blond hair that had fallen over her eyes.

"Billy's a Pious Man, though, isn't he?"

"Aye, he is," I had to say, although he wasn't really. Not exactly, anyway, but I wouldn't show the lad up like that when he had obviously told her different. Bloody Anne kicked me under the table, but I ignored her. "Are you ready to work for me, Mina?"

She nodded, and I paid her the same as I had paid Wolf and I sent her on her way. When the door was closed behind her I gave Billy a hard look, and at least he had the grace to blush.

"Sorry, Papa, I just . . . I like her, you understand?"

"Of course I do," I said. "I was a lad once, too, and not so long ago as you might think. I know how it is, but you mind what you say in front of her. We don't know her and she's not family, so you boast all you feel you need to but only about certain things. And don't you cheek Anne again or you'll be sorry."

"Yes, Papa," he said. "Sorry, Anne."

Her scar twitched as she smirked to say she couldn't care less.

"Forget it," she said.

That was how Matthias Wolf and a girl called Mina came to work for the Pious Men, and that was more important than I knew at the time.

FORTY-SIX

The weeks wore by, and if it had been bad last winter, then now it was worse. There just wasn't enough food in the city, it was as simple as that, and hungry people can be turned to violence very easily. We ate well enough, but the shortages had pushed prices out of the reach of the poorest workers, and then there was trouble. I did what I could to see that my streets were fed and no one went hungry, but I couldn't work miracles.

"It's getting ugly down in the Wheels," Bloody Anne told me, one afternoon at the Tanner's Arms. "Someone's stirring up trouble, telling factory folk how there's no point working at all if they still can't hardly afford to eat. Saying how there's no point paying their taxes, neither."

I nodded at that. Fat Luka had said much the same thing the day before, and I had set him to finding out where this trouble was coming from. My money was on the Northern Sons, on Bloodhands and his Skanian backers. Getting control of the city's workforce had always been the Skanians' main aim, and it seemed that having failed to do it through the underworld they were now trying to do it through simply raising an angry mob. That made sense—it was what I would have done, in Bloodhands's place.

"Aye," I said. "Luka's working on it."

"Best he works quick," Anne said. "Two of Florence's girls got hurt down in the Wheels last night, making their collections."

"What?"

I hadn't known *that*, I had to allow.

"Florence made it right, and she got the taxes," Anne said, and I knew that meant there had been harsh justice done.

That was good. I would have order on my streets whatever it took, and I knew me and Florence Cooper were of one mind about that. I nodded.

"Bloodhands is behind this, you mark me," I said. "I'd lay coin there's no workers' unrest on *his* streets."

Anne just shrugged.

"Not that I've heard tell of, no, but that doesn't mean much. Since Gerta . . . well, you know. These days we've little enough information coming from the west of the city."

I rubbed a hand over my face and said nothing. I didn't want to think about Gerta, especially not after what Fat Luka had told me the previous day. He hadn't been able to be sure, not yet, but he'd thought the chief rabble-rouser down in the Wheels might have been Gerta's widowed husband.

The man had no cause to love me, I knew, but his wife had worked for me, and to my mind if he had sold himself to the Northern Sons then that was a betrayal of both of us. Gerta would never have wanted that, I was sure.

Of course, Gerta had died screaming in some cell beneath the house of magicians, and that had been my fault, so I had to allow that perhaps she would after all. I was still thinking on that with some degree of discomfort when a runner barged into the common room of the Tanner's, breathless and with melting snow on the shoulders of his torn cloak.

"There's rioting up on Dock Road!" he panted.

"Fuck," Anne growled. "Florence's girls are on their own up there."

She stormed upstairs to get her mail and weapons, and I sent the runner back out to rouse some of the hired lads. Once he was on his way again I turned to Black Billy.

"You're coming," I said. "Mika and Hari can mind the Tanner's between them. Go and get mailed up."

"Yes, boss," Billy said.

Half an hour later I was heading north out of the Stink with Bloody Anne and Black Billy and ten armed men at my back.

If those Wheelers wanted a riot, I would fucking give them one.

* * *

Wheelers and Stink folk don't get on; they never have done and that hadn't changed just because they were all my streets now. Deep down even I had to admit I didn't much care for Wheelers, and when we were about halfway up Dock Road I was reminded why.

We could hear the shouting before we saw anything, hear the crash of breaking glass and see the flickering glow of flames around the next turn. Two of the Flower Girls came backing toward us with their blades up, both of them sooty and running with blood, with eight or so angry men giving chase. One of those men hurled a cobble obviously torn up from the road, and it went sailing past the two women and almost hit me.

Black Billy took off like the shot from a cannon, charging them and bellowing with fury as he went. His club rose and fell with a ruthless efficiency, smashing arms and shoulders and heads in its wake. My ten lads were with him, and the two Flower Girls rallied then. It seemed that they had run very short of mercy that day.

"How bad is it?" I asked, when the killing was done.

"Bad, Mr. Piety," one of them said. Jutta, I thought her name was, but I couldn't be sure. "They're breaking everything they can get at, and they've taken one of the factory owners hostage. Some bastard's shouting them on, but they're all around him and we've no bows so there's nothing to be done. Florence is still up there somewhere. We got separated in the fighting, and nothing we could do about that either."

"Aye, riots are ugly things," I said, and nodded to the other woman. She was nursing an obviously broken arm. "Watch over her; we've got this now."

"I can watch over myself," the woman growled. "Go and rally to Flo, Jutta. She needs us all, now."

"Aye, as you will," I said. "Come with us, then."

Jutta nodded and joined us, taking up position on Anne's left flank like it was the most natural thing in the world. She led us back the way she had come, up past the ruins of the Stables toward Old Kurt's alley, and I saw what she meant.

There must have been sixty or seventy of them in the streets at least, men and women who should have been working but were instead smashing windows and trying to set fires in the wet, snowy streets. Two of the Flower Girls were dead on the ground, that I could see. The remaining six had made a ring around Florence Cooper, backed against the wall of a warehouse with blades in their hands but little they could do against so many but defend themselves.

The factory owner had been hanged from a lantern hook.

Her body was turning slowly on the end of the rope, her face purple and the snow beneath her stained dark where she had voided herself in death. All the same, I recognized her. Madame Rainer, her name was. She had come to dinner at my house, once, I remembered.

Destroying your own neighborhood seemed like the work of animals, to my mind, not rational men, but murdering an innocent woman whose only crime had been to give them work wasn't something I even knew how to describe.

Even Wheelers didn't do that sort of thing, but by then I didn't think it had been entirely their own idea. A man was standing on an upturned crate outside the factory they were ransacking, shouting encouragement over the din. It seemed that Fat Luka had been right.

It was Gerta's husband.

"Smash the oppressors!" he bellowed, his face red with fury. "Burn it all!"

He turned then and saw us, fourteen against his sixty or more, and I saw the light of murderous hatred in his eyes.

"It's the devil Tomas Piety," he screamed at me. "Murderer! If you want to leave here alive you'll listen to me, Piety! We demand—"

I stopped listening to him.

I turned and gave Anne the nod she had been waiting for.

She threw back her cloak and raised the loaded crossbow to her shoulder with a fluid ease that spoke of practiced skill. That skill had been honed to a razor edge in the horrors of Messia and of Abingon, and I knew there was no man there before us who was even close to being her equal.

The string slammed forward with a thump as she pressed the lever, and Gerta's husband flew backward off his crate in a spray of blood with a bolt through his chest.

A shocked hush fell over the mob, and in that sudden quiet my words carried loudly enough to be heard by everyone.

"I don't negotiate with animals who hang my people and make demands of me on my own streets," I said. "Does anyone else have any fucking demands they want to make?"

The other lads threw back their cloaks and raised their crossbows now, holding them trained on the mob and ready to deliver a withering volley that would have decimated them in an instant. It seemed that no one else had anything to say.

I have written that I would have order on my streets, whatever it took.

I meant it.

FORTY-SEVEN

I thought perhaps it was time to see about getting another racehorse, for all that Ailsa had just sniffed at the notion. It had been two days since the riot up on Dock Road, and I had spent much of that time thinking about horses.

My da had always loved the track. He wasn't really a big gambler, but I think there was something about the excitement and the passion in the air there that spoke to him. Perhaps it was a way to chase the drinking man's thrill, I didn't really know, but I knew that men who drank often liked to gamble and that the reverse was usually true as well.

Once or twice he had taken me to the races with him, when he had been sober enough. Whatever else he had done to me, on those rare occasions he had actually felt like a father. I hated my da for what he did to me and Jochan, but I cherished those memories all the same, and I've loved horse racing ever since. A racehorse meant status and respect in Ellinburg, and those things were important to me.

The aftermath of the riot would take a lot of effort to clean up, and a lot of coin to repair, and I saw that both of those things were provided. Madame Rainer's eldest son had inherited the factory along with her other businesses, and a couple of days after the riot he came to me to pay his respects and to thank me for what I had done in putting down the trouble and saving as much of his inheritance as I had.

He was a tall, gangling lad with some twenty years to him and a foolish attempt at a beard sprouting from his chin, but he wasn't a child. He had come to me of his own choice, for one thing, and that was wise of him. That showed that he knew how things worked in Ellinburg, and that he understood respect.

"Thank you again, Mr. Piety," he said. He shook my hand and gave me an awkward bow, there in the back room of the Tanner's Arms, while Bloody Anne and Florence Cooper sat at the table and watched him. "I'll pay my taxes, and I won't forget how you tried to help my mother."

"Aye, well and good," I said. "This is Florence Cooper, and it's her crew you'll be paying your taxes to. See that you remember her name, and you show her respect."

"Yes, sir," he said, and he gave Florence another bow. "I've hired some men to keep the peace with the workers. Big men, with clubs. It won't happen again."

"See that it doesn't," I said, and with that he was dismissed.

It came to something when factory owners had to hire their own enforcers, but I only had so many blades I could call on, and as Anne had said in the autumn the City Guard might as well not exist in eastern Ellinburg anymore. Hauer was forcing me to live purely by my own resources, trying to overstretch me until I broke.

Well, I wouldn't fucking break, not for him and not for anyone else either.

Not ever.

I had Matthias Wolf sent to me after that, and I told him to get himself down to the Wheels with Florence and her girls, and to put himself about. He was conspicuous and he was flamboyant and a showman, and people would see him and they would remember his name. I told him to watch and to listen, and I told him to burn the first cunt he heard spreading sedition, without hesitation or fear of reprisal. I told him to do that publicly and in my name, and he nodded and he went to do it.

He might look like a fool, but he wasn't one, and he knew how this worked.

This was what I needed now, I knew, not racehorses but magic. The Northern Sons had magicians on their side, provided by their Skanian backers, and I needed it to be known that I had magicians of my own.

Wolf was a showman, as I say, and when he set to make an example of someone I didn't think it would go unnoticed.

The cunning is a shocking thing, when you're not expecting it, an awe-inspiring thing, and that was good. It was time I made my point, to Governor Hauer and to Bloodhands, and the Skanians and their Northern Sons both.

Shock and awe, that was how it would be done.

The chance came sooner than I had expected. A week after the riot a messenger came to my house bearing a letter from Bloodhands.

Mr. Piety,

A meeting would be in our mutual interests. You are a reasonable man and a man of business, I understand that. My backers are prepared to put a substantial business deal in front of you, if you will but sit down with us and listen to reason. I will meet you in a place of your choosing, if you will agree to discuss terms.

KV

I showed the note to Ailsa, and she frowned over it for a long moment.

"He knows who I am," she said. "He must know you will never agree to a deal."

"Does he, though?" I asked. "Borys sold Billy's secret to the house of magicians, not the Skanians, and he never knew who you were anyway. None of them do, except Anne. He might have sold the Badger's Rest back to the Sons as well, I assume to line his pockets enough to let him get out of my crew and make his way out of the city before I caught up with him, but no, I don't think Bloodhands *does* know who you are. The Sons have never attacked this house, after all, and if the Skanians knew there was a Queen's Man here then I think they would have done. This has always just been business between him and me."

"Perhaps you're right," Ailsa said after a long moment. "*Perhaps*. It's an enormous gamble, Tomas."

"I've made those before," I said.

"Yes, you have, and you know my thoughts on that. I could have skinned you alive after what happened at the house of magicians."

"Aye, well you didn't and that's because I was right and it worked," I said. "I've got a feeling, Ailsa. I think Vhent's days are numbered. The Skanians have the governor in their pay now, so what do they need Vhent for anymore? He was never anything more than their hired man anyway, I'm sure of it. He certainly doesn't have the Skanian look about him. Besides, everything he's done so far has failed. If he can't kill me or buy me very fast indeed, then I think his foreign masters will lose patience with him."

"Perhaps," she said, "but all that means is he will kill you the first chance he gets, and what better chance could you give him than a sit-down?"

"A place of my choosing, he said. He's desperate, Ailsa. Can you fucking imagine what the Skanians will do to him when they decide he's failed them?"

"Yes, I can," she said. "I know *exactly* what they will do to him, and it's no worse than he'll do to you if he can take you alive."

"He won't," I said. "I'll meet him at the Chains, and I've got a plan."

Ailsa sighed and put down her embroidery. She looked up at me with a rare honesty in her eyes.

"I hope for both our sakes it's a *very* good one," she said.

It was.

I brokered the sit-down through Fat Luka, as protocol dictated, but it was obvious that Bloodhands was in a great haste to make this meeting happen, and he agreed to almost everything just to hurry the process along. That in itself made me more and more sure I was right about how little time he thought he had left to him. His only firm demand had been that I left Billy the Boy out of it, and I agreed to that just to get the thing done.

Three nights later the Golden Chains was closed to the public, and I was sitting at a table in the middle of the empty gaming room with Fat Luka standing behind my chair and my brother seated at my right hand. Anne had wanted to come too, of course she had, but as Ailsa had said this was an enormous gamble and if it all went to the whores then someone had to be left to run the Pious Men after I crossed the river. That someone was Anne, to my mind, and that meant she couldn't be there.

"Is this really going to fucking work, Tomas?" Jochan asked me, clutching his glass so tight in his hand it was a wonder the heavy crystal didn't shatter under the pressure.

"Aye, it is," I said, although I wasn't quite as confident as I made myself sound.

A leader must always sound confident in his decisions; the captain had taught me that. Show any doubt and your men will smell it, and then they'll start to doubt themselves. Worse than that they'll start to doubt you, and sooner or later you'll lose them. No decision can be questioned once it has been made and acted on. The time for debate is well and truly past, at that point. Once the decision is made it's the fucking *right* decision and you have to stand by it, come what may.

Jochan gulped his brandy and poured another from the bottle on the table in front of us, and that was his fourth or fifth glass since we had arrived not half an hour before. The liveried serving girl who was waiting by the wall would have to bring us another bottle soon, at the rate he was getting through the stuff.

"I don't like this, boss," Sir Eland said from his place by the door that led out to the courtyard and the shithouse beyond. "There's too many things taken on trust here, for my liking."

"Aye, I know," I said.

"You told him to come unarmed but he won't, nor will his men."

"Nor have we," I pointed out.

"It's a fucking trap, and we've backed right into it," Eland protested. "This place, there's only one way in or out and they'll be between you and it. What would the captain have said about that?"

I snorted. I had to allow him that, I supposed. The captain would have said that was tactical suicide and he'd have been right, on the face of it. There was something else the captain had told me about battle, though, and I didn't think Sir Eland knew that.

Always cheat, always win.

I remembered the captain telling me that, and he'd been right then and he was right now.

"I know what I'm doing," I said.

"But, boss—"

"Listen to my fucking brother!" Jochan roared at him, lurching to his feet with his face flushed red with sudden rage. "Our Lady speaks to him, and he's right! He's always right, so you shut your cocksucking mouth, Eland, or you'll be sucking on my fucking axe!"

"Peace, Jochan," I murmured.

I looked up at him until he spat on the floor in Eland's general direction and sat down again.

Our Lady spoke to me now, did she? That was something I hadn't known, I had to allow. I wondered where my poor mad brother had got that notion from. Our Lady speaks to no one, to my mind, with the possible exception of Billy the Boy and even that I doubted. Priest I may be, but I'll confess that I'm a sight less religious than a lot of my men were.

"Peace," I said again, as Jochan drained his glass and slammed it angrily down onto the table. "Trust me on this."

Jochan sighed and pushed his hands back through his already wild hair, making himself look even more the madman that I feared he was.

"I do," he said, and the light of religious fervor in his eyes gave me pause in a way that his rages never had. "I trust you, Tomas. In Our Lady's name."

"Aye, in Our Lady's name," I had to respond.

Thankfully my guest arrived then and was shown into the gaming room by my guards, sparing me the need to make further conversation with my brother. This was Klaus Vhent, the man folk called Bloodhands. The man who had flayed the head of the Blue Bloods alive and hanged his peeled red corpse from the west gate. He had half a dozen men with him, and I had expected no less. One of them was very tall and very pale, with long white hair pulled back from his face and held in a silver clasp.

That was the look of a Skanian magician, I knew that, and I didn't have Billy the Boy with me.

That was about as bad as this could have gone.

FORTY-EIGHT

"Mr. Vhent," I said, giving Bloodhands as cordial a nod as I could manage under the circumstances. "Do take a seat. Be welcome in my place of business."

He sat across the table from me, a big scarred brute wearing a thick leather doublet under a long black coat and a heavy cloak. He kept that cloak pulled close around him as though he were still feeling the winter cold even in the warmth of the Golden Chains, and it was quite obvious he was hiding weapons under it. His magician stood behind his chair, locking eyes with Fat Luka over our heads. His other five lads kept to their end of the room, each of them marking one of mine in a way that wasn't even close to being subtle. They had very plainly put themselves between us and the only outside door, and there was no subtlety in the way they did that, either. It seemed that the time for subtlety was passed, as I had suspected it might be.

"Mr. Piety," he said, and he gave me a nod.

The serving girl came forward with fresh glasses and another brandy bottle, her long blond hair falling forward over her eyes. She poured for each man around the table, left the bottle there between us, and retreated to her place by the wall without a word.

"So, are you here to buy me or to kill me?" I asked him.

Vhent's mouth curled up at the edges in the suggestion of a smile that was almost lost among the grizzled scars on his cheeks.

"If we're to speak that plainly, then whichever it takes," he said. "Do you know who I work for?"

"Aye, you work for the Skanians and whatever they call their version of the Queen's Men," I said.

"That's right," he said, and I thought there was a flicker of surprise on his face.

Lady willing I had been right about this and he *didn't* know who Ailsa was. All this business would be news to Fat Luka and my brother, I knew that, but again to my mind we were past the time of tiptoeing around such things, whatever Ailsa might think about it. It was time for truths now, and either for bargains or for blood.

"So why should I listen to you?" I asked him. "Your masters want the workforce, I know that. They tried to take over the Ellinburg underworld through Ma Aditi and her Gutcutters, and they failed because I stopped them. They tried again by putting you in charge of the Northern Sons, and again there they've failed because you failed at it. Now they've given up on that and they've given up on you, and they've dug so deep into their coffers they've managed to buy the fucking governor instead. Now they're trying to raise mobs on the streets while the governor's bought-and-paid-for City Guard look the other way, and it's little enough to do with you anymore. You came here to negotiate, but I don't see you've much of anything to negotiate *with*."

"That's where you're wrong," Vhent said. "I didn't come here to negotiate at all."

No, I had never thought for one moment that he had.

Blood it was, then.

The glass in my hand exploded, showering razor fragments into my face. I felt Luka's hands leave the back of my chair as the magician's power threw him bodily backward across the room and into Sir Eland, dropping the pair of them. Blades were drawn all around us, Vhent's men and mine, but he had a Skanian magician behind him and Billy the Boy wasn't there.

Billy the Boy wasn't there because Vhent knew who he was and what he could do and what he looked like, and that had been his one firm condition to meeting me here on my own territory. He was no fucking fool, wasn't Vhent.

But then neither was I.

The blond-haired serving girl stepped forward from the wall, and she raised her hands in front of her.

This is Mina, Billy had said. *She's very strong.*

He'd had the right of that, I had to allow. The Skanian magician slammed backward across the room and into a wall, spitting curses as the girl drove him before her with the force of her cunning.

"Son of a dog-sucking street scrub," she whispered as she walked slowly toward where he was pinned to the wall, her hands still held up in front of her and her pretty young mouth twisting into an ugly shape as she spat obscenities that surprised even me. "You leprous pus-licker, you filthy, putrid sheep's afterbirth, rancid festering fucking . . ."

She passed beyond my hearing then as Vhent lurched to his feet and threw back his cloak, and a moment later he had a shortsword in each hand. The room was already ringing with the sound of steel on steel as Vhent's men and mine went for each other.

Sit-downs between rival bosses aren't common, but they do happen sometimes, and the one rule that is always agreed on is that everyone comes unarmed. That's also the one rule that everyone always ignores or works their way around, just as I had when I had met Grachyev in Dannsburg. Any place where you're told weapons can't be carried is always somewhere you'd be well advised to carry a weapon.

I kicked the table over and faced Vhent, with Remorse and Mercy in my hands.

"Now we'll fucking see who owns Ellinburg," he said.

I supposed we would, at that.

We faced each other, two rival gang bosses with blades in our hands. It never came to this, to bosses dueling each other with steel. That was nonsense from stories, I knew that, not something that ever really happened.

Except it seemed like it was about to.

I'm good with swords. I'm very good, and I've no shame in admitting that, but one look at Vhent's stance told me that he was as well. He was a veteran too, of course he was. Ma Aditi had first met him in Abingon, after all, or so I could only assume. He had a shortsword in each hand the same as I did, and he held them with the same easy confidence with which I held the Weeping Women.

Mina had been my trick, my way to cheat this battle the way the captain would have wanted it, but now she was locked in single combat with the Skanian magician. Vhent was right there in front of me, and all my men were busy fighting his men and no time to spare from anyone.

There was no one left to face him but me, and perhaps it was like something from the stories after all.

We crossed blades once, twice, circling around the overturned table and each of us using both shortswords at once, trying to confuse the other. We even had the same style of fighting, and right then I couldn't have said which one of us was most skilled at it.

Vhent came at me in a sudden surge that answered that question, one of his blades twisting and binding both of mine in a technique so perfect I wish I'd had the time to admire it. He barged at me with his shoulder and his other sword lunged for my throat, and it was all I could do to throw myself backward out of the way.

I landed on my arse on the floor in an undignified heap, losing Remorse as I fell. His blade thrust into the space I had occupied a fraction of a second before. I lashed out with both my legs, trapping his forward knee and twisting hard to send him sprawling beside me onto the brandy-soaked boards.

One of his swords flew from his hand as he fell, but he just spat a curse and dived on top of me. The hilt of his remaining blade crashed into my temple hard enough to make me see stars. He spat into my face as he pinned me with his meaty forearm and tried to bring his blade up and over to do for me.

"I wish I could have fucking skinned you, Piety," he snarled, "but this will do."

I still had Mercy in my left hand, but we were too close for me to get the angle I needed to stab him. The best I could do was slice her along his side, which barely cut the thick leather of his doublet. I brought my knee up between his legs and heaved with my hips instead, sending us rolling into the next table. I could feel his hot breath in my face, smell the rancid scent of his teeth and his sweat as we strained against each other.

This was Klaus Vhent, this was Bloodhands, and I hated him with a passion. I hated him enough to bring out the cold devil in me, the one that had killed my da, but sometimes hatred alone just isn't enough. Vhent was bigger than me, stronger than me, and every bit as good a fighter as I was. That was me done then, and about to cross the river. I could almost see Our Lady opening Her arms to receive me into the gray lands.

We rolled again and now he was back on top and I was half on my side, clutching his wrist with the only hand I had free. His blade twisted in my grip until the edge was against my cheek and drawing blood in a thin, hot trickle. I kept my chin tucked in hard to my shoulder, the way you have to when you're fighting on the ground, protecting my neck and throat as best I could, but I knew it wouldn't do for long. He only had to move my head another inch and I would be done for good and at Our Lady's side. That blade would be into my neck in the killing place any second, I knew, and I was all out of ways to stop him.

"Pray to your fucking goddess," he hissed, and he shifted his great weight and he pushed my head back the inch he needed to expose my throat.

His snarling face exploded in a spray of brains and blood and bone.

Sharp, wet, heavy things smashed into my face and almost choked me on the gush of hot, slick fluids. I blinked the filth of a man's life out of my eyes, and I looked up at my brother. He was standing over Vhent's corpse with his axe dripping in his hands.

"Our Lady's name, Her will be done," he said.

"I'm sorry, Mr. Piety," Mina said to me, afterward. "I can't do it otherwise, not unless I say them filthy things. It makes me feel dirty to talk like that and I don't like it but that's just how it works, for me."

"It's all right, lass," I said. "The cunning's different for everyone, I understand that. If you need to talk when you work, then you talk, and no one will think ill of you for it. You did well tonight, very well indeed."

I was drenched in blood and brains and whatever other liquid comes out of a man's head when an axe splits it in two right over your fucking face. I didn't feel like I was in any position right then to judge the girl for the words she had said.

"I'll allow that it worked," Sir Eland said, "but only fucking just. We've three men dead, and another two wounded."

"Aye," I said. "Aye, we have, but we've fucking killed Bloodhands. That's a fair trade, and a good night's work."

"Is it?" he demanded of me. "Is it fair, boss? Is it really?"

I turned then and I stared at the false knight, and thinking back on it I dread to think how I must have looked. Like some devil from Hell, I could only imagine, dripping with blood and brains as I was. He swallowed, and he dropped his gaze.

"Lady's sake," I said, turning away from him to survey the carnage in the room. "This is going to take some fucking cleaning before we can open again."

I laughed, but it was a cold laugh. A hollow one, with no humor in it.

I felt cold all over, and I knew why that was. The battle shock was coming down on me, of course it was. I had the inside of a man's head running down my cheeks. There were bodies piled on the floor, and blood everywhere. Someone had broken an oil lamp in the fighting, and one of the carpets was on fire because of it and giving off a thick, acrid smoke.

Against the far wall, a Skanian magician had been torn into five pieces by the fury of a young girl's twisted mind. His ruptured entrails were spooled across the floor in the considerable space between his pelvis and his rib cage, and the whole mess reeked of shit.

Abingon had smelled like that, of blood and shit, fire and death. It smelled good.

I threw back my head and laughed, and laughed.

It smelled like victory.

FORTY-NINE

It was three days after the sit-down before I was in my right mind again.

The bout of battle shock that had took hold of me was brutal, worse than I'd ever had before.

Ailsa nursed me through those dark days herself, her soothing words and cool hands probably the only things that kept me from hurting myself, or more likely someone else. If I hadn't loved her before that, then I did by the end of it, and I've no shame in admitting that.

On the fourth day she finally let me get out of my bed, at least, although I suspected that was only because she couldn't turn Bloody Anne away yet again.

Anne was waiting for me in my study, as she had been every morning since that night.

"Lady's sake, you look like shit," she said when I came in.

"Thanks," I muttered, but I had to smile all the same.

Bloody Anne would always tell me the truth; I knew that and I was glad of it. She was my conscience, in some strange way, my view of the world that wasn't filtered through the eyes of that uncaring cold devil. As always she had the right of it, of course she did. I was unshaven, and wearing a loose robe and slippers like some sort of rich invalid, and I could feel that I still wasn't quite of calm mind.

I sank into the chair behind my desk with a sigh and looked at her.

"What's the lay of things?" I asked her.

"It's hard to say," Anne confessed. "Matthias Wolf has put the very fear of the gods into the Wheels folk. That's good enough in itself, I suppose, but I reckon all it means is that those who already hated us now just hate us even more. West of the city . . . oh, the Lady only knows. Sir Eland had Vhent's body fed to the pigs nice and quiet, and those of his men too, so officially no one knows what happened to him. All the same, it's known that he went to a sit-down with you and he never came back, and there's no hiding that."

What the *fuck* was she talking about? I don't hide. I never fucking hide, not from anyone, not anymore. Not since my da.

Never again.

I don't back down, and I don't *fucking* hide!

"I don't *want* to fucking hide that," I shouted at her. "I want it known, Anne. I want it known far and fucking wide what happens to people who cross the Pious Men!"

I was leaning over the desk toward her, I realized, my hands balled into tight fists against the polished wood in front of me. No, I was most definitely not calm of mind yet. I made myself sit back down, forced myself to just breathe, to breathe in the deep, steady rhythm that Ailsa had taught me. That helped some, but it couldn't take the stench of Abingon out of my nostrils. I don't know that anything ever will.

"Aye, well, I reckon everyone knows that now," Anne said.

"Good," I said. Anne grunted in a way that wasn't dissent but wasn't quite agreement either, and I looked up from my hands and met her eyes. "What?"

"Look, Tomas . . ." Anne started, and tailed off.

She was being careful, I realized, very careful indeed about what she said and what opinions she expressed. She was being careful not to rouse my fury, and that made me feel like I had been punched in the guts. She was my best friend, for the Lady's sake, my *only* real friend, and she was looking at me the way I had looked at Jochan after that night the previous winter when he had eaten a man's throat.

"I'm not mad, Bloody Anne," I said quietly. "I'm not my brother. I've had a . . . a bad few days, I'll allow that, but I'm not mad. A lot of men have battle shock; it's nothing to be ashamed of."

"I know," Anne said quietly. "I know, and I'm sorry. I didn't mean to make you feel like I thought it was."

"Forget it," I said. "You were going to say something, so say it. I won't take it ill."

"It's Vhent, or Bloodhands or whatever we're calling him," Anne said. "You and Jochan killed him, and that's good, but it's changed fucking nothing. The Northern Sons are still there. There's still disorder on the streets, and the governor's still doing fuck-all about it."

"Aye, well, he wouldn't," I said. "You remember what I told you that morning in Rosie's room, about the Skanians and the work I do for the crown? Aye, of course you do. Well, those Skanians, the people who owned Bloodhands, I think they own the governor now. I think they worked out that Vhent wasn't going to beat us, so now they're trying something new."

"Fat Luka said as much yesterday," Anne said. "I think you're right, and if we're not fucking careful it's going to work."

A week after the sit-down, Ailsa finally allowed that I was as recovered as I was likely to get, and she let me dress in proper clothes and visit Ernst the barber to have myself made presentable again. That done I was ready to face the world once more, and a good thing too.

When I returned home I finally felt like myself again. I went and joined Ailsa in the drawing room, where she was waiting for me with a letter in her hand.

"We have an invitation," Ailsa said, once I was sat down with a drink in my hand.

"Oh?"

"Yes, and I've been giving this one quite some thought while you've been out. It's from Hauer."

I stared at her. Governor Hauer had been doing his utmost all winter to pretend we didn't exist, and now he sent us a society invitation? That didn't feel right, to my mind.

"He must want to talk," I said, "but the last time he wanted to speak to me he just had me arrested. What's changed?"

"Well, Vhent is gone, of course," she said, "but as you surmised I think the Skanians were all but done with him anyway. Hauer is their new cat's-paw, now. I've been thinking on it, and I don't believe he will move against you again until he really means it. No more false arrests, no more mummer's shows for the people. I think he's serious now. This is the sort of thing Lord Vogel does."

"Hauer isn't Vogel," I pointed out.

"No, he's not, but whoever is behind him on the Skanian side quite possibly is, in their terms. If they have found enough gold to buy the governor, then this must have the sanction of their highest levels. Those people will be no fools, Tomas."

No, I had never thought that they would be.

"So what should we do?"

"We have to accept, of course," she said. "It's a reception, not a dinner, twenty or so people, so he can hardly have you assassinated right there and then in front of everyone. He's not Vogel, as you say. No, I agree he wants to talk, or to threaten, or possibly to put forward an offer of some kind. We have to go, but we shall have to be very careful about it."

"Aye, that makes sense." I nodded, for all that I didn't like it. "Can we get away with bringing Billy with us?"

Ailsa frowned, and looked down once more at the letter of invitation in her hand.

"No, I don't think so," she said. "It's a formal invitation in our names, and *only* in our names. Vhent knew what Billy can do and that means Hauer knows too, and he won't take the chance."

"We could dress Mina up as your maid, perhaps?"

Ailsa shook her head.

"No one brings their own servants to these things, Tomas," she said. "It's a nice idea but we'd never get away with it, and I don't want to risk losing the girl. She's too useful to waste."

Aye, that she was. Mina had saved my life at the sit-down with Bloodhands, her and Jochan, and I wouldn't forget that.

"So we just have to trust him, is that it?"

"I don't trust Governor Hauer as far as I can spit," Ailsa said, and that made me smile. That sounded like *my* Ailsa, that sweet, funny, common girl who didn't exist. The one I had first fallen for. Surely the lioness didn't speak like that. "All the same, we've little enough choice, but I have a man inside the governor's hall now. Not a highly placed man, sadly, but one who frequents Chandler's Narrow nonetheless. Rosie's girls were able to turn him easily enough, and he now reports to me. From what he's said I think it's safe, Tomas, but it's still a gamble."

"Aye, well," I said. "Everything is."

The governor's reception was a tedious affair, as such things usually are. Jon Lan Barkov was there, him of the ridiculous painting, and Madame Rainer's son, and a number of other folk who seemed to be possessed of more money than sense or personality. I knew some of them from the Golden Chains, although few still came in now. When Ailsa and me entered the grand room in the governor's hall the atmosphere became something between awkward and hostile, but no one had the spine to say anything to my face that I would have had to take ill.

I accepted a tall glass of unwanted wine from a liveried footman and Ailsa did the same, and together we began to circulate and play the game of society manners. It *was* a game, I had come to realize while we were in Dannsburg. It was a vicious, deadly game where barbed insults took the place of daggers, but the damage done could be every bit as bloody.

After ten minutes or so Governor Hauer contrived to place himself beside me under the tall windows.

"How was your riot?" he asked me, the corner of his mouth twitching with an amusement that made we want to stab him right then. "I heard your feral whores didn't fare too well."

"Two of the Flower Girls are dead, and another won't fight again," I said, "but you know that. Was it your work, or Vhent's?"

"And how do you suppose it would be *my* work? It is the governor's job to keep the peace."

I turned and leaned close to him.

"I know what you're doing," I told him, lowering my voice to be sure that we weren't overheard. "Withholding the Guard from my streets, trying to turn my own people against me. I know what you're doing, and it won't fucking work."

"Oh?"

"There's a thing you need to understand, my lord governor, and I don't think that you do. We're the Pious Men, and we're the Flower Girls, and we're the Headhunters. We survived Messia, and we survived Abingon while you sat here on your arse and drank wine. We are Ellinburg, and we stand together. You can hurt us, you can even make us bleed, but you can never make us fear."

"Brave words for someone who shot an innocent, unarmed man."

"Unarmed maybe, not innocent. No more than Vhent was. No more than you are."

"And what *did* happen to Vhent?" Hauer demanded. "He's been missing for over a week."

"I heard he died suddenly."

"And what did he die *of*, exactly?" Hauer hissed, his face flushing with drink and anger.

"An axe," I said.

He glared at me for a moment, then turned sharply away. I'd thought he might have had more to say about it than that, but it seemed not.

It came to me then that Hauer didn't much care what had happened to Vhent. We were past that now, I realized, past the time for fronts and blinds and pretending. The time for proxy wars between the governor and me was over and done. It was time now to settle this, and settle it I would, the only way I knew how.

It was time for blood.

FIFTY

The time for blood came sooner than I had expected. Sooner than anyone had expected, I think, even Ailsa. Two days after the governor's reception, the City Guard stormed the Tanner's.

There must have been fifty of the fuckers, and we never stood a chance. I was in the back room with Luka and Bloody Anne when the shouting started, followed by the crash of breaking glass and a brief exchange of steel on steel. A moment later the door was kicked in, and there was Captain Rogan. He had a naked blade in his hand, and ten armed men at his back. Half of them at least held loaded crossbows.

"You're done, Piety," he said. "I'm sorry, but I mean it this time. I have to take you to see the widow."

Going to see the widow, that was what it was called. That was street cant for when you were taken in and it was bad, really bad. Men who went to see the widow usually didn't come back again.

I was on my feet then with Luka and Anne beside me, but there was nothing to be done. There were too many of them and they had crossbows, and I could tell just from the sounds floating down the hallway that the rest of the Tanner's had already fallen. It wasn't worth crossing the river, not yet.

"Aye, as you say, Captain," I said, careful to keep my hands well away from the hilts of the Weeping Women. "Anne, Luka, see that my wife is told of this."

"Yes, boss," Luka said.

Bloody Anne said nothing, just edged closer to me and slightly in front. She was ready to fight, I realized. She had nothing on her but a pair of daggers and she wasn't even wearing her mail, but she was ready to fight all the same. Bloody Anne was like a fucking force of nature in a close-quarters battle, but even she couldn't face this many armed men and hope to live. No one could, not even Cutter.

"No, Anne," I said. "No."

"They'll fucking kill you, Tomas," she whispered.

"No one's killing anyone, not yet," Rogan said. "Put him in irons. He's for the cells, and the governor's justice."

"Stand down, sergeant," I ordered Anne, and she reluctantly did as I said.

I met Rogan's eyes as two of his men relieved me of my swordbelt and locked heavy iron manacles around my wrists. He looked troubled by what he was doing, and I thought that might be a good thing.

"Do you remember what I told you that night at the Golden Chains, Captain?" I asked him. "That if you ever get orders you don't feel you can follow with a clear heart, you should come and talk to me about them before you do something you might regret. Do you remember that?"

"I'm a soldier," he growled. "I follow my orders, and it's not for the likes of you to be questioning them."

"Aye, perhaps not," I said. "Perhaps I thought you had more honor than this."

One of his men hit me then, and I swayed on my feet but shot Anne a look to tell her to stay back. She was a moment away from disobeying orders herself, I knew. There were five or six bows trained on her and Luka, at a range even a child couldn't have missed from. It was no good, and I knew it.

"You'll shut your mouth and come with us in peace or I'll have my men shoot the pair of them," Rogan said, indicating Anne and Luka.

"I'll come," I said. "Don't you worry about me, Captain."

He gave me a sour look but nodded, and his men slowly lowered their crossbows.

"Make sure Ailsa hears," I said again. "At once."

With that I was dragged out of the room, and the door kicked shut behind us.

The common room of the Tanner's was full of guardsmen. Hari and Mika and Emil were standing against one wall with crossbows pointing at them, while Simple Sam was inexpertly trying to stem the flow of blood from a wicked gash in Black Billy's shoulder.

"Sorry, boss," Billy said when he saw me, his dark face looking pale and sweaty from shock and blood loss.

"You did what you could," I said. "There's no shame in not doing the impossible."

"Aye."

Then I was out of the door and in the street, the cold winter wind blowing my open coat out behind me. Another twenty or so of the City Guard were out there, and I started to wonder if there were any more left anywhere else in the city. Some of this lot were the new men Hauer had been recruiting, I saw, not Rogan's old veterans. Almost all of the City Guard had been thrown against the Pious Men that day, and if I'd still had the slightest doubt that Hauer was now in the pay of the Skanians that would have ended it. This was a fucking act of war, there was no other way of looking at it. This was an invasion of my streets by an enemy force.

I was born in the Stink. I lived there my whole life until the war broke out, and I knew those streets like the back of my hand. I knew the people too, the Stink people. I knew what they were like and how they thought, and what they believed in and what was important to them. I was a prince in Ellinburg, as I have written, and a prince looks after his people and he keeps the peace. A prince is respected on his streets, even loved. But when others break that peace and threaten the prince, what then? When they drag him out of his place of business in irons, with crossbows trained on him, how do his people react to that?

How do you fucking think.

It was barely two minutes before the first cobble was thrown.

It slammed into a guardsman's shoulder as they marched me down the road, knocking him off balance and into the man next to him. Then the shouting started. No one saw where that cobble had come from, or the next one, or the one after that. The Stink is all alleys and narrow, winding streets, cramped little houses and shops that lean out over the roads between them until they almost touch. It's all shadows, even in the daytime, and if Stink people know one thing it's how to hide from the Guard.

All the guardsmen wore mail and most of them had crossbows as well as their clubs and shortswords, but none of them had shields. A crossbow won't save a man from a hail of missiles, and that was what they were now facing. One clanged from a guardsman's helmet, sending him to his knees.

"Let him go!"

I didn't know where the shout came from. It was a man's voice, thick with the local accent and echoing from the looming buildings all around us. It could have come from anywhere at all.

"Let him go!"

That was a woman, and not a young one by the sound of her voice. A moment later the chant was taken up by a hundred throats, and I could even hear children's voices in it too. Cobbles and rocks rained down on the Guard from alleys and windows.

"Let him go!" they chanted, and another guard was hit. "Let him go! Let him go!"

The thump of the first crossbow changed everything.

The bolt slammed into an open shutter, hurting no one, but that wasn't the point. That was the moment the City Guard of Ellinburg started shooting at their own citizens, and there was no coming back from that.

The alleys erupted.

The riot took hold like a forest fire in high summer, and the Guard were overwhelmed in minutes. The streets of the Stink are close-packed and overcrowded, with many hundreds of people piled one on top of another in barely a square mile of reeking slums and grinding poverty. Hundreds of angry, hungry, bitter people, whose one bright light in life was their prince and the justice and protection he brought to them. Threatening that prince, putting him in irons, had been very, very fucking unwise of Captain Rogan.

No, I thought, as I watched a guardsman dragged to the ground by a dozen screaming women in patched and stained kirtles gone colorless from wear, not Rogan. He was following his orders, I was sure. Hauer's orders. Hauer was the fool here, and the captain just his cat's-paw.

One of the women was astride the fallen guardsman now, her bonnet askew and wisps of dirty hair falling in her face as she lifted a big rock and brought it down in her work-worn, callused hands. There was a sick crunch of breaking skull and her rock rose and fell, rose and fell, until it was dripping crimson.

A crossbow thumped beside me and she flew backward with a bolt lodged in her chest. Her friends looked up as one, their eyes shining with furious hatred, and as one they charged with their kitchen knives flashing bright murder in their hands.

It was like Messia on the streets of the Stink that day.

Captain Rogan dragged me forward by the chain that linked my manacles, bellowing at his men to fall back, to regroup and make for the Narrows and Trader's Row beyond.

Easier said than done, Captain. Easier said than done.

Twenty men faced the Guard across the street before us, big angry men with hammers and clubs and barrel staves in their hands. Working men, worn lean and hard as old roots by their labors. They'd had no love for the Guard to start with, not a man of them, but that was before. Now there was someone's wife, someone's mother, someone's sister or aunt, dead in the street with a guardsman's bolt through her chest.

Now, oh now there would be blood.

They were like wild animals as they fought, those men of my streets, and I could feel that the Guard were ready to break and run. Only Rogan held them, the hard old soldier with his iron discipline.

"Hold!" he roared. "Shoulder! By the numbers! Volley!"

The crossbows thumped, one after another down the line at punishingly close range, and the Stink men fell before the withering steel rain. It pained me to see it happen, but chained as I was there was little enough I could do to stop it.

"Wheel right!" Rogan bellowed. "Form on me and withdraw!"

He rammed his blade into a Stink man's side with his free hand even as he shouted his orders. He kicked the man's body aside and dragged me into the bottom of Carpenter's Narrow with one meaty hand clamped around the chain between my manacles.

I could hear the guardsmen's whistles blowing frantically for assistance, but I couldn't think they had many men left to call on. Even if they had, they weren't coming.

Of course it had come to blood in the end; these things always do. Rogan's sword was running with it, with the blood of the Stink man he had killed. I wouldn't forget that, or the woman and the men who had been shot down. I hadn't known them, but I promised myself I would find out who they had been and make it right with their families, as much as I could. They hadn't been the only ones to fall, but there were ten guardsmen dead in the streets behind us now, their heads bashed in with barrel staves or cobbles torn up from the road, or with kitchen knives driven between the gaps in their mail.

People are weak, as I have written before, and the poorer and more oppressed they are, the weaker they become—until they just refuse to take it anymore. Then they will rise up, and the gods help their oppressors.

Even as I watched, another guardsman was dragged down by the mob. I didn't think he would be getting up again.

"Can you make this stop?" Rogan hissed in my ear, too low for any of his men to hear.

"No, but you can," I said. "You can let me go."

"I fucking can't, you know that," he said. "I may not be happy about this, you've the right of that, but I've got my orders."

I shrugged and looked over the Captain's shoulder, farther up the narrow, and I liked what I saw.

"Aye, well," I said. "I very strongly suggest you have another think about that, Captain Rogan. Right now."

A runner had obviously reached Ailsa, as I had ordered. Billy the Boy was coming down the narrow toward us, and he had Cutter beside him. I remembered the dream I'd had of the two of them, stalking through the bloody smoke of Abingon with dripping knives in their hands, and I realized it was coming true. Here they came now, their knives still dry but held ready. Billy's smile was every bit the slash of murder it had been in my nightmare.

"You know I—" Rogan started, and then the flames from Billy's hands lit the narrow as they roared overhead in a warning that brooked no argument.

"Let me go, Rogan," I said. "I don't want to kill you, but I think young Billy does. I fucking *know* Cutter does. Let me go."

Rogan looked at his remaining men, cowering from the flames and hopelessly outnumbered by the Stink folk who were still hurling rocks at them from the foot of the narrow, and he nodded.

"You know it can't end here," he said. "We'll be back. You have to understand that."

I gave him a short nod. Of course I understood.

He unlocked my manacles and gave me back my swords, and I stood and walked back down the narrow. A great cheer went up from the massed folk below, a roar of approval that made me smile as I raised my hands to them in acknowledgment. The first battle of the Stink was won, but I knew Captain Rogan had the right of it.

I might not be an educated man but this was war, and I understood that well enough.

They would be back.

FIFTY-ONE

Ailsa joined us in the Tanner's Arms while she could still get there, and that was a relief. If Hauer had taken her hostage I would have found myself in a very difficult position. Billy threw himself into her arms, and she held him close and smiled at me over his head.

The Stink was virtually under siege now, but everyone who mattered was there. Bloody Anne had called the knives, and all the Pious Men had rallied to the Tanner's. That was how it should be.

Matthias Wolf was there too, and Billy the Boy and Mina, the Headhunters and Florence Cooper and most of her Flower Girls, and Stefan and Brak and my aunt. Sir Eland had closed the Golden Chains and left a guard of hired men inside with crossbows and blades. The only one who was absent was Will the Wencher, and that was only because he was holding Chandler's Narrow with five men to protect the girls, and the remaining Flower Girls were holding the Badger's Rest the same way. Rosie was at the Tanner's with us; Anne had insisted, and I hadn't refused her. In truth I was glad to have her there. She was good with a crossbow, was Rosie, and she could think for herself.

There was a big barricade at the end of the main road that led toward the market square now, and another at the bottom of Dock Road, both of them manned mostly by Stink folk. If the Guard wanted to come again they'd have no choice but to come down one of the narrows, where my people could rain anything and everything down on them from the overhanging upstairs windows.

And come again they would.

Hauer had started something now that he couldn't stop. Now that the City Guard had come to blood with the common folk, there was no turning back. I knew that, and so would he.

Jochan was at the main barricade with Cutter and Sir Eland and Simple Sam and Emil, waiting for the chance to kill someone. I didn't think he'd have to wait long. Ailsa was in the back room of the Tanner's with me and Anne and Fat Luka, having finally pried Billy off her and convinced him to rest. Anne knew who Ailsa really was, of course, and that was good. I wanted her at my top table.

Luka *didn't* know, not officially, but he was Luka and I suspected he might have found his way to working some of it out for himself by then. Ailsa didn't object to him being there, at least, and that was good too.

"How long is that barricade going to hold, realistically?" I asked as I paced the room, back and forth like a caged thing. "A couple of old carts and a pile of crates might hold the Guard for a while, stretched thin as they are, but it won't stop real soldiers for an hour. It won't stop a fucking cannon for a moment. How long until Hauer sends to Dannsburg for the army?"

"He won't," Ailsa said. "The very last thing Hauer wants is for Dannsburg to find out what's happening here. He has sold himself to the Skanians, and that makes him a traitor to the crown. It's his magicians we need to worry about, not soldiers and cannon."

"Aye, well," I said, "we've Billy the Boy and Matthias Wolf and Mina, and that will have to do. Old Kurt's fucking disappeared, his house deserted, and we haven't time to go looking for him now. Besides, the last time I saw him we didn't exactly part as friends."

"Are you *sure* the army won't come, Tomas?" Anne asked. "If we need to plan for—"

"*I* am sure," Ailsa snapped, interrupting her, and I remembered again how little the two of them seemed to care for one another. "Hauer does not want Dannsburg to know about this matter, which is precisely why I already have a messenger riding for the capital as fast as she can. He won't ask for soldiers, but I have. All the same, we can't rely on help coming in time, not in this weather."

"No, I know," I said. "This is Pious Men business; we'll deal with it ourselves."

"This is crown business now, *my* business," she corrected me. I shot a sideways look at Fat Luka, sitting at the table and saying nothing, but she ignored me. "A city governor and direct servant of the crown is a traitor to the realm. This cannot be anything *but* my business."

"Aye, that's fair," I had to allow. "What do you want me to do?"

"Exactly what you are doing," she said. "Fight him. Keep fighting him until we win or the army arrives, whichever happens first."

"Well and good," I said, and sighed. "We should go out and be seen, Anne, and you as well, Luka. The people need to see us among them, just now."

When you lead, you have to be *seen* to lead. You might not be at the front of the charge, but you have to be there, so those who fight for you remember who they're fighting for, and why.

"Aye, boss," Luka said, and he and Anne headed out. Ailsa put a hand on my arm to stay me.

"What?" I asked.

"You do realize the army isn't coming, don't you?" she said, keeping her voice low.

"You said—"

"Yes, well, I said that for Anne's benefit. Morale, and all that. Dannsburg will never admit that a crown-appointed governor has sold a major industrial city to an enemy nation. It's absolutely impossible. Sending in the army would be difficult to hide, to speak lightly of it. My messenger will apprise Lord Vogel of the situation, but that's all. This is upon me to resolve. This is what the Queen's Men are *for*, Tomas."

"And that's why you've got me. This is what *I'm* for, isn't it?"

The lioness met my eyes with a pitiless stare.

"Precisely."

The magicians came at dusk.

There were four of them, flanked by twenty of the City Guard, and they didn't come down the narrows after all. They marched straight down the main road toward the barricade, and the shield of their magic turned the crossbow bolts we loosed at them and sent them swerving harmlessly away into the buildings that lined the street.

One of them, a tall woman in a purple robe, raised a thin, pale hand. The cart that formed half the barricade simply exploded, and so did the two men who had been crouching behind it. I heard curses and screams and the sound of someone vomiting. Crossbows thumped uselessly and found no targets.

The woman fell back, looking wearied by her effort, and a youngish man with long hair sent a blaze of flame from his hands through the hole in the barricade. Someone shrieked, burning in their own personal Hell as the fire consumed them.

The Guard charged into the breach and there we held them, blade to blade.

Siege and fire and screams in the gathering darkness, and it was like Abingon all over again. I heard Bloody Anne bellowing orders, and the crank of ratchets as crossbows were reloaded. Chaos and smoke and shouting. I heard a deafening crack and rumble as a house was torn in half by magic to collapse on top of half a dozen Stink folk. Clouds of dust filled the street, choking and blinding us.

Abingon.

Somewhere in the darkness, Jochan was praying at the top of his voice as he fought and killed. Who needed cannon when they had magicians?

Well, I had magicians too.

"Billy, Mina, Matthias! Go!"

The three of them fought as one unit, as I had taught them. That was an old raiding trick of the captain's. When you are outnumbered, you concentrate the strength you have on a single target at a time, and you crush it without mercy and move on to the next. It had worked when we raided the enemy baggage train on the road from Messia, and what had worked once would work again.

My three cunning folk struck together, and the long-haired young man fell shrieking. A second later his heart exploded out of his chest in a gout of blood and shattered ribs.

"Filthy whore's rancid pus-leaking cunt . . ." I heard Mina snarling as she advanced, with Billy at her side.

The Skanians were no fools, though. They knew my trick, and they had tricks of their own. Two of the men turned on Matthias together while the woman threw Billy and Mina back into the burning barricade and held them pinned there by some force of her mind that I can't pretend to understand. Matthias was the only adult among my cunning folk, and they had obviously assumed he was the most powerful of the three.

There I think they were wrong.

"Hold the line!" Anne roared. "Hold, you cunts!" Battle shock didn't seem to touch her. It never had, not in Abingon and not now. Bloody Anne had lived through a lifetime's worth of horror before she ever went to war. "Hold the *fucking* line!"

We held.

Matthias fought well, insofar as I can understand such things. Light flashed between him and the two Skanians, something like lightning that made the dust-choked air feel tight and dry and burned. I rammed Mercy into a guardsman's ribs and ripped her clear as he fell in a spray of blood, then drove my shoulder into another to turn him before he could stab my brother. Jochan's axe split his head and he grinned at me with savage joy while one of Florence's Flower Girls opened a man's throat behind him. Cutter moved like a wraith in the dust-choked darkness, like the very heart and soul of Abingon, and wherever his hands went, men died.

One of the pair of Skanian magicians caught fire and pinwheeled into the middle of the road, waving his arms and screaming as he burned. Matthias hurled something at the other, something black and blurred that shrieked like a thing alive as it moved, but it detonated in the air between them and did nothing. Matthias threw his arms out to his sides and lightning crackled between his hands as he snarled laughter into the face of battle.

". . . plague-raddled donkey-fucking *bitch*!" Mina screamed, and the Skanian woman's intestines exploded out of her mouth in a fountain of blood and filth.

Billy the Boy was free and moving then, but he was a second too late. The last Skanian magician rallied, and Matthias Wolf went in so many directions at once he might as well have been hit by a cannonball. There wasn't enough of him left to bury afterward.

Mina and Billy turned on the remaining magician with hungry murder in their eyes. I cannot bring myself to record here what those two strange, damaged children did to him.

He died, and that is enough.

The Guard were already falling back, and those of us who still had crossbows sent bolts flying after them. More than one found its mark and left a guardsman sprawled dead in the street to be trampled by his fleeing fellows. I turned and saw Bloody Anne and Rosie standing each with an arm around the other's waist and a crossbow in her free hand, looks of grim triumph on their faces. They were made for each other, those two, and no mistake.

That was how the second battle of the Stink was won.

FIFTY-TWO

We nursed our wounded back to the Tanner's Arms and set all the fresh men we had to repairing and manning the barricade, but they didn't try us again that night.

Hari brought out what food and brandy we had left, and I sat and drank until I gradually felt myself begin to relax. That evening had been hard for most of my crew, I understood that. The fight at the barricade had been like Abingon all over again, a window back to a past that none of us ever wanted to see again. For veterans, that was a hard thing.

For the new men, men who hadn't ever been to war, it was much worse. I saw one of Florence's crew cradling a young lad's head in her filthy lap while he wept for what he had seen and done that day. She was a hard, scarred killer with the look of a veteran about her. I didn't know her, but she held that boy while he cried, and for that alone I respected her. That was true comradeship, and it was good to see.

Aunt Enaid was offering what comfort she could as well, soothing brows or telling bawdy jokes, whatever each man needed. There's an art to that sort of thing, to knowing a man and the damage done to him, and how best to approach healing it, and it was something my aunt was very good at.

Ailsa came to me after a while, and she joined me at my table. With the Tanner's so crowded everyone was sharing, even me, and my brother and Sam and two men I didn't even know were at my corner table with me.

"How are you?" Ailsa asked, and I knew what she meant.

"Well enough," I said.

My battle shock hadn't come out anything like so badly that day as it had after the sit-down with Vhent, and I thought I knew why that was. Anne hadn't been there at the sit-down, but today she had. With Bloody Anne bellowing orders in the darkness it had felt like *my* war, the one I knew I had survived, not the one I died in every night in my dreams. Nothing seemed quite so bad when Anne was there beside me.

"I need to speak to you, in private. Come to the back room with me."

I nodded and got to my feet, and stepped over the man beside me who had either fallen asleep or simply passed out from exhaustion. He had his head cradled in his folded arms on the table, and every so often he whimpered in his sleep. I let him be and followed my wife.

"What is it?" I asked, once we were alone.

Crowded the Tanner's might be, but the back room with its long table and twelve chairs remained closed to all but the actual Pious Men. This was our inner sanctum, and some things had to remain sacred even in this time of war.

Ailsa stood with her hands folded in front of her and looked at me, her dark eyes appraising. Those were the eyes of the lioness and no mistake, and the lioness was made of stone and iron.

"I have something for you," she said, after a long moment had passed.

"What? You're giving me a gift, now of all times?"

"No, not that," she said. "Not that at all. This was made for you when we were in Dannsburg, in readiness for the time when you should be given it."

She reached into her belt pouch and took something out, and handed it to me. It was a thick piece of folded leather, and it came to me as I took it from her that I had seen its like before. She carried one herself.

I swallowed. I had to be mistaken, surely? In Our Lady's name, this couldn't be what I thought it was.

"Open it."

I did as she said, and I looked down at what was inside.

The leather was thick and strong but of the very highest quality, butter soft in my hands, and it unfolded around an ornate seal. I looked down at that seal, a white-gold rose set upon a golden crown to represent the royal arms.

I knew what that was.

I swallowed and found that I had no words to say to her.

"I have the Queen's Warrant," she said. "That is an official license to do absolutely anything, with the full and unconditional backing and funding of the crown. It means that I am above the law. I am *utterly* untouchable. Lord Vogel gave me a second one before we left Dannsburg, and told me to wait until the time was right to give it to you. This one is for you, Tomas. Welcome to the Queen's Men."

I stayed in the back room after Ailsa left me. I slept a little, as much as I could, but my head was busy with too many things to allow me the rest I needed, however tired I was.

Ailsa had given me the Queen's Warrant and welcomed me into the Queen's Men.

Me, a Queen's Man.

Do what your father says or the Queen's Men will come and take you away.

The Queen's Men were what people like us used to frighten our children with, like the monster that lives under the bed. That was only in stories, though, the sort of scary stories that children enjoy because they know they're not real.

The Queen's Men were.

The Queen's Men were very real indeed. They were subtle, unseen, and officially nonexistent. The Queen's Men made people disappear.

Now *that* was something to be frightened of.

Was that what I was now, something to frighten little children with?

I had to allow that I probably was.

I felt there should have been more ceremony to it, in some way, some anointing into the knighthood, but perhaps that would come in time. If I survived the week, anyway, and that was in no way a certainty. This felt very much like a battlefield promotion to me, the way the line was filled when an officer fell.

I passed the night in fitful unease, turning and turning in my chair at the head of the empty table and thinking over what Ailsa had given me and the dark implications of it. It meant she trusted me implicitly and that was good, and it must mean that Vogel did too. I supposed that was good as well, to a point, but I had met Vogel and I wasn't sure I wanted to be the sort of man who would earn *his* trust. Vogel was as close to a devil walking as I ever wanted to meet, I had thought at the time, and he had done nothing to change my opinion of him.

I was a prince, in Ellinburg, and I hadn't had a boss since I had turned my back on bricklaying as a young man and become a businessman. I worked for myself, and I liked it that way. I didn't know *who* I worked for now, Ailsa or Vogel. Vogel, I supposed. Ailsa had told me how each Queen's Man ran their own operation like an independent crew and seemed to answer only to him, with no chain of command between them. But then she was right there in Ellinburg with me, so why do this? Why give me the Queen's Warrant now?

An hour before dawn I still had no answers. I gave sleep up for a bad job and went out the back to take a piss, and then had a wash from the freezing water in the horse trough. That woke me up some, and afterward I walked softly through to the common room. Folk were sleeping where they had sat the night before, or curled up on the floor under tables with their coats over them for blankets. I knew Ailsa was asleep upstairs, in the room next to Anne's that Mika had given up for her. Aunt Enaid was sprawled on the floor in front of the fire with Brak wrapped in her heavy arms, holding him close to her heart even in sleep. Mika had the watch at the door and he gave me a nod, but he held his peace for the sake of those sleeping, and I did the same.

In the kitchen I found Billy the Boy and Mina. They were entwined in each other's arms on the threadbare rug in front of the banked fire, both asleep with their clothes in wild disarray. I thought perhaps they had found a closeness together the night before, young though they both were, and that was good. If they were old enough to fight and kill, then they were old enough to fuck, to my mind.

I raided some salt pork from Hari's dwindling supplies and drew myself a mug of small beer, and I sat at the table to break my fast alone.

The sun was coming up outside now, and the kitchen's small window had no shutters. After a while Billy stirred in the light and sat up, disentangling himself from Mina's arms with a gentleness that was quite touching to see.

"Papa?" he whispered.

I saw the look on his face, and I had to smile. I had been his age once myself, for all that it seemed like it had been a lifetime ago.

"Shhh, don't wake her," I murmured, and nodded toward the door.

I took up my mug and my food and led the boy through to the back room where we might talk alone.

"I like her, Papa," Billy said, his face red with embarrassment but with something in his eyes that spoke of pride as well. As far as I knew Billy the Boy had never been with a woman before. "I like her a lot. Please don't tell Mama."

"Aye, that's well and good, and I won't tell your ma if you don't want me to," I said. "There's no shame in it, though, so long as both are willing."

"She was," Billy said, and now he had a shy smile on his face.

"Good," I said again, and found that I had run out of words to say about that. I cleared my throat and looked at him. "You did well last night, both of you, but I need you to conserve your strength in case Hauer has more magicians to send against us."

"He hasn't," Billy said at once, and now he was speaking with the voice of Billy the Seer, Billy who was never wrong when he said that a thing was so. "The cunning is a rare thing. They threw everything they had left at us last night and we beat them, Mina and me. She's very strong. There won't be any more magicians, Papa."

The cunning was a rare thing in Ellinburg, that I had to allow, and apparently it was in Dannsburg as well, but was it so rare in Skania? Billy certainly seemed to think so, but how the fuck would he know? Did Our Lady *truly* speak to him, or through him? I had no idea. I was a priest, not a mystic, after all, and that was a question for mystics.

"Aye, well, I hope not," I had to say. "All the same, lad, you need to rest."

"I'm not so tired," Billy said. "Mina taught me a thing, how to steal another magician's strength, and I can do that now. We feasted on that last one before we pulled him apart."

"That's good," I said, although I didn't really understand what he was talking about.

I didn't understand it, but I wasn't sure that it sounded healthy, to feast on another man. I remembered my brother in the snow-swept moonlight of the previous winter, the blood black around his mouth. I remembered the pieces of human meat stuck between his teeth and how I had thought maybe he had lost his soul for it. Perhaps this wasn't the same thing, not exactly, but it made me uneasy nonetheless.

The cunning was a mystery to me, as I have written. I have no talent for it at all, no more than most people have, and I could only accept on faith that Billy knew what he was talking about. I'm not an overly religious man, priest though I may be, but some things I'll take on faith. Billy's ability was one of them.

I sighed and sipped my small beer, tasting the oaty thickness of it on my tongue, and I put such matters out of my mind. Small beer was the taste of breakfast, the taste of having lived to see another dawn.

It tasted good.

FIFTY-THREE

Three hours after dawn a runner came from the barricade at the end of the street, some Stink man with holes in the elbows of his shirt, and he pushed his way through the groggy crowd in the Tanner's to speak to me.

"It's Cap'n Rogan, sir. He wants to talk to you."

My brother was awake by then, and in a foul temper brought on by brandy and battle shock.

"He can fuck himself," Jochan growled, but I raised a hand to quiet him.

"Be quiet, boy," Aunt Enaid snapped at him, in the voice that we both remembered from our childhood. I thought perhaps her head might be somewhat the worse for drink that morning too, and her mood was no better than his.

"I'll see him," I said. "I'll see him, but he comes alone and he comes unarmed."

"He *is* alone, sir," the man said. "All alone; there's no Guard in sight anywhere on the streets. And he's not wearing his right uniform, neither."

"Aye, well, I suppose what a man wears is his own business," I said. "At least it's not a kirtle and bonnet. Take his blade and get him in here."

That got a halfhearted laugh from the folk in the common room, but no more than that. Keeping morale up was becoming difficult, I had to allow. All the same, ten minutes later Captain Rogan was escorted through the barricade and brought into the Tanner's Arms.

He walked stiffly upright, proud, in a parade ground march. He was alone, as the runner had said, his eyes fixed straight ahead in a way that I didn't know how to read. He was wearing an old-fashioned army uniform, the sergeant's stripes still bright on his tattered sleeve. An empty scabbard hung at his hip where my men had disarmed him, but it hung from an old leather swordbelt that had been polished to a glossy shine.

That uniform was from the last war, I realized, from Aunt Enaid's war. She stood up and saluted him when he came in, and he returned the gesture of respect with such rigid discipline that it was plain he was keeping himself under an iron control.

"What can I do for you, Captain?" I asked him.

"I want to talk to you," he said. "You and the corporal, but no one else."

It took me a moment, but then I realized he meant my aunt. Perhaps they had known each other in their war, perhaps even fought together. Truth be told, I had never thought to ask, but I supposed it wasn't impossible.

I met Ailsa's eyes across the room, and she gave me a tiny nod.

"Aye," I said after a moment. "We can do that."

A minute later Aunt Enaid and me and Captain Rogan were in the back room of the Tanner's where other ears couldn't hear us.

"I am not a traitor," Rogan said, once the door was closed behind us. "I love my country and I love my queen, you have to understand that. These foreign magicians . . . That's not right, it *can't* be. Withholding justice from the streets, shooting at our own people, that's not right either. That's injustice, right there, and that's what I've always tried to stop. That's why I joined the fucking Guard in the first place. Aye, I take bribes and I can't deny that to you, but I don't hold with injustice. Five years I was at war for my country, and no one can ever take that away from me."

"No one here is trying to," I told him. "I respect you, Captain Rogan, for all that we haven't always been friends. I respect you, but I don't respect your boss. Governor Hauer has done things that I can't let pass, you have to understand that."

Rogan nodded, and I could see the pain that it caused him. He was a conflicted man, was Captain Rogan. He was a hard man and a ruthless bully and he had his vices, as I have written, but he was still a soldier and he still had his honor, too.

"I'm no fucking saint of the temple," Rogan admitted, "and I've done things I'm not proud of. I'll work for a corrupt man, aye, if he pays well enough, but I won't work for a traitor. These fucking foreigners, these magicians . . . that's *not* right, I know it's not. Where are they from, and why are they here? Why is there law in half the city and not the other half? That ain't right either, and I don't like it. I had to do it, I had my orders, but . . . but it's not *right*, is it?"

He was close to tears, I could tell. This proud old soldier had reached the limits of what he could overlook for Hauer, of what he could do for silver without his conscience stabbing him in his sleep.

I cleared my throat and looked at my aunt.

"Let us have a minute, Auntie," I said.

She frowned at that, she who had been the one who had served with Rogan, but she took my word and she nodded and stepped out of the room to give us the private moment that I needed.

"Governor Hauer is a traitor," I said. "He's a traitor to the crown, to the queen and the realm and to everything we fought for in our wars. Hauer fucking spits on everything we did, everything we went through. I mean to take him down."

I locked eyes with Captain Rogan, and I reached into my belt pouch and took out the thing that Ailsa had given me.

I held it open so he could see what it contained.

"You see this, Captain?" I asked him. "You know what this means, don't you?"

Rogan's eyes widened as he stared at the Queen's Warrant, and I think that was the moment that I truly realized just how much power I held right there in my hand.

An official license to do absolutely anything.

Ailsa had told me that, and of course she should know.

The full and unconditional backing and funding of the crown.

That was the power of a god, or close enough as made no difference on the streets.

I am above the law. I am untouchable.

Captain Rogan stared at me for a very long time, or so it seemed. Then he straightened up and he stiffened his spine, and he saluted me.

"I'm your man, sir," he said. "I will follow you, and my men will follow me."

I nodded and showed him out.

That done, I called all the Pious Men into the back room. I called them all in, and Florence Cooper and all her Flower Girls, and the Headhunters who had come down from the docks when Anne called the knives. Everyone who mattered was there, everyone I trusted. I left Ailsa out of it; this was between me and my crew, and the less any of them knew about her the better.

They crowded into the room with the Pious Men seated at the table and the members of the vassal gangs standing around the walls, all of them waiting on me to speak.

I took my place at the head of the table, but I didn't sit. I stood there and I took out the Queen's Warrant and I showed it to them, and I told them what it meant.

There was fucking uproar.

I heard cries of disbelief, and anger, and betrayal. I heard rage against the system, against how the common folk were oppressed by what that warrant represented. No one dared to quite come flat out and say it, but reading between their words I heard what a cunt they thought I was. This, I realized, could be about to go very badly for me.

"Quiet!" Bloody Anne bellowed in her best sergeant's voice, and the room fell silent.

I could count on Bloody Anne, always, but even she had nearly stabbed me when she first learned that I worked for the crown. I knew I would have to present this very carefully and in exactly the right way if I hoped to keep the Pious Men at my side.

"Listen to me," I said. "I'm still the devil Tomas Piety, and we're still the Pious Men. This changes nothing, except the amount of power we have. It's no secret now that Governor Hauer is our enemy, and this gives me the means to do something about that. That's all. I may work for the crown, aye, but there's no shame in it. There's gold in it, though, all the gold we need, and the unconditional respect and obedience of anyone I show this to. This is fucking power. This is a good thing for the Pious Men, you mark me on that."

Gold and power and respect, those were the levers that moved the Pious Men.

"He's absolutely right," Fat Luka said. "The whole city will be ours before you know it."

Bloody Anne just nodded, and she glared around the table. Folk looked down at their boots, or up into the air, anywhere but at her, and gradually heads began to nod.

"If there is anyone here," I said softly, "who feels they can't stay, then go now."

It was tense for a moment, but no one moved.

"I never thought I'd see the day," my aunt muttered, but she stayed in her place at the table and that was good.

"Nor did I, Auntie," I said, "but these are the times we live in. Now, this has to stay between us. It's not something the common folk need to hear of, but I don't keep secrets from family any longer than I have to and I wanted you all to know the lay of things. Captain Rogan will be joining us later, and he works for me now. He'll be bringing guardsmen we can trust, and I know it's a strange thing, but we'll be fighting alongside them and I need everyone to understand that. I need everyone to get used to the idea."

Again heads nodded, and I let them file out of the room to think on what I had told them, and what it meant. My brother just gave me a nod.

"In Our Lady's name, Her will be done," he said, and that could have meant anything.

I didn't know how he felt about fighting alongside Rogan, but the captain commanded the lion's share of the City Guard and that was all that mattered.

Hauer had been recruiting new men and those owed no loyalty to Rogan, but they were woefully outnumbered. Rogan's men knew the city and they were veterans too, by and large, tough old fuckers who knew how to break heads and were more than happy to do it.

By the end of that day, they were *my* men.

* * *

We went at midnight.

I never thought I'd live to see a day when Guard fought Guard on the streets of Ellinburg, but I had been wrong about that.

Billy and Mina were both still exhausted, drained by their battle with the Skanian magicians at the barricade the previous day, however much they thought they could steal another magician's strength. Neither was fit to fight, to my mind, but both had wanted to come anyway, and that troubled me. They had an overly bright look about their eyes now, the skin of both their faces seeming as though it were stretched too tightly across the skulls beneath. I had thought that feasting on another man's power sounded unhealthy, and they showed me nothing to change my mind on that. I held my peace about it, but I refused to let them join us all the same and left them at the Tanner's with Ailsa keeping a motherly eye on them.

Billy had assured me there wouldn't be any more Skanian magicians, and when Billy the Boy said a thing was so, then it was so. We would do this the old-fashioned way, just like in the army. Me and Jochan and Cutter, Florence Cooper and Jutta and Bloody Anne headed out in full mail with our lads and Florence's crew behind us.

We met Captain Rogan at the barricade. He was back in his Guard uniform now, the gold stars on his shoulders winking in the lantern light and his heavy breastplate reflecting back a dull sheen. He had a full detachment of fifty guardsmen with him, veterans who I knew would have followed him into Hell itself.

"Captain," I greeted him. "Have you explained the lay of things to your men?"

"Yes, sir," he said, "and sworn them all to secrecy on the matter."

I nodded at that. He had told them I carried the Queen's Warrant, then, and that had been enough.

The full and unconditional backing and funding of the crown.

There were no doors that warrant couldn't open, no loyal man or woman who wouldn't defer to the power it stood for. A command from a Queen's Man carried the same weight as a direct order from the queen herself. Anyone who would refuse such was by definition a traitor to the crown and subject to hang.

That was the power of a god indeed.

"Good," I said, and I stood up on the barricade to address all those there gathered. "Tonight we march on the governor's hall. This will be harsh work we do, I won't lie to you about that. There will be men and women loyal to the governor, who wear the same uniform you do, who will oppose us tonight. Those men and women are traitors to the crown and are to be dealt with as such, does everyone understand that?"

Heads nodded among the ranks of guardsmen.

"Yes, sir!" a thick-bellied sergeant shouted, and the others echoed him.

"Then we march!"

FIFTY-FOUR

Shock and awe, that was how we took the governor's hall that night.

I had over sixty with me, City Guard and Pious Men and Flower Girls together. The Guard's losses had been heavy in the two battles of the Stink, but Hauer had maybe forty armed men and women left loyal to him in the city. That was more than I would have liked, but we still outnumbered them and more importantly they didn't know we were coming.

Captain Rogan had been clever, I had to allow, using his position to make sure his own men held the city gates that night while only the governor's loyalists were on duty in the streets and at the governor's hall itself. We rolled over them like an armored tide, the guardsmen's heavy boots tramping in unison as they marched. They had their clubs slung at their belts and bared steel in their hands, and that night they all carried shields.

A massed rank of well-disciplined infantry is a terrifying thing in the enclosed space of a city street. Form the shield wall and push and stab and push and stab and you drive the enemy before you in confusion and disarray, trampling the fallen beneath your boots. Hauer's men were panicking, unable to understand what was happening. These were their own comrades attacking them, and if some didn't understand why, then that was their problem and not mine. I had no sympathy for traitors to the crown.

After the events of the last few days and the number of bodies we had dragged off my streets I had no sympathy for anyone, that night.

Our column made its way onto Trader's Row and there they were waiting for us, kicked out of their bunks and rallied in haste. They were led by the sergeant who had arrested me and marched me out of my house that summer morning last year. I recognized her, but I couldn't remember her name.

She had perhaps thirty guardsmen of her own behind her, and I thought that was every one they had left, bar the few who had no doubt already broken and run. Rogan's men would stop those ones at the city gates. I knew how that would end, for those who were traitors and deserters both, and I gave them no further thought.

"Sergeant Weaver," Rogan shouted at her across the cobbled expanse between our two forces. "Stand down. That is an order."

"I take my orders from the governor, not from you," she shouted back. "You've turned your fucking coat, Rogan! You're a traitor to this city and to—"

There was a loud thump by my ear, and then the sergeant's head all but exploded as a bolt took her full in the face. Beside me, Bloody Anne was already reloading her crossbow.

Rogan raised his sword.

"Charge!"

It was a massacre.

We took no prisoners on Trader's Row that night, and when it was done the cobbles were running red. When it was done there wasn't a guardsman left alive that wasn't one of Rogan's. We had ten down of our own, nine dead and one trying to hold his reeking guts in with his hands, but done it was.

I looked at the great stone slab of the governor's hall, at the tall iron doors, and wished for a moment that I had allowed Billy and Mina to come along after all. The cunning could have broken that place open for us, but without it I wasn't sure how we were going to get inside. I said as much, and Rogan reached into his pouch.

"I'm still the captain of the City Guard," he reminded me. "I've got the keys."

He marched up the steps with me and Jochan, Cutter and Bloody Anne and ten of his men around him. The big key went into the lock in the iron door and turned with a satisfying click. Rogan reached up and threw the doors open, and only then did I think to wonder why no one had dropped the bar on the inside.

"Down!" I shouted, but it was too late.

The blast of fire from within incinerated Captain Rogan and two of his men where they stood.

"Witch!" Anne roared, her crossbow thumping even as she moved.

I chanced a look, and of course she was right. There he was, tall and gaunt in his long robes, standing in the great entrance hall and flanked by five of Hauer's remaining loyalists. Anne's bolt swerved uselessly around him as he protected himself with the cunning, but it gave us the moment we needed.

The Guard stormed into the hall, bellowing rage and revenge for their captain, and they fell on the men within in a storm of steel. Cutter moved as fast as I think I had ever seen a man move before, his evil little knives glittering in his hands as he went for the magician.

He moved like the wind, but lightning is faster than wind.

That lightning slashed from the magician's hands and across the knifeman's face, sending him screaming to the tiles. Cutter thrashed on the ground with smoke rising from his face. I felt sick to my stomach. I had seen burns like that before, in Abingon, and I knew he would be unlikely to survive it.

Jochan roared like a man possessed, and he charged the magician and damn the consequences. Battle shock and love and grief and rage fueled Jochan's charge, and right then my brother was like some demon from the old stories, some unstoppable god of war and vengeance risen up from Hell itself.

"Cunt!" he bellowed, and his axe rose and fell, rose and fell.

He wrote bloody, screaming slaughter across the walls and the ceiling until the man was nothing but tattered robes and butchered meat, and it was done. My brother dropped his axe and fell to his knees, sobbing as he cradled Cutter's burned head in his lap.

"Yoseph," I heard him whisper.

The governor's hall was ours, but at great cost.

There had been a magician where no magician should have been.

There won't be any more magicians, Papa.

Billy the Boy had told me that, and he had been wrong.

Billy, who was never wrong.

When Billy the Boy said a thing was so, then it was so, but not that night it hadn't been. I thought about the tight look he'd had to his face, and the overly bright shine of his eyes, and how I had thought that feasting on another man's power sounded unhealthy. I wondered if those things might be connected. That was something to think on, but another time.

I drew in a breath and looked at the charred corpse of Captain Rogan, his body almost fused to the remains of the two men who had died with him on the steps beyond the open door. Rogan had found his honor in the end, and look where it had fucking got him.

Where did honor ever get anyone?

I promised myself that I would ensure he had a full military funeral worthy of a colonel, but that too would have to wait.

"Who has the seniority now?" I demanded, my voice cutting over the babble of talk in the hall.

A man stepped forward, the thick-bellied sergeant who had been the first to call me sir at the barricade.

"I have, sir," he said. "Sergeant Miller."

"You've been promoted, Captain Miller," I said. "Detail enough men to organize a search of the ground floor and the cells. I want anyone who's armed killed and anyone who isn't secured. Then you'll come with me."

"Sir."

I left him to it and went to my brother.

"How bad is it?"

Jochan looked up at me and he said nothing, but there were tears rolling down his cheeks. Cutter was alive, but his left eye was gone and half his face with it. His beard was burned away on that side in a mass of blisters and livid, weeping red that hurt just to look at. He must have been in an indescribable amount of pain, but he bore it in silence, with only the flecks of spit that bubbled between his tightly clenched teeth telling of the agony he endured.

"Right," I said. "Fuck this. Take who you need and get him back to the Tanner's, have young Billy do what he can."

"What can he fucking do with *this*?" Jochan hissed at me, his eyes bright with grief and battle shock and murder. "He's in Our Lady's hands now, but She doesn't heal men, does She?"

"I don't know," I admitted, "but Billy will do something. He saved Hari, you remember? I don't understand the cunning, Jochan, but I don't underestimate it either. As you say, he's in Our Lady's hands and She works through Billy."

I didn't know how much I believed that, and Jochan turned and spat on the floor in a way that said he didn't either anymore, but he helped Cutter to his feet all the same. The man groaned in torment as he moved, but no more than that. As Our Lady is my witness, Cutter was not made of the same thing as normal men. Jochan pulled Jutta and two of her girls out of our group, and between them they helped Cutter back out into the street, taking care to skirt what was left of Captain Rogan and his two men as they went.

"Done, sir," Captain Miller said beside me. "The clearing party are about their work."

"Good," I said. "Take us to the governor's study."

Miller led the way up the great stair, in the lead with me and Bloody Anne and Florence Cooper and five of our guardsmen behind. He marched along a corridor and pointed at a door, and I kicked it open so hard it almost came off its hinges.

Governor Hauer was sitting behind his desk in his nightclothes, obviously having been roused from his bed by word of the violence on the streets. His face was pale and sweaty, and he was guzzling wine from a goblet as though his life depended on it.

He wasn't alone.

The other man in the room was tall and lean, and had some sixty years to him, with long iron-gray hair bound back from his face. He wore a plain black coat and an unremarkable doublet, but I knew who this must be. This was the Skanian equivalent of a Queen's Man, standing right there in front of me.

He had the same quality to him that Iagin had, back in Dannsburg, something that put me in mind of a snake in man's clothes.

"Who the fuck are you?" I asked him as Bloody Anne stepped into the room behind me and held her crossbow trained on the governor.

"You don't need my name," he said.

"I'll have it if I fucking want it," I assured him.

He snorted, and there was no hint of fear in his cold eyes.

"This is an act of war, Mr. Piety," he said. "Are you absolutely sure you wish to proceed with it? I assure you, I have the full authority of the King of Skania."

"And I have the Queen's Warrant," I said, "and that means your cock's no bigger than mine. Arrest him."

Miller and his men stepped forward, and the governor's already pale face turned the color of rancid cheese. He dropped his goblet, and wine ran across the desk like blood.

"The Queen's . . ." he whispered. "Tomas, please, I can explain. I can explain everything!"

"Oh, you will explain, Governor Hauer," I said. "At length. In Dannsburg."

I turned to Captain Miller.

"They're for the house of law to deal with. Chain them and throw them both in the cells."

"You can't do this!" Hauer wheezed.

"I have the Queen's Warrant," I told him. "I can do anything."

FIFTY-FIVE

I got no sleep that night.

There were bodies to be cleared off the streets and disposed of, a great number of them, and order to impose. The newly promoted Captain Miller proved competent at least, and I gave thanks to Our Lady for that. For that, and for allowing me to see another dawn.

Ailsa joined me at the governor's hall as the sun was rising. She brought word with her that Cutter had survived the night and was being watched over by Billy the Boy, who was doing what he could. Jochan was with him, refusing to leave his side even to drink.

I thought on that, and I wondered what Jochan's wife would make of it, but that was his affair, not mine. Jochan was caught between two loves, I realized, or perhaps between a love and an obligation. I wouldn't know, and truth be told, it was none of my business anyway. I was just glad that Cutter was still alive.

"Well and good," I said.

We were in Hauer's study and I had taken the seat behind his desk, out of habit more than anything else. It occurred to me then that it should be Ailsa sitting there, not me. I got to my feet and said as much.

"No," she said. "No, sit. It suits you. I thought it would."

I blinked at her. I'd seen hard fighting that night and I'd had no sleep, and I didn't take her meaning.

"Governor Hauer is under arrest and has been relieved of his position," she said, taking the seat across the desk from me as she spoke. "He is going to the house of law, and he won't be coming out again. Someone has to rule here. The crown empowers me to appoint an interim governor of Ellinburg until a permanent replacement can be found and sent from the capital. That will be you, Tomas."

I stared at her, feeling something of a fool.

"Me?" I echoed. "I don't know how to govern a city."

"Of course you do," she said. "You ruled the Stink for years. You *governed* there, Tomas. You set and collected taxes and you spent them wisely, you provided welfare for your people, and you kept the peace on your streets. That's what a governor does. It's no different."

I had to allow that perhaps it wasn't.

"I'm no noble," I said.

"No, but you have at least been introduced to society, and you are well known in Ellinburg and well respected. The common people will accept you."

"And the fucking nobility won't."

"Perhaps not, at first," she allowed, "but you have the Queen's Warrant. You should use it sparingly, Tomas, but it *is* there to be used when necessary. I'd advise you to start with Lan Barkov; he has the most influence in society here. Order him to your side and he will speak well of you to his peers. They will listen to him."

"There's still the Northern Sons to think of, and what's left of the Alarian Kings. They're strong crews even without the Skanians behind them."

She shrugged. "A governor must deal with such things. Broker a peace between them and the Pious Men and draw up a border, or use the Guard to exterminate them. I don't really care. A word of advice, Tomas. You should bring Lord Vogel solutions, not problems. Preferably solutions that you have already successfully implemented."

"Aye, well," I said. "I suppose I can do that. With your help I can. We'll rule together, then. I can be the face of the governor, with you at my side."

"No," she said. "One Queen's Man is enough in Ellinburg, and that's you now. Besides which, I shall need to accompany the wagons that take Hauer and the Skanian leader to Dannsburg. Lord Vogel will want me back in the capital now, to deal with the implications of this. You'll have Rosie, and of course you'll have Luka."

"You're my wife," I whispered. "I . . . I think I love you, Ailsa. *Billy* loves you. Stay with us, please. Please, Ailsa. I don't think I can do this without you."

"I'm sorry, but you will have to," she said, and there was neither love nor compassion nor pity in the eyes of the lioness.

She felt nothing for me, I realized, and she felt nothing for our son either. The lioness was stone and iron, and who was I to speak to her of love anyway? That cold devil in me was no more capable of love than she was. My hands clenched on the table, my fists balling on the sticky wood where Hauer had spilled his wine, and the breath hissed in my throat.

Battle shock.

"Just breathe," she whispered.

"Don't," I told her, in the flat tone of murder that I retreat behind when I don't want to face the world in front of me anymore. "Just don't, Ailsa. When do you leave?"

"Tomorrow," she said. "Miller will give me enough guardsmen to escort the prisoners' wagon. Use Luka, Tomas; he's very valuable. He has worked for us for years."

I stared at her as I worked my way around to understanding this new revelation.

There are only so many shocks a man can take in over the course of one conversation, after all. All the same, in my mind's eye I could already see my hands closing around Luka's fat neck.

"What did you say?"

"He worked for my predecessor. We had him watching you even before the war, while you were spying on the governor for us. Everybody is watched by someone, Tomas. Even me. Perhaps especially me."

"And who watches Luka?"

"I really wouldn't know, but be assured that someone does."

Always someone watching, and always someone to watch the watcher. That was how it was done in the Queen's Men. I wondered who *had* been watching Luka, and I thought about Rosie.

"And what am I supposed to do without you?"

"Govern," she said, and her voice was the cold razor of Vogel's smile. "With war brewing again we must have stability in Ellinburg now. That is all that matters. Taxes must be levied and paid to the crown, and to do that you will need productive industry and strong trade. No more workers' uprisings, no more street violence. We do not want sedition or resistance or thinkers, and the gods only save us from activists. Why do you think Lord Vogel wants to do away with the magicians and the university? Ill-informed and ignorant people are easier to suppress and control. We require a well-behaved, productive, *obedient* workforce, and you will make that happen."

I just stared at her, and I could find no words to say.

Sorrow would keep. Everything would keep, the cold devil told me. Grief, love, betrayal, honor, it would all keep until I could shove it into the strongbox in the back of my mind where it belonged and bury it there until it was forgotten. There was work to be done.

I looked up and met her eyes.

"If you're going, then go. I've got a fucking city to run."

I had my things moved out of our house and into the governor's hall. Ailsa and me were still married, I supposed, for what little that had meant, but I didn't want to see her. She had never felt anything for me; I knew that now. I was the right man for the right job, that was all, and she had been using me the same way I used fucking everyone else. I had to allow that I didn't care for it when it was done to me.

People need to see you and become . . . accustomed to you.

I remembered her telling me that when she had first dragged me into society against my wishes. I had asked her then why it mattered what society people thought of me.

One day it might matter a great deal.

It seemed she had been right, as though she had known even then.

Perhaps she had, at that.

I spent the day in a cold rage, but there was work to be done.

I had Jon Lan Barkov brought to me in the governor's study, as Ailsa had advised, and I showed him the Queen's Warrant and I told him how it was going to be. He was shaken when he left me, pale-faced and scared, but I knew he would do as I told him. Ellinburg society would recognize me as their new governor, and there would be no complaints.

That was what the Queen's Warrant could do.

I wondered just how long the Queen's Men had been planning for this. I remembered the first Queen's Man, before the war, and how even then I had thought it strange just how much gold he had been willing to pay me. Had they been playing such a long game even then, merely hoping that I would survive the war? Perhaps there had been others who hadn't. Perhaps I hadn't even been their first choice for this. I very much doubted that Lord Vogel ever placed all his bets on the same horse.

Could and might and possibly, I thought. That was how the Queen's Men made plans.

I had Fat Luka brought to me as well, and I didn't strangle him after all. I wanted to, but he was too useful to kill, the cold devil told me. Ailsa had had the right of that, at least. The right man for the right job, always, and there were many jobs Fat Luka was suited to. There was a lot to do and little time to do it in, and I needed him. All the same, I spent our entire meeting staring at his neck, and wanting to put my hands around it and squeeze and squeeze and *squeeze* until his head came off in my hands.

I set him to brokering the peace with the Northern Sons and the Kings, and I threw him out before temptation got the better of me. I think he knew how close I had come to violence that day, but I needed him. I needed to impose order in the city, as fast and as hard as possible. I needed to sleep as well, but I couldn't.

I've always said that in Ellinburg I was a prince, but now I wasn't.

Now I was a king, and kings have no time for sleep.

Ailsa left the next morning with her prisoners in irons in the back of a wagon and enough guardsmen to keep them safe on the road. I didn't go out to say my farewells. That was done, to my mind, and the past is best left buried.

Eventually I made my way to the Tanner's Arms under heavy guard. The barricades had been taken down by then, but there was confusion on the streets. Word had spread about what had happened, and who I was now, and I wasn't sure my people knew what to make of that. I was still

Tomas Piety, but now I was riding surrounded by City Guard who did my bidding, and that was too big a change for folk to take lightly.

They would have to get used to it. This was how it was now, and this was how it would stay.

Look at me, Ma, I thought. *I'm the governor of Ellinburg.*

I wondered what she would have made of that. I knew *exactly* what my da would have made of it, and it was nothing good. Da was a working man, when he was sober enough to work, and he didn't hold with nobles or politicians or the City Guard. No one in the Stink did, nor in the Wheels either. Da would never have forgiven me for this, for what he would have seen as a betrayal of who I was and where I had come from.

But then my da was a cunt, so fuck what he thought.

I left the guardsmen outside the Tanner's and went in alone. Bringing them in there with me would have been too much, I knew that. All the same, the busy room fell into an uneasy silence when I stepped inside. When I had been in Dannsburg in the summer I had thought that I could feel the distance growing between me and my crew, and I could see now that I'd had the right of that.

Bloody Anne was waiting for me with Florence Cooper and Aunt Enaid at her side.

"How's Cutter?" I asked.

"Alive," Anne said. "Asleep upstairs with Jochan. Billy is doing . . . whatever he's doing. Mina's with him, and I don't think they want disturbing."

"Aye, perhaps not," I said. "What's the lay of things?"

"Come in the back with me and I'll tell you."

I followed Bloody Anne through to the back room, where we could be alone.

"So?"

Anne rounded on me and I saw the look in her eyes, and I've no shame in admitting that for a moment then I feared her.

"The *lay of things* is that the world is on its fucking head," Anne snarled at me, standing with her hard hands clenched into fists by her sides. "Working in secret for the crown, averting a war, I'll allow you had your reasons for that. Taking the Queen's Warrant, well, that's another thing again, but I can just about see my way to how you might not have had a choice. But *this*? You're the fucking governor of Ellinburg, Tomas, that's the fucking *lay of things*!"

I sighed, and sat down in my place at the head of the table.

"A lot has changed, I'll grant you," I said. "Things have changed too quickly for my liking too, but there it is. I *am* the governor now, if only for a short while. I can't be two things at once, Anne."

"What do you mean?"

I got to my feet again, and I held out the chair for her.

"Sit down, Anne," I said. "Sit here."

"No," she said, and all the anger left her as she took my meaning. "No, I can't do that. All last summer I ran the Pious Men for you while you were in Dannsburg, but I never sat in that chair. I was just ruling as your second, and I did it from the seat at your right hand where I belong. I'm not—"

"I need you, Bloody Anne," I interrupted her. "I need you now like never before. I can't be the governor of Ellinburg and the head of the Pious Men at the same time. There aren't enough hours in the fucking day. Lady willing I won't have to be governor for long, but I can't know that, and while I am I need someone I trust to sit in this chair. You're my second, Anne. You're the one I trust with this."

"I don't know what to say."

"Say yes," I told her. "Say you'll make Florence Cooper *your* second, or my aunt, if you want. You can't have Luka, but there's Mika too, whoever you think fit, anyone but Jochan. I've a long road ahead of me with the workers and the Northern Sons and the Alarian Kings, the nobility and the queen's fucking tax collectors. I need to know my streets are in safe hands. In *your* hands."

Bloody Anne looked at me for a very long time, then took a step toward the chair. I wasn't sure how to read the look on her face, just then. Resignation, aye, and certainly weariness, but I thought perhaps there was something else there, too.

I thought it might be pride.

At last she sat down and took her place at the head of the table.

It suited her.

FIFTY-SIX

I had been the governor of Ellinburg for three weeks, and still the cold rage hadn't left me.

Fat Luka spent his days in sit-downs now, with Bloody Anne and the man who had taken over the Northern Sons after Bloodhands, and with the head of the Alarian Kings. They were working out truces and borders between them, but I couldn't concern myself with that sort of business any longer. As long as it got done, that was good enough.

My business was governing the city now, and there Ailsa had been right. It wasn't so different, not really. A larger scale, perhaps, and different problems, but I found I knew how to deal with them. All but one, anyway.

There was still trouble among the workers, and that was because someone was still *causing* trouble. And I thought I knew who it was.

Old Kurt's sore with you, Billy had told me once. *He'll make trouble, later.*

It seemed that time had come.

"I'm sorry, sir," Captain Miller said, "but can I ask why . . ."

He tailed off and gestured to Billy and Mina, who were sitting there in the governor's study, with him and me and two of his sergeants.

In *my* study.

"Why are there children at a council of war, Captain Miller? That's a good question," I said. "This is Billy, and he's my son but he's also a cunning man so strong that he's fought Skanian magicians and won. The lass with him is Mina, and she's . . . like him."

"I'm his woman," Mina said, and Billy smiled and he reached out and took her hand.

They were young for that, to my mind, but I let it pass. They held hands and their fingers entwined in a way that told me they had found love, and I wished them well of it.

"They're here because it's my belief that the cause of our troubles is Old Kurt, the cunning man from the Wheels. You know who I mean, Captain?"

Miller looked uncomfortable, and he twisted the fingers of his right hand together to make some religious sign that I didn't recognize.

"Aye, sir," he said at last. "I know who that is."

"Well, Old Kurt went missing a while back, after the last workers' uprising I put down, and he hasn't been seen since. Old Kurt believes in the working folk. He could have made himself rich with what he can do but he never did, choosing instead to stay in his hovel down in the Wheels. He made it so Stink folk and Wheelers alike had free access to his door. He believes in equality, does Old Kurt, and rights for folk that don't have any, and other things that make my life fucking difficult."

"He's dangerous," one of Miller's sergeants said.

"That he is," I allowed, "but so are these two. That's why they're here, in case I'm right and we have to fight Old Kurt when we go."

"Begging your pardon, sir, but I still say you shouldn't be coming," Miller said.

"I know, Captain, and I'll take it under advice, but I'm going to ignore that advice and do it anyway. I'm new to the governorship and I need to be seen, and I *will* be seen. I am not Hauer, gentlemen. I'm not a governor who will sit and drink wine and polish the chair under him with his arse while he hides behind his walls. I am a governor that people will learn to fear."

"Aye, sir, as you will," Miller said. "The men are ready. We go when you give the word."

I nodded and stood up.

The Weeping Women hung heavy on my hips. Governor I might be, the most heavily guarded man in Ellinburg, but Lady help me, I needed to kill someone.

Anyone.

Ailsa's betrayal had driven me into a fury so deep and so cold I didn't know if I could ever climb out of it again. I'd had to explain to young orphan Billy that his mother had left us, had left *him*, and he had hugged me and he had wept. He had buried his face in my shoulder and wept great shaking, racking tears of despair and rejection, and for that alone I would never forgive her.

At least he had Mina, and that was good.

I had my cold devil to keep me company, and that was enough.

"We go at first light," I said.

The sun was still coming up above the rooftops when the Guard formed up in the square outside the governor's hall. I joined them there, wearing mail under my coat with the Weeping Women buckled over it. Billy the Boy met me there, and he too was mailed and armed like a man and he had a hard set to his young face.

He had Bloody Anne with him.

The factory was on her streets, after all, and I knew she would want to see this was done right. I could respect that. I nodded a greeting to her.

"I let Mina sleep," Billy said. "I can take Old Kurt down, if I have to."

I thought again how tight the lad's face looked, his eyes overbright under his smooth young brow, but I put it out of my mind. Too much youthful fucking and not enough sleep, that was all it was, and never mind that he had been wrong about that last magician.

Never mind that. Bury it, along with everything else. Forget it and move on.

"Old Kurt was the one who taught you," I reminded him. "Are you sure, Billy?"

"I'm sure," he said, and his voice was flat and cold. "Remember the rats, Papa?"

I swallowed, and nodded. I remembered what Billy had done to those rats, and how that had given Old Kurt the fear so bad he had sent the lad back to me and refused to teach him anymore.

The boy's fucking possessed.

Well, so was Old Kurt, to my mind, possessed by the sort of idealism that wasn't welcomed by the crown.

Fuck idealism. Where had that ever got anyone?

Duty, honor, love.

Fuck it all.

I remembered Captain Rogan, driven by honor and burned to a crisp in the line of duty. I looked at Billy, and I thought of how much he had loved Ailsa. How much he had loved his adoptive ma. She had only left him, in the end.

They always fucking do.

Fuck it all. They only hurt you, in the end.

I would put a stop to it.

All of it.

Maintaining law and order was a big part of my job as governor. People are weak, as I have written, and the poorer and more oppressed they are, the weaker they become until they just refuse to take it anymore. Then they will rise up, and the gods help their oppressors.

I had thought that once, but a great deal had changed since the first battle of the Stink. *I* had changed. That oppressor was me now, I understood that.

I understood it, and I accepted it.

Perhaps law and order is just another way of saying tyranny and oppression, but I wouldn't know. That was a philosophical question, and I couldn't give a *fuck* about philosophy. What I did know was that one of the biggest factories in Ellinburg was closed down because its workers refused to work, and I had a tax levy to pay to the crown at the end of the month.

Those were the things that mattered, not high ideals of duty and honor and love. Hard facts, those mattered. Production quotas, monthly taxes and their due dates. Those were the fucking important things in life.

These men refused to work, and all that meant was that I wasn't oppressing them hard enough yet.

They had set up a barricade in the street before the factory, and they allowed none to cross it. That barricade was coming down before the sun reached noon, and I'd hear no argument about that.

I looked at Bloody Anne, but her eyes were fixed straight ahead in a way that I wasn't sure I knew how to read.

"Form up and sound the march," I told Captain Miller.

We set off in the dawn light, Miller and me and Anne and Billy on horseback with the sergeants, and forty heavily armed guardsmen marching ahead of us. The tramp of their boots echoed in the empty streets.

That was how I governed my city, the only way I knew how.

They were waiting for us.

We had come with the dawn, too early for them to be prepared, but they were waiting for us just the same. They had known we were coming. They had known, and Old Kurt wasn't there.

That told me all I needed to know.

I surveyed the street ahead of us, the rough barricade and the men standing on it with clubs and knives and hammers in their hands. Old Kurt wasn't there because someone had *told* him we were coming.

There had only been me and Billy and Mina, and Miller and his sergeants at that meeting.

They had known we were coming and when, and there was only one way that could be; someone was spying for Old Kurt. Not Miller, I was sure of that. He was clearly terrified of the old cunning man, but someone. One of his sergeants, then.

Or Mina.

She had no family and no last name, so Fat Luka had told me, and Old Kurt was known to take in waifs and strays, like Yan Wainwright's mute boy. Perhaps he had taken Mina in once, and filled her head with his foolish ideals. I didn't like the idea, but I had to allow that it was possible.

A thrown rock whistled past my head.

"It's the queen's bully boy," a man snarled at me, the one I took to be their leader. "The devil Tomas Piety!"

"Go back to work," I said.

My hands were clenched tight on the reins of my horse, shaking with battle shock.

How had it come to this?

What the fuck would my da have said if he could see me now, about to lead a charge of the City Guard against my own people?

Show him a fucking racehorse and a bottle and he'd have overlooked anything, I told myself, but I wasn't sure that was true.

Fuck it all, they only hurt you in the end.

"They won't grind us down if we stand together," the man on the barricade was shouting. "We can hold this place, and we'll be an example to all the working people of this city!"

I rode forward then until I was at the head of the massed Guard, my rich coat flapping around me in the wind.

I fixed him with a look.

"You want to talk to me about working people?" I asked him, my voice taking on the flat tone of murder and loss and despair. "I'm the son of a bricklayer. Everything I've got, I've got because I've worked for it. The only difference I see between you and me is that you're not fucking working."

They turned on us then with weapons raised, these working men who wouldn't work. I nodded to Captain Miller.

"Take them down," I said.

The guardsmen streamed past us, Bloody Anne and Captain Miller and Billy the Boy and me. I watched as battle was joined in the street. I wondered where Old Kurt was, and who had been talking.

I wondered what I was going to say to Billy.

Anne leaned over in her saddle to speak to me.

"How the fuck," she said in a low voice, "has this got anything to do with preventing another war?"

I watched a guardsman break a man's head with his club, and I couldn't meet Anne's eyes.

I had to admit that I didn't know anymore.

I knew one thing, though.

Once this was done, I was going to buy another fucking racehorse.

ACKNOWLEDGMENTS

Book two of a series is often a difficult birth. I owe a great deal of thanks to my wonderful editor Rebecca Brewer at Ace for making me bleed onto the page to make this book what it is, and to my copyeditor Amy J. Schneider for saving me from my own inability to track a timeline properly.

Thanks are as always due to my fabulous agent, Jennie Goloboy at DMLA—if it wasn't for her, you wouldn't have heard of me or be reading these books. Jennie is a guiding hand, editorial voice, cheerleader, and savior in too many ways to count. Thank you.

I'd also like to thank Katie Anderson at Berkley for the wonderful covers, and Alexis and Jessica at Berkley and Olivia and Milly at Quercus for their tireless promotional work. Shout-outs also to all at B&N Sci-Fi & Fantasy Blog ("*Peaky Blinders* with swords"!), Absolute Write, Fantasy-Faction, *SciFiNow* magazine, Fantasy Book Review, and everyone else who welcomed *Priest of Bones* with open arms.

Finally, and above all others, the greatest thanks are for Diane. I wouldn't even be here without you, never mind writing books. Love you, hon.

Photo by Diane McLean

Peter McLean lives in the UK, where he grew up studying martial arts and magic before beginning a twenty-five-year career in corporate IT systems. He is also the author of the Burned Man urban fantasy series.

CONNECT ONLINE

talonwraith.com
facebook.com/petermcleanauthor
twitter.com/PeteMC666